PRAISE FOR
LADY OF SHADOWS

"Heart-pounding danger, sweeping romance, and questions of faith that burn like coals—*Lady of Shadows* is a soul-stirring return to Er'Rets. Jill Williamson and Kelly Fernlake deliver a tale brimming with longing, loyalty, and a love that refuses to be denied. Readers craving a Christian romantasy with high stakes and deep emotion will fall hard for Tara and Carmack's story."

—LINDSAY A. FRANKLIN,
CAROL AWARD–WINNING AUTHOR OF *THE STORY PEDDLER* AND *THE UNRAVELING OF EMLYN DULAINE*

"This story is like an adventure with old friends. It was so delightful to be back in the world of Er'Rets and become better acquainted with the wonderful characters of Carmack Demry and Lady Tara and the wonderful group of characters accompanying them. Adventure, heart, danger, and feels—*Lady of Shadows* has it all!"

—JANE MAREE, GOODREADS

"*Lady of Shadows* was extremely interesting, as it really built out some of the characters who who starred in the original Blood of Kings trilogy. I loved seeing all the characters again, and they were very well thought out. Tara was a fun protagonist to follow, and her inner dialogue was always interesting. Carmack was unique and I liked the tension between the two characters. Five stars, and now I'm really looking forward to the next book!"

—KAETRIANNE, GOODREADS

LADY
OF
SHADOWS

LADY
OF
SHADOWS

←BLOOD OF KINGS: LEGENDS→

KELLY FERNLAKE

JILL WILLIAMSON

sunrise
PUBLISHING

Blood of Kings: Legends

SQUIRE OF TRUTH
LORD OF WINTER
LADY OF SHADOWS
HEIR OF LIGHT

Blood of Kings

BY DARKNESS HID
TO DARKNESS FLED
FROM DARKNESS WON

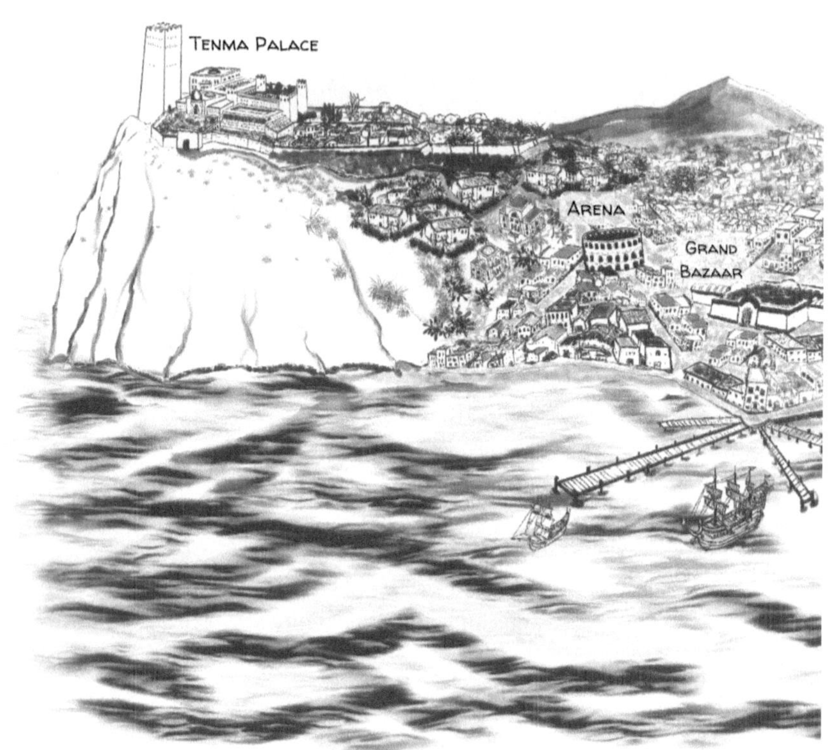

Tenma Palace
Arena
Grand Bazaar

Jaelport
Merchants' Homes
Temple of Zitheos
Slums
Jael Bay

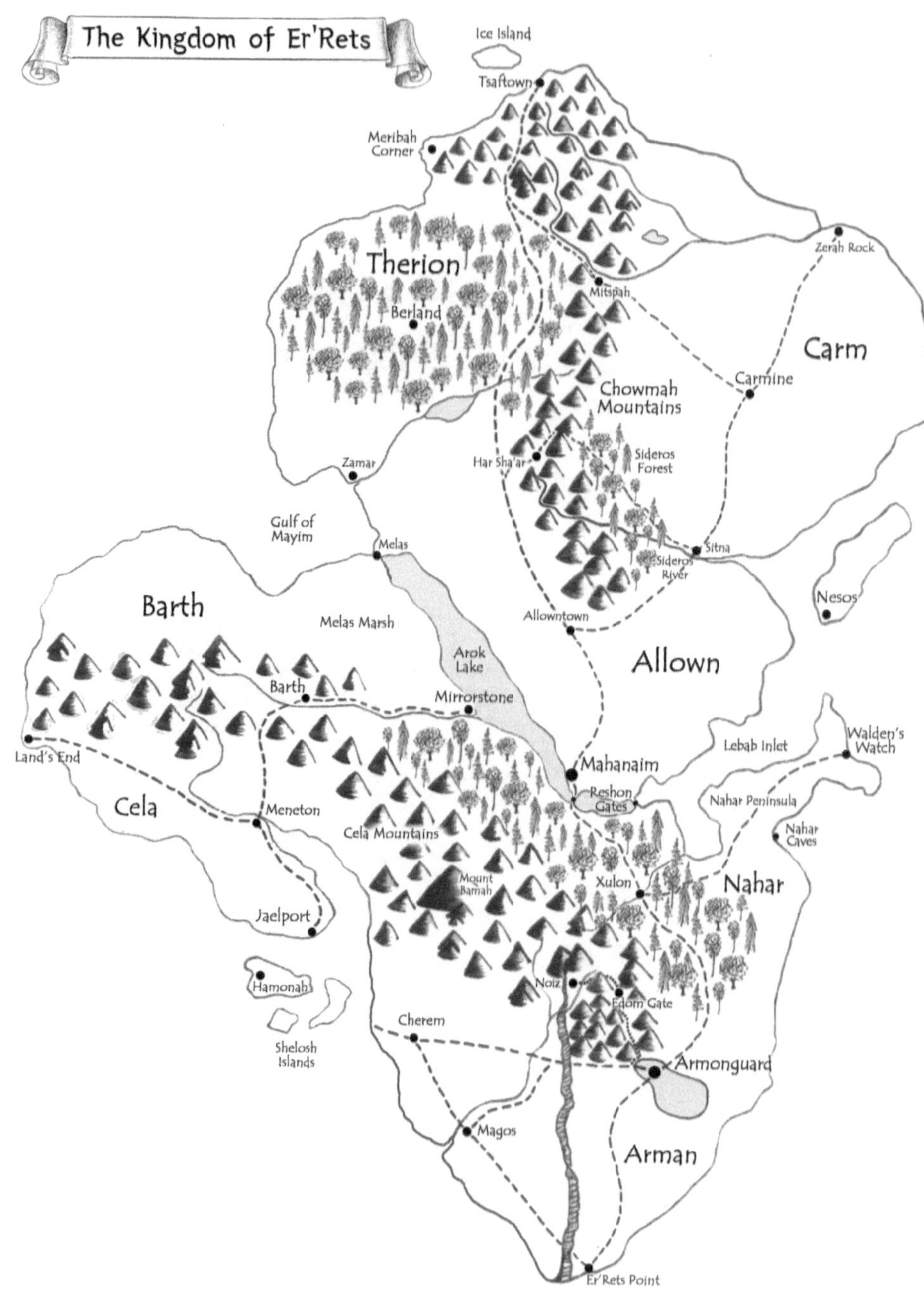

The Kingdom of Er'Rets
Ice Island
Tsaftown
Meribah Corner
Therion
Berland
Zerah Rock
Mitspah
Carm
Chowmah Mountains
Carmine
Zamar
Har Sha'ar
Sideros Forest
Gulf of Mayim
Melas
Sitna
Sideros River
Nesos
Barth
Melas Marsh
Allowntown
Allown
Arok Lake
Barth
Mirrorstone
Land's End
Mahanaim
Lebab Inlet
Walden's Watch
Cela
Meneton
Reshon Gates
Nahar Peninsula
Cela Mountains
Nahar Caves
Jaelport
Mount Bamah
Xulon
Nahar
Hamonah
Noiz
Cherem
Edom Gate
Shelosh Islands
Armonguard
Magos
Arman
Er'Rets Point

For the prayer warriors who lift up writers and our stories,
and for Alex, my leading man.

"Let love and faithfulness never leave you; bind them around your neck, write them on the tablet of your heart."

PROVERBS 3:3 NIV

CHAPTER ONE
TARA

*T*HE FOOL WHO POKES A SLEEPING TAN-*niyn wakes more trouble than expected.*

Her mother's proverb sprang to mind as Lady Tara reached the heavy door separating her from her husband. She wanted her letter, but she hadn't the smallest interest in provoking a giant sea serpent, slumbering or otherwise. Perhaps she should wait for Carmack.

Tara glanced down the corridor toward the great hall where her Shield was meeting with the constable—something about a recent escape from Ice Island. Who knew how long the meeting would take, and Lord Gershom might rouse at any moment. Since his last bout of fever, the ancient man's only predictable habit was to destroy anything that confused him. Nothing was safe, not even Viola's letter lying harmlessly with Tara's sketchbook on the sofa. In his addled state, he would likely toss it into the fire or snatch it for use in the privy.

If only Tara had finished reading her letter during dinner, but as always, she was called away with great urgency, for the cantankerous lord of the house was not to be kept waiting.

Tara pressed her ear against the door. Lord Gershom's snoring easily penetrated the wood, so she nudged it open and peeked inside the solar. Though night blackened the windows, the timber-clad walls glowed with candlelight behind the furniture huddled near the crackling fireplace. Lord Gershom slumped on the brown cushions of the far chair. The waning firelight cast deep shadows into his countless wrinkles, and his mouth hung open, a line of encrusted spittle stretching to his chin.

On the sofa cushion next to him lay Tara's belongings. She gripped the door handle. *Please, Arman, silence the hinges.* Though Tara pushed ever so gently, the iron hardware groaned. Gritting her teeth, she added the traitorous hinges to her lengthy list of unanswered prayers.

Gershom snored on. Tara slipped into the room and nearly choked on the old man's sour body odor. The jasmine-scented candles burning low in the sconces were no match for his poor hygiene, just as the valet was no match for his lord's combative refusal to bathe.

Tara tiptoed across every creaky knot in the hardwood floor, then slowly reached for her belongings on the sofa. Gershom's snoring hitched. She froze, her gaze locked on his chest until its shallow rise and fall resumed. Extending her fingers again, she took hold of the letter and sketchbook then headed for the door.

Snap!

Tara jumped. Only a cinder popping, but with her sudden movement, the letter slipped free and fluttered to the floor. Her skin crawled with the sensation of being watched. A glance over her shoulder confirmed Gershom's foggy eyes were fixed on her. She pivoted, her gaze darting to the side table. There, by the wine decanter, sat his tonics, including a sleeping draught. The lavender bottle seemed impossibly out of reach.

"Good evening, Lord Gershom." Tara curtsied low and scooped her letter from the floor. Slipping it into her sketchbook, she smiled as if welcoming a distinguished guest to Lytton Hall, her childhood home. "May I offer you some refreshment?"

Gershom's skeletal hands twitched. "Who are you?"

"Lady Tara, my lord. Your—" She paused. When she last reminded Gershom that she was his wife, he had thrown a pitcher that narrowly missed her head and hollered a slew of vulgarities about her four dead predecessors. "Your neighbor from Tsaftown."

"Neighbor. Bah!" He broke into a wheezing cough.

Tara rushed to the side table. She set her sketchbook down and poured a generous dose of the sleeping draught into a glass goblet, then added wine to mask its fumes. She offered it to him. "Here, drink this."

His deathlike fingers tightened over her outstretched hand. Tara suppressed a shudder and guided the goblet to his mouth.

Not one drop of the ruby liquid crossed his lips before his hairy nostrils flared. "Poison!" He thrust the goblet away, sloshing its contents into Tara's face.

The liquid stung her eyes, and she rubbed them with her crimson sleeve. "What? No!"

In the blur, Gershom wrenched the goblet away and flung it to the floor, shards of glass pelting Tara's velvet gown. "Liar!" He grabbed hold of her wrists.

Tara lurched back, but he held tight, pulling himself out of his chair. "Lord Gershom, please let go."

"Who are you, trespasser?" he hissed.

Tara's stomach heaved at the stench of his tooth decay. "I'm Tara. Lord Edik Livna's daughter." Her late father's name barely escaped her quivering lips.

"Livna?" A flash of recognition smoothed the creases between Gershom's eyebrows, but suspicion quickly darkened his countenance again. "You are too old to be Livna's girl."

There was no point arguing. Gershom remembered the child

Tara once was, not the nineteen-year-old woman he'd married. His grip on her wrists tightened.

Feeling her bones about to break, Tara yelped. "You're hurting me."

He pushed her away, and she tipped sideways, her feet tangling in her skirt's heavy pleats. The floor knocked the breath from her lungs. Rather than fuel Gershom's anger, she lay still, peering under the sofa toward the door that led to the great hall and willing help to come.

Hinges creaked again, but the sound came from the wrong door—the corner servant's entrance. Rather than Carmack's black boots, two flour-dusted shoes stood rooted on the threshold.

Ghee, the cook.

"Where is my cane?" Gershom grabbed a fistful of Tara's hair and pulled her onto her knees. "You stole it, didn't you?"

"Ow! No, my lord."

The greasy-faced cook stuck his head into the room. "My lord?"

"Help," Tara whimpered, her eyes locked with Ghee's.

"Get out," Gershom snapped, "or I'll have you drawn and quartered."

"Yes, my lord." Ghee withdrew, shutting the door behind him.

Insufferable coward. "Carmack!" Tara's throat burned from the force of her scream.

"Quiet!" Gershom yanked her hair.

Tara clawed at his hands. Cursing, he released her and reached for the fireplace poker. She scrambled to her feet and lifted her hem to run when the iron shaft hit her shoulder, sending a crippling shock all the way to her fingertips. Gershom jerked the hook loose, snagging her sleeve and leaving a searing trail across her arm.

Suddenly, the main door burst open.

A whirl of muscle catapulted over the sofa with the ferocity of an attacking cham. Gershom let the poker fly again, but Carmack caught it mid-swing and filled the space between Tara and her attacker.

Gershom grunted, straining to free his weapon. "Let go, ruffian!"

With one jerk, Carmack claimed the poker and pointed at the sofa. "Sit!"

Tara's legs wobbled, and she peeked around his wide back. Gershom collapsed onto the sofa, clasping his chest and gasping.

Carmack tossed the poker aside and turned his attention on her. His ecru tunic, leather jerkin, and sable pants suited his dark hair and beard, but his thunderous expression darkened his mahogany eyes. "Are you all right?"

Too shaken to answer, Tara nodded.

Carmack's gaze shifted to her torn sleeve.

Half the length of her finger, the bleeding cut on her arm was the worst she'd ever suffered. If her mother were here, she'd be beside herself.

My dear, you are not allowed cuts, scrapes, or skinned knees like your brothers. Scars are repulsive, especially on a lady.

"You shouldn't be here with him," Carmack said, his deep voice gruffer than usual.

Behind him, Gershom sagged against the cushion, his jagged breaths quieted, and his eyes closed. Thank Arman for that. The ogre was falling back to sleep.

Carmack's gaze never left Tara's bloodied sleeve until he hung his head. How typically Carmack, blaming himself instead of her or even Gershom.

What would Mother say if she had caused a mess like this? Not that she ever would, but a saying popped into Tara's head anyway. *Keep conversations light, and your burdens out of sight.*

Tara gingerly pulled the ripped fabric over her wound. "Perhaps it can be mended with some ribbon?"

Carmack jerked his chin. "Ribbon?"

"No, you're right. Lace would be better."

"Lace? To stop the bleeding?"

"Gracious, no. For my dress."

Carmack pinched the bridge of his nose. "This once, might you forget about your finery long enough to notice you need stitching first?"

"Nonsense. It's naught but a hangnail." Tara waved her hand. With the movement, the cut proved a greater pain than the usual suffocating stays or jabbing hairpins. Unable to hold a steady smile, she brushed past Carmack toward her husband. "Now, help me settle—"

Lord Gershom was reclined at an awkward angle. His hands rested slack on his lap, not twitching. No wheezing rattled his lungs.

Tara's breath caught. The old man had turned positively gray. "My lord?"

Carmack stepped forward. "Lord Gershom?" He nudged Lord Gershom's shoulder, then leaned closer, pressing his fingers against his neck.

Why wouldn't the stubborn old goat answer?

"He's dead," Carmack said. "The fit must have finished him off."

She gasped. Dead? He couldn't be, not really. The old man looked like death on a good day, but Tara couldn't deny his pallor was worse now. And Carmack wouldn't mislead her about Lord Gershom dying. Tara's heart skipped a beat. Her husband *was* dead. Freedom.

Cruel heart, how could she be so unfeeling at a moment like this? But she couldn't help it. When she breathed again, it was as if it were for the first time since her father had announced her engagement.

The servant's door creaked open again. Ghee's gaping mouth betrayed his having eavesdropped. He skittered across the room to Lord Gershom's side. "My lord?" Ghee shouted into the dead man's ear. When no response came, he gave Tara a stilted bow. "Sympathies, my lady."

Sympathies was what one said to despairing widows at funerals, not her. Dizzied by her racing thoughts, Tara swayed.

Carmack steadied her, his strong arm around her waist, and she sagged against him, letting his warmth draw the chill from her bones. "Bring a litter to move Lord Gershom to his bedchamber."

"Aye." Ghee glanced at Carmack's hand upon Tara's waist, his eyes narrowing. "I'll help fer Lord Gershom's sake, but not on account of you asking. I know what you've done," he said and scurried out the servant's door.

The weight of Ghee's accusation sank in, and Tara pulled away from Carmack. "I fear what he will tell the others. What if they blame you for his lordship's death?"

Carmack shrugged. "Let them. The senile wheezer had no right to strike you."

"I am—*was* his wife, little more than his property." Tara swallowed the bitterness rising in her throat. "The men of Meribah Corner are loyal to Lord Gershom. Most have not seen how much his illness changed him in these last months." Worse were those who, like Ghee, had witnessed his outbursts and still revered him. "You saw how Ghee looked at us, what he said. He clearly drew the wrong conclusion. If he spins a tale about you attacking his lordship, you could be arrested or worse. You should return to Tsaftown."

He furrowed his brow. "Only if you go too."

"I can't leave, not with a funeral to plan."

"Then I stay." Carmack crossed his thick arms. "Besides, what excuse would I give Lady Revada for abandoning my post?"

"We both know why my mother sent you here." Tara glanced at the gruesome figure slouched on the sofa. Over the course of her marriage, Lord Gershom had kissed her exactly once, at the end of the wedding ceremony when Tara turned her face at the last second, allowing him to peck her cheek. Every other time her husband had looked her way with that detestable gleam in his eye, Carmack had stepped in, distracting his lordship so Tara could make her escape. "I am no longer in any danger of my husband's attentions."

"Gershom isn't the only monster in these woods."

"It's not monsters I fear but men fed lies and thirsty for vengeance. You have to leave. Let me manage this on my own."

Carmack uncrossed his arms, but instead of bowing, he closed the distance between them. "No, my lady. You need me here, now more than ever."

His tender address stunned Tara. When she stared into his eyes, the gathering storm seemed less ominous. Maybe no one would believe Ghee. Though well-known in Meribah Corner, he was only a cook. Perhaps she and Carmack could push through it. Together.

But she remembered Ghee's accusing gaze when he saw Carmack holding her. Saints, had the cook read something untoward into Carmack's simple gesture of support and mistaken it as motive for murder? Or had her own face betrayed her? While Carmack was always a model Shield, hiding her affection for him wasn't easy. Distance would help and was likely the only way to protect them both from scandal. But how to get Carmack to go?

Tara straightened her spine. She had to pull rank. "When my late father arranged my marriage, the only thought he seemingly gave to my future happiness was to ensure that on the day of Lord Gershom's death, I would inherit Meribah Corner."

Carmack scoffed. "Still a lopsided bargain in the elder's favor."

He had always been Tara's fiercest defender, but now was no time to stoke his protective nature, not when she meant to drive him away. Tara turned her voice to ice. "You miss my point. This estate is now mine, and the last thing I need is another man lording over me."

"I am not your lord, Tara. Or anyone's. Nor will I ever be." Carmack's cheeks reddened. "But as your friend—"

"Master Demry, you will call me Lady Gershom." Her heartbeat quickened in her ears, matching the tempo of the unseen mob advancing in her mind. She raised her chin, determined to see him safely away from those who might harm him. "I order you to leave."

Carmack shifted away from her, his eyes stormy and jaw clenched. "Don't do this. Don't ask me to run like a cowardly deserter."

The stricken look on his handsome face tore at Tara's heart. She hadn't considered how it might look if he left, only the danger of him staying. Ordering him to run was asking him to be less than he was, and Tara couldn't, no more than she could say he was wrong about her needing him, because she did. He'd been nothing less than her lifeline, a constant presence standing guard beside her.

But he couldn't stay beside her, not now. His freedom . . . nay, his very life might be at risk. Feeling her facade slip, Tara spun on her heel. "Fine, remain in Meribah Corner if you must, but stay away from me."

"If you wish it." His deep voice turned gruff. "Good night, my lady."

His parting footsteps faded, and the chill seeped back into Tara's bones until she felt no pain from her injuries. Through the leaded windowpanes, she watched Carmack cross the bailey to the gatehouse where he entered the constable's quarters. The mob Tara feared never came. Only Master Ulmer the steward, Constable Becker, and two guards.

After they carried Gershom's body away, Tara retrieved her sketchbook from the side table.

Haunted by Carmack's hurt expression, she numbly unfolded Viola's letter and stood near the fireplace reading the blurry words through unshed tears. Somehow, a winter of trials had ushered in a season of domestic bliss for Tara's brother and his wife.

True love is possible, even for us . . .

For Viola, perhaps, but Tara would not fall prey to that dream again. She finished her letter and dropped the pages on the pile of dying embers, watching them shrivel in a satisfying flash of heat.

An icy draft whistled through the glass panes, and Tara returned to the window. Outside, the late winter wind whipped a dusting of fresh snow into drifts, erasing her Shield's footprints. The bitterly long season had saved its coldest night for last.

Chapter Two

Carmack

REINFORCEMENTS FROM TSAFTOWN couldn't come fast enough. Until they arrived, Carmack needed to stay out of the constable's shackles while he conducted his inquiry into Gershom's death. Whispers of suspicion had grown into a grumbling chorus, every voice raised, accusing Carmack of murder.

He paced along Meribah Corner's curtain wall, peeking through the crenellations at the road weaving through the leafless forest. What he wouldn't give to see a friendly face riding in with the dawn. Instead, a fat-eyed gargoyle wearing a spiked beard of dripping icicles stared back at him. For the first time after years of Darkness, spring had returned to Meribah Corner. Pity the good weather hadn't thawed Lady Tara's frosty mood.

At the end of the walkway, the gatehouse door opened, and Constable Becker, a tall, thin man, appeared. "There you are, Demry. Get in here and be quick about it."

"Are we under siege, Constable?"

"We, no. But you may be."

Nothing Carmack hadn't expected. The people of Meribah Corner were grieving their lord and wanted someone to blame.

If he was their scapegoat, so be it, so long as a web of rumors and circumstantial evidence didn't turn into a murder charge. Carmack followed Becker down the gatehouse's stairway to his office.

Racks crammed with polearms, bows, swords, and other assorted weapons lined the narrow room. Carmack squeezed around Becker's desk to claim the rickety stool between two doors. One led to the holding cell in the front room, while the other opened into the gatehouse's main passageway.

"Any word about the fugitive from Ice Island?" Carmack asked, steering the conversation to a subject other than Gershom's death. The slave smuggler and his likely escape route through Meribah Corner had been the buzz of the stronghold until Gershom died.

"No." Becker sat in his weathered chair behind his desk. "The slippery eel likely sailed right past us. He's probably halfway back to Cela by now."

"Not without help."

"Slave smugglers always seem to have more friends than they deserve, but it's not the smuggler I wish to discuss. People are talking, Demry."

So much for distracting the good constable from his investigation. Carmack shrugged. "People always talk. A sensible man like you knows it's not always worth listening."

"Sometimes, a man charged with maintaining peace is forced to listen, even when he'd rather not."

"Becker, you've never been one to mince words. No need to start now."

"So be it. You admitted you struggled with Gershom and were there when he collapsed. Why didn't you assist him?"

Carmack shifted and the stool creaked. "As I said before, I didn't realize he was dying. I was preoccupied with Lady Tara's injuries."

Becker's eyebrow quirked upward. "Mm, the entire estate is buzzing about your preoccupation with Lady Tara."

The same old charge dropped on his lap. Carmack had been

denying his feelings for Tara for years, so he met Becker's stare without flinching. "Everyone knows I serve the house of Livna. Her well-being is my sole responsibility."

"Steward Ulmer just informed me that Lady Tara's marital contract provided somewhat more than the standard widow's share. Did you know she is to inherit the whole of Merbah Corner?"

Carmack's pulse quickened. Becker had not raised *this* before. He was sniffing around for a sinister motive. Carmack's knowledge of Tara's inheritance wasn't going to bolster his claim of innocence, but neither would a lie told in fear. "Lady Revada mentioned the terms when she hired me."

"Were you not surprised?"

More than surprised. Gutted. But the generous terms helped explain what was otherwise unthinkable. "Considering the bride's worthiness, and that the man was old, sick, and desperate, no."

"Some would say this proves you had motive to kill him."

"His lordship's death brings me no benefit. If anything, it makes my job more dangerous."

"How so?" Becker asked.

"Everyone dies eventually, and Lady Revada feared his lordship's health would fail sooner rather than later, leaving her young daughter vulnerable to marriage hunters. It's why I'm here." Among other reasons.

"Has the nature of your relationship with Lady Tara changed? You can't deny she has spent more time with you over the course of her marriage than she did with his lordship."

Carmack's ears turned hot, but he couldn't deny it. "I've only done my duty."

"So, there is no intimacy between the two of you?"

"There is not, nor will there ever be." Carmack met the constable's gaze. "On my honor."

Becker stared him down, as if waiting for some break in Carmack's expression, some hint of a lie. He wouldn't find it. Impatience? Absolutely.

Carmack stood, holding out his wrists. "If you mean to arrest me, get on with it."

Becker sat back in his chair, a long breath gusting from his nose. "For the time being, you're free to go. But I warn you, Demry, Terr Ulmer is on the warpath. Normally, the steward would not have authority over my inquiries, but with the accusations of murder flying around and with the local families' support, he has invoked the authority to speak in the lord's place, which puts me in a tenuous position. If there is any evidence to support these rumors, you will bear the charge of murder. And Lady Tara best be careful too. Some, including Ulmer, suspect her of conspiring—"

The rumble of a galloping horse turned Becker's head. Carmack strained to hear the voices outside, but the conversation was muffled.

Someone pounded on the door.

"What is it?" Becker said.

A guard poked his head into the room. "There's a large, shifty-eyed man at the gate. Name's Dunn. Says he's here for Demry."

Praise Arman, Lord Livna had received Carmack's letter. The common folk might feel emboldened to rebel against the young Lady of Meribah Corner, but she was a member of the nobility, a Livna, and sister to the Lord of Tsaftown. Her family had its own, much larger, group of fighting men ready to settle any dispute over Tara's rights to inherit. Carmack knew them well. He used to serve among them.

"My guess it's Lovell Dunn," Carmack said. "My former trainer." And the only man that Carmack requested by name.

Becker's eyes widened. "*The* Lovell Dunn?"

"Strong arm of the Fighting Fifteen?" the guard whispered.

"That's him, but he no longer serves with Tsaftown's fighting men."

"What's he doing here?" Becker asked.

"I sent news of Lord Gershom's death to Tsaftown. I assume Dunn rode ahead to prepare us for Lord Livna's imminent arrival."

"Demry!" Dunn's voice boomed from outside. "Get your scrawny carcass out here and open this gate!"

Carmack bit back a laugh. "He's seldom as violent as he sounds."

"Heads are going to roll!" Dunn's warning echoed off the bailey walls.

Becker signaled the guard. "Don't just stand there. Let him in."

Carmack followed the departing guard but stopped on the threshold. "Constable, about what you said before . . . You're too smart to confuse which of the Gershoms is the victim here."

They locked eyes.

"Then do us both a favor and lie low until this mess is sorted," Becker said.

"I plan on it." Carmack swung the door shut and jogged out to the gate to meet his former trainer, a mountain of a man, dressed head to toe in black that matched his thick hair and beard.

"Finally, you thankless scamp." Dunn dismounted, pulled his horse through the gate door, and lifted Carmack in a rib-crushing bear hug. "Some welcome I get after I busted my backside to make the trip. In record time too."

Carmack slapped Dunn's broad back. "If you'd let me breathe, I'd thank your horse and offer you a handshake."

"A handshake?" Dunn dropped him and stood nose to nose with Carmack, something few men could. "Might as well punch me in the face and insult my mother."

"How is Lady Mildunn these days?"

Daxon Lovell Mildunn, known only as Dunn to most, cast him a sideways look, his green eyes twinkling with no indication of the disease slowly stealing his sight. "Fine, but if you dare mention that name again, I'll be halfway back to Tsaftown before you come to."

Dunn's identity as the youngest son to the lord of Har Sha'ar was a closely held secret. With two older brothers and a slew of nieces and nephews, Dunn had no aspirations of inheriting his father's estate and left nobility behind, determined to make a new name for himself as a soldier. To say he had succeeded was an understatement.

"Can I offer you a trencher of breakfast with my apology?" Carmack asked.

Dunn gave him a playful shove. "Make it two, and I'll let you live."

Carmack led the way to the kitchen where the yeasty aroma of fresh baking bread billowed out of the ovens. A young woman peeling vegetables took one look at Dunn and elbowed her friend.

Dunn must have caught them staring because he winked at them. "Hello there."

Both women dissolved into a fit of blushing and giggles.

Carmack shook his head. "What women see in you, I'll never know."

"Same thing they see in you. Muscles and a good head of hair."

Carmack chuckled and grabbed an empty basket. He filled it with a slab of smoked ham, jars of canned fruit and jelly, a warm loaf of bread, and a jug of ale. Nothing less would do for a soldier built like Dunn. On the kitchen's main table, he spotted the covered dishes used to serve eggs.

Behind it, Ghee wielded his rolling pin and sneered up at him. "What're you doing down here? Breakfast ain't fer another half hour."

"We have a hungry guest who just arrived from Tsaftown. May I offer him a few boiled eggs?"

Ghee sized up Dunn. "Aye, fer your guest, not—"

"For me. Yeah, I get it." Carmack opened the nearest dish and grabbed a handful of eggs, still warm from the pot.

He led Dunn through the timber columns into the diamond-shaped great hall where a dozen men had gathered for the morning meal. Several stared as they walked past three rows of trestle tables, six tabletops long, but no one offered a greeting or a place to sit. When Carmack claimed an empty seat at the fourth row, three guards sitting nearby picked up their trenchers and crossed the room.

"I'm glad to find Meribah Corner lives up to its reputation for hospitality." Dunn turned a slow circle. Like any well-trained guard, he was probably reading the room, taking in every detail from the glowering faces to the number of stairs leading to the second-floor balcony that bordered the hall. He plopped onto the opposite bench and shivered. "Is it just me, or has the temperature plummeted since we came inside?"

"I should have warned you. You're dining with Meribah Corner's pariah. If you sit with the others, I'm sure you'll receive a warmer welcome."

Dunn glanced over at the hostile crowd, then stretched his massive arms wide. "And give up all this room?" He slugged Carmack's bicep and raised the jug of ale. "Thanks be to Arman for this fine feast and good company!" His roaring voice bounced off the hammer-beam ceiling, startling several onlookers.

While Dunn chewed through the basket's contents, Carmack spilled the details of Gershom's death and the rumors swirling around Meribah Corner.

"I'd ask why your brother isn't here instead of a weak-eyed, retired sword-slinger," Dunn said, "but I heard he sailed out with Vexley Larr and Cerdic Ironblade on the *Brierstar*."

"Aye, he wrote. Apparently, Captain Chantry needed some extra fighting power before joining the Jaelport blockade."

Dunn chewed. "Did you two patch things up after you left the Fifteen?"

Far from it. Besides, Carmack had heard all Roxburg had to say. Nothing he did would ever meet his older brother's approval. "I didn't bring you here to negotiate a peace treaty with my brother."

"Fine, I'll keep my nose out of it. Anything else I should know?"

"The constable and I were chatting when you rode up. Seems I'm suspected of murder, and Lady Tara, my rumored conspirator."

Dunn's chewing slowed. "Am I wrong to assume you two have been thick as thieves since your days with the Fifteen ended?"

"Shut it." Carmack grabbed a boiled egg and smacked it against the table.

Dunn grinned. "And how is the lovely Lady Tara faring?"

Carmack picked away the shattered bits of eggshell. "Stubborn woman hasn't left her blasted room in four days."

"Wasn't asking you." Dunn rose from his seat and bowed. "M'lady, nice to see you again."

Carmack spun from his seat, knocking his bench backward. He stopped it from tipping and bowed stiffly in one awkward movement. Lady Tara barely glanced his way. Praise Arman. If she'd overheard, she wasn't in the mood to scold, despite her up-tight outfit. Her whitish blonde hair was in a tight knot, and her gray dress dulled her pale skin. Tara would always be beautiful, but the pretty, carefree girl Carmack had first met at Lytton Hall seemed long gone.

"Master Dunn, I thought it was your voice I heard." Tara smiled. "I am relieved to find my ears did not deceive me."

"My sympathies on the loss of Lord Gershom," Dunn said.

Tara's smile faltered. "Tell me, when can we expect my family?"

"I'm afraid your mother has taken to her bed with a bad cold. Her healer advised she not travel until it passes."

"Oh no, I am sorry to hear she won't be coming, though I'm glad her illness isn't serious. Well, at least I will still have my brother and his family here." When Dunn winced, Tara's shoulders sagged. "He's not coming either, is he?"

"Unfortunately, Lord and Lady Livna cannot attend Lord Gershom's funeral due to some pressing business in Tsaftown. He asked me to pass along his sincere apologies."

Tara's face fell, along with Carmack's hopes of Lord Livna's support, and she massaged her upper arm.

"How's the cut?" he asked.

She dropped her hand. "Naught but a hangnail, Master Demry." Without making eye contact, she added, "I will leave you to enjoy your breakfast."

Dunn's gaze skipped between Carmack and Lady Tara as she walked away. "What did I miss?"

"She's avoiding me to stop the gossipmongers." Carmack noted the faces that turned hostile as Tara crossed the room.

"It won't work." Dunn plopped back down. "Not with you staring at her like a lovesick goat."

Carmack didn't blink. Across the hall, the pimple-faced tanner whispered something to Spratt, a guard at his table, then stuck his boot into Tara's path. She fell to her knees and yelped.

Carmack bolted over and helped her to her feet. "You okay?"

She nodded, blushing as the men surrounding them snickered. Carmack clenched his jaw and sized up his morning work. The tanner first, then his friends.

Dunn rushed to his side. With one glance at Carmack, he said, "Right. M'lady, I recommend you enjoy breakfast in your chamber."

While Dunn directed Tara to the stairs, Carmack lifted the tanner from his seat and pushed him against the nearest timber column.

The tanner's face reddened. "You going to kill me too?" Above him, Lady Tara scrambled up the steps, taking two at a time. Gasping for breath, the tanner laughed. "There goes your clumsy tart, off to nurse her guilty conscience."

Carmack punched once, and the tanner crumpled into a silent heap. Benches grated across the stone floor as the blacksmith, a stableman, and Spratt and Jenkins, the two guards who had been sitting with the tanner, rose from their seats.

Dunn fell in next to Carmack. "You had to knock him out in front of his friends?"

Four against two. Easy. "Never stopped you before."

"Right." Dunn turned to the men, his arms outstretched. "Now, gentlemen . . ." Like a battering ram, he charged forward and drove Jenkins and the stableman backward. The empty bench caught their knees, and the three slammed into the tabletop, knocking it from its trestles.

Carmack aimed a quick jab at Spratt's nose. Spratt reared back, and Carmack's knuckles grazed his turned cheek. Spratt wound up. Carmack ducked his oncoming fist, caught his arm, and shoved him away.

A strong blow to Carmack's ribs knocked the air from his lungs. He grunted, then spun out of the blacksmith's reach. The spasm in his lungs released, and Carmack returned a quick uppercut to the blacksmith's chin, sending him to the floor, out cold.

A groan grabbed Carmack's attention. Dunn and his opponents had found their feet. Judging by the way the stableman was stumbling away, he'd tasted Dunn's right hook, but Jenkins was closing in on Dunn's left side.

"Look out!" Carmack shouted.

Dunn spun, spotted Jenkins, and buried his fist in his gut.

Knuckles smashed Carmack's cheek. His eyes watered, blurring his view of Spratt's ugly smirk. Carmack punched the mouthful of crooked teeth. On impact, Spratt reeled. Carmack leaped over a fallen bench and trestle, giving himself more room to maneuver. Spratt barreled after him. Dunn, who had Jenkins by the scruff of his neck and waistband, hurled him into Spratt, sending both guards crashing onto what remained of their dining table.

The room fell silent, apart from the moaning of the men lying on the floor.

"Is there a problem, Demry?"

Carmack's head snapped up.

Becker stood beside the head table, surveying the bodies, either unconscious or writhing in pain, splayed out across the hall.

Carmack straightened his leather jerkin and started toward the exit. "We were just leaving, Constable. Weren't we, Dunn?"

Dunn smoothed his wild hair and followed. "Yes, delicious breakfast, sir," he said, pausing to shake Becker's hand on the way out. "Wonderful conversation."

They exited into the diamond-shaped bailey, lined by outbuildings with clapboard shingles peeking through a blanket of melting snow. Carmack scooped up a handful of slush from along the keep wall and pressed it against his swelling cheek. "Sorry I got you into this mess."

"I'm not. Best day of retirement, yet." Dunn patted Carmack's shoulder. "Like old times."

"Except it's morning, and we're stone-cold sober."

Dunn laughed and dabbed blood from his cut lip. "Thanks for watching my back in there."

"Arman knows, I owed you one."

Dunn had looked out for Carmack in Tsaftown and used to always see the next blow coming. But after the false prince Esek had murdered Tara's father on Dunn's watch, Dunn had written to Carmack, confessing his failing eyesight and his decision to resign his post. "How are the eyes?" Carmack asked.

"'Bout the same as yours, according to that bruise on your cheek," Dunn said, never one to admit weakness. "So, what's the plan?"

Carmack shrugged. "Lie low until his lordship arrives."

"Well, that's not happening anytime soon." Dunn looked back toward the great hall. "Something tells me you'll be needing a fallback, and you better not say—"

"Improvise," they said together.

Dunn groaned. "Why not hunker down in Tsaftown? I could

guard Lady Tara until she settles into her new role and the rumors die out."

Not a bad idea, but not one Carmack favored. Although he trusted Dunn to watch his back, Tara was Carmack's responsibility—one he wouldn't surrender to Arman Himself, much less a man going blind. Besides, when Carmack ran from trouble, people he loved paid the price.

He tossed the slush aside. "I'm not going anywhere."

CHAPTER THREE
TARA

W e walk in the light when we follow our Guide.
The Light of the World is Câan.

TARA SAT AT HER DRESSING TABLE, humming the tune and tapping her toes while her maid, Kressy, brushed her hair.

Alas, funerals were not supposed to be happy occasions. She had a role to play, that of a mourning widow. Anything less would cause a scandal. Tara glanced at the endless azure sky outside her window and sighed. She'd rather kiss a cham bear than pine for the Darkness that once plagued Er'Rets, but she'd welcome a heavy blanket of gray clouds, stiff wind, and freezing drizzle to anchor her spirits.

The perils of stormy weather turned her thoughts to her brother, somewhere at sea aboard the *Brierstar*. Tara studied her embroidered rendering of the mighty sailing ship hanging near the window. What adventures might her brother Leif be having onboard?

"Would you prefer the crowned braid or two side loops, m'lady?" Kressy asked.

"Neither." Tara dabbed her wrists with the bottle of jasmine perfume. "The nape coil will do."

"But you wore it that way yesterday."

"And I shall again today, and for the foreseeable future."

Her honey-blonde maid wrinkled her freckled nose. "The coil isn't very pretty."

"Exactly why I chose it. I'm no longer a young maiden. I'm Lady of Meribah Corner and a widow, not the queen of Er'Rets." Though, if fate had been kinder, she might have been.

In the mirror, Kressy frowned.

"You disapprove?" Tara asked.

"Hiding your curls like an old woman won't change how people see you, m'lady."

Tara almost laughed at the irony. Nothing would change the fact that people didn't see *her* at all. Her face, her hairstyle, and her wardrobe, yes—but not who she really was inside.

"They're already wagering on who you'll marry next," Kressy said.

Tara's temples pinched while Kressy twisted her hair into a tight knot. "Then they will be disappointed. I have no plans to remarry."

"Why not? You're not yet twenty. Plenty of time to start a family."

Tara's dream of having a husband and children once guided her every step across banquet halls throughout the kingdom, but reality had proved marriage nothing short of a nightmare. "I prefer to remain alone."

"I'm not sure people will understand your preference."

"They don't need to understand. They simply must accept it. Aunt Nitsa managed Carm Duchy alone for years after Lord Amal died, and the people love her."

Kressy jabbed a pin into the tight knot of hair, her gray eyes darting sideways.

Tara winced. "Surely, you can't disagree with me on that?"

"As you say, m'lady."

Tara turned in her seat. "Don't you dare 'as you say, m'lady' me, Kressy Linwood. If you disagree, then say so. I won't have my maid hiding her true feelings."

Kressy's face fell. "I mean no disrespect, Lady Tara, but your circumstances are different from your aunt's. The duchess was older when Lord Amal died, and she had children." Not to mention her bloodvoicing gift, but Kressy didn't need to know about that. "Yet even she and your cousins lived under constant threat until she married Sir Eagan."

The only thing that made a woman more vulnerable to ambitious men than beauty was wealth. Aunt Nitsa had both and had been harassed by Lord Nathak, who had sought to gain control of Carm through marriage. "Well, no one's going to abduct me, not with Master Demry around. Did you happen to see him earlier?"

Kressy opened Tara's wardrobe. "He's right outside the door."

Tara rose. "I might have guessed after yesterday's excitement."

"They should lock that troll in the stocks for tripping you. Lord Gershom's not yet resting in his grave, and already the men have forgotten you're the lady of this house." Kressy grimaced, pulling the gray gown from the hanging rod. "I assume you'll be wanting to wear this one again."

"I don't have much choice. The dressmaker supposedly didn't have fabric to make me a black gown for the funeral."

"Hogwash. I'd bet Master Ulmer hasn't paid for your last gown."

Tara barely heard Kressy's words. How often had her mother preached a lady's power depended on her presentation? When Tara had worn her plain gray dress and hair in a simple knot, people hadn't seen her as more demure, only less noble. "On second thought, how about the aubergine?"

"For the funeral?"

"It's somewhat close to black." And was by far Tara's most extravagant gown. If people had forgotten her station, she would provide a reminder.

"As you wish, m'lady." Kressy shoved the gray silk back into place. Once she had gathered all the pieces of Tara's elaborate ensemble, she began lacing, pinning, and tying everything into place.

When she finished, Tara asked Kressy to rearrange her hair in an intricate waterfall braid, woven with golden ribbon to match her gown's embroidery.

Tara stepped in front of her mirror transformed, but she couldn't shake the feeling she'd need more than a fancy dress to improve her standing in Meribah Corner. Tara's father often attributed the marked decline of Lord Gershom's estate to some level of mismanagement. If he had been correct, and Tara could right the estate's affairs, perhaps she could earn the people's respect. Master Ulmer's delinquency in paying the dressmaker seemed a prudent first step.

She put her wedding ring on last. "I am ready."

"Wait." Kressy retrieved a black mourning veil from the wardrobe. "You'll need this for the procession."

"Not yet. I must speak with someone first."

Kressy's eyes twinkled. "Master Demry?"

"No." Tara arched her eyebrow. "Master Ulmer."

Kressy sobered. "You're not going to confront that horrible man because of what I said about the dressmaker, are you?"

"In part. To manage this estate, I will have to deal with its steward, no matter how vile a creature he may be." Tara gave one parting look to her reflection. She couldn't remember the last time she had dressed so well. Perhaps the gray gown would have been more fitting. Or, better yet, a suit of armor.

Tara swung open her chamber door, and her mouth went dry. Carmack stood inches away, dressed head to toe in black. The straps crossing his doublet accentuated his broad chest, while his trousers skimmed his muscular legs. Tara marched past him. Out of the corner of her eye, she saw him take a second glance at her gown.

His heavy steps followed her. "Going somewhere, my lady?"

"Obviously."

"To the funeral?"

"Eventually."

"And until then?" Carmack asked.

"I will be inspecting the estate's ledgers."

Carmack followed Tara to the steward's study. "I am no expert in ladies' fashion," he said, "but you look overdressed for accounting."

Tara whirled around. Her nose grazed his doublet, catching an intoxicating blend of leather and pine. "As you said, you are not an expert. In the future, please keep such opinions to yourself." She stepped back. "And do not follow so closely. You nearly ran me over."

"Perhaps you should save your pirouettes for the dance floor."

When they reached Master Ulmer's office, Carmack swung open the door.

Tara swept past him. "Wait here."

The steward's office looked as though an Eben giant had ransacked the archives. Scrolls and ledgers littered two long tables along each side of the room. Others lay in makeshift piles. In the middle of the chaos, Terr Ulmer perched on his stool behind a tall desk. Dressed in an oversized brown tunic and small woolen cap, he resembled a rat holding court over stacks of ledgers, coin bags, and dirty tankards.

Though his quill scratched to a stop, he failed to stand and bow. "Are you not leading the funeral procession this morning?"

How dare the gaunt little miser speak to Tara as his equal? The warning Master Dunn had whispered as she fled the great hall the previous morning proved true. *They're testing you.* First the tanner, now the steward. Tara's mother had the perfect unspoken response for such breaches in etiquette—chin up, nostrils slightly flared, and one eyebrow arched. Tara did her best impression and did not answer.

The steward grimaced, hopped off his stool, and bowed, his bald head disappearing behind the mess. "M'lady."

Honey traps more flies than vinegar. Tara relaxed her scowl. "The procession is not for another hour. I thought I should use this time to better acquaint myself with the business of Meribah Corner."

Master Ulmer slid whatever he'd been writing under the nearest book. "All is well taken care of."

"I never suggested otherwise, although it has come to my attention that the dressmaker's bill remains unpaid. I was quite certain you would not have overlooked it, so a quick confirmation of your ledger will suffice."

"This is no time to trouble yourself with maddening columns of numbers."

Tara gritted her teeth. "How thoughtful. However, numbers are no trouble to me. My mother kept careful accounting of Lytton Hall and has taught me well." Master Ulmer would have known as much had he not blocked her previous attempts to manage the estate, citing Lord Gershom's instructions—a feeble excuse that had expired with her husband.

Tara spied a thin, wide, leather-bound book resembling a ledger and pulled it from the stack. "Ah, here we are."

Master Ulmer slapped down the cover. "Your time is better spent mourning your husband." He snatched the book, sending a prickling sting through Tara's wounded arm, and retreated to his desk.

Insufferable impertinence.

Yes, dear, her mother would say, *but do not raise your voice. No one heeds a shrill woman.*

Tara fought to rein in her temper. "I best honor Lord Gershom's memory through the impeccable management of his—rather, *my* estate."

"I disagree, my lady. Your sole responsibility is to remarry and quickly."

Tara's jaw slackened. Surely, discussing remarriage twice before her husband's funeral luncheon was as insupportable as humming a happy tune. "I have neither the need nor the intention of remarrying, sir."

"You fail to appreciate how vulnerable young widows of means are to unscrupulous fortune hunters."

"Some may be, but not I. The stronghold is secure, and Master Demry is a very capable Shield."

"Master Demry takes prodigious care of you; however, I fear he will not be a free man for long."

A rap on the door answered, and a squat man with thinning red hair and a thick fur coat stepped sideways into the room. Over his shoulder, Carmack shot Tara a look, but she waved him off. As the lady of the house, she could stand on her own and would command the proper respect from every person in her house, even without her Shield's intimidating presence to ensure they showed it.

Master Ulmer's eyes lit up. "Ah, what fortuitous timing. Master Thusk, allow me to introduce you. Lady Gershom, Master Thusk owns the local shipping fleet that takes our goods to market." He dropped his voice. "And is a highly eligible bachelor."

Tara's head whipped sideways. Though she had never met her wealthy neighbor, she had overheard enough about Thusk's cutthroat business methods and womanizing to know she did not want an introduction. Master Ulmer couldn't possibly view him as a potential suitor for her, but the gleam in his beady eyes said otherwise.

Master Thusk wobbled over, smelling of brine and fish. He clasped Tara's hand and pressed it to his wet lips. "My lady, how unfortunate we are to meet on such a sad occasion."

Tara's skin crawled. As if meeting a disreputable man could ever be deemed fortunate. If Arman knew the day would bring this odious beast to Meribah Corner, why in Er'Rets had He allowed Tara to wear her best dress? She forced a grin and jerked her hand free. "Excuse me, sir, my steward and I have private business to discuss." She nodded toward the door. "If you would please wait in the great hall, we will have sufficient opportunity to become acquainted after the funeral."

"I would like nothing more. Master Ulmer, we can discuss the terms of the next, er, shipment later. Having inspected the goods, I'm eager to get underway." Thusk winked at Tara.

Tara's smile slipped. Was there anything more uncouth than flirting with a widow on her husband's burial day?

"Shipment?" Master Ulmer's face went blank until Thusk gave him a pointed look. "Ah, of course, sir. As promised, I am doing everything to arrange expedient delivery."

"See that you do." Thusk bowed, his eyes remaining level with Tara's bodice instead of dropping to the floor. "Until later, m'lady."

As soon as the door closed behind him, she whirled around to Master Ulmer. "Lest you entertain any foolish notions, I would sooner marry a whale than a scoundrel like Magnus Thusk."

Master Ulmer's countenance darkened. "The match would benefit Meribah Corner and restore your tattered reputation. As things stand, many suspect that you and Master Demry conspired to murder Lord Gershom so you could marry each other."

"That's a wicked falsehood! Master Demry merely prevented Lord Gershom from inflicting serious harm upon me. He didn't so much as touch his lordship."

"Nonetheless, a rumor's potency lies not in its veracity but in people's desire to believe it. Unless you convince them otherwise, Master Demry will bear the full weight of the law." Master Ulmer craned his head toward Tara's ear. "And consider how your unusual familiarity might support the charges against him."

Tara recoiled. "Master Demry is my Shield, nothing more. He has served my family for years."

"I'm afraid that only supports the speculation." Master Ulmer tapped his quill's feather against his lips. "As does Master Demry's constant presence at your side, your frequent disappearances into the woods together, and his incessant interference with Lord Gershom. Some say Master Demry prevented the consummation of your marriage. Even if the charges against him fail, the validity of your marriage and right to inherit may not survive the challenge."

Tara saw red. She could not deny Master Ulmer's charges, nor would she change anything if she could, but she wanted nothing more than to dismiss him from his position. "You overstep, sir. Not only have you wandered well beyond your area of expertise, but you have assaulted the bounds of decency. Shall I presume this offense serves as your notice of resignation?"

"No." Master Ulmer straightened. "As steward, I am responsible for the administration of justice in the lord's absence. Should my employment be terminated before the inquest into his death is completed, the shadow of guilt hanging over you would, I fear, darken."

"So, you repeat baseless and inappropriate speculations to what end?"

"Only to remind you that our late lord was not always the afflicted man you knew as your husband. His tenants remember him fondly and would rather his lands be forfeited to the crown than pass to another unworthy lady."

"I was Lord Gershom's wife. How dare you imply I am unworthy?"

"I'm not surprised that your parents kept that piece of Meribah Corner's history from you. You see, your late husband was not the first Lord Gershom to die under suspicious circumstances. Lord Alexei Gershom was believed to have perished on an adversary's sword after a humiliating bout; however, locals regard his jealous wife as his true killer. I believe Lady Adira Gershom was a distant relation of yours."

"A very distant relative, who has nothing to do with whether or not I inherit."

"Had Lady Adira been tried and convicted, she would have been put to death and this estate forfeited to the crown. Back then, no one dared speak up against the murderous lady, and people believe Meribah Corner is cursed because of it. Eager to reverse their misfortune, they will not allow history to repeat itself."

Sweat formed along Tara's hairline. No wonder the tenants and servants had turned hostile.

"Mark my words," Master Ulmer said, "you will not be Lady of Meribah Corner long unless you dispel the salacious rumors surrounding you and your Shield by marrying Magnus Thusk."

His ridiculous ultimatum killed Tara's desire to inspect her estate's records. "I will consider your advice, Master Ulmer, but even you must appreciate the impropriety of remarrying before the customary mourning period ends." Tara headed for the door.

"I would not wait, my lady," he called after her, "for justice does not bow to decorum."

Tara had nothing to fear from justice. She and Carmack were innocent. But another loveless marriage? She refused to suffer that miserable fate again.

CHAPTER FOUR
CARMACK

CARMACK FELT LIKE A CHAINED BEAR standing in the cramped corridor outside Ulmer's office. The reek of fish still lingered, though Magnus Thusk had wobbled back to the great hall. On the other side of the door, Tara's muffled voice hit a higher octave, and Carmack fought the urge to check on her. She'd said to wait, so wait he would.

The door suddenly flew open, and Tara stormed out of Ulmer's office like her hem was on fire. Carmack hurried after her.

She ignored at least a dozen bows and curtsies from the funeral guests gathered in the great hall. Not like Tara at all. That weasel Ulmer must have said something despicable to make Lady Hospitality forget her manners. If he had threatened Tara in any way, Carmack needed to know about it. He sped his steps to match hers as she fled the hall and sprinted out of the keep, making a beeline for the chapel, a one-room building mere steps from the front door.

Once inside, Tara plopped down in the window seat closest to the open coffin. One sniff became a series of sniffs, and she dabbed tears from her eyes. Other than the wood altar and Gershom's coffin, the chapel offered no furnishings to stop her choked sobs from echoing off the brightly painted walls and arched ceiling—the sound eerily similar to her wedding day.

Tara usually kept her emotions tucked behind the impassive mask of dutiful daughter, wife, and lady. Most days, Carmack resented that mask for hiding her spirit, though he preferred it to listening to her crying. She probably wished he wasn't there and wouldn't talk to him until she pulled herself together anyway. He headed for the door.

"Don't go," she whispered.

"I thought you'd prefer to be alone."

She stared blankly at the coffin. "You, of all people, should know me better than that."

He did, but his bruised ego had its own complaint. "Lately, you've made it obvious that you do not want me around."

"I'm sorry. I thought distance would stifle gossip, but I'm convinced now nothing will. Please, stay."

Carmack's heart pulled him toward the empty spot on her bench, where he might easily hold her hand. Better to steer clear. He leaned against the wall. "What has you so upset?" It certainly wasn't the old man in the pine box.

"Magnus Thusk."

"I knew I should have followed him into Ulmer's office."

Tara sniffed. "It seems I must marry him."

Over Carmack's dead body. The ugly thug was rich, but he was way below her station. Why would Tara even entertain the thought? The notion was closer to an insult, one that undoubtedly put those tears in her eyes. "Let me guess. Ulmer's idea?"

"He thinks marrying Master Thusk is the only way I can assure the people of Meribah Corner that I am a worthy lady."

"He's mad. You are a nobleman's daughter, and a Livna."

"My lineage only complicates matters. Apparently, people here believe my great-aunt Adira killed her husband, a previous Lord

Gershom. They view Meribah Corner's decline as their punishment for not bringing her to justice."

"Superstitious fools." Carmack pushed away from the wall and paced. "Darkness is to blame, not your aunt."

"Master Ulmer advised that Master Thusk's shipping fleet would be a boon to Meribah Corner, and if I married quickly, I could silence any speculation that you and I . . . that we . . ."

Carmack froze in his tracks. "No need to repeat it." *Stay away from thin ice.* "We both know the rumors aren't true."

"What if the truth isn't enough?" Tara's eyes filled with fresh tears. "When Lord Gershom was still alive, I often imagined what it would be like to be his widow. I certainly didn't expect another loveless marriage with someone as despicable as Magnus Thusk."

That wasn't going to happen. Carmack's job keeping her out of Lord Gershom's clutches had been hard enough, and he had been a doddering old fool. Should she remarry a scheming walrus like Magnus Thusk, Carmack would be helpless to prevent the inevitable. He had to kill the notion at its root. "You should be asking what your steward has to gain. What does Thusk have that Ulmer wants, not just for Meribah Corner, but for himself?"

"How should I know? The only thing Master Ulmer seems interested in is money."

"And Thusk has plenty. Ulmer likely saw an opportunity and offered his matchmaking services for a generous fee."

"They did seem to share some unspoken understanding about an imminent delivery of goods. Could they have meant me?" Tara shook her head. "I hardly set the hook. I was practically uncivil in dismissing Thusk."

As if a few curt words would distract any man from everything else she had to offer. "He's no gentleman. You could have insulted his grandmother, and he would have overlooked it."

"If he is not a gentleman, why would he be gracious to me?"

"Because you're young, kind, wealthy, and beautiful beyond

compare. How many similar women do you think roam Meribah Corner?"

Tara's mouth popped open.

Blasted tongue. He'd said too much. Her tearstained, sapphire eyes were already softening, pulling him in. Carmack forced himself to look away. The one thing he could not do was give her the impression *he* saw her that way. She could never know the depth of fondness he felt for her. "Or so the song goes."

"Song?"

"No particular song. I only meant that people have been praising your beauty since your first banquet."

Her face fell. "How tiresome to have one's appearance valued above all else."

Tara would know. It happened everywhere she went. Strangers fawning over her, complimenting her looks, never commenting about how clever or kind she was. Not to mention resilient, like a velvet-covered brick.

But everyone had a limit, and Carmack hated to see Tara reach hers. Only Arman could change her circumstances, but Carmack hadn't prayed in a while. He squeezed next to Tara on the window seat and nudged her shoulder. "Ignore Thusk. With any luck, he'll come to his senses, like King Gidon did, and fall deeply in love with a more suitable bride by year's end."

Tara's cheeks reddened. "A more suitable bride?"

Carmack fought to keep a straight face. "Aye, I'm sure our young king praises Arman every time he remembers slipping the noose of his first marriage proposal."

"Slipping the noose! Am I as bad as that?"

"Well, no," Carmack said, and Tara relaxed slightly. "But you would have made a rubbish queen."

Tara gasped. "Carmack Demry!"

"You asked, my lady, and I won't insult you by lying."

"So, you resort to cruelty instead." She slouched back into the window seat. "Do you really think I'd have been a rubbish queen?"

"Only on those days you'd pout over how hard it is to be so beautiful." He winced, clutching his chest in mock distress.

Tara's eyes flashed, and she elbowed him. "How dare you tease me!"

Carmack grinned.

She swung her elbow again, faster, and fine strands of hair along her face broke free from her braid.

His fingers itched to reach out and tuck them behind her ear. Instead, he caught her arm midair. "Careful. You're mussing up your hair."

Tara wrenched free, huffed, then smoothed her hair and skirts. No sign of tears remained.

Success.

She crossed to Gershom's coffin. "It's quite shocking to see him like this."

Carmack went to her side. Lord Gershom was laid out in a fine linen shirt with frilly laced cuffs and collar. A sumptuous robe of crimson brocade and gleaming ebony fur disguised his frail stature. His cheeks were stretched smooth, stuffed with embalming herbs, and caked with rouge. Ruby wax colored his lips.

"The real shock is that he smells better dead, and his color has improved," Carmack said.

Tara pressed her handkerchief to her mouth, stifling a snort.

"Brace yourself for the undertaker's bill. He must have used up all his herbs and face paint."

With that, Tara doubled over with laughter, one hand holding her handkerchief against her stomach and the other gripping his forearm.

"Demry!" Constable Becker called from the back of the chapel, his angry tone sending a shock down Carmack's spine.

Uh-oh. His stomach sank. This wasn't good. The two of them

caught unawares, Tara holding his arm and both laughing over her dead husband. Horrible, foolish mistake. Carmack sprang away from Tara so abruptly she stumbled.

Becker marched up to them and bowed stiffly. "M'lady, if you're ready, the crowd has gathered in the inner bailey for the procession."

"Thank you, Constable." The glint of mirth hadn't completely left her eyes. "As soon as my maid arrives with my veil, we can depart. Master Demry, will you please fetch Kressy?"

Carmack bowed his head, but Becker gripped his shoulder. "Stay here, Demry. We need to talk." He withdrew his hand and motioned toward the chapel door. "Some of the guests are waiting nearby. It would be best if you both cooperated."

Carmack's stomach sank. Had the funeral guests heard Tara and Carmack laughing? "How long have they been there?"

Becker gave him a knowing look. "Long enough. Forgive me, m'lady, but what could have possessed you to behave so recklessly? Today, of all days!"

Tara frantically looked to him.

Put on your Lady Tara mask, Carmack silently pleaded, and stepped forward. "This was my fault. Lady Gershom was grieving, so to cheer her, I made a joke."

Becker frowned. "You best fetch your maid, m'lady."

"So long as Master Demry escorts me."

Carmack's heart swelled, but Becker shook his head. Carmack wasn't going anywhere. "I should stay. We don't want another scene like yesterday's in the great hall. Besides, Master Dunn is desperate to make himself useful."

Tara sighed. "When you put it that way, it's hard to argue."

Becker bowed as she departed.

"I appreciate your cooperation, Demry, though it won't do you much good," Becker said. "Master Ulmer has ordered me to arrest you for the murder of Lord Gershom."

Carmack crossed his arms. "He has no authority to make such an order. You're the constable."

"In the lord's absence, his steward may serve as his substitute to maintain law and order. Until the circumstances of his lordship's death are sorted, what choice do I have?"

Anything but this. If Carmack were stuck behind bars, keeping Tara away from knaves like Thusk would be impossible. "Choose to do what's right, man!"

"Ulmer pays my wages and those of every person here. We have families to feed, so while you may question his authority, do not underestimate the power he wields." Becker lowered his voice. "I know you're no murderer, Demry, but until I clear your name, my holding cell is the safest place for you."

CHAPTER FIVE
TARA

EVERYTHING LOOKED BLEAK WHEN viewed through the black mesh of a mourning veil. Tara followed closely behind the eight guardsmen carrying Lord Gershom's coffin through the crowded bailey. Dozens of tenants, vassals, and their families clumped together, everyone donning their best tunics and wraps. When their pall of silent reverence gave way to whispers, Tara stepped sideways into Master Dunn's shadow. Like Carmack, he was tall and fit, with a few gray hairs in his beard and more creases around his green eyes as they scanned the bailey. Tara pulled Kressy's arm tight against her other side as she scanned the bystanders.

One woman's icy stare seemed to slice through Tara's veil and pierce her very soul with unspoken hatred. Tara whipped her gaze away and kept her eyes fixed straight ahead. On each side of the gatehouse, guards lined the sentry wall, their heads bowed to pay their respects to their lord as the local priest led the burial procession into the forest outside the stronghold.

"Slide two steps to the left, m'lady," Dunn said.

Tara guided Kressy on a leftward course beneath the first of the gatehouse's two portcullises. Something dropped through the nearest murder hole. Eggshell and a blackened yolk splattered against the cobblestones, missing Tara's gown by mere inches. The rancid smell of sulfur filled the air.

Kressy's pert nose wrinkled. She raised a fist, but Tara lowered it. "Mother always says, 'Vengeance is Arman's.'"

"No disrespect to Lady Revada or Arman, but those mules need to know their place."

"I need your arm more," Tara said. "This path is slippery, and I refuse to create a spectacle by falling in the mud." Her laughter in the chapel would be enough to unhinge the tongues of gossip-mongers. "Let's just get through this without drawing any extra attention."

Kressy frowned. "Then the gray dress would have done."

Indeed, it would have.

Once Tara passed under the second portcullis, the crowd thinned, lifting a weight from her shoulders. The crisp air scented by woodsy pine, damp moss, and thawing earth cleared her mind. Weeks had passed since she and Carmack had taken their last ride outside the walls of the stronghold, a pastime both had enjoyed on the rare occasion the weather and Lord Gershom's temperament cooperated.

Of all the forest paths Tara had explored, the one leading to the Gershom family crypt was her favorite. It meandered through a wide gorge, bordered by cliffs and filled with ancient pines. Along the way, a footbridge crossed a narrow stream fed by the glossy cascade of an icy waterfall, where, drop by drop, the spring sun freed the water from its frozen state. From there, the snowy path descended to a lake, set like a brilliant turquoise gem cradled within prongs of frosted rock. Ice, polished by the wind, covered half the water while wisps of steam rose from the portion warmed by hot springs. A spectacle so breathtaking, Tara could not behold it without wonder at the beauty of Arman's creation. How sad that the lake had spent so many years hidden by the thick shroud of Darkness, unable to reflect its Maker's glory.

As the procession followed an uphill fork in the path, Tara faced a less scintillating view. The stoic priest climbed a series of stone steps in the cliff face to the crypt's opening. Two pillars carved into the mountain framed each side of the door, with a pediment bridging them, creating a temple-like facade.

The funeral party gathered around the priest as he opened his prayer book and read, "O Arman, since the first sunrise, you have loved your people. Your hand forms us, in your hand we live, and to your hand we return. Throughout time and space, you have revealed yourself, and ultimately, your word dwelt among us in the body of your son, Câan. In his life, death, and resurrection, we find our calling in this world and our hope for Shamayim, the world to come. In this great hope, we commend to you our brother Lord Vadin Gershom and commit his body to this resting place."

The priest sang the opening notes of a hymn, and the crowd joined in. When the singing stopped, the pallbearers carried the coffin into the crypt, and the priest followed them.

Tara whispered to Kressy and Dunn, "Please see everyone returns to the great hall for the banquet. Should anyone wish to offer condolences, I will receive them there. For now, I wish to be alone."

Kressy curtsied. "As you wish, m'lady."

"Take as long as you like," Dunn said. "I'll wait here for you."

The guards reemerged without the coffin, and Tara ascended the stairs and went inside. Her eyes adjusted to the crypt's darkness as the priest pressed a cloth sack into her hand. Gershom's coffin sat in a long hole cut into the vault's wall. Tara approached and emptied the soil from the sack onto it.

The priest left. His parting chant drifted in, joined by the voices of those gathered outside.

"*Arman hu elohim, Arman hu echâd, Arman hu shlosha beechâd.* Arman is God. Arman is One. Arman is Three in One."

Tara tugged her wedding band from her finger, and her wounded shoulder twinged painfully. She set the ring on the coffin. *Now we shall both be at peace, my lord.*

The assembly's murmuring faded, shushed by the afternoon winds. As much as Tara wanted to flee the crypt, she remained. If she left too soon, she might encounter some disgruntled townsfolk or their rotten eggs. Better to wait a while longer.

Tara read the names carved into the crypt walls. She could not imagine her name being among them one day. Not one night had she slept next to Gershom when he lived. Why should she spend eternity beside his bones in death?

A woman's hooded figure darkened the doorway. How had she snuck past Master Dunn? "I'm sorry," Tara said, "but I am not receiving visitors. Please proceed to the great hall with the rest of the funeral party."

The woman stepped closer. "I never go out of my way for that kind of party."

A waft of spicy perfume and the woman's southern accent gave her identity away before she lowered her hood, revealing tight braids, glowing skin, and sharp cheekbones.

Tara lifted her mourning veil to see what she never would have believed otherwise. "Jaira!"

"Hush! I hope marriage hasn't made you prone to hysterics."

Tara's heart leaped at the sight of Jaira's familiar scowl, and she embraced her childhood friend. "I'm not hysterical, only surprised. Whatever are you doing this far north? And how in the depths did you get past my guard?"

"You mean the strapping lout at the bottom of the steps?" Jaira's eyes sparkled. "He was quite insistent that I do not disturb you, but in the end, I persuaded him."

The hairs on Tara's arms rose. Like all Hamartano women, Jaira was a mage, and though such women rarely used their potions and powders outside Jaelport, Jaira never hesitated to bend any rule if it suited her.

"Do not tell me you enchanted him," Tara said.

Jaira smirked. "Wasn't going to."

Tara rushed from the crypt and spotted Dunn slumped against the cliff face at the bottom of the steps, snoring. "Jaira Hamartano, we aren't children anymore. You can't go around incapacitating my guards." Tara hurried down to Dunn.

Jaira sauntered after her. "Says who?"

"I believe I did—several tournaments ago, when a poor young guard slept for three days straight and woke up weak and starving. He nearly lost his post on account of it." Tara tapped Dunn's cheek. "Master Dunn?" His eyes fluttered open for a moment, then closed again. Tara poked his ribs. "Master Dunn!"

"Don't trouble yourself," Jaira said. "I used the merest pinch. He'll rouse within a half hour."

Tara planted her hands on her hips. "And what if I require his help before then?"

"Relax. I can deal with any ruffians luck brings our way." She looked around. "Shall we take a walk in the woods, like old times?"

Tara glanced down at Master Dunn. "I can't just leave him like this."

"Of course you can." Jaira unhooked her necklace and fastened the silver chain around Tara's neck. "When we return, you can pour this on his tongue. He'll come right to."

Tara lifted the pendant—a glass vial wrapped in silver filagree and filled with a bright orange fluid. "What is this?"

"Mandzee's panzehir. Her antiserum works the fastest and lasts the longest. It's the only thing she's good at."

"I shall give it to him now."

Jaira tugged Tara's elbow. "Don't be a ninny. You'll throw away your one chance at unchaperoned freedom in gods only know how many years. And don't expect me to answer any of his questions."

Master Dunn would have questions, and how would Tara ever make him understand her friendship with a mage? She hardly understood it herself. Still, Tara didn't dare leave Master Dunn for long. If he awakened while she was gone, he'd be sick with worry. She tucked the necklace under her gown's neckline. "Perhaps a short loop to the lake and back."

"Excellent," Jaira said. "Lead the way."

Their footsteps crunched through the slushy snow on the path to the shore. "What are you doing so far from Jaelport?" Tara asked.

"I have been to Ice Island," Jaira said matter-of-factly. "My father fell ill last month and never recovered. We received word that we could collect his body for burial, so I volunteered to bring him home."

Though Jaira's steely expression bore no emotion, Tara's chest tightened. When her own father was murdered, Lord Gershom's ill health prevented her from traveling home. At least, that was the excuse Tara had given. No one would have stopped her from going, but at the time, she hadn't cared to attend her father's funeral. Not so soon after he'd placed her gloved hand in the iron grip of Lord Gershom. "My sympathies, Jaira. It speaks well of him that you would travel all this way to bring his body back to Jaelport."

Jaira shrugged. "Whatever happened to your faithful shadow?" she asked. "The swarthy one you couldn't take your eyes off of. Carmack, wasn't it?"

"Master Demry to you. And that was years ago."

"He's probably gotten fat and lazy, as men are prone to do."

The notion of Carmack being either of those things was ridiculous. The lake view reminded Tara of the times Carmack had removed his tunic to swim. Her cheeks flushed, and she waved her hand, doing her best to look bored by the subject. "The constable requested Master Demry stay at the stronghold."

Jaira chuckled. "No need to avoid hot porridge with me, Tara.

In Jaelport, when a man is behind bars, we simply say so. Gods know, it's hardly a novelty."

"He is not imprisoned." Yet.

Jaira's eyebrows rose. "I'm glad to hear at least one of the three rumors I heard is false."

"Let me guess, the second was that I conspired to kill my husband, which I didn't."

"Shame. That's the one I hoped was true."

Tara's jaw dropped. "Jaira Hamartano, you haven't changed a bit."

"Zitheos forbid it."

"What was the third rumor?" Tara asked.

"Utter nonsense. Something about you having a torrid affair with a portly old sailor and planning to elope after the funeral. The man had no title, so I didn't pay much attention to his name."

The memory of the man's fishy odor made Tara's stomach churn. "Magnus Thusk."

Jaira paled. "That's it. I know you have a thing for lowly commoners, but please tell me this isn't true."

"It's not. Rumors in Meribah Corner outpace wildfires. I only met him this morning. For his own nefarious reasons, my steward wishes me to marry the man. I fear he will use false charges against Carmack to force my hand."

"Your senile husband finally departs this world, granting you much-deserved independence, and already another man is treating you as his puppet. Why have you not thrown this meddlesome steward out?"

"It is not so easy. For all of Lord Gershom's warts, the people here respected him, but they view me with suspicion." Tara turned to walk back. "This is all my fault, really. Since the wedding, I have been so miserable, I failed to win the hearts of Meribah Corner's people. If I were to dismiss the steward amid these baseless accusations, I would lose all credibility."

"So, instead, you let it be known a lady will kowtow to her lowly subject to keep the peace?" Jaira shook her head. "What a backward life you live! Honestly, I'm never so proud of Jaelport as when I am reminded of what little power women hold elsewhere."

"It won't be forever. I fully intend to hire a new steward, one who is loyal to me. Once Eric arrives, he will help me negotiate the transition."

Jaira wound their arms together, pulling Tara into a quick march. "What you should do is leave this frozen wilderness for good."

As the crypt came into view, a screeching flock of rat-bird gowzals abandoned their perch in a giant, budless tree, one of many bare skeletons standing as grim memorials of the Darkness that had covered half of Er'Rets for nearly a decade.

Dunn stirred.

"I told you he wouldn't be out long." Jaira's sharp elbow nudged Tara's ribs. "I should go. Larkos is waiting with the cart near the main road. He will wonder what's keeping me."

"You're not staying?"

"Unfortunately, my grand tour of Meribah Corner ends here. I must keep moving. Our boat is meeting us on the coast at sunset."

"What a shame you cannot visit longer after traveling so far."

"I only stopped to see how you were faring." Jaira lowered her voice to a devious whisper. "Besides, my city is under royal blockade. The last headache you need is your cousin in Armonguard finding out you've been consorting with a Hamartano."

Tara hadn't thought of that. She had been so caught by the surprise of seeing an old friend, she forgot Jaira was a sworn enemy of King Gidon and Queen Averella. Not without good reason. Almost a year ago, Jaira had tried to bewitch the king when he was still known as Achan Cham. Since then, Achan had won the war, taken his rightful name, Gidon Hadar, and been crowned. Jaira had lost her two older brothers in the war. Now, her father too.

"Wait, Jaira." Tara threw her arms around her old friend. "Thank you for visiting me. None of my family came to the funeral, so that you did means a great deal, especially when you are mourning too. You are a true friend."

Jaira stiffened and pulled away. "I've fought with whether I should burden you with this, but I'd be a wretched heel if I didn't warn you."

Tara's stomach sank. "Warn me about what?"

"Rumors are not the only thing flying around Meribah Corner. I overheard threats too—oaths men have sworn to take your life and Carmack's. Watch yourself." Jaira squeezed her arm. "Remember what I said. If your circumstances do not improve, come to Jaelport. You'll find freedom there you never dreamed possible."

Dunn groaned again, and Jaira bolted up the rise, disappearing through the trees. Tara returned to the crypt stairs as her befuddled guard stood, swaying on his feet.

"Did you enjoy your nap, Master Dunn?" she asked.

"Forgive me, m'lady." He shook his head, blinking. "I feel absolutely jug bitten, but I swear, I haven't touched a drop." He cursed. "Ahh, forgive me again, for swearing."

Tara had never seen Dunn so discomposed. She fidgeted with the silver chain hanging around her neck. It might restore his senses, but questions would follow. She tucked it under her neckline. "We should head back. Wouldn't you agree?"

Tara took Dunn's arm, steadying him as they went. By the time they reached the footbridge, his bloodshot eyes had cleared, but he didn't stop mumbling his apologies until footsteps thumping through the forest sent another flock of gowzals shrieking into the sky. Dunn unsheathed his sword.

When Tara recognized the blue woolen frock waving through the trees, she raised her hand. "It's only Kressy."

"Lady Tara!" Kressy hunched over, bracing against her knees. "Come."

Tara hitched up her skirt and sprinted to her maid's side. "What is wrong?"

"It's Master Demry. He's been arrested."

Tara's stomach plummeted. Master Ulmer had wasted no time moving his plan forward. "Let's not panic." She struggled to keep her voice steady. "Once my brother arrives, the charges will be dismissed."

Kressy shook her head, her eyes filling with tears. "That's just it, m'lady. I overheard Master Ulmer talking to a man at the banquet. He said, clear as day, 'By the time Lord Livna arrives, it will be too late. Demry won't make it to trial.'"

"What?" Tara broke into a cold sweat. "He can't possibly mean..." *They were going to kill Carmack.* As she stood there, grappling with Ulmer's words and finding no other plausible meaning, Master Dunn stalked off. He was ten strides up the mountainside before Tara caught up with him. "What are you going to do?"

"Improvise," he growled.

"Wait!" She pulled him to a stop. "You cannot storm in there and get arrested too. We need a plan."

He eyed her. "Do you have one?"

Tara stared up at the diamond-shaped stronghold. Huge blocks of stone stacked into imposing walls and towers, every inch of them rightfully hers. Her mind raced with ideas. "I will before we reach the gatehouse."

Dunn extended his arm. "Then, by all means, ladies first."

CHAPTER SIX
CARMACK

CARMACK WAS A DEAD MAN, OR ABOUT to be, according to the rumors that had reached Constable Becker's ears. Carmack paced tight circles around the gate-house's holding cell until he was too dizzy to keep going, then took measure of the door that separated him from Becker's office. Even if he could get past it, attempting escape would only make him look guilty, and that wouldn't help Tara.

Underfoot, musty rushes provided little cushion and were heavily sprinkled with rodent droppings. Likely fleas too. Carmack would rather sleep standing upright than wake up covered with itchy bites. He leaned against the door where moonlight from the side wall's arrow loop touched the tip of his right boot.

Dunn's voice drifted in from outside, near the outer portcullis. "Either of you blokes interested in some arm wrestling?"

Carmack tensed. What was Dunn doing out there? He should be in the banquet hall watching over Tara.

No one answered.

"Come now," Dunn said. "I've got a bronze for any man who can outlast Strongarm Dunn to the count of one hundred."

One hundred? Carmack shook his head. No one in Meribah Corner could hold Dunn to the count of ten.

"Let's see the coin first," a raspy voice, likely Lugg Sipton's, answered. Sipton was a guard often posted at the main entrance. After a moment, Sipton said, "You're on."

"Grab hold," Dunn said. "Ready…go!" Dunn started counting while Toomis, Sipton's partner, cheered on.

Outside the cell, the office's outer door creaked open. Becker and his family must've returned from the funeral banquet. When the constable's heavy footsteps didn't thump across the outer room, Carmack pressed his ear against the cell door.

"Five, six…"

Carmack heard nothing over Dunn's counting. Whoever had entered the outer room was being quiet—too quiet to be Becker. A metallic scraping warned of a key turning inside the lock.

"Ten, eleven…"

The lock clicked, and Carmack's heart pumped faster. Whoever was on the other side of the door wasn't supposed to be there. Becker had warned Carmack that he had made enemies. Could it be one was paying him a visit? If so, Becker may have overestimated the safety of his holding cell. Carmack backed against the adjacent wall, glancing around for a makeshift weapon. The empty cell offered none. In the bare room against an armed visitor, Carmack had zero good options. His best hope was to get a jump on whoever was sliding the door's padlock from its hasp.

The door pushed open. Carmack spotted an arm in the moonlight, grabbed hold, and pulled the intruder into his cell, taking far less effort than he'd expected. He wrapped his arms around his shorter, and much lighter, trespasser. A woman. A waft of jasmine hit his nose at the same time her back crashed into his ribs.

Tara screamed.

"Shh!" he hissed in her ear, and she slapped her free hand over her mouth.

Outside, Toomis asked, "Did you hear something?"

"Only a stupid gowzal screeching," Dunn said.

"Didn't sound like a gowzal to me," Sipton said. "Let go of my hand."

"You quitting already?" Dunn asked. "How about I restart the count at twenty to give you a sporting chance. Twenty, twenty-one . . ."

Tara elbowed Carmack. "Let me go," she whispered.

He released her. "What are you doing here?"

She swung around, a hand on her hip. "What do you think I'm doing? I'm helping you escape."

Just the sort of half-baked idea that would land them both in serious trouble. Carmack took hold of Tara's shoulders, turned her toward the open door, and gently, but firmly, pushed her forward. "You need to get out of here and return Becker's key before he realizes it's missing."

She extended her arms and braced against the doorframe. "I didn't steal the constable's key." She wiggled a skinny skeleton key in her right hand. "I stole Ulmer's."

Carmack wanted to wring her pretty neck. He slid his hands down her shoulders, pinning her arms to her sides. Through gritted teeth, he whispered in her ear, "You need to put that back where you got it. I won't run away like a guilty coward."

Tara spun around again and poked him in the chest with the key. "You don't have a choice." Her quaking voice broke. "Kressy overheard Ulmer plotting to hang you without a trial."

So, Becker hadn't been exaggerating.

"You have to fetch Eric," Tara said, her tone less clipped. "Ulmer may not listen to me, but he won't dare cross the Lord of Tsaftown."

"Thirty-three, thirty-four . . ."

Tara pulled Carmack's arm. "Master Dunn's horse is saddled in the stables."

Carmack should have known Dunn was in on this. "I won't leave you here unprotected."

"You will if you're hung from a noose!"

She had a point. "First, we get you out of this gatehouse." Carmack left the cell and stepped into Becker's office. "If anyone sees you here, they'll assume the worst." Again.

He glanced in the direction of the spiral stairs. The elevated route along the sentry walk to the stables offered the best route back to the keep without being seen. From there, Tara could sneak through the keep's side door, but she would have to jump off the stables' roof first. Too risky for a lady.

Carmack took Tara's hand, trying to ignore the tingling sensation that spread down his arm when her delicate fingers laced between his, and crossed to the door leading out to the bailey instead.

Tara tugged his arm. "Not that way. Guests are leaving the banquet. We'll be spotted." She pointed to the staircase. "Better to take the sentry walk and jump from the stables."

If she was game to jump, he'd be sure to catch her. Carmack rushed upstairs. Tara followed and stopped behind him when he cracked open the upper door. As Carmack expected, the sentry walk was deserted. The penny-pinching steward had pruned the night watch to a skeleton crew and halved the number of torches along the curtain wall.

"Remind me later to thank Ulmer for tightening the purse strings." He pulled Tara into a crouch on the narrow walkway. The gatehouse cast a long shadow that hid them from the moon's glow. "Get ready to run to the stables."

Dunn's count echoed through the gatehouse's entrance. "Eighty-six, eighty-seven . . ."

Besides the two men Dunn was entertaining at the main gate, only one guard stood post near the keep's open door. "Was this Dunn's idea or yours?"

A grin danced on Tara's lips. "Mine, though he suggested arm wrestling as a diversion."

Loud cheering drowned out Dunn's count. The guard by the keep crossed the bailey toward the commotion.

Carmack kept his voice low. "Now!" He ran along the parapet to the first lean-to built between the gatehouse and the south tower. Carmack dropped to the stables' roof then grabbed Tara by the waist and lifted her down. Her body warmed his hands through her thin woolen dress. "What in the depths are you wearing?"

"Kressy's frock and cloak."

Carmack took her hand and shuffled down the roof. "Why aren't you wearing your own?"

"If you must know, Kressy is posing as me at the banquet. No one will suspect her with that dreadful mourning shroud. How else could I be two places at once?" When they reached the roof's edge, Tara sat down, her feet dangling. "Really, Carmack, until today, you've never shown the least interest in what I wear. This is no time to start."

Tara jumped feetfirst into a snow-covered pile of stable muck before he could warn her about it. She whimpered her way out of the smelly slush, reminding him of the young tagalong with blonde ringlets he used to see trailing after the Livna brothers in Tsaftown, always crying, "I can do it too." And she usually did, even if it meant falling headlong into trouble.

Becoming Lady Gershom hadn't killed her off entirely.

Carmack lowered himself off the roof onto a stack of firewood. Careful not to disturb the pile, he jumped down and followed Tara through the stables' double doors. "You okay?"

She shot him a dirty look. "You could have warned me I was about to plummet into a pile of horse—"

"Shh!" Footsteps approached. "Someone's coming." He grabbed the only tool dangling from a nearby hook, a measly hoof pick slightly longer than his hand. He pressed Tara into the dark corner of the first empty stall as one of the doors swung open.

Moonlight filled the aisle, spilling a man's shadow across the hay-covered ground like ink.

Carmack slowly turned his back to Tara, readying his feet. When the cloaked figure came into view, Carmack jumped out of the stall, wrapped his arm around the man's neck, and pressed the pick's sharp point against it.

The man lifted his arms in surrender. "I didn't throw away a piece of bronze for a hug, Demry."

Dunn. Carmack released his breath and his hold on his friend. "Good, because you're not getting one."

Dunn pointed to the pick in Carmack's hand. "What were you planning to do with that? Clean my teeth?"

"How about I rearrange a few while I'm at it." Carmack returned the pick to its hook. "What were you thinking, involving Lady Tara in this?"

"Like I had a choice. Have you ever tried arguing with—"

"Ahem." Lady Tara shot a quick glance at the open door. "Shall we focus, please?"

"Sorry, m'lady." Dunn flung his fur-lined cloak over Carmack and drew the hood over his head. "The guards are expecting me to ride out on Mace. After losing my small fortune, I told them I had to nurse my pride back to health down at the local watering hole."

Dunn pulled his gleaming black horse from its stall.

Carmack slipped his foot into the stirrup, and a sour taste filled his mouth. He lowered his boot to the ground. "I can't leave." Something bad always happened when he left Tara. "I promised Lady Revada—"

"Mother will understand," Tara said. "The best way to help me now is to go. Bring back my brother."

Those words sounded hauntingly familiar. "My father said something like that the night he fell through the ice." He gazed into Tara's eyes. She already knew the rest of the story. As a young boy, Carmack didn't have the strength to pull his father from his watery grave. By the time he had returned with Roxburg, their father was gone. After all these years, Roxburg's rebuke still stung.

You shouldn't have left him. You should have tried harder.

Now Carmack faced a similar problem. If he left to summon the help Tara needed, who would protect her from Ulmer? She needed to escape the troll as much as he did. "Come with me."

"Meribah Corner is my estate." Lady Tara backed away. "If I go, I will lose any chance of winning the people's fealty. Master Dunn is here now. He will be my Shield until you return."

Did Tara really consider Carmack that easy to replace?

"With all due respect, m'lady, I agree with Demry. You're too vulnerable here." Dunn's voice turned gruff with emotion. "Though I'd watch over you as best I can, my best might not be enough."

Despite Dunn's bravado, Carmack always sensed the limitations of Dunn's failing eyesight pained his friend. This was the closest Dunn had come to admitting it. "That settles it," Carmack said. "Either you join me, or I'm not going anywhere."

Tara wrung her hands. "But we just helped you escape. What do you plan to do? Walk back in and say, 'Sorry, I changed my mind'?"

"That will be the gist of it, unless you get on your horse and spare me the embarrassment."

Outside, a trio of children's voices broke into song. By the sounds of their high-pitched tones, they were young children, like Constable Becker's. If he and his family were returning to the gatehouse, the alarm bell would soon ring news of Carmack's escape. The portcullises would drop, and his trip to Tsaftown would end before it started. "Time's up. I'm going back to my cell."

Lady Tara heaved a sigh. "Fine, I'll go."

"Wise choice, m'lady." Dunn beamed. "I'll ready your horse."

"No time for the saddle. Just give me a boost." Tara retreated to the stall of her stallion, Tempest.

When Dunn quirked his eyebrow upward, Carmack shrugged. "She learned to ride bareback with her brothers. I only wish she had a more reliable mount. That hot-blooded beast of hers can out stubborn a mule."

"Hmm, just her type," Dunn muttered and ducked into the stall.

While Dunn bridled Tempest, Carmack boosted Tara onto her horse's back.

Dunn handed Tara the reins, then pulled Carmack aside. "I need a little something to help me explain to the constable how you ended up with my cloak and horse."

A wicked shiner would serve Dunn right for aiding Tara in her crimes. Needing no further invitation, Carmack smashed his knuckles into Dunn's left cheekbone. A restrained punch, sort of. Dunn staggered back, hissing a curse, and Carmack shook the sting of impact from his fist.

Tara gasped. "What did you do that for?"

"Tell you later." Carmack climbed into Mace's saddle. "Remember, no turning back. You can't get caught helping me escape. I'll be right behind you."

"You go first," Tara said. "The guards are expecting Dunn, not a woman."

Dunn pushed open the stable doors and signaled the path was clear.

No time to argue. "Fine. Next stop, Tsaftown." Carmack squeezed his heels, and Mace bolted on cue.

Behind him, Tara and Tempest gave chase. Carmack steered Mace through the opening between the gate towers. The clattering of Mace's hooves echoed off the stone walls, mimicking a stampede. The guards stood back, giving Carmack a wide berth. As he cleared the outer gate, a woman screamed behind him, and Tempest whinnied. Carmack glanced backward. On the opposite side of the gatehouse, Tara's spirited horse balked. She held fast, clutching fistfuls of Tempest's mane. Whoever had screamed, it wasn't her.

Carmack spun Mace around, his heart pounding in his ears. The alarm bell rang out. Carmack raced his mount back, but the metal clad spikes of the outer portcullis dropped in front of him, punching into the ground and trapping Tara inside. Mace reared back, and Carmack clung on, his mind spinning.

He couldn't leave Tara. She'd pay the price for helping him escape. He had to get back in to take the blame, though what excuse he could give for her riding out after him, he didn't know. He'd have to think of that later.

Mace stomped an impatient circle, and a whoosh of air brushed Carmack's cheek. An arrow pierced the ground beside him. Blast, the archers were already shooting at him. Dressed in black against a backdrop of snow, Carmack was an easy target. He wouldn't live to long enough to clear Tara's name.

Whirling Mace around, Carmack dug in his heels and sped the animal down the winding road into the forest. Arrows rained down around them, but Carmack did not look back. He wouldn't stop until he reached Lytton Hall.

The Lord of Tsaftown may have dodged his brother-in-law's funeral, but now he would come to Meribah Corner and remind everyone that by the king's authority, the nobility governed the land, not greedy stewards. And his lordship would come whether he wanted to or not.

CHAPTER SEVEN
TARA

WHAT A CRUEL TWIST. IN HER AT-tempt to free Carmack from his cell, Tara had landed in another, albeit a gilded cage of her own choosing. By claiming sanctuary in a chapel, she had avoided the constable's custody. Barely. When news of Carmack's jailbreak had spread through the keep, it had taken Dunn's sword, the constable's badge, and the priest's holy book to turn the angry mob away.

Tara paced the short length of the room, her footsteps ricocheting off the bright frescoes and stone arches that crisscrossed overhead. Though the chapel was only slightly longer than the keep's solar, the high ceiling, stained-glass windows, and sparse furnishings made it seem much larger. Over the past two days, Tara's long skirt had polished the mosaic floor between the altar and the door to a high sheen. Prompted by her surroundings and pure desperation, Tara had even resorted to prayer to speed the time.

If Arman showed mercy, Carmack would reach Lytton Hall that very morning, and Tara would not be confined much longer. But if the arrows had wounded him or his horse? He might have fallen in the forest. Freezing. Bleeding to . . . no, Tara would not think it. Two more days until he would return with Eric. By then, she would wear a trench in the tiles.

The door cracked open, and Kressy peeked inside. "I've come with your afternoon tea, m'lady."

Tara sighed. "I am not sure I can last another day cooped up in this chapel."

"I can't help but feel this is my fault." Kressy set her tray on a window seat, filled a cup, and handed it to Tara. "If I hadn't screamed, you would be safe in Tsaftown with your family right now."

Tara took the cup and sat down. "If you hadn't screamed, Master Thusk would have likely abducted you, and I could never have borne the guilt, knowing I put you in that situation."

What had the man been thinking? Had he conspired with Master Ulmer to kidnap Tara and force her into a wedding? She shuddered at the very idea.

Tara's temple prickled, and she heard a familiar voice.

Lady Nitsa, Duchess of Carm.

Tara's skin broke out in goosebumps. She sprang from her window seat, hot tea spilling down the front of her crimson gown as she looked around her. "Aunt?" Every inch of the chapel was in plain sight, except for the space behind the altar, and Aunt Nitsa would never stoop behind that. Tara and Kressy were alone, but Aunt Nitsa's voice had been so clear.

Kressy's eyes narrowed. "Are you all right, m'lady?"

My dear niece, do not fear. I am speaking to your mind through my gift.

Aunt Nitsa had demonstrated her bloodvoicing ability to Tara before, but such communications were rare. "Is something wrong, Aunt? Why have you reached out to me this way?"

Kressy clutched her apron. "Arman, preserve us. Her mind has snapped."

"Hush, Kressy! I'm talking with Aunt Nitsa."

Kressy inched to the far end of the window seat. "Whatever you say, m'lady."

Tara rolled her eyes. She'd have to explain Aunt Nitsa's blood-voicing magic to her maid later.

Your mother sent word of Lord Gershom's passing, Aunt Nitsa said. *Due to her illness, she has asked me to come in her stead. Though I am a poor substitute, I hope that I might be of some comfort. We are approaching Meribah Corner now.*

Tara's heart soared. She wasn't hallucinating. "I'm thrilled you've come, Aunt Nitsa, and would love nothing more than to greet you at the gate myself. However, I have been forced to claim sanctuary. Lord Gershom's steward has turned everyone against me, and I dare not leave the chapel."

What about Master Demry? Your mother said he was with you.

A lump settled in Tara's throat. "The steward was plotting to execute him for Gershom's death, so he fled to Tsaftown."

Oh, dear. This is a most shocking development, but take heart. We will see each other soon.

Tara set aside her half-empty teacup and felt Kressy's wary eyes follow her to the chapel door. The sound of a carriage entering the bailey rumbled through the stained-glass windows, and Tara twirled her long braid through her fingers, fighting the urge to throw open the door.

Instead, Dunn did. The bruise on his left cheek had deepened from red to purple. "The Duchess of Carm to see you, m'lady."

Aunt Nitsa swept into the chapel dressed in a rich emerald gown that flattered her auburn hair and fair complexion. Tara sprang into her open arms. Though her aunt was shorter than Tara, there was strength in her embrace, and Tara leaned against her, afraid her own legs might give way.

"Oh, Aunt . . ." Emotion choked her words. Remembering her manners, Tara pulled away. "Would you care to sit?"

"Thank you, but no. I've been confined to a carriage seat for too long. Now, tell me everything."

Tara wasted no time recounting her experiences since Lord Gershom's death. Through it all, Aunt Nitsa listened calmly, though her lips pressed into a thin line several times.

"So, you see," Tara said, "I fully intended to escape to Tsaftown with Carmack until I heard Kressy's scream. She was supposed to be at the banquet, pretending to be me so I could slip away."

"I was wearing Lady Tara's gown and mourning veil," Kressy added. "Whenever someone spoke to me, I made like I was crying, just like Lady Tara told me to. No one was any the wiser, m'lady—not even the mongrel that grabbed me while I was taking a breather in the bailey. It wasn't until he hauled me off to his carriage, and I called him a yellow-bellied, cod-kissing—"

Aunt Nitsa raised a hand. "I see. Then what happened, Tara?"

"I reined in Tempest and shouted for help," Tara said. "Poor Constable Becker. I'm afraid I delivered him quite a shock, riding bareback dressed in a maid's frock."

Aunt Nitsa paled. "I can imagine. Perhaps I need to sit after all." She settled on the nearest window seat. "Continue."

"After Constable Becker sounded the alarm, guards flooded into the bailey and lowered the portcullises. The guards shot arrows after Carmack, and I just sat atop Tempest, imagining the worst until Master Dunn staggered out of the stables, shouting about horse thieves. When he saw me, he pulled me down and told me to stay in the chapel until help arrived." Tara blinked away her tears. "I don't know if Carmack ever reached Lytton Hall."

Aunt Nitsa took a long breath. "That, I fear, is the least of your problems, and one easily solved. I shall ask him. Give me a moment, please." She closed her eyes.

Her aunt was using her magic again. Of course she could ask Carmack. Finally! Tara would have answers to the questions eating her alive.

Kressy nudged her. "Is she napping?"

"My aunt has the ability to bloodvoice," Tara told her.

Kressy's eyes widened. "Like the king? Oh! She was talking to you before when you spilled your tea." She frowned. "But surely you don't have the magic too?"

"No," Tara said.

Aunt Nitsa's sculpted eyebrows crumpled together. "No!"

"What is it, Aunt?"

When she didn't answer, Tara fought the urge to pester as the pressure of not knowing Carmack's fate built up inside. Had he arrived healthy? Wounded? Not at all? Every beat of her heart stretched longer, louder in her ears.

After several minutes, Aunt Nitsa's eyes flew open, and she inhaled sharply. "Carmack arrived in Tsaftown before daybreak."

Why was her aunt frowning about happy news? "Oh no. He's injured."

"Master Demry is in perfect health," Aunt Nitsa said. "Kressy, please take some refreshments to my advisor and driver. They are waiting in the bailey."

"Of course, Your Grace." Kressy bobbed a quick curtsy and left.

Once the door had shut, Aunt Nitsa said, "I didn't want to say too much in front of your maid, but Master Demry had dire news."

Tara's heart pounded. "Tell me."

"Before he arrived, your brother Eric received word that the *Brierstar* has disappeared."

Leif. Uncle Chantry. Tara collapsed on the bench next to her aunt. "Are they . . ." Dead?

"No one knows for certain. The ship was last seen near Jaelport. No flotsam was found, so the fleet believes both ship and crew have been captured."

"By whom?"

"That is what Eric intends to find out. He set sail early this morning, and Master Demry is with him. Not by his choice, as I understand it, though Captain Roxburg Demry is among those lost."

Tara's heart stung. Typical of Eric to put her last, but to take her Shield to Jaelport too? Carmack would be gone weeks . . . months. Aunt Nitsa said it wasn't his choice, but that didn't seem possible. No one, not even Eric, could restrain Carmack if he was set against going. But his brother was missing too. Naturally, part of him would feel compelled by duty to rescue Captain Demry. Tara cradled her head in her hands. "How can I possibly wait in this chapel until they return?"

"My dear niece, you cannot. I fear for them all, our brothers and the Demrys. You know that as Lady Chairman of the Council of Six, I am privy to sensitive information. The *Brierstar*'s sudden disappearance in calm seas suggests the involvement of the Hamartanos and their dark magic. We must face the likelihood that none of the sailors will return."

Tara shook her head. Jaira had made no mention of the *Brierstar* or the blockade during her short visit. As a friend, she would have told Tara if she knew anything about the ship and crew. Or would she? Jaira always had been selective about her truth telling.

"If only we had a trusted source to relay information from Jaelport, we might know more," Aunt Nitsa said. "Unfortunately, several men have been dispatched to Jaelport, never to be seen again."

Several men . . . all men. Tara's stomach fluttered with the beginnings of a crazy—no, a worse-than-crazy idea. "Aunt, is it too late to get me aboard Eric's ship?"

"Whatever for?"

"He's not the right person for this rescue. I am."

"My dear Tara, you know I am the first to support a woman willing to tackle a man's job, but you're not a soldier or a sailor. You are a young lady."

"That's exactly why it must be me. Averella told me women are not susceptible to Jaelportian magic. That enabled her to save King Gidon when Jaira tried to trap him into marriage with her magic."

"Yes, however, Averella was in disguise. Jaira had no reason to suspect her." Aunt Nitsa folded her hands. "I'm afraid it would be far too dangerous."

What other argument could Tara make but to confess her secret? "With respect, Aunt, you are mistaken. Jaira will not suspect me either, because she invited me to Jaelport during her recent visit."

Her aunt's jaw slackened. "Lady Jaira was here? When?"

"The day of the funeral. She was on her way home from Ice Island with her father's body."

Aunt Nitsa rose from her seat, wringing her hands.

"Aunt Nitsa, I've known Jaira since we were girls. Admittedly, our friendship has been as volatile as Jaira herself, but I believe I have her trust. If the Hamartanos captured the *Brierstar*, then I am the one person in Er'Rets who can get close enough to find it. As you said, I am not a soldier or a sailor, so no one would ever suspect me of being a spy."

"Do you understand what you are asking? If you are discovered, King Gidon will not negotiate for your release. The Hamartanos have proven too many times that they cannot be trusted to uphold their end of any bargain."

"I have to try." For her brothers, her uncle, and especially for Carmack.

Aunt Nitsa stroked Tara's cheek. "You love him, don't you?"

Had Tara accidentally uttered his name out loud or had Aunt Nitsa read her mind? Bloodvoicers could do that sort of thing, though they had an unspoken code that they would not abuse the gift. "My days of being a lovesick romantic are over. Carmack is my Shield. Nothing more."

Aunt Nitsa arched her eyebrow. "Averella mentioned you had

become a skeptic of love, and yet you use Master Demry's given name."

Tara's cheeks flushed. "Everyone assumes there is something untoward between Carmack and me, but there is not."

"I never suggested anything untoward. I, too, was once a young widow, convinced fate would forever deny me my true love, but I was wrong." Aunt Nitsa squeezed Tara's shoulder. "Do not harden your heart against the possibility of similar happiness. Now, let me see where Eric and his ship are and inform him of your intentions." Her aunt sat again and closed her eyes.

Tara watched her as she silently used her magic. Aunt Nitsa's advice, though well-meant, rang hollow. She and Sir Eagan had fallen passionately in love with each other before she married Duke Amal. Aside from exchanging fleeting glances, Tara and Carmack had only ever danced with each other, and their last was three years ago. She knew better than to suspect any mutual attraction existed between them. Those fleeting glances were just part of his job to watch over her. Undoubtedly it was for the best, as Tara had a hard enough time maintaining formality around her handsome Shield. Besides, Carmack was driven by duty, and time had proved nothing else kept him by her side.

Aunt Nitsa's eyes opened. "Anillo is readying the carriage, and I've sent Master Dunn ahead. We have just enough time to get you to the docks, but I'm afraid you'll have to go as you are."

"What if the constable won't let me leave Meribah Corner?"

"Nonsense." Aunt Nitsa linked arms with Tara. "Let me do the talking. I assure you, neither the constable nor that detestable steward would dare stand against the Duchess of Carm."

Never estimate a lady's power by her stature. Mother's proverb had never rung truer than when Tara's petite aunt parted the group of guards gathered outside the chapel door like an Eben giant stomping through the muddy bailey. She and Tara walked straight up to her carriage where Kressy stood with a tray of refreshments next to a wiry older man—Anillo, Aunt Nitsa's trusted advisor.

Terr Ulmer, who was lurking by the keep's door, scurried down the steps after them. "Your Grace, Lady Gershom is not to leave Meribah Corner."

"Kressy," Aunt Nitsa said, "fetch Lady Tara's and your outer wraps. Make haste."

"Your Grace, I insist," Master Ulmer said. "You cannot—"

Aunt Nitsa spun around. "Who are you?"

The mousy steward stepped back. "Ah, I am Terr Ulmer."

"So, you're the troublesome steward." She turned her back to him. "Anillo, deal with this man's complaint." Aunt Nitsa ushered Tara into the carriage first, then sat across from her.

Ulmer continued sputtering his protests until Anillo shut the carriage door in his face. "The Council of Six requires Lady Gershom's assistance. If you wish to bring a complaint, you may request an audience with the king, though I doubt he will grant it."

Ulmer turned pea green and shrank back. Tara pressed her hand to her smiling lips. She didn't like leaving the city in this man's care, but she could do nothing here. At least in Jaelport, she could make a difference.

Anillo opened the door again, allowing Kressy to climb in, her arms full. She passed Tara her cloak. As they each threw their cloaks around their shoulders, Anillo closed the carriage door. He returned to his seat next to the driver, and they were off.

"Our short journey to the docks doesn't give much time to prepare you," Aunt Nitsa said. "How much do you know about Jaelport and its mages?"

"Well, I know many Jaelportian women are trained as mages," Tara said. "Most fast from meat and paint runes on their foreheads when they wish to practice their dark arts. They train their eunuchs too. Together, they use botany, alchemy, and enchantments. Poisons that mimic diseases. Curses that control one's mind, steal health, sedate, and who knows what else. The terror such magic inflicts is not easily forgotten."

"Mercy," Kressy said. "We're not going to Jaelport, are we?"

"You need not worry, Kressy," Tara said. "Jaelportian magic does not work on women." Judging by Kressy's wide eyes, the information brought little comfort.

Aunt Nitsa pointed to Tara's braid. "May I have your hair ribbon?"

"Of course." Tara pulled it free and handed it over.

"Though I can use my gift to communicate with you and Carmack because I know you both, this ribbon will help me connect with you faster. I hope to check in on you from time to time, though I cannot promise it will work once you reach Jaelport."

"Why ever not?"

"Shortly after King Gidon defeated Lord Nathak, Armonguard's bloodvoicers lost contact with the city. We cannot communicate with anyone there—even our allies—and when our spirits travel there through the Veil, a thick fog overtakes us, and we are blinded."

"So, you cannot see what happens there?"

"We cannot, and our blindness makes us more vulnerable to magical attacks."

Tara and Kressy fell into an uneasy silence as Aunt Nitsa shared more facts and history of Jaelportian mages, some of which was familiar to Tara from previous conversations with the Hamartano sisters and her sister-in-law Viola, whose mother was Jaelportian.

When the carriage reached the docks, Aunt Nitsa threw the door open, and Tara and Kressy climbed out into the brisk, salty air. Meribah Cove was a jagged, tooth-shaped inlet of deep blue waters separating the steep mountainsides. A dozen local fishing boats and the occasional merchant ship requiring repairs were moored in the quiet waters, tucked away from the winds and storms of the open sea. Along the eastern edge, two rows of the fishermen's clapboard homes and watering holes lined the docks.

"With my gift, I saw the captain charting a course close to the northern point." Aunt Nitsa said, lifting her chin to the mountain rising on her right. "The ship should pass not far from the inlet's mouth within the hour. Do your best to get in front of it. Though I informed Eric of your intentions, he insisted he would not stop to take on passengers."

Headstrong man, and as dismissive of Tara as ever. "Typical."

Kressy tightened her wrap against the sea breeze. "Arman, preserve us."

Aunt Nitsa lifted the seat cushion in her carriage and retrieved from beneath it an extra blanket and a small velvet purse. "Here, take these for your journey."

The heavy pouch settled into Tara's hand, clinking of coins. She peeked inside, surprised to find several were gold. "Aunt Nitsa, this is a small fortune."

"Though money cannot solve every problem, I find that, with its help, most crises can be averted." Nitsa wrapped the woolen blanket around Tara's shoulders, while Tara tightened the purse strings and wrapped them around her wrist.

"Now, hurry along. Once I see Eric's ship, I will tell him where you are. Let's hope that convinces him to drop anchor."

"And if he doesn't?"

"Then we'll know this mission wasn't Arman's plan for you."

Tara embraced her aunt, sure Arman didn't care one way or another. "Wish us luck."

"I can do better. I will pray Arman goes with you and keeps you safe."

Tara and Kressy jogged down to the docks where Master Dunn waited beside a weathered boat with a single tattered sail. Tara's stomach rolled as she pushed aside an empty bucket and took a seat onboard. Hopefully, Arman proved more attentive to Aunt

Nitsa's prayers than her own. Dunn raised the sail, and their tiny boat pulled away from the dock toward the Yâm Sea.

A line of black clouds loomed on the horizon, and white caps rose, even higher as the boat approached the inlet's mouth.

Tara's stomach wasn't the only thing rolling as the small boat finally left the cove to battle the swells of the open sea. As the boat pulled past the northern point, Tara spotted a three-masted ship cutting a southwesterly course through the waves. True to Aunt Nitsa's warning, Tsaftown's second fastest ship, the *Zephyr*, showed no signs of slowing.

"There she is!" Tara pointed, straining her voice to carry over the wind. "We must go faster, Master Dunn."

Dunn gripped the rudder with both hands. "I'm doing my best, m'lady, but if I'm not careful, this death trap will capsize."

"Unless we catch that ship, 'this death trap' will be our only ride back to shore."

"Point taken." Dunn adjusted the sail, and the wind tugged their boat forward into a sharp lean. "Look out!"

A large swell crashed into their bow, spilling frigid water into the boat and soaking Tara's feet with icy water. The measly craft offered no hope of catching the ship if it was waterlogged. Tara grabbed the small bucket and started bailing. She pitched water until her shoulders burned and her fingers were frozen stiff.

"Kressy, help!" she cried, but Kressy had crumpled into a heaving ball of seasickness.

Sourness rose in Tara's throat too, so she kept her eyes trained on the full white sails drawing closer. Dunn pulled their boat in line with the *Zephyr*, close enough for Tara to count the men on deck as the ship bore down on them. On its forecastle, the sight of a tall muscular figure standing like a sentry made her heart swell.

She stumbled to the bow. "Carmack!"

His head turned, and he hollered, pointing in her direction.

"Stop!" Tara shouted into the wind, waving both arms.

Carmack sprinted for the stern. When next she spotted him, he had reached the quarterdeck and grabbed the helmsman manning the ship's wheel. A skirmish broke out as the smaller vessel coasted into the oncoming path of the larger ship. Tara held her breath. *Yes, Carmack! Make them stop. Don't leave me here.* Finally, the *Zephyr*'s anchor plunged from its bow and splashed into the sea.

Tara grinned back at Dunn. "They're slowing down."

"Not fast enough!" Dunn jerked the rudder and yanked at the sail. As their boat turned, a wave caught it broadside, pitching it at a sharp angle.

Kressy screamed.

Tara grabbed the hull's side and stared up at the carved figurehead that resembled Tara herself—a woman with pale windswept braids, a determined chin, and brilliant blue eyes. When Cetheria, the goddess of protection, passed overhead, Tara's mouth went dry. "She's going to—"

A violent lurch and the splintering of wood cut short her words as the mighty *Zephyr*'s bow crashed into their tiny boat.

CHAPTER EIGHT
CARMACK

THE FOOLS HAD DROPPED THE ANCHOR too late! Lord Livna should have known better. Since when had Tara ever agreed to be left behind?

Carmack bolted to the railing and leaned over as the *Zephyr* spun the small boat, its tiny keel crunching and splintering. The boat listed, and water poured in. Tara clung to its half-submerged side as it slid along the *Zephyr*. Dunn shouted, but Carmack couldn't hear him over Kressy's shrieking.

Carmack grabbed a coiled mooring line. He tossed it over the side and into the path of the boat. Both Tara and Dunn lunged for the rope, and their boat tottered. Tara yelped as the line slipped through her hands, but Dunn caught hold. Carmack wrapped his end around a wooden cleat, then clambered over the railing and down the treads of the ship's fixed boarding ladder. The icy sea spray from the waves pricked his skin. He stopped before his feet reached the water, wrapped an arm and leg around the ladder's side rope, and pulled the mooring line toward him. On the other end, Dunn braced against the bow.

Carmack pulled again, trying to drag the small boat closer. Instead, the sinking boat's weight stretched his arms to the breaking point. "No good!" he shouted.

"Grab the rope, ladies!" Dunn shouted. "Abandon ship!"

Three bodies splashed into the water, not a strong swimmer among them. Shouts of "souls overboard" echoed above.

Carmack frantically pulled the mooring line. At the other end, three pale faces bobbed in the waves. What had they been thinking to sail so far from shore in that tiny boat?

Kressy reached the ladder first. Dunn was another three feet down the rope, with Tara trailing behind.

"Climb up, Kressy!" Carmack yelled, keeping a firm hold of the line running between him and Tara.

Chunks of Kressy's blonde hair hung wet in her eyes. The young maid flailed her arms and did not release the mooring line to grab hold of the boarding ropes. Carmack climbed down below the waterline to the lowest tread, every nerve ending firing in alarm as the frigid water seeped into his boots and through his pants. Though it had been several days since his last swim, he knew how to fight through the shock. The others wouldn't. He controlled his breathing and caught Kressy by the back of her dress, lifting her partially out of the water. She grabbed hold of the side rope, but her feet slipped off the tread, dragged down by the weight of her soggy clothing.

"Dunn! Help!"

With jerky movements, Dunn swam over and gripped the boarding rope. "Hold on, miss."

Carmack pushed off the ship and splashed into the breathtaking cold to make way for them. Kressy clutched Dunn's shoulders, and he pulled them both onto the ladder's lowest tread.

Just beyond Carmack's reach, Tara slipped below the surface. He yanked the line toward him, and the loose end hurtled out of the water. No! If Tara drowned in the Yâm Sea, it would be his fault, just like when Pa had broken through the ice. As a young boy, he had been powerless to help, unable to swim and too weak to pull his father out.

Not this time.

He clutched the line and dove underwater. As he scanned the depths, a blurry patch of white and crimson drifted below him. He dove deeper, snagged Tara's torso, then kicked hard for the surface. When he reached it, he flipped onto his back with Tara against his chest, keeping her head above water.

She coughed and gulped in air.

Praise Arman, her lungs weren't full of seawater. "I've got you." Carmack held fast to her. Seconds felt like hours as the crew pulled the mooring line back to the *Zephyr.* Together, he and Tara grabbed the boarding ropes.

"Feet up." Carmack steadied Tara as she put her feet on the ladder's lowest tread. Every second in the freezing water would push her closer to shock. They couldn't afford any slips. His arms were shaking from the exertion of pulling the rope, and Tara's arms were likely too numb to make repeated attempts. She wouldn't like it, but he put his boots beside hers, then scooped her cloak and skirt over his shoulder.

Her trembling jaw dropped. "W-what are you d-do—"

"On my honor, I promise you I won't look." And he meant it. "Trust me, if a swell hits, the weight of your clothes will drag you back in."

Tara nodded shakily, her lips blue. Rung by rung, she climbed out of the deathly sea and up the side of the *Zephyr.* Carmack stayed right behind her, sometimes helping place her boot on a rung. Finally, they spilled over the railing and collapsed onto the deck in a tangled heap.

A cabin boy rushed over with a blanket. Carmack tucked the scratchy fabric around Tara's shivering body, then pushed her wet hair off her face.

Her brow relaxed. "G-glad to see you, Master Demry. As always, your timing is impeccable."

Carmack's heart skipped a beat. He wished his arms were the blanket wrapped around her. Instead, he settled for sheltering her from the wind as she stood. She shivered against him, her teeth chattering. She was onboard, safe. He rubbed her hands to warm them. She winced, and he turned them over. The rope had scratched her palms raw. "Blast it, look at your hands."

Tara formed fists. "Naught but a hangnail."

Lord Livna approached and removed his cloak. "Someone fetch Miss Wepp to assist my sister." He wrapped his cloak around Tara, his face nearly as pale as hers, then clasped Carmack's hand. "Good man, Demry. Now, both of you, out of this wind."

Carmack had done everything he could think of to get Tara safely onboard the *Zephyr*. Now he would stop at nothing to get her off. He ran to his bunk, changed into dry clothing, then rushed back to Lord Livna's cabin, chilled but starting to warm now that he wasn't sopping wet. Judging by the raised voices coming from inside Lord Livna's cabin, Tara was catching some heat too. Not the type her body needed, but the scolding she deserved. If Lord Livna couldn't get through to his sister, then Carmack would. No matter what it took, he'd make sure Tara returned safely home. He knocked.

Lord Livna opened the door. "Good, it's you. Come talk sense to my sister."

Carmack entered the cabin that ran the ship's width. Beyond a small round table and chairs, Tara sat in a wide bunk under a mountain of fur blankets, with Kressy nestled beside her. No doubt Tara had made sure her maid was comfortable before she had settled in.

Lord Livna gestured to his sister, a crease in his brow. "As my aunt warned, Tara intends to sail to Jaelport with us. What do you say, Demry?"

"Absolutely not."

Tara's nostrils flared, and she stared him down. "At least allow me to explain."

"There is nothing to explain," Lord Livna said. "Enough of our family is in peril. Nothing could possibly convince me to add to the number."

"The trip is too dangerous, my lady," Carmack said.

"For you two, it may be," Tara said, "but as a woman, I cannot be bewitched by Jaelportian magic. Queen Averella told me so, and Aunt Nitsa confirmed it."

"So, that's what sprouted this outlandish scheme," Lord Livna said. "I'm sorry, Tara, but feminine immunity from the dark arts of mages will not protect you from the steel swords of their eunuchs."

"The Hamartanos' eunuchs will have no reason to threaten me."

Carmack rubbed the knot of tension forming between his eyes. "They'll have every reason. Northerners like us do not visit Jaelport, especially now that it's under royal blockade. If we're discovered, the Jaelportians will instantly suspect wrongdoing and treat us accordingly." Then what? He'd been asking himself that question since leaving Tsaftown. Jaelportians were known to be merciless in punishing outsiders. For that reason alone, he needed to get Tara off the ship.

"So, we agree," Tara said. "You two cannot simply waltz into Jaelport and expect to go unnoticed. You'll end up no better than the missing crew, which is why I must go instead."

"The Yâm has frozen your brain," Lord Livna said. "If I, with my darker coloring, cannot blend in, how will you with that blonde hair of yours? Tara, what you need—"

"What I need is for you to listen, or the two of you are sailing on a one-way trip to Shamayim. When you do not return, who will preserve our family's rights to Meribah Corner? Who will rule Tsaftown?" Tara threw back the covers and stood, dressed in a sailor's tunic, gray vest, pants, and stockings. "Remember, *Lord Livna*, my estate helps feed your people. Furthermore, unlike anyone else on this boat, I do *not* need to blend in, because I have been invited."

Carmack and Lord Livna exchanged looks.

"By whom?" Lord Livna asked.

"Lady Jaira Hamartano," Tara said.

"When?" Carmack asked.

Tara's chin rose, the expression that always preceded words he didn't like. "At Lord Gershom's funeral."

A sinking weight settled on Carmack, and he pressed his hands against the table.

Lord Livna straightened. "Lady Jaira was in Meribah Corner three days ago? How did she get past the blockade?" He pulled at his black beard. "For Lightness' sake, Demry, how did she slip past you?"

Carmack met Lord Livna's stare. "She didn't." Neither Dunn nor Tara had bothered mentioning Jaira's visit before, but Carmack saw no need to drag Dunn's name into the conversation. The man was in enough trouble for putting Lord Livna's sister on a collision course with his ship.

"Then explain how my sister received a Hamartano as a funeral guest."

"Carmack wasn't there, Eric," Tara said, her voice rising. "He was in a holding cell, waiting for your help. And to be clear, I did not receive Lady Jaira. Not formally. She found me in the family crypt. After hearing the death threats flying around Meribah Corner, she stopped to warn me and offered refuge in Jaelport at Tenma Palace." Tara slouched, arms crossed. "Isn't it ironic that Jaira, supposedly one of Er'Rets most conniving villains, diverted from her trip out of concern for me, yet my own brother couldn't find time in his busy schedule?"

"I had just received word that our brother and uncle had gone missing and needed to decide the best course." Lord Livna stepped closer to her. "You are being tremendously unfair, Tara."

"Do not speak to me of fairness!" Tara stood her ground, her loose clothes shaking as her body trembled. "Was it fair when Father took you sailing, riding, and hunting, but never once took me? Was it fair on the night of my first banquet that he announced to the entire hall, that as pretty as I was, he would have preferred all sons? Maybe you can explain how fairness paid for your tournaments and Leif's commission but left nothing to feed the village except my dowry. Not that I ever cared about it—the art, the silver, the jewels. I would have gladly sold it all to help Tsaftown, but instead, Father auctioned me off to a mad old badger." Her voice broke. "And you said nothing."

Lord Livna's cheeks flushed.

For years, Carmack had longed to see Tara stand up for herself. He might have clapped but for the effect her outburst was having on her brother. Carmack wanted Lord Livna to acknowledge his sister's pain but not if it changed his mind about letting her go to Jaelport.

"My lady, please return to bed," Carmack said. "You're shivering."

Tara's flashing eyes swung his way. "I'm not cold, Demry. I'm angry. Furious that I have risked everything to give this mission the best chance of success, and neither of you will listen."

"We have listened, Tara," Lord Livna said, his voice much softer than moments before. "But you must consider the disadvantages of bringing you along."

Tara crossed her arms. "Because I am a lady?"

"No, because you tend to overlook the evil in people, as proven by your recent encounter with Lady Jaira. You are more interested in accommodating others than protecting yourself."

Carmack rocked back on his heels. Perhaps he hadn't given Lord Livna enough credit for how well he knew his sister.

Lord Livna continued, "You are too trusting, Tara. You always have been."

Tara's lip quivered. "Take heart, Brother. You are quickly curing me of the habit." She spun on her heel, climbed back into bed, and jerked the covers to her chin.

Carmack had never seen Tara this angry before. The exhaustion and shock of the day's events were taking a toll. He whispered to Lord Livna, "We should allow her to rest."

Tara muttered, "I wish Viola were here."

"What of my wife?" Lord Livna asked.

"She would understand." Tara rolled, turning her back to them. "The only ideas you heed are your own."

Lord Livna's brow creased, a sure sign Tara's barb had hit its mark, and he hesitated on the threshold.

But there was nothing to reconsider, and Carmack would not let Lord Livna jeopardize Tara's life by allowing her to tag along one last time. Carmack nudged him through the door, closing it behind them, then the two returned to the deck.

"She makes a powerful argument," Lord Livna said.

Carmack's pulse quickened. "She's tired and angry. She would not say those things otherwise."

"Doesn't make them untrue," Lord Livna said. "When she needed me most, I abandoned her, and I am about to do it again."

Carmack's gut tightened as he crossed the quarterdeck. Below, on the main deck, the crew readied the anchor and the rowboat.

"We'll have the ladies on shore within a half hour, my lord," Captain Strumgerd said.

"Thank you, Captain," Lord Livna answered.

Carmack inhaled the briny air. So little time until Tara boarded the rowboat, likely to be their last goodbye. She would drift away, hurt and angry, never knowing how much she meant to him. In a voice thick with regret, he said, "It's the only way."

Lord Livna slapped the railing. "This feels all wrong, Demry. Tara is not safe in Meribah Corner without my protection. You and my aunt have convinced me of that. If I don't help her now, I may never have another chance." He paced. "But at what price? Every hour we delay may cost lives."

Unease prickled along Carmack's spine. He had to convince Lord Livna of the only plan that would keep Tara safe. "There can be no delay, sir. You and your guards should go with your sister, and I'll sail to Jaelport in your place."

Lord Livna halted and stared at Carmack. Neither man blinked. "A noble offer, Demry, but how will you manage it alone?"

"I won't be alone. I'll take Dunn."

"I presume Lady Jaira's visit occurred on Dunn's watch."

Carmack's jaw tensed. The answer lodged in his throat.

Lord Livna shook his head. "I cannot send you and Dunn to rescue the entire crew of the *Brierstar*, any more than I can send Tara ashore alone." He stared toward the distant snow-capped mountains. "I only hope Arman will provide the way to save us all. Excuse me." Lord Livna walked to the bow, where he knelt with his head lowered.

Prayer seemed a natural response for a man like Eric Livna, but Carmack's prayers hadn't helped when his father had fallen through the ice or when Lady Revada had announced Tara's engagement, so Carmack wouldn't rely on Arman now. He'd find a way to save Tara and Roxburg on his own. The only thing he needed Arman to do was stay out of his way.

All too soon, the *Zephyr* reached Meribah Cove, and the crew released the anchor. Lord Livna went belowdecks and reappeared with Tara, still dressed in sailor's garb, with the addition of a midnight blue jacket. Kressy was not with them, probably gathering their wet clothing.

Color had returned to Tara's cheeks, and she had tied most of her damp curls in a loose tail. She looked far less like Lady Gershom without her fancy gowns and complicated braids. More natural. Even more beautiful, which Carmack hadn't thought possible. Blast, he found it hard to breathe. He mulled over the goodbye he had sworn he would never say and wished Lord Livna and the swarming crew would disappear. Maybe then the right words would come. Instead, his last precious seconds with Tara slipped by in awkward silence.

"They're ready for you, my lord," the captain said.

Carmack offered his hand to help Tara over the railing. "It's been my pleasure and honor to serve you, my lady."

Her eyebrow quirked up at her brother. "You have not told him?"

Lord Livna shifted in his boots. "I'm afraid my sister still requires your service, Demry."

Carmack's heart caught. Lord Livna was sending him with Tara, the very outcome Carmack had begged for when he'd first boarded the *Zephyr*. But that was before he'd learned Roxburg was missing. "My lord, I'm sorry, but I must help my brother. And I cannot serve Lady Gershom in Meribah Corner while everyone thinks I'm a murderer."

"I agree," Lord Livna said, "and I could not entrust my sister's safety to anyone else."

Carmack's stomach crashed as though the deck had dropped under his feet. Words flooded his mind, none suitable with a lady present. "Sir?"

"I changed my mind. My sister is going to Jaelport in my place."

Lord of Tsaftown or not, Carmack pulled Lord Livna aside. "You cannot do this! This mission, it's too dangerous."

"Do not remind me." Lord Livna held up his hands. "This is

Arman's will. In truth, I never wanted this journey. Viola convinced me that surrendering the *Brierstar* and its men to their fate would be a heavy blow to Tsaftown so soon after the uprising. She felt this rescue attempt was a sacrifice we needed to make as a family to fully win the hearts of the townspeople, but I prayed for another solution. Now, as I was praying again, King Gidon bloodvoiced me."

Carmack steeled himself at the mention of that particular young man. "The king?"

"He ordered me to Meribah Corner and my sister to Jaelport. Knowing my extended family, you can thank my aunt and Queen Averella for our king's expedient intervention." His voice dropped. "My concerns have not changed. Tara has had no training for something like this. Use the journey to prepare her." He squeezed Carmack's shoulder. "Make sure she comes home alive."

King Gidon may be Arman's chosen king, but what was he thinking, sending a lady like Tara into enemy territory? Nothing Carmack could say would change things. So, Tara would go to Jaelport, her Shield with her.

"She will return safely, sir. I promise you." Even if it meant Carmack would not.

CHAPTER NINE
TARA

S HE HAD DONE IT! TARA STOOD WITH Carmack at the railing amidships, bound for Jaelport with her brother's blessing. She waved goodbye to Eric, and he returned a wave from the dock. The fate of forty-some-odd men, including Leif, Uncle Chantry, and Captain Demry, now depended on her. The saltwater she had swallowed earlier threatened to come back up, and she pressed her hand to her lips. What had she done?

"This is a mistake." Carmack gripped the railing next to her. "You should stay here."

"Eric will deal with Master Ulmer and have Meribah Corner in order by the time we return. Besides, I have two brothers, and Leif needs me." She was the only northerner with a plausible excuse for visiting Jaelport. "Even without training or experience, I am still his best hope."

Carmack shook his head. "Just like your father, you always put your brothers first."

Her cheeks flushed. "You have done the same for Captain Demry."

"That's different. With Lord Livna at the stronghold, you do not need my protection or the people's suspicion that comes with it." Carmack clutched the nape of his neck. "I intend on finding my brother—*both* of our brothers—but how in Er'Rets am I supposed to do that and protect you at the same time?"

Foolish mistake, assuming Carmack would serve her in Jaelport as he had in Meribah Corner. Of course, his sole duty should be his brother's rescue. "My aunt warned me of the risks, and I accepted them," she said. "Your priority must be your brother, so consider yourself my Shield only to keep up appearances."

"Nice thought, but I'm honor bound to always make your safety my priority." Carmack's eyes locked with hers. "Your ladyship cannot command otherwise." He strode across the deck.

Tara hurried after him. "I can take care of myself, Master Demry."

Carmack spun on his heel, looming over her. "Really? Say I'm a Hamartano guard who discovered you wandering in a room where you do not belong, and the mainmast is your only door out, show how you will escape."

Tara lunged to the side, but Carmack caught her waist. She twisted away, but he grabbed her hands. The more she pulled, the tighter he held on. She grunted and tugged until her arms burned. Exhausted, she stopped struggling.

"You'll need to try harder than that," he said.

She huffed. "This is silly. As Jaira's guest, I will not need to fight her guards. She promised I would enjoy more freedom in Jaelport than I do at home."

Carmack released her with a hollow chuckle. "Do you honestly think that snobby minx will throw open every door and give us a tour?"

Tara bristled. Jaira just might provide one if *he* asked. Jaira enjoyed flirting with handsome men, and though she usually ignored anyone without a title, she had remembered Carmack. "Well, what were *you* going to do? Pick every lock, beginning with the main gate? Say what you wish, but your odds of finding our brothers are better with me."

Carmack gestured to the docks in Meribah Cove. "Take a long look, Tara. Odds are you will never see your eldest brother or Meribah Corner again." He stormed away.

Tara clenched her fists. "Carmack Demry, I have not dismissed you!"

He did not turn back, climbing both ladders until he reached the stern deck. Fine, he was angry, but how dare he ignore her!

"Weigh anchor!" the captain shouted.

Some of the crew circled the capstan, and the *Zephyr* headed back to sea.

When Tara could no longer see Eric on shore, she walked to the ship's bow and watched the sunset's golden rays pierce through the purple rain clouds on the horizon.

Master Dunn joined her. "Have you lost your shadow, m'lady?"

"He's sulking at the other end of the ship."

Master Dunn chuckled. "He's not used to being outmaneuvered."

"I fear I will need several lessons before I manage that." A gull flew past, scolding her with its sharp squawks. "Master Dunn, do you think I was wrong to come?"

"Doesn't matter. You're here. The only thing worth thinking about now is how we're going to find those missing men and get them home."

Right. Mistake or not—whether Carmack liked it or not—Tara had to focus on their next steps. "We need a plan."

Master Dunn flashed a waggish smile. "Shall I drag the ornery bird off of his perch?"

Tara glanced back. Carmack had climbed part of the mizzenmast and was standing on the ratlines partway up, watching them. "Tempting offer, but I believe a more subtle approach is necessary."

"I'm afraid subtlety is not among my specialties."

"If we exchange our ideas over dinner, the discussion may coax our friend back into the conversation."

Master Dunn cast a sideways glance over his shoulder, then clasped Tara's hand, raising it to his lips. "I look forward to it." His prickly beard tickled her knuckles as he held them to his lips. He winked and walked away.

Tara froze, her hand suspended in the air. Had she given Master Dunn the wrong idea? She flexed her outstretched fingers and shoved them into her borrowed jacket's pocket. As Tara marched back toward her cabin, she felt Carmack's gaze follow her the length of the ship, maybe because she always assumed that whenever he was nearby, he was watching over her. Imagining otherwise left a hollow feeling in her chest, but if dinner went as planned, she wouldn't have to assume anything. Her Shield would soon be standing beside her once again.

If only Tara could get Carmack to see her as a true asset, not a helpless liability. Convincing him wouldn't be easy, especially if he was still sulking, but she stood at the threshold of the captain's mess, ready to try.

Inside the dark-paneled room, six people sat around a long table set with mugs and steaming bowls. Four men, including Master Dunn and the captain, along with a half-giant woman, who matched the tallest of the men in height, and the ginger-haired Miss Wepp, who had helped her and Kressy change into dry clothes. Beyond them, a large chart of Er'Rets hung on the wall. The chairs on either side of the captain remained empty. One for her, and the other, she guessed, for Carmack. He wasn't there.

Tara straightened the oversized jacket she wore and tightened the rope holding up her pants. She had been forced to wear her salt-crusted hair loose around her shoulders because Kressy was in no condition to help her look more presentable. At the first mention of dinner, the poor girl dove for the bucket and eventually confessed a history of severe seasickness. Tara gave her strict orders not to eat her evening meal in the crew's mess, rather take in plenty of fresh air and sip only broth until the nausea passed.

Truth be told, the ship's constant movement was making Tara queasy too, but skipping dinner was no option. This trip to Jaelport had been her choice, the first major one she had made. For too long, she had dutifully followed others. If her life was to be her own, she had to voice her thoughts and opinions, though she hated the conflict she had created. Carmack's empty seat reminded her that he was far more comfortable with conflict than she was. What if he refused to resolve their difference in opinion?

Drawn by a peal of laughter, Tara stepped into the room.

Master Dunn rose from his seat. "Ah, Lady Gershom, allow me to introduce Captain Alfrid Strumgerd."

The other men stood as Tara approached the table, but the white-haired gentleman bowed, his eyes twinkling like his vest's shiny buttons. "Glad to have you aboard in one piece, my lady. Please, call me Captain Strum. Hope you don't mind we started without you. I wasn't sure you'd feel up to a meal."

"Nor did I, if I am honest, and my poor maid feels even worse."

"The seasickness usually passes in a few days. Please, sit."

Strum pulled out the empty chair to his right, and Tara sat between him and Master Dunn. The captain made introductions, and Tara exchanged smiles with Cole Tanniyn and Mistel Wepp, two freckled minstrels from Armonguard, while Dunn fell into easy conversation with their traveling companions, ZolZanna tan Quelle, the half-giant woman next to him, and Kurtz Chazir, a broad-shouldered man at the end of the table.

"Always a pleasure to meet another northerner, eh?" Master Chazir said.

Tara spread her napkin on her lap. "Are you from Tsaftown, sir?" She sipped a spoonful of steaming broth.

"Born and raised." He smiled, his deep dimples puckering his beard. "Had the pleasure of lodging at Ice Island for a spell."

The savory bone broth in Tara's mouth lodged in her throat, and she coughed.

"Not to worry, m'lady," Dunn said. "Master Chazir is Sir Gavin Lukos's cousin and a member of the Old Kingsguard. That's what landed him in such fine quarters, courtesy of that traitor Nathak's scheming."

"That does put a different spin on it." Tara laughed.

Carmack strode in and claimed the empty chair directly across from hers. His intense brown eyes glanced her way, and she fell silent. Honestly, how could he speed her heart like a smitten schoolgirl simply by entering a room?

Master Dunn leaned closer. "You all right, m'lady?"

She nodded and took a steadying breath. "Captain Strum, can you share more about our journey south? My brother suggested I discuss the details with you."

"Our first port of call will be Land's End in five days."

"That's on our account, my lady," Cole Tanniyn said. "Our next engagement calls us there."

"Will we stay in port long?" Tara asked.

Captain Strum filled her mug with ale. "Only a few hours. Long enough to drop off our passengers and procure additional supplies."

Tara took another sip of broth and set her spoon aside. "Then on to Jaelport?"

"I'm afraid sailing into Jaelport is not possible due to the ongoing blockade," Captain Strum said. "At the time Lord Livna boarded, he had not yet settled on his destination. I believe he was still weighing his options." Strum raised his mug to his lips.

"Which were?" Tara perched on the edge of her chair, waiting for the captain's answer.

After four swallows, Captain Strum set down his ale and wiped his whiskers. "An additional two-day voyage to Hamonah, and from there, hiring a smaller vessel to cross the channel into Jaelport."

Master Dunn squirmed. "Can't say I love that option after the day we've had."

"Nor I," Tara said. "I fear simply suggesting it may cost me Kressy's service forever. What do you think, Master Demry?"

"Navigating the pirate-infested waters around Hamonah will likely cost you more than your maid," Carmack said coolly.

Tara dabbed her mouth with her napkin, hiding the smile that pulled at her lips. Pirates were nothing to smile about, but at least Carmack was talking again. "Then we agree. Hamonah is out. What other options have we, Captain?"

"We could land along the southern shore of Cela, which is west of Jaelport, and you could cover the remaining distance on foot."

Walk? "How long will that take?"

"Depends on your route. The southern coast of Cela stretches some seventy leagues between Land's End on the northwest tip and Jaelport to the southeast. The blockade chokes the southern channel between Cela and Hamonah on the Shelosh Islands, so the closest we could land would be two days from Land's End, sixteen leagues west of Jaelport."

Tara nearly dropped her spoon. "So far?"

"That's not the worst part." Carmack tore off a piece of his flatbread. "If we hike along the coast, we'll have to withstand hours in the brutal sun by day, an onslaught of biting insects at night, wade through tidal pools brimming with sharks, and scale the cliffs west of the city." He popped the bread into his mouth, chewed, and swallowed. "Of course, we could hack our way through the jungle, home to countless venomous spiders and snakes, where we might stumble upon fresh water. We'd have to fight off flesh-eating fish and reptiles to take a drink, though, and still scale those cliffs. No avoiding those."

"I'd advise against the jungle, I would," Master Chazir said. "Darkness rotted much of Cela's vegetation, which gives off a noxious odor in the sweltering heat. People have fallen deathly ill from breathing the fumes, they have."

"May I suggest a third alternative?" Carmack said, taking a drink of ale.

Thank Arman, Carmack had another idea, because nothing thus far sounded feasible. "I'd gladly hear it," Tara said.

Carmack put down his cup and leaned across the table. "You come to your senses and, at Land's End, board another ship bound for home."

Movement at the table ceased, and Tara sensed everyone was awaiting her response. As Carmack's superior, she could give him a firm set down, but that would hardly resolve their differences. What would Mother do?

Humility begets civility.

Tara swallowed her irritation. "Thank you for your suggestion, Master Demry. I shall keep it under consideration."

His eyes narrowed, and the party resumed eating.

Master Dunn cleared his throat. "Master Chazir, why don't you fill us in on the latest from Armonguard?"

"Certainly," Master Chazir said. "It took some time to repair the damage done to the castle, but it was in top shape when we left, it was."

Tara wasn't the least bit interested in the happenings in Armonguard. She studied Carmack's set jaw. Deference hadn't coaxed a snippet of his cooperation, so Tara finished her broth and turned her attention to a yellowed map of Er'Rets hanging on the wall. Specifically, the one road running east from Land's End to Jaelport, by way of Meneton.

During a lull in the conversation, Tara pushed back her chair.

Master Dunn rose to pull it out of her way. "Retiring so soon, m'lady? I can escort you back to your cabin."

Carmack's features darkened as his gaze darted between them. Not the look of a man open to discussion, but of one spring-loaded for a fistfight.

Arman help her, her Shield wasn't making this easy, but she wasn't about to surrender. "No, Master Dunn," Tara said. "I want a closer look at that map." The men stood as she crossed to it. She pointed to Cela's coast due west of Meneton. "Captain, how long would it take to sail from Land's End to here?"

Captain Strum approached, with Masters Dunn and Chazir close behind. "A half day, at most."

"And what type of land lies between the sea and the road?" she asked.

"Rocky hills covered with thorn bushes," Captain Strum said.

Dunn squinted and pointed to a spot close to her fingertip. "Except along this riverbed."

Better and better. "If we got an early start and followed the riverbed, could we reach the road by nightfall?" Tara asked.

"Aye," the captain said. "It wouldn't be overly difficult on foot."

Master Dunn traced a line from her finger to the road. "This is a heavily traveled trade route. Should be plenty easy to hitch a ride and make Meneton by the following afternoon."

The men returned to the table, but another broad shadow fell across the map. "Why Meneton?" Carmack's voice was low, and his breath warmed the back of Tara's neck.

"There are no cliffs between it and Jaelport."

"It's a den of thieves and kidnappers."

"But not sharks and flesh-eating reptiles, and a city promises better shopping."

Carmack pinched the bridge of his nose.

"I'm joking, Master Demry."

"You should be taking this situation seriously."

"Kingdom knows, you are serious enough for both of us," Tara said. "This is Er'Rets—if it were possible to avoid danger entirely, you would be out of a job."

"What I wouldn't give for that to be true. If I could trust you to stay clear of trouble, maybe I could catch my breath." Carmack tipped his head closer, his intense gaze making the rest of the ship fade away. "I was afraid I failed you today. When you went under, I thought you might drown like . . ."

Like his father. "But I didn't, thanks to you." Carmack carried enough guilt and responsibility to sink an entire armada. Tara never intended to add to it. "I do not mean to be difficult. I have information and ways to help this mission, but we must work together."

Carmack shook his head and stepped away. "We'll discuss it tomorrow. It's time to turn in. Goodnight, Captain."

So much for settling their conflict.

"Dunn, go easy on the ale," Carmack said. "Starting tomorrow, we have a lot of training to do."

Dunn lowered his goblet from his mouth. "Aye, sir."

"And *I* will escort Lady Tara back to her cabin." Carmack ushered her out the door so fast, she doubted he noticed Dunn grinning at them.

CHAPTER TEN
CARMACK

CARMACK WAS RUNNING OUT OF TIME. After five days at sea, he had taught Tara just enough to last to the count of ten in a fight. The *Zephyr* was anchored in the harbor off the port of Land's End, which bustled with sailors and merchants exchanging cargo for money.

The minstrels had disembarked earlier, bidding them traveling mercies. Kressy, desperate for solid ground under foot, had volunteered to assist the captain on his trip ashore. What help she could offer, Carmack couldn't fathom, but he was thankful she had left. One less distraction for Tara, who was still signaling every other move with telltale glances and checking her strikes.

Carmack stood on the main deck, watching Tara weave and duck around a piece of driftwood Dunn wielded like a knife. Her movements were sluggish, but otherwise, Tara looked healthier than she had in months, eyes bright and skin glowing. She had stayed clear of Dunn this round, but he was going easy on her. Probably because she'd been practicing for hours under the morning sun.

Dunn took a slow step forward, practically begging her to

pound his chin. Instead, Tara feinted left, then right. Carmack drummed his fingers against his biceps, willing her to hit her burly target. Suddenly, the heel of her hand struck Dunn's jaw.

Dunn staggered back, blinking furiously and rubbing his face. "Ow!"

Tara immediately relaxed her stance and reached for him. "So sorry, Master Dunn. I—"

Dunn grabbed her wrist and spun her around, holding the driftwood to her throat. "No apologies, m'lady."

Tara slouched against him. "Drudge. I always forget that part."

Carmack wanted to pull his hair out. "You're supposed to be fighting for your life, not chitchatting. What next?"

Tara flopped her arms at her sides. "Say my prayers? He supposedly has a knife to my neck."

"No time for prayers," he said. "Grab his arm and throw him over your shoulder."

"No time for prayers, yet you are cracking jokes," she said.

"It's not a joke. Take hold of his forearm against your chest with both hands and drop to your knees. As you drop, twist your body like you're sheathing a sword, and he'll topple right over you."

"What sword?" Tara held out her empty hands. "Weapons and I are not a winning combination, remember?"

That was an understatement. The afternoon spent teaching Tara basic blade skills had nearly driven Carmack overboard. "It's a figure of speech to help you remember the twisting motion toward your waist. Dunn, demonstrate."

Dunn dropped Tara and passed the stick to Carmack. "Sorry, I'm on break." He waggled his eyebrows. "You show her how easily she can tip a man, seat over teakettle."

"I should have left your sorry carcass in retirement," Carmack muttered.

Dunn laughed. "You can thank me later."

Carmack watched Dunn retreat to the shady foredeck. He'd

forgiven him for bringing Tara to the *Zephyr* and for that long kiss to her hand. He suspected Dunn had done it only to taunt him, much like he was doing now.

"Can we call it a day?" Tara wiped the sweat from her brow. "I cannot seem to do anything right, and we still need a plan for when we reach Jaelport."

"Later. You're doing fine."

Tara rolled her brilliant blue eyes. "No, I am not, and we both know it. You said to listen to my gut. My gut tells me I am horrible at self-defense."

Her gut was right, but giving up wasn't an option. "You can do this. By 'put away your sword,' I meant pull across your body, from shoulder to waist." He showed the movement, then beckoned her closer. "Trust me."

Tara sighed and stepped into his shadow.

He pulled her back against his chest and wrapped his arm around her throat, her hair tickling his neck. He tried to ignore how well she fit against him, the top of her head grazing his chin. His body no longer seemed oversized, but framed hers perfectly, like Arman molded him to be her armor.

Tara grabbed his arm with both hands and leaned against him, pressing her ear to his heart.

Beads of sweat broke out along his spine. Carmack tucked his chin to brush his cheek against her hair. Memories of her sweet jasmine perfume mixed with sea spray.

Tara tilted her head back, so their noses nearly touched.

Carmack's breath hitched, his throat suddenly dry. "When you're ready, drop to your knees, and pull your hands down diagonally. Don't release my arm."

Tara didn't move. "Now?"

Not yet. He wanted this moment to last. He gazed down at her pink lips. Her eyes drew him closer. Curses, he needed to get out of this drill and clear his head. "Stop asking questions and—"

Tara dropped, and the world spun out from under Carmack's feet. His back pitched against the deck, knocking the breath from his lungs. He blinked, and Tara's beaming face blocked the sun. She let out a whoop, loosening her grip on his arm—the one clutching the driftwood. Carmack checked his impulse to tap the stick against her abdomen. The kill move would erase any confidence she had gained by executing the throw. Instead, he glanced at his hand. Tara caught the hint and shifted her knee onto his arm, bending his wrist the way he had taught her during their otherwise unsuccessful knife session. She pried the makeshift weapon from his loosened fingertips.

"I did it!" Tara waved the piece of dried wood above her head. "I can't believe that worked!" She helped Carmack to his feet, then wound his arm around her neck. "Let's do that again."

"No." He backed away. His arms still tingled from embracing her, and he shook them. "Enough."

Tara frowned. "Is something wrong?"

Carmack took a deep breath, trying to coax his heart back where it belonged. "We can practice again later. Right now, it's your turn to teach."

The corner of her mouth ticked upward. "Teach what? Is this to be a sewing, drawing, or dancing lesson?"

"I already know how to dance."

"It's been ages . . ."

Three years and four months, to be exact, since Carmack had foolishly asked for two dances in a single night. Roxburg had noticed and had immediately promoted him to the Fighting Fifteen, separating Carmack from Tara. He did not see her again until Lady Revada hired him to escort Tara to her wedding in Meribah Corner and remain there as her Shield.

"I assumed you forgot," she added.

Carmack's chest tightened. "It would be better if we both did." Tara's face fell, and Carmack wished he hadn't said it. The best piece of his soul would die without that memory. "We need to focus on other things," he said, his words clipped. "Like our plan to find our brothers and outwit your mage friend."

"Right. Duty calls." Tara sighed. "How different our lives might be if duty had called someone else." The soft expression of longing in her eyes wrenched Carmack's heart, and she left him to join Dunn on the foredeck.

Duty. Honor. Providence. It didn't matter which was to blame. The life that might have been was never theirs to choose.

CHAPTER ELEVEN
TARA

N O ONE EVER SOUGHT TARA'S OPINION about anything important.

Well, that wasn't exactly true. Carmack usually did, but at the moment, he was too busy pacing the foredeck while she hid in the shade of the foremast. "I'm telling you, Dunn," he said, "we should focus on finding the men first. We'll need the help of Roxburg, Ironblade, and Larr to free the ship."

"We don't know whether we'll need their help, not if we don't know where the blasted ship is or how heavily it's guarded," Dunn said.

It didn't matter whether they looked for the ship or the crew first. They needed to find both before they could escape with either. Tara needed to take charge and end their bickering. That's what her mother would do. Trouble was, she was having a hard time finding the right words, when all she really wanted was to throw herself into Carmack's strong arms again. But she'd gone too far with her flirting comments about dancing, much to his mortification and hers. Rightfully so. Tara's cheeks burned.

"You disagree, my lady?" Carmack asked.

Finally, the opening she needed, but her mind went blank. "I'm sorry. I lost track of the conversation. What were you discussing?"

"Possible locations of the *Brierstar*."

What had she missed? The answer seemed obvious. "Won't she be in Jaelport's harbor?"

"Exactly," Carmack said. "A ship that size can't be moored in some shallow backwater. And we can assume the Jaelportians aren't sailing her under their flag, or the blockade would have spotted her."

"If she's in port, she'll be crawling with Jaelportian guards," Dunn said.

"They'll have guards posted no matter where she's anchored," Carmack said, "which is why we need to locate Roxburg and the crew first. We'll need extra manpower to free the ship."

Tara stared at the canvas folds of the spritsails tied to the yards in front of them. "What if they've stripped the sails or it's not seaworthy?"

Carmack squirmed. "We improvise."

"In other words, pray Arman will deliver us," Dunn said.

Tara shouldn't have asked. Time to change subjects. "About the crew, can we agree Tenma Palace is their most likely location?"

"I expect it will be infested with guards," Dunn said. "Probably houses Jaelport's entire army."

Carmack asked Tara, "Has Lady Jaira ever described her home to you?"

"In tiresome detail," Tara said. "It sits on cliffs overlooking the Eversea and is the only fortified structure in Jaelport. Jabal Tower rises several stories above the rest of the palace and is indeed the city's garrison. The family's residence spans the middle, with size-able gardens and the trades quarter within the outer curtain wall. All visitors enter the main gate and are presented in the throne room. That is where we will meet the family and request their hospitality."

"I thought you were invited," Carmack said.

"Invitation or not, we must abide by their customs," Tara answered. "We must also present gifts."

"Gifts?" Carmack asked. "For what?"

Dunn waved him off. "We'll leave protocol to you, m'lady. Kingdom knows, Demry's manners aren't up to snuff."

"There is another custom I should warn you about," Tara said. "At Tenma Palace, men and women are housed in separate wings. You will stay in the east wing, and I will stay with the Hamartano women in the west."

Carmack straightened. "Over my dead—"

"Allow me to explain," Tara said. "The west wing is the private residence of Queen Torrezia and her daughters, Lady Mandzee, the presumptive heir, and Lady Jaira, which reminds me—in Jaelport, they are considered princesses and addressed as 'Your Highness.' The only men allowed in their private residence are the eunuchs chosen as their personal guards, and there is no shortage of those. I'll be perfectly safe."

Carmack set his jaw. "With us in the east wing."

"Be reasonable. I cannot possibly stay with you and leave Jaelport with my reputation intact."

"It's your body that has to leave intact," Carmack said, "not your reputation."

"Both are at risk if I stay with you," Tara snapped. "Every male guest in the palace will assume I am a strumpet and that you are not above sharing."

Carmack's face reddened.

Tara Emmaline Livna Gershom! Aunt Nitsa's voice thundered through Tara's mind.

She clapped a hand over her mouth then lowered it. "Sorry."

My dear, what has come over you? I meant to see how you were faring, only to hear you speaking like a coarse sailor.

"I didn't mean for that to come out so bluntly."

It's not like you, Tara.

"Moving on," Carmack said.

Tara held up her hand. "One at a time, please." Carmack and Master Dunn exchanged quizzical looks, and Tara pointed to her ear. "Aunt Nitsa is talking."

Understanding dawned on their faces.

I take it things between you and Master Demry are not going as smoothly as we hoped. Remember, I can hear your thoughts. No need to speak aloud.

This time Tara thought her reply. *Erratic, to say the least.*

Be patient, my dear. He cares deeply for you.

He cares deeply for his job. We mustn't confuse the two.

I see you've reached Land's End. Where are you headed next?

To Meneton, then south into Jaelport. We should reach it within three days.

Excellent progress. I will leave you now.

"Wait!" Tara shouted, making both Carmack and Master Dunn jump. She slammed her eyes shut and thought the rest of what she wanted to say. *Aunt Nitsa, how did Averella best Larkos and Jaira?*

Larkos blew anabas dust in Averella's face, to no effect, since it only works on males. The eunuch suspected antiserum at first, then ultimately, deduced she was a woman. Before he could recover from his surprise, she knocked him out with the pommel of her sword.

A lump formed in Tara's throat. *Her sword?*

Yes, dear. As to Lady Jaira . . . Averella never fought her directly. She bloodvoiced Sir Gavin. He and the other knights saved her. Why?

Just curious. Thank you, Aunt.

May Arman continue to bless you, dearest niece.

Tara opened her eyes. Both of her guards leaned closer.

"What did she say?" Carmack asked.

That Tara didn't stand a chance. She managed a shaky smile. "We briefly discussed Jaelportian magic. Now about the palace gardens—"

"Skip to the magic, please," Carmack said.

"Blast it, Demry," Master Dunn said. "Stop interrupting. Although in this case, he has a point, m'lady."

"Very well. What little I know comes from a variety of sources, including Jaira, Queen Averella, Aunt Nitsa, and Lady Viola, whose mother was a Hamartano."

"Is every noble family in this blessed kingdom related?" Carmack muttered.

"Er'Rets is an island," Master Dunn said. "What do you expect?"

Tara shared what Aunt Nitsa had said about the runes mages drew on their foreheads and the various potions and powders the mages used to control and incapacitate men. "Each new generation of mages studies their craft, not only to preserve it, but to improve their capabilities. Every year, they compete to measure their advances—which potions work the quickest, last the longest, and so on."

"A tournament of witches," Master Dunn said. "Please tell me we will not be attending."

"Not to worry, Master Dunn. The event happens in late summer. We will be home by then."

"Arman willing," Carmack mumbled. "Who are the top contenders, so we know who to avoid?"

Jaira's boasting left little doubt. "Over the past three years, Jaira has won every contest but one—magical remedies and antiserums," Tara said.

Carmack pinched the bridge of his nose, a sign he was reaching the limit of how much bad news his broad shoulders could carry.

Tara wished she hadn't ended on a sour note. Or had she? "Antiserum," she repeated, remembering her aunt's words. "When Jaira's eunuch thought Averella was a boy, he mentioned antiserum. That must be how eunuchs do not fall victim to their own potions.

Perhaps antiserum could prevent you two from succumbing to such potions in the first place."

"Where would we find it?" Carmack asked. "If antiserum can protect men from mage poison, the mages wouldn't make it readily available."

Master Dunn nodded. "Even if they did, we don't know what to look for."

Tara did. Jaira's chain and glass vial, still tucked under Tara's neckline, chafed against her skin. The imagined echo of her mother's voice, reading from the *Book of Arman,* rang as clearly as Aunt Nitsa's. *"If we claim fellowship with Arman while we walk in darkness, we are liars not living in truth. But if we walk in the light and truth with Him, we have fellowship with each other, and the blood of his son Câan washes us clean of wrongdoing."*

"I must confess something," Tara said. "Master Dunn, you did not simply nod off after Lord Gershom's funeral. Lady Jaira bewitched you. I am sorry I did not tell you earlier. I believed secrecy was necessary for her sake." Tara pulled the chain and its tiny vial out from under her bodice's neckline. "I should have given you this."

Carmack took it from her hand and held it up in the sunlight. An orange flash shimmered across his face. "What is it?"

"An antiserum called panzehir. Jaira gave it to me to revive Master Dunn, but I didn't use it. He woke on his own."

"I'm thankful you didn't," Master Dunn said. "I wouldn't drink any concoction from a mage's hand."

Carmack handed the panzehir back to Tara. "Any other secrets you've been hiding?"

Tara winced at his stern tone. She'd never kept secrets from him before. Not dangerous ones like this. "No."

Behind her, the ringing bell announced the captain's return to the ship.

"We should rest. This will be our last opportunity to sleep for a while." Carmack left without the slightest glance Tara's way.

If only she had been honest from the start.

Master Dunn cleared his throat, startling her. "Confession is never easy, and for what it's worth, all is forgiven between us."

"I am grateful for your understanding, Master Dunn."

As Carmack descended belowdecks, Tara hoped he, too, would find a way to forgive her. Until then, she had little hope of winning his trust or playing a meaningful role in finding their brothers. Much like her family, Carmack would go on seeing her as helpless Tara, sure to bumble headlong into trouble. All beauty, no wit.

Tara was capable of far more. And it was high time Carmack Demry saw it.

CHAPTER TWELVE
CARMACK

GUARD HER BODY AND LOSE YOUR heart; guard your heart and lose your mind.

Carmack's makeshift boxing dummy stood strapped to the mainmast, its bucket head wobbling on top of the mop handle that served as its spine. Carmack jabbed his fists into the dummy's stuffed jacket—left, right, left. Right, left, right.

The early morning sea breeze cooled the sweat trickling down his bare back and face, reminding him of the way Tara's hair had grazed his cheek. His fingers itched to hold her again. Carmack wanted off the ship as fast as possible, to get some space between them, but with dangerous days ahead, there was still so much he needed to teach her.

Right hook. Carmack flexed his hands, took aim, and sent the bucket flying across the deck.

"What did that poor bucket ever do to you?" Dunn stepped out from the shadows of the quarterdeck.

"I thought you were sleeping."

"I'll sleep when I'm old."

"You're old now." Carmack picked up the bucket, tipped it upside down on the mop handle, and resumed jabbing.

"You'll feel differently in seven years when you're my age." Dunn leaned against the closest railing where Carmack had left his shirt airing in the breeze. "Listen, I hate to peddle unwanted advice, but as your former trainer, I suggest you tell Lady Tara the truth."

Carmack glared at him. "About what?"

Dunn's eyebrow quirked upward. "Her training, for starters. I saw that throw, or should I say dive?"

Hopefully, that's all Dunn saw. "You know how throws work. Tara followed my instructions and gravity did the rest."

"Sure, she tossed you, but you surrendered the weapon."

Carmack unleashed his fists on the dummy. "A trained soldier would never have held the knife to the front of her neck, so either way, she'd be dead." He punched out each word. "Is that what you'd have me tell her?"

"Not exactly in those words, but you do her no favors by withholding correction."

"She was giving up. I had to boost her confidence."

"Confidence comes through solid instruction. Anything less will only get her killed."

That and countless other possibilities. Suddenly, his stuffed jacket was not a tool for exercise, but a Hamartano guard looming over Tara, and Carmack was the only one who could protect her. Once again, he sent the bucket flying but did not stop pummeling the dummy.

"Maybe," Dunn said, "your feelings are affecting your judgment."

"My feelings are completely under control." Carmack delivered a spinning kick, and the mop handle snapped under his boot. Broken in two, the dummy crumpled, its fish net innards sagging out of the jacket into a heap at Carmack's feet.

"So I see." Dunn scooped up the nets and tossed them aside. "Then what's keeping you awake?"

"A toss-up between your snoring and Jaelportian magic." Carmack pulled on his shirt and walked over to the railing. "When I first heard rumors of love spells, I imagined something like a strong drink. That a man caught by the poison would stumble around, befuddled. But then the king grew violent when someone got in the way, and that tells me the magic changes a man's motives."

Dunn joined him. "Cruel magic, to turn a man's heart into an instrument of hate."

"Cunning too. I can't think of a better way to fully wield a man's power." Carmack rubbed the knot of tension forming at the back of his neck. "Is there anything a man won't do to protect the woman he loves—or thinks he loves?"

Dunn shrugged. "I'm a sworn bachelor. You're the one who left everything to pursue Lady Love. Though now that Lady Tara is single again, you've turned into an utter boor. Has your fever for her cooled?"

"If only." Carmack fixed his gaze on the coast of Cela, unable to look his friend in the eye. "You should have seen her put Lord Livna in his place. I knew she hid a fiery spirit under that cool exterior, but I hadn't seen it in so long, I was starting to think marriage had killed off that side of her completely." With fresh evidence to the contrary, Carmack was having a hard time ignoring how it fed his own hidden flame, one he worked very hard to contain. One of longing for her.

For several minutes, neither man said anything. A line of light pink sand widened along the horizon. On the quarterdeck, the first mate turned the wheel, pointing the *Zephyr* landward.

"You should tell her you're smitten with her," Dunn said. "That you've been waiting for old Gershom to drop so you could marry her and have the family you've always dreamed of."

"I can't marry her." Carmack released a hollow laugh. "I'm more of a sworn bachelor than you."

"Bah! Since when?"

"Since I vowed lifelong celibacy to ensure she survived her marriage."

"You did what?" Dunn's eyes widened. "Why?"

Desperation. Guilt. Maybe if he hadn't left, things would have been different. But that wasn't what Dunn was asking. "Lady Revada is a shrewd woman. Like Roxburg, she guessed my feelings after Tara and I danced together twice in one evening. It's why she summoned me back to Lytton Hall. Who better to entrust her daughter's safety than the soldier who loves her? But Lady Revada would not send me to Meribah Corner as Tara's Shield without a vow protecting both houses from the potential scandal of an illicit romance."

"Why didn't you refuse?"

"And leave Tara's protection to someone else? That's what I did when Roxburg promoted me, and look how that turned out for her."

"You can't blame yourself for that. Lord Livna would have given his daughter's hand whether or not you were there."

You've thrown your life away, chasing after a woman who'll never be yours.

"You sound like Roxburg." And it didn't matter if Dunn was right. Those months apart were torture, even when Carmack had assumed Tara was safe at home. "I couldn't have lived with myself, knowing she was under that lunatic's roof."

"But Lady Revada had to know Gershom was failing. She couldn't have intended to bind you forever. Besides, vows are only words." A gruff bitterness tinged Dunn's speech, making him sound like a man haunted by heartbreak. "Easily made, easily broken."

"Not vows made before Arman, recorded by the priest, and governed by the Northlander Charter." The archaic charter set forth the governing customs in the northern range of the Chow-mah Mountains and dictated harsh consequences for those who violated their code.

Dunn winced. "You bound your honor."

"Aye, and if I marry, neither my bride nor I could set foot in Tsaftown or Meribah Corner again. Even if I could stomach the disgrace, I could never ask Tara to abandon her family and estate—everything she values—to join me in squalor."

"This definitely explains your mood swings. I take it Lady Tara doesn't know."

"How could I tell her without admitting why the vow was necessary? Nothing good can come of it. Better she thinks I'm an unfeeling sack of muscle."

"Hate to tell you this, but I believe Lady Tara is attracted to unfeeling sacks of muscle." Dunn scratched his beard. "Even when you're a despicable grump, her eyes follow your every move."

Carmack had noticed enough of Tara's lingering stares to suspect some regard, but the thought of Tara loving him sent warmth pulsing through his veins until shame doused it. It was cruel to hope she suffered as he did.

"If you accept that your vow is Arman's will, all the more reason to tell Lady Tara about it," Dunn said. "Spare her heart so she can move on."

Move on? Why would Dunn torment him with the thought of Tara falling in love with anyone else? The vision of his friend kissing Tara's hand sprang to mind. Maybe there had been something behind it, after all. "With you?"

"Don't be daft." Dunn shoved his shoulder. "The Poroo and Ebens get along better than romance and me, but Lady Tara doesn't strike me as the spinsterly type. If you don't tell her, you risk binding her heart to a lost cause, like you did."

A sour taste filled Carmack's mouth. Confessing his vow to Tara would be a complete surrender, forever burying the dreams he'd cherished for so long. Fibers deep in his soul strained against the idea. "For someone who supposedly doesn't peddle unwanted advice, you sure shovel it out."

"Then I'll say no more." Dunn left Carmack alone on the deck.

Carmack's heart *was* a lost cause, but he would not make matters worse by encouraging Tara's affection. When the time was right, he'd tell her about the vow, but not now. Close quarters had blurred the line between them, but their mission could restore distance. Whatever happened, Carmack had to keep Tara at arm's length, or better yet, out of his arms entirely.

Chapter Thirteen
Tara

WAGON BEDS WERE NO MORE FIT for sleep than beds of nails. Tara thanked Arman when the wagon finally stopped, and its splintered boards no longer pounded her tired muscles and aching ribs. A light hand shook her shoulder.

"We've arrived in Meneton, m'lady," Kressy said.

Tara raised her head. Kressy sat at the end of the wagon, and Carmack and Master Dunn stood mere paces away. One deep breath choked Tara with the fumes of onions and bird droppings. Moaning, she buried her nose in the crook of her elbow.

"Are you sick?" Kressy asked, her cheeks pink with sunburn and her pale gray dress turned dingy beige from dust.

"Only tired." Tara sat up, bumping the crates piled alongside her.

"BAWK!" A chicken at the top of the wobbling stack flapped its wings in protest, and others in the caged brood joined her.

Tara scooted away from them and the mound of green onions taking up most of the wagon bed. She wiped the grit from her hands, her purse swinging from her wrist, and the sleep from her eyes with her sleeve. The rank odor of salt, sweat, and soil trapped in the crushed velvet fibers made her nose water. "And filthy." She pulled a stray chicken feather caught in a curl dangling between her eyes. Her fingers tangled in the matted curls as she raked them back. She whimpered. "And crusty."

Five days on a ship without a bath had been bad enough. After a full day's hike through Cela's wilderness, a night's rest in a dusty ditch, and a half-day's ride alongside a load of dirt-covered onions and mite-infested chickens, Tara could no longer stand herself. "First chance I get, I am going to burn this dress."

"Good, because I'm no miracle worker." Kressy held out her hand, steadying Tara as she climbed down into a narrow side street tightly packed with sandstone shops, most fronted with faded striped awnings and capped with russet clay tiles. At the street's far end, the Yâm River glistened under the midday sun. To the south, Meneton rose with the hillside, its residents' homes stacked against the steep slope as haphazardly as the crates housing the farmer's incensed chickens.

The wiry farmer turned in his wagon seat and cleared his throat, clearly awaiting the compensation promised for their ride. Tara fished through the clinking contents of her purse and handed him a silver gora. "Thank you, sir, for making room for us among your . . ." Tara's gaze slid sideways, and she held her breath. If she ever ate another onion, it would be too soon. She forced a smile. ". . . fine goods."

The farmer flipped the coin over in his calloused palm, and his bulging eyes dropped to her purse. "Would you be interested in buying any of my chickens? They're the best you'll find. Dependable egg layers, all of 'em."

"No, thank you."

"How about some green onions, then?" Though Tara shook her head, the farmer hopped down, grabbed a fistful of wilted onion tops, and waved the pungent clump in her face. "I'll give you a fair deal, better than the bazaar's swindlers."

Tara reared back and bumped into a broad chest.

Carmack's tunic was stained with sweat. He stepped around her, his imposing shadow darkening the farmer's dusty face. "Her ladyship said no. Be on your way."

The farmer clambered onto his wagon. "Hee-yaw!" He slapped the reins against his mule's back, still clutching his onion tops as he rode away.

"I suggest we find the nearest tavern and order some grub." Master Dunn turned a slow circle, rubbing his hands together, then pointed at a series of signs. "Let's see, we've got The Dancing Swine . . . Four Barrels . . . or might I suggest The Blind Monk?" His thumb stayed raised at the painted caricature of a monk wearing a blindfold hanging behind him. "Something tells me he's a good bet."

Carmack shot a disapproving look at Master Dunn. "We'll find a proper inn with private rooms."

Master Dunn let out a low whistle. "Finding one in the cesspit of Cela will be about as easy as finding a cuddly mama cham."

"Let's not waste daylight, then." Carmack strode ahead. "Our best hope is along this main road."

"Shouldn't we visit the market?" Tara hurried after him. "All of us need new clothing before we reach Jaelport, and it couldn't hurt to freshen up first."

"Contrary to your upbringing, a new wardrobe is not a necessity. Food and lodging are."

"Surely, no innkeeper in his right mind will rent decent rooms to us in our bedraggled state."

"Your aunt's coins will change minds faster than our clothing." Carmack marched on.

Typical man, putting his stomach before sense. Considering Tara reeked of onions, she'd be lucky to find quarter in the town stables, but she bit her tongue. Carmack's foul temper was bringing out his controlling side. Better to let him have his way than to challenge him and make matters worse.

Tara had not walked far when she sensed others watching her. After years of being put on display by her parents, she was used to heads swiveling as she passed by, but this was different. In a banquet hall, she might meet a stare and receive a smile or bow in return. Instead, haunted faces and unblinking vacant eyes leered from shadowed doorways and through ragged curtains.

Outside one crumbling hovel, a young boy dressed in a long threadbare tunic waved a dirty rag at Carmack. "Shine your boots, sir? One rutah each."

"No." Carmack blocked the boy's attempt to grasp hold of his boot, sweeping his skinny arm aside.

The boy followed. "A bargain for you, then. One rutah for both." Carmack walked on, and the determined twinkle left the boy's brown eyes.

Poor thing was nothing but dust-covered skin and bone. Only Arman knew when he had last eaten or what. Tara reached into her purse and pulled the smallest coin she could find. A copper worth twenty rutah. She flipped the coin, and it landed at his feet.

The boy snatched it from the dust and gave a toothless grin. "Spankin' copper! That's right nice of you, miss," he shouted and scurried away.

Carmack scowled over his shoulder. "Quit tossing coins, or we'll be tripping over every street urchin in town."

Tara rolled her eyes. After two days of travel and many unsuccessful attempts to moderate his surly behavior, she lacked the willpower to make another.

Near the center of town, Carmack pointed out a two-story building painted a cheery, albeit faded, yellow. On its sign, "Happy Rosie's Inn" was written in magenta around a yellow rose.

"This looks promising," Carmack said.

Master Dunn stationed himself on the perch, while Tara, Kressy, and Carmack stepped inside. The room was tolerably clean, with fewer flies than most inns, and two of the tables were empty.

"Out!" A rotund woman charged through the back doorway, brandishing a cleaver. "Be gone with you."

Carmack raised his hands. "Happy Rosie?"

The woman didn't appear one bit happy, but she nodded. "Aye, and I've paid my dues, I have, so I'll not put up with the likes of your kind blighting my establishment."

"We'll pay you for your trouble." Carmack nudged Tara.

Tara shook her purse so the contents jangled loudly. As if she'd rung a gong, the few patrons seated at the tables turned in their seats.

Carmack's hand clamped onto her wrist, stilling the purse. "Not. Like. That," he said through clenched teeth.

"Flush with plunder, are yeh?" Rosie's eyes narrowed. "You and every other scurvy pirate looking for favors."

"Me?" An unstoppable peal of laughter rose up from Tara's belly. "A pirate?"

Kressy's hand went to her throat. "Sweet saints above, m'lady's mind has really cracked this time."

"You misunderstand us, madame." Tara stifled her giggles. "We are not pirates. Only weary travelers from the north. I am Lady Tara Gershom from Meribah Corner."

"Ooh, Lady Tara, is it?" Rosie drawled. "Well, beggin' your pardon, Lady Tara, but I don't shelter pirates or their harlots, no matter how profitable their excursions may be. And I don't care if you're the queen of Magos, you won't be staying here, reeking up the place worse than a pot of rancid fish stew." Rosie gripped her cleaver with both hands. "Now get out, or I'll chop you to bits!"

Kressy launched forward. "How dare you disrespect m'lady, you pug-faced crone!"

Carmack caught Kressy around the waist, hoisting her out of

range of Rosie's cleaver. "We're leaving. Now." He jerked his chin at Tara, and she hurried out the door.

"Let me go," Kressy said. "I'll teach her a lesson in hospitality."

Rosie's voice followed them into the sun-drenched street. "And don't come back, or I'll report you to the guild for harassing an innkeeper!"

While Carmack scolded Kressy, Tara sagged in a sliver of shade under the neighboring roofline. Not the slightest urge to laugh remained.

A young girl with long brown braids approached. Several pairs of dull gemstone earrings dangled from a grungy red scarf around her neck. "Buy a bauble, pretty miss? Two for the price of one." Faded yellow and purple bruises mottled her arms and left cheek.

"You poor dear, who has done this to you?" Tara reached for her shoulder, but the gangly girl reared back. "Don't be afraid. I won't hurt you."

The girl snarled. "They all say that." As she bolted away, Tara grabbed her scarf, wheeling her around. "Let go, you dirty scupper!" The girl bared her teeth and pulled Tara's hand toward her mouth as if to bite it.

"Stop!" Tara yanked one hand back, holding the scarf with her other. "I only want to talk to you."

"I've heard that before too." The girl yanked Tara around in a circle.

"Enough!" Carmack stepped between them, and the girl kicked his shin. He grunted and snagged one of her braids. She screamed an obscenity that enflamed Tara's cheeks.

"Don't hurt her," Tara said. "She's only a child."

The girl buried her fingernails into Carmack's arm, and he gave her hair a small tug. "More like a feral cat."

Tara shoved her hand into her purse, grabbed the first coin she felt, and thrust it under the girl's nose. "Will you take us to the market?"

A flash of gold turned the girl's wide brown eyes amber, and she stilled. Not the coin Tara had intended to offer. A copper would have paid a week's room and board; one silver gora would cover a month's; but a gold coin, worth ten gora, would only land a street girl in trouble. Fate had pulled a trick on them both.

"A poor bargain." Carmack scowled and released the girl. "The bazaar will be in the town center, and we decided to find an inn first."

Poor bargain was an understatement, but Tara raised an eyebrow. "We? You mean, *you* decided."

The girl reached for the coin, but Carmack snatched it first. "Not so fast, girl. How do we know you won't take it and run?"

She crossed her arms, glaring. "How do I know you won't cheat me?"

"If I may." Tara rested her hand on Carmack's bicep, and he jerked back as if her fingers had singed him. What had gotten into him lately? Since leaving the *Zephyr*, he had treated Tara as if she were covered in pox. "I'll pay one rutah now, another when reach the market, and once you lead us to a suitable inn, I'll exchange the gold for the rutahs."

"I don't believe you," the girl said.

Tara shrugged. "Then you're out the two rutahs."

The peddler girl sized them both up, then held out a grubby palm. "Fine, but my name's Betzi, not Girl."

"Pleased to meet you, Betzi. I am Lady Tara." She sifted through her purse, searching for anything smaller than a copper. "Master Demry, I don't suppose . . ."

Carmack huffed, then stuck his hand in the small leather pouch hanging from his belt and handed Betzi one rutah.

A sly grin crept across her face. "The bazaar is a block away in the central plaza."

Carmack shot Tara a look that said, "I told you so."

"I know all the best booths. Any trinket you can imagine and cloth fit for a queen." Betzi led the group farther down the same road, with Carmack alongside and Kressy close behind, spilling details into Betzi's ear about every item they required.

Tara fell back into step with Master Dunn and in a low voice asked, "Is something wrong with Master Demry? He's been out of sorts lately."

"Like his stomach, he growls when he's hungry." Master Dunn's mouth ticked slightly. "Besides that, I can't say. You might ask him."

"I will." Something more than hunger was bothering Carmack. Master Dunn knew it too.

Out of the corner of her eye, Tara glimpsed someone watching them from the rooftop, but when she looked up, no one was there. Maybe in the fog of exhaustion she had only imagined it. A chunk of her salt-stiffened hair fell in her face. She pushed it back, catching a sour whiff of body odor. Was that horrendous smell coming from her?

Disgusting. She needed a bath, a hot meal, and a candid conversation with her Shield. But first, shopping.

Amazing how a handful of kebabs could boost morale. Tara chewed a mouthful of savory lamb, satisfied with her shopping successes. Now all she required was a decent night's rest. She marched with her companions through the bazaar. Around her, canvas booths filled the plaza like tiles pressed into a slapdash mosaic. A broken chorus of calling peddlers filled the air, along with the aromas of curry, cinnamon, and dried flowers.

Kressy and Master Dunn held bundles of new clothing—dresses and undergarments for the women and new tunics, trousers, and leather jerkins for the men. Hidden safely in the folds of Tara's skirt were three bracelets for Queen Torrezia Hamartano and her daughters. The only item the bazaar failed to offer Tara was a mourning dress. Hardly surprising. Such expensive garments were usually made-to-order. The one dress Tara had found herself—a pale blue kirtle—had been custom made for a merchant's wife. After several rounds of negotiating with the tailor, he had agreed to sell it for three times its original price. As a result, Tara's purse hung lighter from her waist.

Tossing her empty skewer aside, she dug out a gold coin and pressed it into Betzi's hand. "For a job well done."

Betzi stared at it, eyes glistening. "But I haven't taken you to an inn yet."

"You have my trust." Tara rested her hand on Betzi's shoulder. "A coin like that can buy many things, maybe even a fresh start. Now, off we go before I drop."

"This way." Betzi hadn't gone far when she turned around and headed back the direction they'd come.

"What's the matter?" Tara asked.

"Wrong way." Betzi broke into a jog. "Follow me. Hurry!"

"Hurry?" Carmack stiffened, scanning the surroundings. "Dunn!"

The men formed a barrier of muscle. Tara craned her neck, trying to see around them.

"Aye. Two to the north, three on our tail."

"Don't be missing the trouble straight ahead," Kressy said.

When Betzi bolted past two shabbily dressed men, one grabbed her arm and tossed her over his shoulder.

"Betzi!" Tara screamed. "Help her, Carmack."

"She's not my main concern." Carmack pressed his hand against Tara's back, speeding her steps to the plaza's edge. Halfway there, he stumbled forward. Tara wheeled around. A man wearing a grimy red headscarf was clutching Carmack's neck from behind.

"Run," Carmack rasped, then pulled his attacker over his shoulder. The man landed on his back on the cobblestones at Carmack's feet, and Carmack punched him.

"This way, m'lady." Kressy grabbed Tara's hand and took off, weaving between the vendors' booths.

Tara tried to keep up, but her stiff velvet dress weighed on her with suffocating heat. Pinpoints of light flashed across her vision. If she didn't stop running, she would faint. Tara ducked into a shady triangle of hanging tapestries, pulling Kressy with her. She sank to her knees on the cobblestones and closed her eyes, willing herself not to pass out.

"I can't see what's happened to them," Kressy said. "Stay here, m'lady."

Finally, the dizziness stopped. When Tara opened her eyes, the bundles of clothes were on the ground around her, but Kressy was gone. Tara peeked through the tapestries and saw her maid grab a clay flowerpot from a neighboring pottery booth and launch it into the melee.

The tapestry behind Tara flapped. An arm snaked around her waist, and a hand grabbed her face. She screamed into the sweaty palm as it clamped over her mouth, pushing and pulling at the massive arms covered in sweaty hair. The man dragged her from the bazaar through a solid wooden gate.

The hairy-armed captor wasn't alone. A short, bald man barred the gate behind them, then the two men wrestled Tara down an alley into a deserted courtyard. At the far end, the dome of a boarded-up shrine cast a serrated shadow across the uneven cobblestones.

Would the throw Carmack taught her still work with the man's arm around her waist? Tara tried to drop into a squat, but instead of pulling her captor off-balance, she hung like a limp rag doll over his arm.

He yanked her purse off her wrist, and she screamed. His fat hand clamped over her mouth, while the shorter man raked her clothing. He pulled the wrapped bracelets from her skirt's inner pocket, his black eyes gleaming. "What other treasures might you be hiding under your frock?"

The taller man's arms tightened around Tara. She thrashed her head and kicked her feet, tears blurring her vision. No one had ever spoken to her in such a coarse way before, but she could do nothing to stop the thieves.

"That's no way to treat a lady." A tenor voice came from a shadowed figure who stepped between the shrine's pillars.

Tara's captor snarled, revealing a row of blackened teeth. "This don't concern you, whoever you are."

"Aye, we caught this dove on our own," the short man said.

"Tsk, tsk, tsk." A slender man stepped out of the shadows, and the sun glinted off his golden hair and the extravagant embroidery trimming his blood red jacket. Saints, he looked so much like Viola's brother, Sir Rigil, Tara almost sighed with relief, but something was off. Though this stranger was undeniably handsome, there was a hardness to his chiseled features. Perhaps it was his pointier chin or squinty eyes. Whatever it was, an uneasiness gripped Tara's heart. "I am afraid chivalry commands me to intervene."

Chivalry?

Tara's captor went rigid. "Is that who I think it is?"

"Eel's breath." The short man dropped Tara's valuables and fled.

Her captor lifted her like a shield, and Tara thrashed her feet. "Don't come any closer," he said, "or I'll . . . I'll . . ."

"You'll what? Fell me with your rotten breath?" The gentleman's laughter reverberated through the narrow courtyard like discordant wind chimes. He pulled a dagger from his belt. "Put her down gently, and I won't fling this into your skull."

The man did as he was told. Tara's knees gave out the second her feet touched the ground, the thick folds of her skirt cushioning her fall. Her captor ran away, a corner of red handkerchief waving from his back pocket.

The gentleman in the red coat gathered Tara's belongings and handed them to her. "I apologize, miss. Had I arrived a moment sooner, I might have spared you the shock of such violence."

Tara tucked the bracelets into her purse. She attempted to retie its strings around her wrist, her fingers shaking.

"Allow me to assist you." He flashed a toothy smile, then tied the purse cords with his long fingers, giving Tara a close look at his gold ring. The band was covered in tiny scales, sculpted like a tanniyn. The miniature sea serpent had a ruby eye and diamond fangs that swallowed its tail. Such a fine piece of workmanship must have cost a small fortune, far more than the man's shiny boots and embroidered brocade coat.

"Who are you, good sir?" she asked.

"A bold question in the backstreets of Meneton." The gentleman chuckled. "To a fetching young miss like you, I am Captain Myck." He bowed. "May I have the favor of your name?"

Fetching? Filthy was more like it. Something in the back of Tara's mind pressed her to remain silent, but that would have been rude considering the man had rescued her. She extended her hand. "Lady Tara Gershom."

Captain Myck pulled her to her feet. "So, it *is* you! I thought it might be."

Prickles ran along Tara's spine, and she pulled away from his grip. "How do you know me?"

He grinned. "Word of visitors spreads fast, especially well-to-do ladies dressed in red velvet with corn silk hair and eyes like shallow seas. I wager you need lodging during your stay."

Lodging. In the midst of everything, she'd nearly forgotten. "I'm afraid so. Happy Rosie turned us away."

"The old sow thinks Meneton a grand city rather than a backwater slum. Don't take it personally. I keep a suite of rooms at the Juggler's Inn. You are welcome to stay there as long as you like."

Goosebumps spread up Tara's arms. Chivalry was one thing, but obscene generosity? And to stay in a stranger's personal suite? "I couldn't possibly oust you from your own bed."

"What gave you that idea?" Myck asked.

Tara's cheeks warmed. "Sir!"

"I'm only teasing." Myck laughed. "You will have the whole place to yourself. My crew and I sail tonight."

"Crew? Are you a sea captain?" He bowed his head, and she smiled. Providence? "Now, there is an offer I cannot refuse."

"Tara!" A pounding racket thundered from the alleyway.

She jumped at the sound of her name. Captain Myck reached for his sword, but Tara raised her hand. "That is Master Demry, my Shield."

"Then I shall escort you until you are safely reunited."

Tara's knees wobbled from exhaustion, and she tripped on a cobblestone.

Captain Myck caught her arm and wound it around his. "Lean on me. Poor girl, you've had a terrible shock."

Saints, this man was bold. Her mother would throw a fit if she caught Tara walking arm in arm with a strange man, but Mother was leagues away. Besides, Captain Myck had saved her from the thieves, returned all her valuables, and solved her lodging problem. Why should Tara refuse a strong arm to lean against? She found it strangely comforting, though the captain's bicep was noticeably thinner than Carmack's. Something else about this man niggled at her. "Captain, how did you know my name, when I am merely a widow from Therion?"

"A widow from Therion?" Captain Myck looked aghast but did not drop her arm. "Bart's blood, I have you confused with another Lady Tara."

Tara's head spun. "Another?"

"Indeed, an infamous harasser of innkeepers." Laughter danced in his gray eyes. "And reputed pirate."

Tara's mouth dropped open, and she laughed with him. "One and the same, I'm afraid."

CHAPTER FOURTEEN
CARMACK

TARA!" CARMACK POUNDED AGAINST a tall gate. Its solid planks stretched all the way to the stone arch above it—the plaza's only exit point near Tara's last known location. "Dunn, help!" Carmack threw his shoulder against the gate, and Dunn followed suit. Kressy dropped their purchases and joined in, but even with three of them pushing, it barely moved.

"No good," Dunn panted. "Must be barred on the other side."

Carmack spun in a circle, scanning the assorted pottery, textile, and weaver booths nearby. The scuffle hadn't lasted long, but by the time Kressy had bashed a flowerpot over the head of Carmack's last attacker, Tara was gone.

"Kressy, are you sure this is where you left her?"

"She was kneeling there, between those tapestries at the weaver's booth with our parcels." Kressy pointed, and her face crumpled. "When I went back to collect them, she was gone, like she was snatched, body and all, into the Veil."

"Keep your wits, miss," Dunn said. "Shall we go 'round to the other side?"

A faint noise from the other side of the gate caught Carmack's ear. "Wait, I hear something." He pressed his ear against the wood. A man's voice, then a woman's. Tara. By the sound of her musical laughter humming through the wood, she was okay . . . more than okay. Who in the depths was she talking to?

Kressy knocked loudly, pounding Carmack's ear away from the gate. "Lady Tara? Are you safe?"

"Yes!" Tara answered from the other side. "All is well."

The gate swung open. Kressy sprang forward, arms outstretched, but pulled back when a man in flashy clothes stepped through. Tara's hand was curled around his elbow.

Carmack grabbed the man by his silky lapels and pinned him to the alley wall, pressing a forearm against his throat.

The stranger raised his hands, his pale eyes flashing. "Easy on the jacket, chum."

"Master Demry!" Tara huffed. "Is this any way to treat my rescuer?"

The stranger's thin lips ticked upward, stuck between a smirk and a snarl. "I believe she's talking to you."

"Let the captain go, Carmack!"

He slowly released the man, eying this *captain* carefully. "He had your arm, my lady."

Tara blushed. "I was unsteady on my feet."

"Hardly your fault, Lady Gershom." The captain smoothed his rumpled collar. "Meneton's cobblestones are notoriously crooked."

Carmack spread his stance. "I've heard the same said of more than its cobblestones."

The captain faced off with Carmack. "Better crooked than square."

"Mind if I cut in?" Dunn extended his hand. "Captain, I'm Lovell Dunn."

"Forgive me. I should have introduced you sooner," Tara said. "This is Captain Myck. Captain, Master Dunn and Miss Kressy Linwood, my lady's maid."

Myck bowed low enough to kiss his own knees. "An honor."

Kressy twittered with nervous laughter, then retrieved their bundled purchases.

"And Master Carmack Demry," Tara said, her gaze darting between Carmack and Myck. Carmack didn't extend a hand. Neither did Myck. "Captain Myck saved me from two thieves who took me from the marketplace, and he has graciously offered us rooms at the Juggler's Inn."

"Awfully nice of you to help, Captain." Master Dunn smacked Carmack's shoulder. "Isn't it, Demry?"

"Awfully." Carmack stared down Myck. "Do you often lurk in deserted alleys hoping to assist young ladies in distress?"

Myck's smile didn't reach his eyes. "Just a lucky coincidence."

"Indeed, lucky for me." Tara took Myck's elbow, turning him away, but shot Carmack a warning look over her shoulder. "Which way to the inn, Captain? I am dying to freshen up."

As Myck led them through the plaza to a quiet side street, shouts and chanting pealed across the crowded marketplace. "Save our children! Save our children!"

"What's that ruckus?" Kressy asked.

"Another cursed protest," Myck said. "Don't you worry. We'll be beyond the noise once we reach the inn."

"What are they protesting?" Tara asked.

"The fools are clamoring for the town council to crack down on the slave trade and hire more rooftop watchers."

A deep crease marred Tara's forehead. "Why do you think them fools? The king himself ordered the end of slavery, and I understand Meneton has suffered greatly because of it."

"Did I say 'fools'?" Myck asked. "I meant hypocrites."

Sure, he did.

Myck continued, "Sadly, this town was built on the despicable business of slavery. There isn't an adult in Meneton who hasn't considered trading a child for a bag of rice."

The so-called captain had misread Tara if he thought she had no compassion for the less fortunate. But to Carmack's astonishment, she let the subject drop. Had the cad's good looks and rich clothes blinded her?

Acid churned in Carmack's stomach all the way to the Juggler's Inn, where Myck led them to the top floor. He opened the only door, revealing a large parlor filled with plush sofas, lounging cushions, and elaborately carved tables. Potted palms stood in the four corners of the room, their leaves swaying with a breeze flowing in from open clerestory windows that ran along the top of the walls. Such luxurious lodging didn't come cheap. Whatever Myck's trade, it was highly lucrative, most likely illegal, and that made him dangerous. Carmack exchanged looks with Dunn before following the others into the suite.

"The staff is at your disposal," Myck said. "You need only ask for food and bath, and they'll assist you."

"I'm desperate for both," Tara said, and Kressy promptly headed downstairs.

"Smaller chambers are off to the left." Myck threw open the largest of three doors leading off the right, revealing an enormous bed covered by a thick red blanket and satiny gold pillows. "This is my personal chamber for your use, my lady. I hope you find it suitable."

Tara gaped. "Suitable? It's positively palatial."

"Especially for a sea captain," Dunn said under his breath.

"I assume you are sailing south?" Tara asked.

Carmack bit his cheek to keep from cursing. He did *not* like where this question might be leading.

"All boats out of Meneton must sail south to reach the Eversea." Myck's eyes narrowed slightly. "Why do you ask?"

"We are bound for Jaelport, and I am willing to pay for our passage. In gold."

Carmack stepped in front of her. "A word, my lady."

Tara glared at him. "It can wait."

He stepped back, the tips of his ears burning. Tara had always heard him out. This was a dangerous time to stop, and she seemed to be clueless about the danger she was courting.

Myck cocked his head. "As much as I would like to help you, I couldn't in good conscience take you to Jaelport."

Carmack's ears cooled. Perhaps he'd misjudged the captain.

Tara blushed. "Forgive me. I had no right to presume an impeccable gentleman such as yourself would run the blockade for money."

Impeccable gentleman? Why was Tara paying her compliments as if the rooster needed his feathers puffed?

"You are too polite." Myck strode over to a side table and poured himself a glass of whatever burgundy liquid sat in the crystal decanter. "Regretfully, I am exactly what you suspected. My destination is Jaelport. Beneath all this gentlemanly pretense lies a blockade runner." He slugged back his drink in one gulp. "At least, I can claim the distinction of being the best."

Carmack tensed. So, his read of Myck had been dead right.

"I see nothing regretful about it," Tara said, "for I have little use for a gentleman and greatly need a blockade runner. Are you sure you have no space for us?"

"There is plenty of space, so long as you're willing to sleep above deck, but that is not the issue. The journey is simply too dangerous for a lady of your, er, delicacy."

"Considering I have traveled all this way from Meribah Corner," Tara said, "I can assure you, I am not so very delicate."

Myck's gaze raked every inch from Tara's dusty hem to her disheveled hair. A week of grime and sweat would dull any diamond's shine, but Tara's sun-kissed complexion couldn't mask her fine features. Neither did her crumpled dress hide her figure.

The captain's grin deepened. "Perhaps I underestimated you."

Whatever Tara was up to, Carmack had seen enough. "My lady, I believe you would enjoy the view from the balcony."

"Not now."

"It will only take a moment." Carmack all but dragged her out the balcony door. "Coming Dunn?"

Dunn shook his head. "I should check on Kressy."

Coward.

As soon as Carmack closed the balcony door behind them, Tara spun around. "What is wrong with you?"

"You think I'm the problem? You are flirting with an admitted criminal."

"Were you not listening? Myck sails tonight. We could be in Jaelport before sunrise."

"He's a smuggler draped in expensive threads. Do you even know what sort of goods he trades to pay for rooms like these?"

"It doesn't matter—"

"Any cargo so lucrative is worth killing for, and I would bet your captain has spilled plenty of blood to pay for his lifestyle."

"He's not *my* captain, and the blood I worry about being spilled is my brother's and uncle's."

"Always thinking of your family, their needs, their lives. What about your own? What about Kressy or Dunn? Or me, Tara? After all this time, does my life mean nothing to you?"

Tara reeled back, her hand covering her heart. "Of course, you mean a great deal to me. I thought . . . well, it doesn't matter what I thought. What have I done to make you despise me so?"

He meant a great deal to her. A fire rekindled in Carmack's chest. "I don't despise you, Tara." He ached to tell her how wrong she was and how it was driving him mad to be so close and never close enough. "When I became your Shield, I swore I would . . ."

Tara gazed at him with such longing Carmack felt himself slip deeper into the hole he could never fill. He had to stay true to his vow. He'd have agreed to almost anything to stay near Tara and protect her. But she hadn't made a vow like Carmack had, and he never intended to burden her with the hopelessness that came with it. He gripped the balcony's iron railing as if it was his only tether to solid ground.

Tara rested her hand on his, sending a bittersweet tingle into his fingertips. "You can tell me, Carmack."

He pulled his hand away. "I swore I would protect you with my life." Protect her body, heart, and soul. "You might consider that before you flirt your way into deeper trouble with a smuggler."

Tara's mouth opened and closed. Finally, she said, "I was only trying to help, but if you believe sailing with Captain Myck is too dangerous, then we will find another way."

Guilt stung Carmack's conscience, but he swallowed the urge to take back his words.

With her head hanging, Tara returned to the salon, and Carmack followed her.

"Captain Myck," she said, "after further consideration, I believe it best if we forego your kind offer."

Myck lifted his eyebrows. "I understand." He tipped his head, locking eyes with Carmack, then smiled at Tara. "If *you* believe it best, then I won't tarry long."

Kressy reentered the suite, carrying two pails of steaming water. When she set them down by the small chamber door, Carmack reached in his pack and slipped her a ball of soap, one he'd bought from a stand adjacent the tailor's while Tara haggled. He pressed a finger to his lips. His gift would have to stay a secret, or Tara might get the wrong idea.

Kressy sniffed it and smiled, then picked up her buckets. "M'lady, your bath is nearly ready."

Tara curtsied to Myck. "I bid you goodbye, sir, with my gratitude for your help."

"I am honored to have met you, Lady Gershom. I do hope our paths cross again." Myck bowed, his eyes following her to the smaller chamber until the door closed. "Before I go, can I interest you in a drink, Demry?"

"No."

"I can't say I'm surprised." Myck sloughed off his red jacket, tossed it over a sofa, and poured himself another glass. His cool grin didn't detract from the challenge in his eyes. "There are no guarantees in my business, and I would hate to see Lady Tara in peril. In truth, I'm relieved you talked her out of it."

Myck didn't look it. Better to not poke at the snake that was housing them. "Like most women, Lady Tara is prone to changing her mind without warning," Carmack said.

"Ah, but if you and I could agree on anything, it would be this—Lady Tara is *not* like most women." Myck locked eyes with Carmack, downed his drink, and set his glass aside. "I fear we got off to a poor start. Perhaps I can make amends." He crossed to his chamber and returned moments later in a long black coat. He reached into the pocket and handed Carmack a tiny vial. "If you continue onto Jaelport, you'll need this."

The simple glass vial stopped with cork held bright orange liquid, like the fancy silver one Tara had. Carmack could barely contain his surprise. Antiserum. He raised his eyebrows. "What for?"

"Keeps the mages at bay. My boat the *Ruby Tanniyn* is moored at the docks. You can find me there until midnight, should you change your mind." Myck turned on his heel and swept out the door.

Of all the swindlers in Meneton, the smooth-talking captain was in a class of his own. Carmack slipped the vial into his pack and stood outside Tara's chamber. The sounds of water splashing penetrated the door along with the soft fragrance of jasmine soap, making his own musk of stale sweat, street dust, and garlic from the kebabs more repulsive.

Dunn returned with a tray of food and two mugs of ale. He claimed an empty chair next to Carmack and offered him the extra mug. "When I said help Lady Tara move on, I didn't mean alienate her by acting like an insufferable brute."

Carmack waved the mug away. "How am I supposed to protect her when she swings her purse for all to see and fraternizes with back-alley scoundrels?"

"She got us these rooms, didn't she? And she would have gotten us a ride to Jaelport if your jealousy hadn't gotten in the way." Dunn set the extra mug down and took a sip from the other. "You still haven't told her about the vow, have you?"

The knot of tension between Carmack's eyes tightened. "Not now. I have to keep my head clear."

"Your head hasn't been clear since Lady Tara came of age." Dunn wiped foam from his beard. "Her flashy admirer could have delivered us to Jaelport in less than half the time it will take us to get there by land."

Her admirer. Carmack's chest burned at the thought. "I see slick Myck has hoodwinked you too."

"Don't be daft. An asp with shiny scales is still an asp."

"Then why should we get on a boat with one?"

"First, we have an advantage. Lady Tara has charmed this particular snake, so we might as well use him. If he meant to hurt her, he could have done so. Second, the hours we would save could decide the fate of our missing friends, including your brother."

Roxburg had used far more cutting words than Dunn about Carmack's inability to keep his heart in check, and Carmack's response had been even worse. Unless they reached Jaelport soon, those ugly words might be the last his brother heard from him.

"And third, what happened to bolstering Tara's confidence?" Dunn downed his ale and traded the empty mug for the second. "After two days of your snapping at her, she's reeling."

"You made your point, *Master* Dunn." Carmack pulled the mug from Dunn's grip and dumped it into a potted palm. "Don't overdo it. We have a boat to catch."

CHAPTER FIFTEEN
TARA

DEAR ARMAN, NO. THE *BRIERSTAR* wasn't in Jaelport! A crushing weight settled into her stomach as Tara stood at the bow of the *Ruby Tanniyn,* Carmack at her shoulder, searching the lavender haze of Jael Bay.

None of the boats moored in the harbor had more than two masts. Leif, Uncle Chantry, Captain Demry—where could they be, other than the bottom of the Eversea? Hot tears pooled in Tara's eyes. "Have we come all this way for nothing?"

"We can't assume the worst," Carmack said, his voice low. "Ships searched these waters within hours of the *Brierstar*'s disappearance. They would have found flotsam—some trace of her sinking."

His words smoothed over Tara's fears like the gentle waves lapping over the pink sandy beach. "So, we stay the course?"

Carmack nodded. "We will search the palace for the crew first. Once we find them, they are likely to know the ship's location."

"And if they don't? We have no hope of outrunning the Jaelportian guard on foot."

Carmack took a long breath. "One battle at a time."

"Be not anxious about anything, but with prayers of thanksgiving,

present your concerns to Arman, and His peace will guard your hearts and minds in His son, Câan."

Mother had made Tara memorize the verse from the *Book of Arman*, but it had been ages since Tara had tested its truth. Her heart tugged. It was time.

"Will you pray with me?"

Carmack nodded and folded his hands on the railing.

Tara did the same, bowing her head and closing her eyes. "Father Arman, thank You for bringing us to Jaelport safely and quickly. We praise You for providing our every need and for those who have helped us. As we face new challenges and dangers, be our light and guide. Help us find the lost, and until then, keep us all safe, for You are our fortress and shield."

"In the name of your son, Câan, may it be so," Carmack said.

The tightness around Tara's heart eased, and she opened her eyes.

The sun peeked over the sea, splashing orange rays across the imposing towers and sprawling walls of Tenma Palace. Like a massive boot stomping on the highest cliff, its walls loomed over the city of Jaelport and its bay. Below it, pinpoints of flames dotted the hillside, and a smoky haze blanketed the buildings and docks. One of the flames took the shape of a fire bowl hanging from a pole at the end of a long pier. Its gray smoke carried the scent of burnt resin and potent spice across the water.

Captain Myck's crew trimmed the sails as the ship approached the pier. Their clandestine journey had spared Tara from conversing with the captain—silence a necessary measure to avoid the blockade and a blessed relief to Tara. The string of profuse compliments that had spilled out of Captain Myck's mouth when she first had come aboard, freshly bathed and in her new pale blue gown, had made her cheeks burn. To make matters worse, he had refused payment, as if she were a poor damsel and he her gallant benefactor. But by delivering them safely to Jaelport, the man had proven he was not all bluster. "I should bid farewell to the captain."

"Wouldn't a wave from the pier suffice?" Carmack muttered.

"I'm afraid not." She started toward Captain Myck, Carmack on her heels, and as soon as Captain Myck saw her approaching, he shushed the pock-faced man next to him and gave her a toothy smile.

"Lady Tara, I hope you were able to rest during our short journey."

"I was, thank you. We will trespass on your generosity no longer. I am ever so glad we met, Captain."

A flowery compliment delivered without a kind expression is like a letter without a seal—no one will believe its authenticity. To appease her mother's imagined critique, Tara forced her smile to reach her eyes.

The captain's smile brightened. "Will you require any assistance finding a suitable inn?" he asked.

"No, I am staying with a friend."

"How fortunate for Jaelport's innkeepers." He winked. Despite his eccentric clothing, this man could out-charm the most polished courtier. "Though I am curious, with whom could the Lady of Meribah Corner claim acquaintance, other than the infamous Hamartano sisters?" The captain's gaze never left her face, but when Tara hesitated to respond, he grinned sheepishly. "Bart's blood, that's none of my business. My apologies. I could not fault you for denying a friendship with known mages. I imagine it would be a source of gossip, even shame among your peers."

Why did she get the impression he was testing her? "I have denied nothing, nor am I ashamed. Princess Jaira is a lifelong friend. She invited me here to escape my bereavement." Tara's cheeks flushed. That was not what she had practiced. Saints help her, she made it sound like she intended to kick off her widow's weeds a month early.

Myck's cheek twitched. "My sympathies, my lady. You did not mention your beloved having departed recently."

"Escape was not the word I intended to use." Intended to use? Why not just admit to rehearsing her lines? Tara wanted to jump overboard. *When words fail, curtsy.* Mother would be pleased, knowing her training came second nature when nothing else would. Tara curtsied. "Goodbye, Captain."

"Not so fast, Lady Gershom."

She popped back up. "Is there some problem?"

"Only that your goodbye is as premature as the last. I, too, am headed to Tenma Palace."

Carmack, who had obviously been listening in, straightened. "Don't you have cargo to unload?"

"My first mate has everything in hand. Don't you, Axe?"

Axe cracked his knuckles.

"Not that I don't appreciate your concern for my affairs, Master Demry." Myck smirked. "However, I must speak with the palace's purveyor before I unload my cargo. I've already arranged for a carriage that can carry us all."

Something was off. What was this mysterious cargo bound for Tenma Palace that prevented Tara from going belowdecks and now could not be unloaded without inspection? Tara pictured her back-alley kidnapper's wide eyes when he recognized the captain, like death itself had called upon him.

"Are you unwell, my lady? You suddenly look pale." Myck offered his arm. "Allow me to see you to the carriage."

Tara recoiled before she could stop herself, and Myck's eyes narrowed. She fanned her face. "Best stand clear, Captain. I fear our journey has unsettled my stomach."

"To shore, my lady?" Carmack crossed the plank to the pier, then reached back for Tara.

She grabbed hold, pressing her building panic into his strong hand. He squeezed her fingers briefly before his grip eased, the smallest gesture of reassurance. Enough to steady her nerves and make Tara wish she never had to let go.

How in the depths would Tara search such a massive palace? She peered out the carriage window as it ascended the steep road that ran along Tenma Palace's curtain wall. The wall itself seemed to wind on forever. High above, a flock of gowzals flew rings around Jabal Tower, and guards dressed in black uniforms peered down between its crenellations. Ahead, a line of wagons blocked the way to the iron-clad gate. A half dozen guards inspected the first wagon's crates, while one wearing a gray sash shouted questions at the cowering driver.

Tara fanned her face. "It seems we will be waiting in this heat for a while."

"Nonsense," Captain Myck said. "I know all of the palace's gate-keepers." He climbed out of their carriage. "Follow me." Once Tara and the others stepped into the road, Myck sauntered past the wagons, ignoring the jeers of the waiting drivers. "Commander Seetin!"

The guard in the gray sash swung his head their way, and the furrow between his brows deepened. He signaled his men to allow the wagon through, then marched straight toward Myck.

"Your friend doesn't look pleased to see you," Carmack said.

"He's thrilled, believe me," Myck said.

Master Dunn and Carmack exchanged looks and positioned their hands near their swords.

"Captain"—Seetin bowed—"the family will be surprised that you've returned with another shipment so soon."

"Fortune smiled on me. More importantly, I bring Lady Tara Gershom, who has traveled all the way from the northern tip of Therion."

"Will you please let Princess Jaira know I am here to see her?" Tara asked.

The commander peered down his beaky nose at her. "With all these wagons arriving, I do not have time to play message boy. Captain, you may go through, but the rest of you will have to wait until the end of the week."

"But I have brought gifts for Queen Torrezia and her daughters," Tara said. "At least allow us to pay our respects."

"Your visit is ill-timed," Commander Seetin said. "The palace is already full."

First, no *Brierstar.* Now their chances of searching the palace for the missing crew seemed slim. What next? She looked to Carmack for help, but before she could speak, Myck stepped forward.

"Come now, Seetin, you can't turn this beautiful lady away when she's come so far." When Seetin's expression remained stony, Myck leaned closer and whispered, "Should Princess Jaira learn her childhood friend was rejected at her gates, I fear she may view it as a black mark on her reputation."

The commander's throat bobbed. "Very well. If you vouch for this lady and her men disarm, they may proceed to the throne room, but be warned. The princess regent is unlikely to receive them."

Myck cocked his head. "Princess Regent?"

"Due to Queen Torrezia's failing health, Princess Mandzee has been elevated to princess regent," Commander Seetin said, frowning. "The family is hosting a banquet in her honor."

"So, that's what the fuss is about." Captain Myck chuckled. "Don't worry, friend. All is not lost." He turned to Carmack and Master Dunn. "You heard him. Hand over your weapons."

Carmack glowered while unbuckling his sword belt and removing the sheathed knife from his waistband. Master Dunn followed suit. Commander Seetin took their blades and waved them all through.

Beyond the gate, Tenma Palace's bailey bustled with activity. Dozens of servants unloaded crates from the wagons parked around a massive fire bowl, its smoky bonfire unnecessary on such a sultry day.

"Why did he allow *you* to keep your sword?" Carmack asked Captain Myck as they strode into the shade under the massive portico.

"A privilege I've earned."

"How, exactly?" A rough edge tainted Carmack's tone.

Captain Myck's lips curled. "By not asking foolish questions."

Tara's eyes locked with Carmack's, silently pleading with him not to antagonize Captain Myck further. He was clearly in league with someone powerful within these walls, and until Tara figured out who, she and her friends needed to be on their best behavior.

Tara and her party followed Captain Myck into the vestibule. The spicy resin aroma seemed to trail in after them.

Above, the masonry ceiling was carved like an intricate honeycomb between the jagged spikes that dropped like icicles of stone, some all the way to the floor, forming pillars. A circle of hanging fire bowls illuminated the stucco, and rust-colored etchings decorated the doorframe.

Captain Myck led Tara up to two gilded doors flanked by guards. A woman in a white wrap and silver sash stood behind a high table with a quill, ink pot, and scroll. A figure of curved and straight lines was drawn in brown on her forehead.

"Only two are allowed from each party," she said.

"Kressy and I will stay here," Dunn said.

Captain Myck dropped back. "This is as far as I go too. These receptions can be quite tedious, and my business with the purveyor cannot be delayed."

This time, Tara smiled easily. "Farewell, Captain."

Once the woman recorded Tara's and Carmack's names on her scroll, the guards opened the doors. Tara stepped inside a throne room so filled with people that she found herself facing a wall of backs. The ceiling was high, the walls covered with vivid mosaic. A carved baldachin rose along the side wall, but Tara saw little else apart from the audience and the occasional guard, dressed in black with sashes like those who had manned the gate and tower.

"Presenting Lady D'argon and Lord D'argon," a man announced. "And their son Master Ormo."

Tara tugged on Carmack's sleeve. "Is Jaira there? Can you see?"

"Not Jaira," he said. "Only her older sister Mandzee and her eunuch."

"Can you get us closer to the dais?"

"Presenting Lady Iros, and her daughter Lady Fateema Iros," the herald droned.

"Follow me." Carmack wedged his shoulders between two shorter men. One of them scowled but didn't object.

Push by push, Tara and Carmack reached the middle of the room. She peeked around him. Under the baldachin's canopy, Mandzee closed her hand fan, and her eunuch, bare-chested and wearing a long burgundy skirt, stepped forward.

"That concludes today's reception," the herald said, and the audience dipped into curtsies and bows.

Tara had to do something—anything—to get Mandzee's attention. She pushed past Carmack, then jumped and waved her arms. "Wait! Your Highness!"

"Something tells me that wasn't proper protocol," Carmack said.

Six palace guardsmen closed in on her.

"Who dared to shout at me?" Mandzee's husky voice carried over the crowd.

The crowd parted like a portcullis was about to drop. Tara locked eyes with Mandzee, who stood on the edge of the dais. Though not blessed with Jaira's exquisite features, Mandzee had an aura of quiet dignity in her lilac gown, her arms and neck wrapped in gold chains and amethysts. "Lady Tara?"

"It is I, Lady Tara Gershom."

Mandzee waved her ringed fingers. "Stand down, guards. I will speak with Lady Gershom privately in my sitting room."

The guards peeled back, creating an open path to the throne.

As Carmack shifted closer to Tara, a guard in black stepped in his way. "Men may not enter the princess's sitting room."

"I'll be fine," Tara whispered. "Go tell the others what has happened. I'll return or send word as soon as I can."

Carmack looked uneasy but left the throne room. Was she imagining it, or was he being much more cooperative since scolding her on Captain Myck's balcony?

Mandzee beckoned Tara, her bracelets jangling. She led Tara through an arched doorway into an opulent parlor with green silk wall coverings and rich mahogany furnishings. "Zitheos' horn, why are you in Jaelport?"

Though Mandzee had always attended the same tournaments and social gatherings as her younger sister, Tara couldn't recall exchanging more than a dozen words with her in the past. The five years that separated her from Jaira might as well have been fifty, for the two sisters had little more than their family name in common. "Princess Jaira invited me."

"Did she?" Mandzee's eyebrows rose. "How unlike my sister, and at the same time exactly like her for not consulting me."

"As you've heard, my husband recently passed. Jaira promised I would find a respite from my trouble here."

Mandzee sat on a settee and tapped the gold brocade cushion beside her. "And exactly what sort of trouble are you in?"

Tara sat. Best stick to the truth. The fewer lies she told, the fewer she would have to remember. "Not everyone tied to my late husband's estate believes me capable of managing its affairs. I found myself the target of false accusations and plots to undermine my control."

"A universal trouble. With power comes the struggle to keep

it." Mandzee sighed deeply. "I wish I could help, but this is not a good time."

The curtains blocking a doorway parted, and Jaira sashayed through, wearing a sleeveless green gown with a high gold-stitched collar. "I disagree. Lady Tara's timing couldn't be more perfect. She can help us celebrate your grand promotion." Jaira pulled Tara from her seat and embraced her.

"Jaira, what a relief to see you," Tara whispered into her ear.

"I believe it," Jaira said. "I spotted Master Demry through the screens from the observation gallery. Best gift of the day, assuming I don't have to share him with Mandzee." She winked.

Tara bit her cheek. "Master Demry is not a gift, though that reminds me. These are for you." She pulled the packages from her purse, unwrapped the bracelets, then gave the orange topaz to Jaira and the others to Mandzee. "The lapis is for the queen. I was sorry to hear she is unwell."

Mandzee stared at the lapis bracelet with glassy eyes and a far-away look. "It was generous of you to think of Mother. She would thank you herself if she could."

Jaira held up her bracelet, inspecting it against the light streaking through one of the high windows. "Orange topaz. A talisman of good fortune."

"And friendship," Tara added.

Jaira linked arms with Tara. "Come, let's get you settled. We still have a few hours before the banquet to find you something suitable to wear."

Apparently, Tara's blue kirtle didn't pair with Jaira's tastes.

"Jaira, she cannot stay," Mandzee said. "The palace is already bursting at the seams."

Jaira led Tara toward the velvet curtains. "Don't blame that on me, *Your Highness.* You're the one who invited half of Cela. Surely we have room for one more."

"I'm afraid not, little sister." Mandzee's tone rose a notch.

Jaira whirled around. "How can you be so selfish? You have filled every cranny with people you don't even like. Am I not allowed one friend at your precious party?"

Tara dipped her head. She'd ignited a row she would have rather not witnessed. "Perhaps I best lodge at a nearby inn."

Jaira held fast to Tara's arm. "If my friend is not welcome here, then neither am I. Is this how you wish to begin your reign, Mandzee? You've already alienated the eunuchs. Must you alienate me too?"

Mandzee's stony gaze faltered, her shoulders sagging. "Very well. Tara may stay, but you'll have to find a place for her."

"Done. Larkos!"

Jaira's brawny eunuch stepped through the curtains. His head and face were shaved, and he wore a long burgundy skirt held up by leather belts that crisscrossed his bare chest. "Yes, Your Highness?"

"Show Lady Gershom's Shield to the east wing," Jaira said.

"What about my other guard and my maid?"

Jaira pressed her lips together. "My, you've brought half of Meribah Corner to us. Not to worry, as you will soon see, Tenma Palace can house all of Cela and then some. Larkos, show the *two* guards to Silvo's old room, then bring the maid to my suite."

Larkos bowed and left, and Jaira pulled Tara through the curtained door and down a short corridor. At its end, they entered a courtyard. A reflecting pool spanned its length, and around it, doors opened into the shaded walkway.

"Mandzee always makes things more difficult than they need to be," Jaira said. "How anyone believes her capable of ruling Jaelport is beyond me."

Tara struggled to match Jaira's pace while craning her neck to see through every doorway. Each gave a glimpse of an opulent room, some sitting parlors, some for dining. Several opened into a long ballroom. What a strange palace, its rooms joined by an open courtyard rather than under one roof like the other keeps in Er'Rets.

"Larkos tells me you arrived with Captain Myck. Lucky you!" Jaira nudged Tara in the ribs. "I will invite him to join our table at my sister's ridiculous banquet. A party can never have too many handsome dance partners."

Only one handsome dance partner came to Tara's mind, and it wasn't the captain. "Please do not invite him on my account. I'm sure he's glad to be rid of me."

"Nonsense. You are just his type, and though he is not a knight, he's rich, single, and a half-century younger than your late husband. See how right I was? Jaelport will give you a fresh start and the romance you've always desired."

At the end of the reflecting pool, Jaira turned, and Tara followed her into a three-story building with turrets at its corners. "This is the west wing," Jaira said.

A wonderful floral fragrance filled the spiral staircase to the second floor, giving Tara a respite from the smoky incense. Maybe this could be a start to her search. "Ah, I have not smelled fresh flowers in so long. How lucky you are to have flowers blooming when our winter is only just ending up north. May I explore your gardens?"

"What you smell is the queen's private garden." Jaira smirked. "It is not open to guests."

Tara gritted her teeth. Jaira always seemed to enjoy denying a simple request. When they reached the second floor, Jaira pointed. "This door leads to Mandzee's suite. Mother's is at the end of the hall. You mustn't go down that way. Noise agitates her condition."

"Your mother's illness . . . how bad is it?" Tara asked.

"Very. Few expect her to live out the week."

"I am sorry. What a shock to have just lost your father, and now this."

Jaira sniffed, turning a corner. "It's no shock to me. Her madness is the price she agreed to pay to practice powerful magic."

Tara stutter-stepped. Jaira talked of her mother's madness like it was rain on a tea party.

At the end of the hall, Jaira threw open a wide door, and Tara entered a sumptuous chamber. Floral motifs covered the walls, and green silk draperies framed the windows. Wide lounging sofas flanked a tall fireplace, and a massive canopy bed spread with magenta silk dominated the far end of the room.

"Exquisite," Tara said. "We shall be quite comfortable here."

"You ninny! This is *my* room." Jaira cackled. "You'll want your privacy." She walked to a small panel door on the back wall. "My maid's chamber has its own door out to the hallway, so you won't disturb me should you need the privy at night. I'll send her to sleep in the kitchens, so you and Kressy can stay nearby." She opened the door to what looked like a large closet. The scant light coming from a small lattice window near the ceiling revealed a dull rainbow of hanging gowns and a door at the far end.

It *was* a closet. Yet in the middle of the cramped space, a folded cot sat on a threadbare rug. Tara's back ached just looking at the rickety thing. "Surely, you don't expect two people to sleep on that."

Jaira raised an eyebrow. "Really, Tara, I thought you'd show a little more appreciation after I saved you from being thrown into the street."

A sour taste filled Tara's mouth. This was the side of Jaira she despised. A massive room full of empty sofas, all twice the width of the cot, and Jaira expected Tara to be satisfied with her paltry generosity. She had no choice but to feign gratitude, long enough to find her brother. The sooner she did, the better.

"Forgive me. I am so exhausted from the journey that I forgot my manners. I am grateful." Tara turned away from the dismal little room. "Will you give me a tour of the rest of the palace? You've told me so much about it that I am dying to see it."

"You will have to die a little longer. We have a banquet to prepare for."

"That won't take long. You already look beautiful, and Kressy needs no more than an hour to make me presentable." Even as a young girl, Jaira preferred more dangerous exploits. "What about your secret passages?" Tara asked. "A palace this grand must have dozens."

"It does, but several house my mother's exotic pets, and I can never keep them straight. The snakes I don't mind, but I have had too many close encounters with the lion and cham. Poor Larkos caught such nasty scratches last time, I had to ask Mandzee to patch him up."

"Oh." Tara swallowed. "But you're far too smart to make the same mistake twice."

Jaira's eyes narrowed. "A moment ago, you said your journey had left you exhausted, and now you want to explore beast-infested tunnels. What are you up to?"

Tara's skin crawled like she had walked into a spider web. She waved her hand flippantly and giggled. "Nothing. I never make sense when tired. An afternoon of pampering is just what I need." And for the *Brierstar* and its crew to magically appear before Jaira figured out the real answer to her question.

Chapter Sixteen

Carmack

Never trust a eunuch bearing gifts.

Carmack's skin crawled. His entire outfit felt a size too small. The fitted dark moss jacket, snug black pants, and crisp shirt with its chafing collar were a gift from the princess, or so the eunuch had said, without specifying which princess Carmack could thank for his misery.

He stood with Dunn at the edge of the Fountain Courtyard, near one of the thin pillars separating the large patio from its covered perimeter like bars on a marble cage. Across from him, Mandzee sat alone under an ornate pavilion. None of her honored guests remained at the head table beside her. Under a web of smoking glass lanterns, other guests lounged on rugs and cushions spread throughout the courtyard. The entire place reeked like someone had tossed a bottle of perfume into a campfire.

Carmack watched a twirl of dark blue silk and shiny blonde curls near the fountain. At least Tara was in her element. Surrounded by luxury, rich food, and lively music, she appeared rested and refreshed, her beauty outshining all the Jaelportian women with their sheer dresses, glittering jewels, and darkly lined eyes.

Most had symbols painted on their foreheads. The place was crawling with mages.

Carmack's gaze returned to Tara and her partner, Captain Myck, whose blue jacket nearly matched Tara's gown, except for the ridiculous silver stitching ruining its collar.

"You know, if you would have asked her to dance, you wouldn't need to spend the night moping," Dunn said.

"Things don't turn out well when we dance together." The last time Carmack had dared, his brother had promoted him to the Fighting Fifteen. Two dances in one evening had broken some rule, or so Roxburg had said in his long-winded scolding. The promotion had been more like a punishment, separating Carmack from Tara until Lady Revada summoned him back to Lytton Hall for Tara's wedding to Lord Gershom. "And I'm not moping."

"Your face disagrees. We are on the grounds of Tenma Palace. Few outsiders have ever stepped inside this place. You should be celebrating."

"That would be easier if a certain ship had been in port. Did you make any progress with the guards?" Carmack asked.

Dunn had a way of getting people to talk. His easygoing swagger, coupled with his offbeat sense of humor, quickly put people at ease, especially fighting men. He knew their lives, spoke their lingo, and within the span of an hour, could make all but the most cynical think he was one of them.

"I've made a start," Dunn said. "Seems Tenma Palace is a house divided. Though the eldest sister is the heir and has the support of most of the soldiers, the eunuchs believe the younger is better suited to rule. As for our missing friends, no leads yet. I'll try again tomorrow. What about you?"

"From what I saw, there are only two palace gates, both heavily guarded—the one we came through and one in a remote corner of the orchards that's of no use to anyone but the fruit pickers. Jabal Tower is a fortress. The only part of Tenma harder to penetrate than the tower is the west wing. Every corridor to it ends at a red-skirted eunuch."

"No need to worry about the red-skirts. If we're not allowed into the west wing, our missing friends wouldn't be there either."

Carmack's gaze landed on Tara's head, her long curls spreading like beams of light around her as she spun. "That's where Lady Tara will be staying, and I have no way to reach her should something go wrong."

"As long as we don't raise suspicions, nothing will," Dunn said.

The smell of strong spice wafted over Carmack, and he sneezed.

"To health, Master Demry," a woman said from the covered walkway behind him.

His spine stiffened. Besides Mandzee, Carmack knew only one other woman in Jaelport. He pasted on a grin and turned, coming face-to-face with Jaira Hamartano. "And to yours, Your Highness."

Most of her skinny black braids had been coiled on top of her head. A polished crystal sparkled from a thin gold chain around her neck, drawing Carmack's eye toward the plunging neckline of her clingy olive-green gown. Her eunuch Larkos stood in the shadows behind her. How long had they been standing there? More importantly, what had Jaira overheard? Her severely sculpted eyebrows gave no clue. Between her eyebrows, she had painted two triangles stacked tip to tip, like many of the other women sitting around the tables.

"I have it on good authority you are the finest dancer in Tsaftown," she said.

Carmack's stomach sank. If he were the last unoccupied man at a ball, Jaira Hamartano wouldn't initiate conversation about dancing with a lowly guard. She was up to something. He forced a grin. "If true, that would be a slight on Tsaftown."

"I confess, I hardly believed it. Strapping men such as yourself are built for combat, not twirling around a dance floor in satin slippers."

Carmack sighed, trying to sound bored. "I cannot argue with you there."

Jaira stepped closer, filling his nose with her spicy fragrance. "Has Lady Tara been lying to me?"

The nerve of this conniving woman to discredit the one person who considered her a friend. "Lady Tara can be overly generous, especially with her compliments. I believe she simply lacks the ability to see people for what they really are."

"Then I will judge for myself." Jaira held out her hand. "Shall we?"

No way was Carmack going to get any closer to the devious mage. "A man of my station knows better than to dance with a princess."

"A man of your station should know better than to refuse one."

He did, but why show courtesy to someone who never practiced it? "One of my greatest failings, unfortunately. My duty is to serve Lady Tara, not entertain myself by dancing."

Jaira snapped her hand back, her nostrils flaring.

"Forgive me for interrupting, Your Highness," Dunn said, "but I believe Princess Mandzee is trying to get your attention."

Across the crowded courtyard, Mandzee rose from her gilded chair wearing a golden gown and tiara. Her stare locked with Jaira's, and the air between them seemed to crackle. She beckoned Jaira with an insistent wave of her hand.

"I was wondering if you might introduce me to your sister," Dunn said, "so I can pass along my gratitude for her invitation to join this grand party. And it's Dunn." He bowed.

"What's done?" Jaira spat.

"That's my name. Lovell Dunn. I thought I should mention it because we have not been formally introduced either."

"I know who you are." Jaira's sharp tone turned the heads of several guests, and Larkos approached Dunn, glowering.

Dunn merely grinned like everything was fuzz on peaches. Lord

Mildunn's son knew better than to introduce himself to a lady, but Carmack owed him a pint for his timely gaffe.

"Follow me." Jaira spun on her heel and marched with Dunn and Larkos, cutting a line through the crowd to the pavilion. When Dunn bowed before Mandzee, he won a rare smile from the stoic princess, then walked off and struck up a conversation with one of the guards milling about. Meanwhile, Jaira plopped down on her cushion at the head table and snapped her fingers at the nearest eunuch until he refilled her goblet.

The musicians strummed the song's last note, and the crowd applauded. Pairs exchanged places on the dance floor, except for one. Judging by the way Tara was shuffling her feet while Myck clutched her arm, they were not in agreement. Tara's gaze swept the room, finally finding Carmack and silently pleading with him.

Carmack was at her side by the time the jingling tambourine announced the start of a new song.

"Aha! Here comes Master Demry, just as I was saying," Tara said.

Carmack glanced at Myck's fingers still wrapped around Tara's forearm, then stared down the captain, wedging his body between the two. "My lady, may I assist you to your seat?"

Myck's eyes narrowed.

"Oh dear, how embarrassing. You have forgotten," Tara said.

Carmack studied her blushing face. "Forgotten?"

"That you requested the third dance." Again, her eyes pleaded with him.

Of all the excuses she could have given. The drums rolled with the prelude, and Carmack blinked. "Of course, my lady, I apologize. Captain, that is our cue."

Myck released Tara's arm, his mouth puckering like he had swallowed rotten fish. "So you say." He stormed off the floor.

"Forgive me, Carmack," Tara said. "Captain Myck insisted on a third dance, and I panicked. Mother always taught that one dance per partner was best—two only in cases of a special regard—but three? Absolutely scandalous. It was bad enough he tricked me into the second."

Special regard? So, a second dance with the same partner wasn't always forbidden, though Roxburg hadn't minced words. *She is a well-born lady. You are a guard with nothing to offer.* Apparently, a lowly guard had been enough to earn her special regard back then.

Tara fanned her face. "Arman knows what I wanted to say, but I didn't dare be rude. I do apologize. I know you don't care for dancing."

When the prelude ended with a rousing chord, Carmack bowed. "I never said I don't care for dancing." He just didn't care to dance with anyone but Tara.

She curtsied, and Carmack clasped her hands while she walked a small circle around him. "Well, you should not feel compelled out of a sense of duty."

"I don't." Along with honor, duty pulled him in the opposite direction—away from his lovely partner where he could watch at a distance, safe from her charms.

Tara completed her circle and blinked. "You don't?"

Carmack could have made his excuses, but caught in the light scent of jasmine and her desperate sapphire eyes, his heart refused. He stepped around her. "As your guard, duty required nothing more from me than to toss your previous partner aside and escort you off the floor." He completed his circle and met her gaze. "I am dancing with you only because I wanted to." Carmack extended his hand.

Tara rested hers on top, sending a warm tingle up his arm. "Oh." A blush brightened her cheeks as they turned to promenade across the floor. "Well, good. We haven't danced together since the Midwinter Banquet at Lytton Hall three years ago."

His pulse quickened. She remembered. "We haven't had many opportunities since."

"True," Tara said, as they passed the last couple in line, parted, and turned to face each other. When they came together and joined hands again, sadness edged her voice. "You were away all those months, training, and then . . . well, Meribah Corner was so very dull without music."

Carmack squeezed her fingers, so soft and delicate, wanting to chase those dark memories away. "And a little too exciting with it. Remember when you hired that harpist to help Lord Gershom fall asleep?"

Tara's gaze flitted up to meet his, a slight grin on her lips, as he spun her around. "Skies, yes. His lordship threatened to toss the poor man and his 'infernal racket-maker' into the cesspit."

"Even after his lordship retired, it took us two hours to convince the harpist it was safe to climb down from the mantle." Carmack shook his head and led her through the steps, his hand resting on the small of her back. "How those scrawny arms and legs managed to climb up the fireplace stones so quickly, I still don't know."

Her tinkling laughter sounded sweeter than the band's soft melody, and Carmack smiled. As he moved through the dance's pattern in lockstep with Tara, something in his soul clicked into place. He and Tara fit together, whether sparring on the deck of a ship or swaying with music at a grand party. Not once during her two dances with Myck had the suave captain made her smile like Carmack had. He pulled her waist a few inches closer, and she seemed to melt toward him. Her pretty face relaxed as she swayed with the music. An invisible weight lifted from his shoulders. It would come crashing back eventually—it always did—but for the moment, all of Tenma Palace, its mysteries and splendor, faded away as he and Tara glided across the marble tiles in perfect unison.

"Where did you get that outfit?" she asked. "I don't recall a green jacket being among our purchases in Meneton."

"A gift from the princess."

"Which one?"

"Mandzee, or at least, I assumed so."

"Don't be so sure," she said, her tone strained. "Jaira fancies you."

"I doubt that, though she did ask me to dance."

Tara stutter-stepped. "She did?"

"You're shocked she'd ask an ogre like me?"

"You're no ogre. You are exactly what a lady like Jaira would want, except without a title. Take care. She means only to trifle with you."

Because an untitled guardsman could hope to be no more than a lady's plaything. So said Roxburg. Tara spun away from him, and when she twirled back, Carmack locked his elbows, keeping her at arm's length. He needed to focus. "Were you able to explore the west wing?"

"No, my request for a tour was not well received. I had hoped to see the underground tunnels that connect different areas of the palace, but apparently, Queen Hamartano's menagerie of exotic beasts roam free in some of them. Not even Jaira knows which to avoid."

Carmack's pulse quickened as the music slowed. "Promise me you won't go searching on your own."

As they turned, Tara glanced at the head table. "Oh dear, Jaira and Captain Myck are squabbling."

"Looks more like she's scolding him."

"Probably for his lack of decorum," Tara muttered, "but she's glaring at me. I better go smooth things over. We need to stay on her good side."

"If she has one." Carmack dropped Tara's hands and followed her back to her place of honor, next to Jaira at the head table.

"Join us, Master Demry." Challenge flashed in Jaira's eyes as Tara sat down. "Larkos, fetch an extra cushion. Move over, Tara. Make room between us."

Though the hair on his arms stood on end, Carmack sat on the cushion Larkos placed between the two ladies, and Jaira's lips curved upward. "So, the truth was not stretched, Master Demry.

You are a fine dancer, which makes me wonder what your other hidden talents may be."

A server filled the goblet closest to him, and Carmack sipped the minty punch. "As I told you before, I am a man of duty and service alone."

Tara fidgeted with her satin napkin.

Jaira ripped a chunk off a piece of flatbread but did not eat it. "Larkos tells me you were scurrying around the palace all afternoon. Like Lady Tara, are you overly eager to uncover Tenma Palace's secrets?"

His jaw tensed. "I'm not sure what secrets you are alluding to, Your Highness. I was merely getting my bearings as a Shield with a noblewoman to protect."

Jaira turned to Tara. "You're quiet all of a sudden. I know how to cheer you." She snapped her fingers. "Larkos, fetch him."

"Fetch who?" Tara asked. "Gowzal? I haven't heard his barking and wondered where he might be hiding."

Carmack bit his tongue. Hadn't Arman put that spoiled mongrel out of its misery? The only hair on the bony creature sprouted from the end of its whiplike tail and tips of its oversized ears. How perfect that the bat-like dog was named after a bat-like bird.

Jaira's lips twisted into a sly grin. "Gowzal is a delight, but I have a far better surprise for you."

When Larkos reappeared through a nearby archway, a slender, hooded figure followed him, too tall to be a woman. The pair crossed the pavilion and stopped at the head table. Jaira rose from her seat, handed a goblet to the cloaked man, and whispered something into his hooded ear.

The man walked to the front of the table and raised the goblet in Mandzee's direction. "To Her Royal Highness, the Princess Regent," he shouted.

The violins screeched to a stop, and the entire courtyard stilled. Everyone, including Carmack and Tara, lifted their wine.

"By the power of Zitheos," the man continued, "may she rule her people courageously in the proud tradition of the mothers before her, and may Zitheos add to her flock, even as I pledge myself to her royal service."

Mandzee sat as though carved in stone, a symbol inked on her forehead, similar to her sister's. Her knuckles whitened around the arms of her chair. She shot a scathing sideways glance at Jaira, then looked back to the hooded man. "Your pledge pleases me," she said through clenched teeth, "though I insist you delay your purification until I am queen."

The corners of Jaira's mouth twitched upward, her sister's displeasure clearly her delight.

Larkos stepped forward and presented the man with a folded garment bundled with leather straps like those attached to his own skirt. "We welcome your pledge, and very soon, you will join our proud order."

Orders were for priests, and Larkos was certainly not one of those. "Arman, help him," Carmack said. "The fool is consenting to become a eunuch."

"But his accent doesn't sound Jaelportian. He sounds like . . . oh no." Tara's hand began to shake, and she quickly lowered her goblet to the table.

Larkos lowered the man's hood, revealing a mop of curly blond hair and a familiar boyish face.

Tara gasped. "Leif."

Leif's body, perhaps, but not his soul. The younger of Tara's brothers had a wild streak, but his faith in Arman had always been strong. He would never willingly serve another god, much less sacrifice his masculinity to do so.

Larkos unsheathed his sword. Lifting a handful of Leif's golden curls, he sliced them off and threw them into the fire bowl in front of the pavilion. The pungent smell of burnt hair wafted over their table. Were the theatrics to mask the stench of Jaelportian magic? Not that Carmack needed further proof Leif had fallen victim to it.

Tara's hand flew to her mouth. Under the table, Carmack clutched her other hand.

Leif, his eyes glassy, knelt at the end of their table.

"Why so quiet, Lady Tara? Are you not pleased to see your brother?" Jaira stuck out her lower lip. "This was to be a happy reunion."

Carmack exchanged glances with Tara, unspoken understanding passing between them. No, this was a clear reminder of exactly who they were up against.

CHAPTER SEVENTEEN
TARA

O F ALL THE CONNIVING, BACKSTAB-bing . . . Jaira had poisoned Tara's own brother! Like a befuddled fool, Leif knelt before Jaira, utterly transfixed, making the truth viciously apparent. Jaira not only knew about the *Brierstar*'s fate, but she also somehow felt it acceptable to parade the spoils of her plunder before Tara. The only thing that kept Tara from screaming was Carmack's warm hand squeezing hers as tightly as she held his.

"Isn't this thrilling?" Jaira gushed. "Once your brother completes his rites, we'll be nearly family." She tapped her ringed fingers against her goblet. "Well, Tara? Say something."

Had she already guessed Tara's true motivations for visiting Jaelport? If so, why not immediately throw Tara's entire party into the stocks, or whatever other form of punishment the Hamartanos favored?

Tara willed her face not to twist like her heart. "Forgive me. This surprise was so wildly unexpected . . . My dear brother, I have not seen you since before my wedding." She reluctantly released Carmack's hand, pushed to her feet, and walked toward her brother.

Leif stood as she approached, and she embraced him. He did not lift her off the floor in his usual manner. Instead, he leaned away.

"Whatever are you doing in Jaelport?" she asked.

"I am here at the request of Princess Jaira," he said.

Odd. No excuse given for his absence on the worst day of Tara's life. "As am I, Brother." Tara forced a grin and guided Leif away from the head table. "But why are you not sailing with Uncle Chantry?"

His pupils flickered slightly. His skin, usually a golden tan, looked dull, as if he hadn't seen the sun in weeks.

"Leif?"

His chapped lips twitched as if his mouth was fighting itself. "Captain Chantry fell ill. We sailed into Jaelport to seek a healer's assistance."

Oh dear, was there any truth to Leif's words? If so, wouldn't the ship still be in the harbor? And if Uncle Chantry was ill, where was he? Too many questions, and Jaira's ear was turned their way. "Go on."

"He recovered and sailed for Hamonah."

That would answer why the *Brierstar* wasn't in port. But the fleet imposing the blockade would have seen their sister ship sailing for Hamonah, unless they'd sent word later. How could Tara know that? Aunt Nitsa might have received such news after Tara left, but it seemed unlikely. Her aunt would have bloodvoiced such an update before they had reached Jaelport. Besides, Leif—Uncle Chantry's most loyal officer—would never willingly abandon his post.

Tara lowered her voice. "Have you resigned your commission?"

Leif's cheeks turned red. "Stop questioning me, Tara," he seethed. "I serve the house of Hamartano, and no one else."

Tara shrank back, trembling.

"Everything all right?" Jaira asked.

"Yes, Princess." Leif bowed to her. "May I return to my chamber?"

"You may." She waved her hand, dismissing him, and he left through the archway.

Tara wanted to follow him back to the west wing to see where his chamber was, but she caught Jaira watching her.

Mandzee rose from her seat. "Sister, a word."

Jaira rolled her eyes. "Can't it wait? I'm actually enjoying myself."

"Now." Mandzee left the courtyard through the same archway, with Jaira stomping after her.

Captain Myck drained his wine. "Never a dull moment at a Hamartano party." He beckoned the nearest server. "Care for another drink, Lady Tara?"

"No, Captain." Tara fought to steady her voice. "I am afraid all the excitement has left me exhausted. Please tell the princesses that, with regret, I retired early."

Captain Myck sat up. "Allow me to escort you."

"No, thank you. I insist you stay and enjoy your wine. Master Demry will take me."

Captain Myck's eyes flashed, but he collapsed back on his cushion.

Carmack stood and quickly escorted Tara through the crowd in the opposite direction Leif and the princesses had gone.

"What did your brother say?" he asked.

"Hardly anything." Tara repeated what Leif had said. "He didn't even sound like himself. Did you see the way he greeted me?"

"Both your feet remained on the ground, and for the first time, I didn't fear he'd break your ribs."

"He displayed none of the effects of love powder Averella described." Tara whisked past the three-tiered fountain, each stone layer carved to look like a piece of dripping wet lace. "What if he has changed since I last saw him?"

"Your brother has always been a wild card, but Jaelportian magic seems the more likely culprit. Whatever enchantment Jaira used, she turned your brother into a zealot for Zitheos."

"But why?"

"You know her best. Could she be testing your loyalty?"

Tara's memories of Jaira flowed through her mind like the water cascading over the fountain. That very afternoon, they had conversed easily through hours of beauty treatments, sharing their common burdens as younger daughters of noble houses. Jaira shared Tara's sense of duty to family and the pain of living in older siblings' shadows, while each coveted control over her own destiny—Tara as Lady of Meribah Corner, and Jaira? What did she truly seek?

Tara glanced back to where the Hamartano sisters had retaken their places under the royal pavilion. Mandzee, the next mage queen of Jaelport, sat forlorn on a gold chair, while Jaira perched beside her on her floor cushion, her head held high, as if her braids were a crown of royal jewels.

Tara whirled around and marched out of the courtyard with Carmack at her side, her mind replaying Jaira's confidences.

This succession is ludicrous. Mandzee has neither the mind nor the backbone to rule Jaelport. Everyone wishes I were the firstborn, even our eunuchs. They despise Mandzee since learning she plans to abolish their order.

"It is not the *Brierstar* Jaira wants," Tara said when they reached the vestibule. "She wants to be queen of Jaelport. This wasn't our test. It was Mandzee's, to see if she would decline Leif's rite in front of her subjects."

"What if it's both?" Carmack asked. "Jaira could have bewitched any man in Jaelport, but she chose your brother. My first thought was that she knows why we're really here."

Tara slowed her steps. "Then why would she reveal her hand?"

"To force ours," Carmack said. "She's toying with us."

That sounded exactly like Jaira. As a young girl, Tara had watched Jaira dangle mice by their tails in front of hungry cats, letting them swat and jump at the poor rodents until she tired of the game. The mice never lasted much longer.

As Tara passed the throne room entrance, she said, "We have to free Leif first thing. Jaira suggested an excursion to the bazaar tomorrow so I wouldn't need to borrow any more of her gowns." Frankly, Tara hadn't seen the need when her Meneton dress fit so well, but one gown was hardly enough for an extended stay. It didn't matter that Tara planned to leave Jaelport soon. She had to keep the ruse going. "Larkos will go with us. Can you free Leif while we're gone?"

"Bad things happen when I leave you alone," Carmack said as they turned down the hallway to the central courtyard between the east and west wings.

"From what Jaira said, the queen is deathly ill. This may be our only opportunity to save my brother." Tara stopped at the end of the long reflecting pool. "While I'm out, I can make inquiries about the *Brierstar* and look for more antiserum."

Carmack seemed torn but eventually nodded. "Fine, but only to the bazaar. Take Kressy—she's been helpful in dodgy situations—and don't dawdle." Under the moonlight, Carmack gently brushed a wisp of hair from Tara's face, and she caught a glimpse of the young man she used to pine after. "I won't be able to breathe until you return."

Her heart lifted. The dance had shifted something between them, awakening a hope that Tara had let die years ago. An impossible hope—for untitled men without means could not court ladies. Then again, as the Lady of Meribah Corner, Tara had means enough to court whoever she liked. But she and Carmack needed to survive Jaelport first.

⟵　　⟶

"I could not imagine a bazaar grander than this," Tara shouted over the cacophony of haggling surrounding her. Nor one more difficult to navigate. How was she ever going to find tiny vials of antiserum in the never-ending maze of stalls and shops? Jaelport's bazaar made Meneton's look positively provincial. The entire length of the colonnade was covered by a series of painted domes, lined with merchant bays. Every possible good filled them—from fabric to raw metals. Ahead of her, Jaira sashayed down the city's main thoroughfare, her hairless dog Gowzal straining at his leash and yipping at everything that moved.

Captain Myck picked up a silk embroidered sash, frowned, and threw it back. "I'm afraid the current offerings are paltry in comparison to a year ago."

Jaira scowled at Tara. "The stray king's ridiculous blockade is strangling us, but not for too much longer."

"Zitheos be praised," Larkos muttered.

Leave it to Jaira to not only insult the king's tragic past by calling him a stray, but to openly mock his rule, as well. Kressy's mouth dropped open. Tara nudged her, and she closed it.

By the way Kressy's nostrils flared, Tara expected to hear her full opinion about Jaira's treasonous words later. "You say the blockade is ending soon. Does that mean Jaelport is emancipating its strays?"

Jaira flicked her hand as though irritated. "Oh, let's not spoil the day by talking politics." She sighed. "It's a pity Master Demry couldn't join us."

"I don't see why. Carmack detests shopping. When he complained of a headache this morning, I insisted he return to bed."

Jaira edged close to Tara and lowered her voice. "Without your Shield hovering, you and the captain can get better acquainted."

Eager to change the subject, Tara pointed at a stationer's bay stocked with inkpots, quills, parchment, and rag pulp paper. "Oh, it has been ages since I've drawn anything." She went inside and before long had selected a set of pastels, two charcoal sticks, and a bundle of parchment. She paid the stationer using the smaller coins Carmack had procured from the palace treasurer. He had insisted. No more gold coins after Meneton. Tara slipped her purchases into the basket she had borrowed from Jaira.

Captain Myck shadowed her through the stationer's bay, and the moment she exited, asked, "Might I carry that for you, Lady Tara?"

"Thank you, but I shall manage."

"You need only ask, should you change your mind." Whether it was the absence of wine or Jaira's tongue lashing at the banquet, Myck was acting more gentlemanly, quite different from his boorish behavior on the dance floor.

Jaira led Tara to a series of tables piled high with bolts of opulent fabric.

Tara ran her fingers over a slippery black silk. "I ought to be wearing a mourning frock. We couldn't find one in Meneton."

"Why? You are no more grieving your dead husband than I am." Jaira pulled a bolt of sumptuous black lace from the pile. "If you must, buy a color and make an overlayer with something like this." She tossed it near Tara. "In Jaelport, widows wear green, not black. How about this?" Jaira lifted a bolt of lime-green satin.

Tara didn't hate the idea of wearing a color under black lace, but she grimaced at the green. "I will look absolutely sickly in that shade."

Jaira draped the end of the lime satin over her arm. "Isn't that the point of widow's weeds?"

Tara spotted a rich emerald silk and pulled it from pile. "Would this do?"

"You might as well wear purple, like at the funeral." Jaira laughed wickedly. "That was the first flash of rebellion I had seen in you since you kissed the stray at the prince's coming-of-age banquet. Hopefully, not the last."

Tara remembered the glaring woman at Lord Gershom's funeral

and shoved the silk back in its place. She would not be repeating that mistake. She also didn't miss how Jaira had called the king a stray again and had referred to the pretender, Esek, as the real prince. What warped reality did Jaira live in?

Eventually, she and Jaira agreed on a pine-green taffeta. The wrinkly fabric was Tara's least favorite but was the only flattering shade that met Jaira's approval. Tara handed the bolt of fabric to Kressy to oversee the measuring and cutting. Once the purchase was complete, Tara and her party continued their trek through the bazaar.

Captain Myck again fell in next to Tara. "I can't help but notice you do not seem overly excited about your purchase."

"A keen observation, Captain. Few ladies are giddy about purchasing new mourning clothes."

"Ah. That does paint things in a different shade, though not even a black shroud could hide your beauty." His laughing eyes and broad smile transformed his face, reminding her again of Sir Rigil. If Tara were the girl she once was, she would be quite smitten with the captain's easy charm and good looks.

But she wasn't a romantic anymore, and nothing could make her forget their morbid topic of conversation. "A kind compliment, sir, but you've never seen me in black."

"I believe you could make puce look fetching."

Tara laughed. "I cannot decide which is more ridiculous—that compliment or the fact that a sea captain knows what puce is."

"Hate to interrupt the fun"—Jaira winked at Tara—"but you will have to wait for me here. My next errand is with Isbelda." She tipped her head toward a black door between two bays. *Apothecary* was written in script above it. "Being from Magos, she does not allow adult men in her shop."

Of all the shops in the bazaar, this looked like the most promising place to find more panzehir. "May I join you?" Tara asked. "Perhaps Isbelda can recommend something for Carmack's headache."

Kressy grabbed Tara's hand and squeezed.

"You can remain here, Kressy," Tara said.

Kressy's wan face broke with relief, and she released Tara's hand. "Thank you, m'lady."

"Isbelda is nothing like the apothecaries in Tsaftown, you know," Jaira said.

Tara forced a grin. "Only the best in Jaelport, right?" She entered the dark shop, where a potent mixture of incense and foreign smells made her nose water. A dingy layer of soot dulled the constellations and etchings painted on the plaster ceiling. As Tara's eyes adjusted to the low light, she glanced down the rows of shelves jammed with bottles, jars, and baskets.

Jaira marched over to the shopkeeper's counter.

A woman, presumably Isbelda, sat behind it. Everything about her was dull, from her hair and pasty skin to her tattered wrap. She bowed her head. "Your Highness, how may I help you?"

"I need more honey and a few other things." Jaira slid a scrap of parchment across the counter.

Isbelda gave it a skimming glance, then shuffled to a heavy door at the back of the shop. She unlocked it, and Jaira walked through. But when Tara approached, the old woman's sinewy arm shot out from under her wrap, barring the way. "Not for you." Isbelda craned her neck as she glanced around the shop and yelled, "Mez! Where are you?"

A young boy wearing an orange tunic popped out from the far row of shelves. "Here, Auntie. Restocking the bat's blood like you asked."

The old woman sneered at Tara. "Keep an eye on our guest."

"Yes, Auntie," the boy said.

Isbelda slammed the door shut, and Tara stepped back, accidentally bumping a jar of yellowish-green sludge on the table behind her. It teetered precariously before tipping over the edge. She flinched, expecting to hear glass shatter. Instead, two small hands snatched it from midair.

"Careful, miss." The young boy set the bottle back in its place. "Toad's skin jelly leaves a nasty rash."

"Thank you. Mez, is it?"

"No, I'm Zeke. Mez was the name of Isbelda's last stray. She hasn't bothered to learn mine."

So, she wasn't his aunt either. He was most likely her slave, considering Jaelport refused to abolish the practice of slavery, even after King Gidon had imposed the blockade.

Tara scanned the labels on the shelves. Unable to find any orange liquids, she asked Zeke, "Do you have any panzehir?"

Zeke gaped at her. "That's a royal serum. They hang anyone caught buying or selling it." He leaned closer. "I've heard rumors a mage down at the docks sells it, but no telling if hers actually works. Just be careful who you ask." He drew his finger in a line across his throat.

Tara swallowed a tight knot. Seems she would have to be more cautious in her search. "I appreciate your warning."

So much for purchasing more antiserum. With that goal on hold, Tara pulled her parchment and charcoal stick from her basket and began to draw. When her rough sketch of the *Brierstar* was done, she found Zeke straightening jars on another set of shelves.

"Do you like ships?" she asked.

"Nay, they're bad omens."

They would be to a young boy smuggled away from his family. "Not every boat is bad." Tara held out her drawing. "This is my uncle's ship—my real uncle—the *Brierstar*. It came to Jaelport not long ago. Did you happen to see it?"

When Zeke glanced at the drawing, his eyes widened, and he turned back to his work.

"Please." Tara placed a small silver coin, worth one gora, on the shelf next to his hand. "My brother and uncle are on the ship, and all are missing. I worry so for them."

Zeke stared at the coin. "I can't say." Across the shop, the door creaked open. "She'd be cross," he whispered.

"Mez! What are you whispering about, boy?" Isbelda said. "You better not be pestering that young lady."

Tara stepped out from behind the shelf, coming face-to-face with the scowling shopkeeper. "He's no bother. Quite the opposite."

"How's that?"

"I was asking him for suggestions on what I might sketch during my visit to your lovely city."

"Psh, it's not my city. I only live here. What did Mez say?"

"He, er . . . well, he recommended several wonderful spots, such as . . ." Tara's mind went blank.

Zeke stepped forward. "I told her the palace is the prettiest sight, especially the south view when the stars come out."

The boy had offered no such advice, but his mention of stars gave Tara hope. She beamed. "Tenma Palace at twilight. It even sounds like a masterpiece."

Isbelda's beady eyes narrowed. "Back to work, Mez."

"I hope I won't have to wait long for my order," Jaira said, closing the heavy door behind her.

Isbelda returned to her counter. "The magen will be delivered this afternoon, Your Highness."

"I'm counting on it," Jaira said. "Tara, this is for you." She tossed her a small indigo pouch.

"What is it?" Tara asked.

"Headache herbs, for Master Demry." Jaira nodded toward Isbelda. "Hurry up and pay the woman."

"Of course. How much?"

"One copper." Isbelda held out her gnarled fingers. "Sniff one pinch per hour."

Tara handed her the coin, then turned to say goodbye to Zeke, but the boy and the silver gora were gone. His clue about the south side of the palace had to mean something. Carmack wouldn't like it, but Tara would simply have to do some sightseeing before returning to the palace.

She and Jaira rejoined Kressy, Captain Myck, and Larkos outside. "I have an idea. Why don't we all enjoy a leisurely luncheon, then go for a sail? Jaelport, especially Tenma Palace, must look spectacular at sunset. Captain, would you take us?"

Captain Myck glanced at Jaira, who shrugged. Then he bowed. "I would happily take you anywhere you wish to go, Lady Tara."

"Thank you, Captain. You will come too. Won't you, Jaira?"

Jaira smirked. "I'd only be in the way."

"But we can't go without you," Tara said. "An unmarried couple sailing alone is highly improper."

"Don't be a ninny, Tara. No one cares a fig about such things in Jaelport. Besides, you have your maid with you."

Except that Tara needed to keep Jaira and Larkos away from the palace while Carmack rescued Leif. She got the feeling Jaira wanted Tara to spend more time with the captain. Perhaps if she played along, Jaira would too, but if she and Larkos returned to the palace early, Carmack's search for Leif would be in jeopardy. Tara needed to warn Carmack. "Kressy must deliver that fabric to the dressmaker so she can get started on my dress. In fact, she best return straight away. Here, Kressy." Tara handed her the fabric. "Be sure to inform Master Demry of our change in plans."

"Yes, m'lady." Kressy curtsied and hurried away.

Tara pulled Jaira aside. "Please say you'll come. The captain is dashingly handsome. I want to get to know him better, but I don't dare go alone."

Jaira rolled her eyes and dug into her reticule. "Take this." She pressed a small purple pouch into Tara's palm. "If necessary, simply blow a little love powder at him, and he'll be utterly helpless. Now, be a big girl and get on with it."

The thought of using love powder against any man, even Captain Myck, turned Tara's stomach, but she had to choose. Either she abandon her search for the *Brierstar* and call the day a complete loss—one she could ill afford—or make a risky move, sure to infuriate her Shield.

"Very well." Tara tucked the pouch in her basket. "Wish me luck."

A devious smile on Jaira's face rose goosebumps on Tara's arms. "With that little pouch, you won't need luck." Jaira sauntered away with Larkos, Gowzal yapping at her heels.

Tara prayed that Arman would keep her safe with the captain. Hopefully, Carmack and Dunn's plan to get Leif out of the palace had worked, because their time was nearly up.

Chapter Eighteen
Carmack

CARMACK HAD ZERO FAITH IN HIS plan, but Dunn had insisted upon one. After a night of brainstorming, their best strategy seemed more like a desperate ploy likely to end in frantic prayers.

Among the army of servants cleaning the Fountain Courtyard after the banquet, Carmack meandered his way around the courtyard's edge. Nearby, a eunuch paced in front of the southern archway where Leif had made his exit the night before.

Dunn's unmistakable whistle drifted closer, and when no one was looking, Carmack slipped into position behind a potted palm. Through the thick fronds, he caught a glimpse of his friend's arms, full of banquet decorations. Instead of joining the line of servants clearing away the mess, Dunn approached the eunuch.

"I have orders to return these lanterns and cushions to the west wing," Dunn said.

"You cannot enter here."

"Fine, I'll leave them with you."

"No, you canno—"

Dunn dropped everything. Glass lanterns popped, shattering against the tile.

"Fool!" the eunuch said. "Clean up this mess."

Carmack bit back a chuckle as Dunn kicked at the broken lanterns, his heavy boots crunching the glass into finer pieces.

The eunuch pushed him back. "Not like that!"

"Okay." Dunn raised his hands. "I'll leave you to it." Then he rushed away.

"Come back here!" The eunuch raced after him.

Carmack bolted through the archway, silently thanking Arman that there were no other eunuchs or guards posted inside. He raced down the corridor and rounded a corner into a longer hallway. At its end, he found a massive staircase. Footsteps were descending from above. A nearby door stood open to the outside, so he darted through it, onto a gravel path in a walled garden.

Trees, bushes, and flowering plants of all heights masked the walls and provided a shady canopy. Though sickly patches of decay from Darkness still marred a few tree trunks, every plant bore fresh green leaves and colorful blooms.

Carmack followed the meandering path, searching for another door into the west wing. Crunching footsteps and a creaking noise approached, and he dove behind the nearest clump of flowering shrubs. The spiked purple flowers released a flurry of pollen that settled on Carmack's black sleeves like fine snow. A sweet aroma filled his nose, and he pinched away a sneeze.

He held his breath as the footsteps slowed, then stopped, and finally, passed him by.

A warm calm washed over Carmack. His limbs relaxed. What a comfortable place to rest. He rolled onto his back, bumping the plants again, and enjoyed another blast of their heady perfume. Why had he been in such a hurry? Carmack wanted nothing more than to spend every day surrounded by this beauty.

He sneezed and shivered from the tingles running from his scalp to his toes. The footsteps and creaking returned.

"Who is there?" a female asked, sounding trustworthy.

"Carmack Demry," he said, hoping his name would meet with approval.

The footsteps came closer. "Come out at once."

Without hesitation, Carmack crawled into the sunshine. Or was he floating?

He met the shimmering folds of an ivory gown and sat back on his heels. An attractive woman stood on the path, like a vision sent from Shamayim, her skin glistening with golden flecks.

"Master Demry, you are in the queen's private garden."

"Garden?" Everything blurred except her face. The warm notes of her voice lulled his senses. "Who are you?"

"You know me perfectly well."

Yes. Princess Mandzee. Beautiful. Powerful. Carmack scrambled to his feet and bowed deeply. "Your Highness, I am at your service. How may I please you?"

Her sparkling brown eyes rolled, and she pointed to the ground. "Fetch a piece of root from that bush you were hiding under."

Whatever she wanted, her desires were his own. He dropped to his knees and plunged his hands into the soil, which was unyielding at first, but with his frantic digging slowly became pliable. He dug until his fingers found a gnarled root. He traced it deeper, swept away the dirt, and snapped off a thin piece. He stood, presenting it to Mandzee on his open palms, and dared to gaze into her intoxicating eyes.

"Take a bite and chew," she said. "Do not spit it out until you are in your right mind."

Desperate to please her, Carmack bit through the root's gritty skin, breaking a piece free. He crushed it between his molars, and a vile bitterness filled his mouth.

Darkness streaked across his vision and dulled the bright colors of the garden. He noticed a wrinkled woman sat hunched in a roll chair under the shade of a nearby tree. Her wrists and ankles were shackled to the chair.

Carmack's eyes and nose watered, and mucus thickened his throat. He gagged, but something compelled him to keep chewing. Suddenly aware Mandzee had discovered him sneaking around, Carmack broke out in a cold sweat, yet he could not stop obeying her wishes. His stomach heaved violently, the weightlessness disappeared, and he dropped to his hands and knees, spitting out the bitterness in his mouth.

When he had recovered, he sat back on his heels. "Forgive me," he panted. "I . . . don't know what came over me."

"You were intoxicated by that innophoria plant. Fortunately, you sneezed as I passed by, or who knows how long you would have lain there or who you might have sworn allegiance to. Trespassing in my private garden is dangerous, Master Demry. What are you doing here?"

Carmack slipped the rest of the root behind his belt and stood. By what miracle was he still there, instead of being dragged off in chains to the dungeon? The garden's high walls and trees blocked the watchtowers from view. No eunuchs hovered nearby, but Mandzee was not alone. His gaze settled on the gaunt woman in the roll chair, dressed in night clothes, her head wrapped in a scarf. "This must be your mother."

"Don't speak to her." Mandzee turned him away. "The garden soothes her, but the slightest irritation can send her into a frenzy. And you need not worry of her reporting your presence here. She speaks coherently so rarely, no one pays any attention to what she says even when it isn't gibberish ranting."

"I'm sorry. That must be difficult for you."

Mandzee's eyes turned misty. "Thank you. It is, but she would not listen to the warnings. All I can do is bring her here for a few moments of peace." She blinked away her far-off look and faced him. "Now, tell me what you're doing here."

Mandzee hadn't called out to anyone upon discovering him. Instead, she'd restored his sense. He could lie, but perhaps he didn't need to. "I am searching for Leif Livna."

"Why?"

Tara better have been right about the strife between the Hamartano sisters and the root of it. "I wanted to talk some sense into him. With all due respect, Your Highness, I do not think he would make a good eunuch for Zitheos. Since Leif was a young boy, he has followed the Way."

A wrinkle formed between Mandzee's sculpted brows. "By that, you mean young Livna forsook all other gods to worship Arman alone. You think it impossible for my sister to have convinced him that Arman is not the only god and to follow Zitheos as well?" Mandzee clasped her hands. "What person's faith is so sure that it cannot be shaken?"

Certainly not Carmack's. "I can't speak to another man's faith. Life's challenges can raise doubts in anyone's heart, no matter how steadfast." He felt the distance that had grown between him and Arman since his father had drowned, but despite it, Carmack never could forget His promises. "My father used to say that when our faith wavers, Arman's faithfulness remains." Wonder what Papa would tell Carmack now, because when it had mattered most, Arman had been noticeably absent.

"A God faithful to subjects who are not? What a foreign notion!"

Carmack scratched his beard. "It's strange, isn't it? But who am I to question Arman's nature." Though, in his heart, he just had.

"Nor do I require you to," the princess said. "It is Master Livna's loyalty at issue, not Arman's."

Carmack remembered something Roxburg had taught him. "The *Book of Arman* says He won't let His followers be tempted beyond what we can bear. Arman is a jealous God, and Leif Livna loves Him and His son Câan with a zeal that I've always admired. So, to answer your question, no, I do not think it possible Arman allowed Leif to abandon Him for Zitheos, not willingly."

"Nor do I." Mandzee met his gaze, then looked away. "Tell me, what does your holy book say about younger siblings who reject an older sibling's leadership."

Carmack fought to keep his expression plain. "I don't think it addresses that explicitly. If it did, my brother Roxburg would have certainly drilled it into my head."

One side of Mandzee's mouth quirked up. "So, in your family, you are the brash fool who jumps into trouble with both feet?"

This time, Carmack couldn't keep a dry laugh from escaping. "Roxburg would say so, without admitting he's never satisfied unless I do things his way."

Mandzee sniffed. "Maybe his way keeps you safe."

Carmack stared into the distant sky, remembering the last words he had shouted at his brother. *I don't need you constantly telling me I'm doing everything wrong! Leave it to Câan to save me from my mistakes, if He gets around to it.* Carmack had ached for Roxburg's forgiveness but had not thought about it in a long time. "Arman's son Câan is my Savior, not Roxburg."

"But will your God's son save Jaira?"

Carmack blinked. "Forgive me, Your Highness, I thought we were discussing my family." What else could he say? Though Carmack's hope in Arman seemed to shrink as his faith wavered, he clung to the shred that remained. His soul couldn't face the future without it. But the Hamartanos did not follow the Way. They had no hope apart from themselves. "You and Jaira are in a more difficult situation."

"Difficult I could handle, but Jaira has long outgrown that description."

A piercing shriek made them both jump. Queen Torrezia rattled against her shackles, screeching and hollering.

"You must go." Mandzee grabbed his arm. "This way." She hurried down a split in the path to a long, arched arbor supported by a wall of trellises that disguised the garden's rear wall with a thick tunnel of flowering vines. Carmack ducked his head as he followed her. Halfway through, Mandzee stomped on an iron peg near the path's edge, and a section of stone wall popped open, revealing a descending ladder.

Carmack's stomach tightened. "Feeding me to the lions?" he asked.

A slight grin danced on Mandzee's lips. "This passageway is free of beasts—the queen's emergency escape should Tenma Palace ever come under siege. It also connects to the eunuchs' tower. Those awaiting the rite of Zitheos are housed on the top floor. You'll find Lady Tara's brother there. Then follow the passageway downhill to the edge of the city. You should all depart at once, before you end up villager pieces on my sister's Citadel game board."

Carmack stepped into the gap. "I don't understand why you're helping me, but thank you."

"Once the headache hits, you won't be thanking me. Now hurry. The last thing my palace needs is another eunuch."

"Wait, what headache?" he asked, but Mandzee kicked the iron lever, and the wall closed between them. Back in darkness, the air was cool. Almost homey.

Carmack held his breath, listening for any noises. Nothing. Small gaps in the outer wall let in spots of light. He let his eyes adjust, then descended the ladder and followed the dots of sunlight through a dank passageway to a spiral staircase. He climbed the steep steps. After two rotations, light from a small keyhole window revealed a wooden door. He waited, ensuring no one was about to emerge, then proceeded. Four more rotations took him past two other doors. On the seventh turn, sunlight poured down the stone steps.

A dull ache hit his temples, and he winced. Oh, *that* headache.

Above him, the beams of the tower's ceiling exposed a clay tile roof. A loft. As soon as Carmack climbed the last four steps, he'd be visible to anyone there. Had Mandzee sent him into a trap? Her concerns about Jaira had seemed genuine. Either that or she was the best actress in Er'Rets. He crept upward until his eyes were even with the floor.

Leif sat facing one of the six lattice-covered windows spread evenly like numbers on a dial along one half of the circular room. Alone, with no door, guard, or chains to keep him there.

Given his own recent run-in with Jaelportian magic, Carmack knew a similar enchantment must be to blame, though it didn't matter which one. Carmack would carry out Leif on his shoulders if he had to. "Leif," he whispered, "it's time to go home."

Leif didn't move. "I wait for my queen."

Carmack knew he wasn't talking about his cousin, Queen Averella. "Princess Mandzee wishes us to leave Jaelport," Carmack said.

Leif sprang up and grabbed Carmack's jerkin. "Mandzee will never be queen." His blue eyes were glassy. "You're an intruder!"

Carmack raised his hands. "Easy, friend. It's me, Carmack Demry."

Leif's grip slackened slightly. "Carmack Demry is my sister's Shield."

Good, Leif's mind wasn't completely gone. "That's me." Carmack pulled from his pocket the tiny vial of antiserum Myck had given him. "I brought you a gift."

"I do not want gifts." Leif pushed Carmack. "My queen would not wish to find you here. Leave me."

"This gift is from Princess Jaira. Would you like to see it?" He held out the vial of orange liquid in his open palm.

When Leif glanced down, Carmack closed his fist. With his other hand, he grabbed Leif's tunic, swept Leif's legs out from under him, and pinned him, face to the floor, with Carmack's chest against Leif's back. Carmack snaked his forearm under Leif's neck and squeezed, hard enough to stop the man from yelling. Leif bucked against Carmack and swung his arms, but captivity had weakened him. When Leif's flailing slowed, Carmack rolled him onto his back, using his weight to pin Leif to the floor. He pulled the vial's cork out with his teeth and pinched Leif's nose. As soon as Leif's mouth opened, Carmack dumped the orange liquid under his tongue.

Leif sputtered and writhed against Carmack. What if Myck had given him counterfeit panzehir?

Carmack's dull headache grew into a splitting pain, and his muscles burned from restraining Leif, who would soon need a deeper breath. As soon as his jerky movements stopped, Carmack eased off.

Leif's face relaxed, his scowl gone. "Carmack? Is it really you, or am I dreaming?" He blinked like he was trying to clear his eyes. "Why are you trying to kill me?"

Praise Arman! The panzehir must have taken effect. "It's me, and I'm not. You're trying to kill me."

Leif coughed. "I know better than to fight a Demry."

Carmack released Leif and helped him to his feet.

Leif raked his fingers through what was left of his tangled blond curls. "What in the depths happened to my hair?"

"You don't remember last night?"

"My memories hang in twisted shreds. Though now that you mention it, I had a nightmare that Tara was here." Leif paled. "That wasn't a dream, was it? When my mother finds out you've brought her to Jaelport, you'll be sacked."

"She's here with your brother's permission and the king's. It's a long story. Tara insisted on searching for you, your ship, and the crew. So far, you're the only one we've found. Now that you're in your right mind, I'm hoping you can help."

"Gah!" Leif rubbed his face. "It all bleeds together, so many hallucinations. My last clear memory on the ship, I was at the helm, taking the night watch. We were within sight of Jaelport, on flat seas, barely a breath of wind. That's the last I recall."

Carmack's heart sank. Would he ever find the *Brierstar*? He had to. Another way out of Jaelport seemed unlikely. As soon as the palace eunuchs discovered Leif was missing, they would begin a manhunt, but that was a problem to solve later. "What about the crew?"

"I have visions of all of us lying on our backs, staring at a small piece of the sky, waiting for sweet crackers to rain down on us."

Sweet crackers? A strange choice of food for prisoners. "You were outside?"

"No, in a round room with a domed ceiling. There was a hole at the top where daylight and food came through."

The crew had to be somewhere in the palace, but all the domed ceilings Carmack had seen were in the state rooms. What Leif described sounded like an underground chamber. A dry cistern, perhaps.

"It was a nightmare. I couldn't move the smallest muscle, not even to blink. The only comfort was the perfume." Leif walked back to the window. "Sometimes, when the breeze blows, I can still smell it."

Carmack joined him, rubbing his forehead. Mandzee had warned of a headache, but the pain had him seeing double as he gazed through the lattice. He pressed his temples and brought the world back into focus. Terraced gardens stretched out from the base of the eunuchs' tower. Below, several workers were picking fruit from the trees and hoeing the dirt between vegetable plants. One woman pulled a rope that hung from a pulley and tripod of poles positioned above a large hole surrounded by stacked stones.

Likely a well. Carmack counted ten similar circles spread throughout the surrounding terraces, some with tripods and pulleys, some without. The woman reached toward the hole, but instead of retrieving a bucket of water, a basket filled with a mustard yellow substance emerged from the hole. So, not a well after all, but a silo for storing harvested crops.

Carmack's heart jumped. Or prisoners.

"It's time to go," he said. And he meant it. For all of them.

CHAPTER NINETEEN
TARA

GENTLEMEN REQUIRE FORTITUDE IN *battle, but well-bred ladies require it for uncouth company.*

If Mother only knew what Tara had endured that afternoon, she would be quite proud.

In a dodgy tavern, reeking of old grease and spilled ale, Tara stared at her untouched trencher of gristly meat bits while Captain Myck droned on about his exploits. Carmack had once teased Tara that an anvil dropping out of the sky couldn't crack her mask of politeness. Well, she was about to prove him wrong.

Captain Myck said, "Since that day in Hamonah, I'm practically a king."

Tara pushed away from the table, unable to stomach anymore. "My, it's getting late. Shall we make our way to the docks?"

"Of course. As I said earlier, I am at your disposal." His uneven smile left Tara's stomach as unsettled as their unpalatable meal. As if he, too, wore a mask that had slipped.

They left the public house and walked down to the harbor, where they boarded a small sailboat moored next to the *Ruby Tanniyn.*

Captain Myck removed his jacket, untethered the ropes from the dock, and rowed out to deeper water. "This spry little bird is the smallest boat in my fleet, but she can catch up to anything on the water."

Behind him, the deck of the *Ruby Tanniyn* appeared deserted, except for a slight figure leaning against the mizzenmast. As the boat floated away from its slip, Captain Myck unfurled the sail. When the afternoon breezes pulled the smaller boat farther into the bay, the person—a young woman with long black braids and eyes lined like a Jaelportian mage—stepped out from the mast's shadow. She looked like Tara's young guide in Meneton, except Betzi wasn't a mage. And why would she be on Captain Myck's ship?

Tara shielded her eyes from the water's glare, trying to get a better look.

Captain Myck glanced back over his shoulder. "See something?"

Whoever the woman was, she ducked behind the mast, like she did not want Captain Myck to see her. It seemed wrong to point her out. "I thought I saw a fish jump, but the waves have tricked my eyes."

Captain Myck stowed the oars and took hold of the rudder. "At lunch, you mentioned sailing to the south side of Tenma Palace, but we'll enjoy smoother seas if we stay in the harbor."

Staying to the north of the palace was no good. Zeke had specifically mentioned the southern view. Jaira's pouch of love powder would work to convince Myck, but Tara would rather not use a mage's method of persuasion. Tara had her own skills, courtesy of her mother.

A vain man will never refuse a parade.

Tara sighed with feigned boredom. "I suppose the harbor is a safer choice, if one lacks the stomach for excitement."

Captain Myck's grayish eyes flashed. "Have you forgotten that I'm the best blockade runner in the south seas?"

"You *did* suggest we stick to the harbor. Perhaps *you* have forgotten that I am not one to run from an adventure."

Captain Myck flashed a toothy grin and steered their boat to the south.

The fresh ocean breeze provided a delightful reprieve from Jaelport's smoke. As the waves swelled higher at the harbor's opening, one splashed over the side. Tara gasped as the water sprayed against her back.

Captain Myck laughed. "You should sit closer to me if you want to keep dry."

She nearly declined, but saltwater drops glistened on her new bundle of parchment. Rather than risk ruining the lot, she picked up her basket and wobbled to the stern. Captain Myck held out his hand, and she grabbed hold, then sat next to him.

His thumb traced a lazy circle along her wrist. "Better?"

Her pulse quickened as his leg pressed against her own. How in the depths was she to keep a respectable distance between them on a boat? Her gaze fell to the basket in her lap, and the answer practically jumped out of it. "Captain, may I draw your portrait?"

He squeezed her hand and released it. "Only if you call me Myck."

Saints, if only Jaira were there to check the man's impropriety, but the set down the captain deserved could not come from Tara. She needed his cooperation. "Thank you. Myck." Tara pulled parchment and a charcoal stick from her basket, slid to the far end of their bench, and busied herself with drawing.

He frowned. "If I'd have known you'd sit way over there, I might have answered differently."

"Capturing your true likeness proves difficult if I sit too close." Tara poured over her parchment, sketching Myck's profile.

A sharp knock reverberated through her head. *The Duchess of Carm.*

Tara's hand jumped, dashing a dark line across the page. "Au—" Tara covered her mouth with her hand.

"Something wrong?" Myck asked.

Very. Tara's cheeks burned. Her aunt had just caught her alone with a strange man. "I made a careless mistake."

Take comfort, niece. Though I am shocked to find you in such a situation, I trust you have good reason. I have been sick with worry trying to connect with you. Did you not hear me knocking?

Not since before Meneton, Tara thought.

I surmised as much. Some enchantment hides the city of Jaelport and blocks my gift. Through your eyes, I see only thick fog. Have you found the Brierstar?

No, only Leif. He said the ship sailed on to Hamonah.

I am thrilled you found your brother, but this cannot be. We would have received word. Could Leif be mistaken?

Worse. We believe he's under some spell.

Tara shifted her focus to the changing scenery behind Myck. Tenma Palace sat high on a narrow point that jutted into the Eversea, creating a small cove on the back side. Her heart fell. The perfect spot to anchor a ship like the *Brierstar*, and it was empty.

"Have you finished?" Myck peered over the top edge of her parchment.

She snatched it away. "Not quite." With her hand shaking, Tara resumed drawing and avoided eye contact by studying the scenery behind him.

"I thought you were drawing my portrait, not a landscape."

Be careful, Tara.

"I am," Tara answered both of them. "I must find a fitting back-drop." And, if Zeke had sent her on a wild chase, where else the *Brierstar* might be. Could she have misunderstood the boy? "What's around the next bend?"

"Another cove much like this one."

"Will you show it to me?"

"It's getting late. We should head back."

"Please." Tara slid next to Myck and squeezed his hand on the rudder stick. "It is nearly sunset. The colors will be spectacular." His eyes flickered back and forth as if unconvinced, so Tara leaned closer. "And very romantic."

You should not speak of romance to a strange man, Aunt Nitsa bloodvoiced.

Tara forced herself to stare into Myck's eyes while her thoughts drifted. *Please, Aunt,* she thought, *I can't explain now.*

Then stop this nonsense! He grows suspicious.

Tara nodded. "Fine."

Myck's chin jerked. "Fine what?"

Tara wanted to bury her face in her hands, but that would hardly explain away her bungle. "I don't wish to spoil our afternoon by arguing." With no choice but to return to the palace without finding the ship, she put down her charcoal. She bit her quivering lip, tasting nothing but bitter frustration. The whitewashed limestone cliffs beneath Tenma Palace were slowly turning orange in the waning hours of afternoon, except for a large patch of gray. There, under an arch of rock, a slatted gate of worn timber stretched all the way into the water, covering a large hole. So large, a tall ship could pass through it.

Aunt, do you see it? Tara thought.

See what?

That strange door in the cliff. Then she added aloud, "There."

Myck scooted closer. "There, what?"

Drudge. He'd heard her.

"The colors are changing," Tara said.

I see only Jaelport's fog, Aunt Nitsa said. *Unfortunately, I must leave you. I am traveling to the Council meeting in Armonguard, and my attention is needed elsewhere. I will reach out for you again at sunrise. May Arman keep you safe.*

Tara scribbled frantically at her sketch. She needed more time.

Why couldn't she just demand her way, like Jaira? Or perhaps flirt. Aunt Nitsa wasn't watching anymore, and it was worth a try.

Tara batted her eyelashes. "What a shame we cannot stay. The scenery befits so handsome a subject."

"Well, when you put it that way . . ." Myck's gaze dropped to her lips. "I suppose we can circle around so you can admire the view awhile longer."

"Thank you, Capt—I mean Myck." Tara picked up her drawing parchment, holding it like a wall between them, and frantically replicated the gate, paying close attention to its location along the south wall of the palace. Once those details were done, she realized they drew the eye straight to the gate instead of her supposed subject. Tara spent the rest of the journey sketching Myck's likeness, finishing his eyes and nose. The boat's bobbing was making her dizzy. When the boat rounded the point and entered Jaelport Bay again, Tara tucked the parchment and pastels away.

"Are you not going to show me your masterpiece?" Myck asked.

"Not until I finish."

"Then we must arrange another sitting." Myck wound his fingers between hers and pressed her hand to his lips. He leaned closer. A shiver raced down Tara's back when his boozy breath warmed her ear. "I have looked forward to a moment alone with you."

A salty taste flooded the back of Tara's mouth, and her entire body broke out in a sweat. She lurched to the side of the boat, heaving the contents of her stomach into the water. When she recovered, Tara withdrew a handkerchief from her basket, wiped her lips, and sheepishly faced Myck again. "I'm sorry. Just a bit of seasickness. You were saying?"

Myck grimaced. "It can wait until you are well."

Tara turned her scalding hot cheeks toward the Eversea and lifted a prayer of gratitude for Zeke and his hint, for Aunt Nitsa watching over her, and for new hope that the *Brierstar* might be within reach. Above all, she thanked Arman for perfectly timing her seasickness.

Perhaps He had not left Tara entirely on her own, after all.

When Tara reached the west wing's entrance without a glimpse of Carmack, another wave of nausea hit. What if he and Dunn had gotten caught trying to free Leif? She would never find them in this fortress by herself.

Tara tiptoed past the door to Jaira's suite. Inside, Gowzal started yapping. If Jaira happened to be in her room, she'd want to hear all about Tara's excursion with Myck, and Tara would much rather find Carmack. Tara slipped into her chamber, praying Jaira would not follow.

Kressy nearly tackled her. "Praise Arman, you're safe!"

Tara hugged Kressy back and whispered in her ear. "Shh, I don't want Jaira to hear, but I have good news. I think I've found the *Brierstar*. I must tell Carmack. Did you find him when you returned?"

"Aye," Kressy whispered. "When I told him where you were, he threatened to chase you down, but I insisted he wait for you in his chamber. Poor man looked as green as that hideous taffeta you bought."

Tara's stomach fell. "Was he not able to rescue Leif?"

"Your brother is safe, but Master Demry is feeling poorly."

Oh no. Just when it seemed Arman was smiling upon them. "I must go to him."

"I can take you. I helped him get there earlier." Kressy led the way into the corridor.

A knot of tension formed between Tara's shoulders. "He must have felt near death if he allowed you to help him."

Kressy scoffed. "He had plenty enough strength to snarl at me the whole way, as if he could scare me into a fit of prissy vapors."

Tara's lips twitched, and the knot between her shoulders loosened. That sounded more like her Shield, always trying to be the strongest one around, though clearly, Carmack had underestimated her maid. Perhaps Tara had too. "Kressy, you are a wonder."

They snuck through the east wing's hallways. Kressy rounded every corner first to check their path was clear, and it was, all the way to Carmack's door.

"Go back to our chamber," Tara said. "I'll return soon. If anyone asks why I'm not at dinner, tell them I fell asleep early." She opened the door and hesitated, about to commit another egregious breach of propriety. But the day would soon be over, and this was urgent. She could dwell on her misdeeds tomorrow. Tara slipped into a spacious suite, lit by a solitary oil lamp next to the distant bed where Carmack lay. Funny, and unsurprisingly, Jaira had been far more generous with his accommodations.

If Carmack was sleeping, Tara didn't want to startle him. She tiptoed past a couple of overstuffed chairs. As she approached the bed, her heel caught on the thick rug. She fell and spilled her basket. A warm hand caught her shoulder, preventing her face from hitting the bedframe.

Carmack lay on his side, his muscular arm stretched between them. "Why are you sneaking around my room?"

"I came to check on you." Tara scooped the mess from under the bed back into her basket. "Kressy said you were sick."

"It will pass." He collapsed back on his pillow and pinched the bridge of his nose. "You broke our agreement. You were only supposed to go to the bazaar, not sail alone all afternoon with a suspected pirate."

"I was following a tip about the *Brierstar*." Tara plopped her basket on his bed and went to the window. "Wait until you see what I found." She pushed open the curtains, but the dusk's light barely penetrated the lattice window screen.

Carmack groaned. "She said I'd have a headache, but this is torture."

"She?" Tara returned to his side.

"Mandzee caught me searching for Leif in the garden."

Her stomach dropped. "What happened?"

"I'm not entirely sure. I remember hiding behind some bushes with purple flowers. They stunk like cloves. The next thing I know, I'm on my hands and knees, heaving that bit of chewed root from my mouth." Carmack pointed to his bedside table.

Next to the oil lamp's low flame lay a shriveled root. In the scant light, Tara studied the root's hairy tendrils. Teeth marks revealed a milky core under rust-colored skin.

"Mandzee must have poisoned you."

"I don't think so. My best guess is the plants I dove into had magical properties, and she gave me the root to clear my senses. Afterward, we talked, and I told her I planned to find Leif."

Unbelievable. "You scold me for spending time with Captain Myck, while you confess our plans to Jaira's closest sibling!"

"According to you, Jaira is after Mandzee's crown. How close can they be? Besides, the risk paid off. Mandzee showed me to a hidden passage with instructions on how to escape. Without her help, I never would have found Leif and gotten him out of the palace so quickly."

"Was he okay?"

"He's well enough. Dunn took him to find a hiding spot until we locate the ship. Now, what did you find?"

"I want to show you." Tara flipped through the loose pages.

Carmack sat on the side of the bed and groaned. "Can't you just tell me?"

"Look in my basket for a small indigo pouch. I purchased head-ache powder at the bazaar. Sniff a pinch. Maybe it will help."

Carmack rummaged through her basket. He palmed a cloth pouch, dipped his fingers inside, then cast it aside. Tara extended the lamp's wick, and as the room brightened, Carmack lifted his fingers to his nose, sniffed, and sighed. "Whoa, I'm already starting to feel better."

She pulled her sketch from the disordered pile of parchment. "Look."

Instead of studying the sketch, Carmack set it aside on his pillow, then ran his hand up her arm, causing her to shiver. "Have I told you how well that new dress looks on you?"

"No."

He stood, resting his hands on her shoulders. "Somehow, it makes your eyes even more beautiful, like twilight skies on a clear day."

Were her ears deceiving her? Carmack had never spoken this way before, though she had often wished that he would.

"And your hair shimmers with every flicker of candlelight . . ." He touched the curls alongside her face. "Like silk." He brushed his cheek past hers, his beard tickling, his nose buried near her ear. A low vibration rumbled deep in his throat. "Mm, jasmine. How you torture me."

Tara's mouth went dry. "Torture? I never meant—"

"I know." His breath warmed her temple, and his eyes locked with hers. "You're far too kind to purposefully torture anyone. You're the most beautiful woman in Er'Rets, and yet your kind-hearted ways—they're why I love you."

Could her dream be coming true? Finally, a man who saw Tara for who she really was and wanted her for more than her beauty or title. And not just any man, but Carmack Demry. "You love me?"

"My heart, Lady Tara, has always been yours. You are all I want. All I ever wanted." Carmack slid his hand around her waist, pulled her close, and whispered, "Please, let me kiss you."

Tara's heartbeat quickened. His strong hands cradled her neck, and the scents of leather and pine mixed with her jasmine. Her entire body tingled. She nodded only once before his beard brushed her chin and his lips found hers.

So, this was what a kiss felt like. Carmack's thumb gently stroked her cheek while his strong fingers spread into the hair behind her ear. A controlled restraint gave way to urgency as his lips quickened against hers. Every fiber of her body was tuned to his subtle movements yet losing touch with the floor underneath her feet. Caught in this dizzying blend of contradictions, Tara sensed they'd skipped a step, but she didn't care.

She slid her hands up his chest, and he lowered his, his arms tightened around her waist. Their kiss deepened, until Tara's lungs ached to breathe. Finally, she turned her head sharply, breaking the kiss. Tara opened her eyes and gasped.

"Carmack, wait."

His embrace slackened, but he kept dabbing her cheek and ear with kisses. "Don't make me wait any longer." Carmack dropped to one knee. "Marry me, now."

"Now?" Tara shook her head, unable to trust her ears. The kiss had been a surprise, but for Carmack to propose marriage in Jaelport made no sense.

"Yes, now," he said, his chest rising. "Duty be damned."

Her body stiffened. These were not the words of the man she knew. Tara caught a trace of spice in the air, like a baker's tray had passed by. Soothing. Delicious. But not at all like Carmack. She shifted her stance, allowing the lantern to shine on his face. A smudge of silvery powder rimmed the edge of his nose.

No.

Carmack studied her with heavy-lidded eyes. "What's wrong, my love?"

"Show me the headache powder you used."

He turned to the bed and lifted a pouch from the basket.

Tara held up the lamp, its light revealing Jaira's love powder.

"Carmack, this is purple, not indigo! You opened the wrong pouch."

He frowned and studied the pouch, his eyelashes casting sharp shadows on his cheeks. "It was the only pouch. Isn't indigo your way of saying purple?"

Tara combed through her basket, through the sheets of parchment, the charcoal pencils, and pastels. Where was the other pouch? How could she have made such an awful mistake? Tara dropped to her knees and swept the floor under the bed with her hands until her fingers hit a swath of fabric. She pulled out the indigo pouch, still tied tight.

"Why?" she whimpered at the ceiling.

"It's fine, love." He pulled her from the floor and guided her to sit beside him. "My headache is gone. It doesn't matter what color the pouch was."

But it did. The wrong pouch made Carmack's sweet words meaningless, every one a product of poison. So was his kiss. She had been a fool to think she didn't want true love, and a bigger fool to think she'd found it.

Duty bound Carmack to her. He may have denied it on the dance floor to spare her embarrassment, but he had confirmed it to Jaira. Carmack loved duty and service. He loved his job. He did not love Tara.

There was only one remedy for this terrible mistake. Tara pulled the panzehir from underneath her neckline. "Drink this."

"May I have another kiss if I do?"

Carmack's sultry smile pulled at her heart. How long had she dreamed of this moment, for him to admire her like they belonged together? She wanted nothing more. But her dream was his living nightmare, and she needed to wake him from it.

Her eyes filled with tears. "Drink, please."

Without argument or even a wary look, Carmack cracked open

the vial and emptied the elixir into his throat. Immediately, his face twisted, and he turned, coughing.

Tara pressed her fingers against her trembling lips, still tingling from his kiss, waiting for the antiserum to shatter the illusion that trapped his mind. When Carmack faced her again, he backed away, confusion replacing the longing in his watery eyes.

Tara's heart ached, thumping like a hollow drum. The kiss had taunted her with what might have been, but it was all a lie. Though Carmack had no title, he was more chivalrous than most gentlemen—far too disciplined to seduce a lady into a forbidden kiss. And he wasn't the romantic fool Tara was.

Would she ever learn? No matter how recklessly she pursued love, like a mirage of land rippling beyond the waves, it remained fixed on a horizon that never drew nearer. Not to Tara. Arman's smile never stretched that far.

CHAPTER TWENTY
CARMACK

POISON! CARMACK'S TASTEBUDS STUNG, and his nose watered with vapors of fermented roses, as if he'd gargled an old woman's perfume. He stumbled over to his washbasin and spat, but the bitterness didn't fade. Something sharp jabbed his palm. He opened his fist to find Jaira's vial empty.

"Why did you give me the panzehir? I only had a headache." The skull-splitting pain was gone, but his brain felt like a sponge bobbing in a sudsy bucket.

"You opened the wrong pouch."

"What was in it?"

Tara winced. "Love dust."

The air left Carmack's lungs. He closed his eyes, trying to recall exactly what had happened. Tara had tripped and dropped her basket. The sweet smell. And then? His lips tingled, and a vision of her upturned face flashed through his mind. His mouth had been pressed against hers. Her smooth cheek in his hand. His fingers tangled in her silky curls.

Warmth erupted in his belly and sent a flush up his chest and into his ears. Carmack ran his hand down his face. "What in the depths were you doing with love dust?"

"When I told Jaira I didn't dare go sailing with Myck alone, she gave me that pouch. I assumed she meant it for self-defense, but the more I think about it, she likely hoped I would use it for other reasons. She has been pushing him on me at every opportunity."

"So, you poisoned me instead?"

Tara's cheeks darkened to crimson, likely burning as hot as Carmack's. "It was an accident. The headache powder fell out of my basket when I tripped, but I didn't realize you grabbed the wrong pouch until you . . ."

Until he'd kissed her. And she had kissed him back. His heart jumped at the memory of her upturned face, her parted lips. She had *wanted* his kiss. Arman, help him. Even in his right mind, the urge to kiss her again was powerfully strong. The images flashing through his foggy memory did not satisfy. Carmack wanted to taste and feel the proof of what seemed lost in a dream.

But the haunted look in Tara's eyes stopped him. Was her conscience shaming her for wanting to kiss a man beneath her station? Was it the guilt of wanting what was forbidden? She didn't even know the half of it.

"Well, none of that matters," Tara said plainly. "The panzehir worked, so we can forget the whole episode." The quiver in her chin suggested Tara wouldn't be forgetting their kiss anytime soon, but she was right.

They faced enough complications. Best to blame dark magic and leave the moment behind them. "Fine," he said. "What was it you wanted to show me?"

Tara handed him a sheet of parchment from his bed. "Below the palace, along the southern cliffs, there is a gate, taller than a galleon's mast." She pointed at the cliff on her drawing. "Look how it dips into the water."

Carmack studied her drawing, appreciating every detail from

the palace windows above to the ridges and ledges in the cliffs below. "This is good work, Tara. The *Brierstar* could slip through a gate like that, but what about what Leif said? That the ship sailed to Hamonah?"

"Aunt Nitsa confirmed it never sailed to Hamonah."

"When did you speak with the duchess?"

"When I was sailing with Myck."

Carmack's stomach sank. If Tara's aunt knew she'd spent the afternoon alone with a strange man, Lady Revada would soon hear about it and sack Carmack at the first opportunity.

Well, look at him, entertaining the possibility that he'd actually survive this mess. Facing Lady Revada was much preferable to spending the rest of his days bewitched in Jaira's underground menagerie.

"I need to confirm the *Brierstar* is there, but climbing down those cliffs at night is too dangerous. I'll go first thing tomorrow."

Tara sighed and set her drawing on the bed. "Even if the ship is there, we have no crew to sail her."

"Leif remembered being held underground, and I spotted ten large holes in the southern gardens. The workers were using them to store crops. An empty silo would match Leif's description. Once Dunn finds him a safe place to hide, he'll return to search them."

"Why would they keep prisoners in the garden instead of the dungeons?"

"I wondered the same thing. I think you're right about Jaira testing Mandzee, but Mandzee has no idea what her sister is up to. If Jaira has gone rogue, better to keep her prisoners in a remote area with only a few loyal eunuchs to guard them, rather than in Jabal Tower, where one soldier loyal to the crown could ruin her plans."

"If Master Dunn finds the crew, will he free them tonight?"

"We can't attempt it until we have more panzehir. Leif would not leave his prison until the antiserum cleared his mind. He was ready to kill me. I'm sure the others will be the same."

Tara's forehead wrinkled, and Carmack wished he could chase her worries away. "You found panzehir for Leif? Where?"

Carmack hadn't meant to let that slip. "A gift from Myck. I didn't mention it before, in case it was counterfeit. I didn't want you to rest your faith on it." Or Myck.

"Well, I'm glad it worked." Tara slumped down on the edge of the bed. "The boy at the apothecary shop told me they hang people for buying and selling it and warned me not all formulas work equally. I wonder how Myck . . . Wait. That's it!" She straightened her posture. "The boy also shared a rumor about a mage selling panzehir at the docks, and when we sailed out, I saw a Jaelportian woman on the *Ruby Tanniyn*. She might be the one. I should go find her."

"Absolutely not. If the mage is in league with Myck, we can't trust her, especially if she saw you with him."

"What choice do we have? We need more panzehir."

What choice *did* they have? Carmack stared at the oil lamp as if it could shed light on the problem. His gaze fell to the mangled root on the table. "I'll get more roots. Mandzee used them to clear my mind, so they might work for the others."

"And if not?"

When Carmack failed to answer, Tara went to the window. The moonlight pouring through the holes in the lattice highlighted her silhouette. Downcast, she wiped her eye.

He almost preferred his latest headache to the way her tears gnawed at his soul. "Don't lose hope, Tara. We'll find a way back to Meribah Corner."

Her lip quivered. "I have grown weary of hope, how it yanks at my emotions."

"We knew our mission would be difficult, but overall, Arman has blessed it."

"Has He? Sometimes, I feel He is mocking me. One minute

we're dancing, and the next, everything turns to dust. Nothing is as it seems."

From dancing to dust. Tara was talking about *them*, not their mission. Carmack remembered her resting in his arms, returning his kiss, and the troubled look in her eyes after his mind cleared. Had he misunderstood? Yes, she wanted the kiss, but did she want more, something he could never give her? Dunn had warned him of her affection, that hiding the truth would only bind her heart to a lost cause.

"Arman is not mocking you. Things are exactly as they seem."

Tara rolled her eyes. "This coming from a man who, only moments ago, told me I am all he has ever wanted."

No. Carmack could not let his fears sow her doubts, not in him or their God. He joined her at the window. "Jaelportian magic made me kiss you, but that doesn't mean I don't care for you. You are everything to me." When her face brightened, his stomach sank. He'd said too much. *Don't give her false hope.*

"Why have you never said so before?" Tara asked, her voice shaking.

"Because it changes nothing."

She grabbed his hand. "My dearest Carmack, it changes everything."

Her *dearest.* His heart clenched. He had to regain control of this conversation and his emotions before both got away from him. Tara needed to know why he could never act on those feelings. Neither of them could.

Carmack guided her to one of the chairs in the corner. "Please sit, and I'll explain."

"Very well." She sat, and he took a seat in the chair facing hers.

"Remember the Midwinter Banquet two years ago?"

She sniffed. "The night you joined the Fighting Fifteen without saying goodbye."

"I was under orders. After my brother saw us dancing together, he guessed I was smitten with you and promoted me to prevent me from seducing a highborn lady."

Tara reared back. "I did not realize . . . well, I'm glad he changed his mind and allowed you to return as my Shield."

"That was your mother's doing, not Roxburg's. He and I nearly came to blows when I told him I was resigning my post to take the position. I haven't spoken to him since."

"I'm sorry, Carmack. I suspected you and your brother had a falling out—you mention him so little—but I had no idea it was on my account."

"Please, don't blame yourself. Roxburg has always treated me like a child, incapable of making good decisions. He's second-guessed my every move since the night my father drowned."

Tara reached for his hand. "I'm sure he doesn't blame you for that tragedy."

"As I breathe, I can do nothing right in Roxburg's eyes. When I left the Fifteen to become your Shield, he was beside himself, convinced I would act like a lovesick fool. Turns out your mother was way ahead of him."

"How so?"

Carmack sucked in a deep breath. "As a condition of my employment, she required me to take a vow of celibacy before a priest. Should I pursue a love relationship with any woman, the Northlander Charter dictates that my lover and I will be banished from the duchies of Therion and Carm, forfeiting all property within them. Any trespass would be punishable by death, which would mean never visiting home, famil—"

"No, don't tell me." Tara sprang from her seat and paced. "I have heard enough."

He watched her walk, the way her curls fluttered, his chest so tight he couldn't breathe. "Now you understand why my feelings change nothing," he said. "They only add to your troubles."

Tara spun on her heel. "Your feelings do not trouble me. My

parents' betrayal does, as if selling me off into a hideous marriage wasn't bad enough. At least Father could justify that because he only delayed my future happiness until Lord Gershom's death, but how could my mother rationalize a vow that forfeits love forever? I can scarce believe she contrived something so cruel."

Carmack shook his head. "You know how she loves you. She hired me to protect you and wisely used my vow to safeguard your reputation."

"A lot of good it did, considering what happened before we left Meribah Corner." Tara plopped back down in her chair. "You are right though. Mother is wise, not heartless. There has to be a loophole, some way to release you from your promise."

As Carmack had feared, his vow had become an ill-timed distraction. "We have bigger problems to solve. Even Mandzee advised we leave Jaelport immediately, before we're trapped in whatever Jaira is scheming."

"We cannot leave, not without the ship and crew. So, you better tell me exactly where you were in Mandzee's garden."

"Why?"

"Because, while you explore the sea cave, I will collect more roots."

"But—"

"Master Carmack Demry…" Tara lifted her chin. "Do not make me pull rank and issue an order. If you insist on doing everything yourself, you will only delay our departure."

The playful challenge flashing in her eyes warmed his heart. Blast it, she was a force he loved to reckon with. He rose from his seat, crossed his arms, and peered down at her. "Why so high and mighty all of a sudden?"

Tara did not shrink back an inch. Instead, she stood to meet his stare. "Because I am in a hurry to return home. I have a complaint to raise with my mother." She squeezed his forearm. "Now, the queen's garden … I want every detail."

Praise Arman for Tara's attention to detail! Her drawing proved accurate. The turreted south tower stood at the lowest point along the cliffs.

Carmack peered over the precipice, still shadowed by the subtle light of early morning. He couldn't see the sea cave below, but according to the sketch, it was a short swim from the end of his rope. *If* it reached the water.

He'd picked up two ropes, each ten fathoms long, from the roper's shop in the trades quarter. After knotting them together, he secured one end around a sturdy horn of rock and unfurled the rest over the cliff. He rappelled down until his feet found purchase on a craggy rock a dozen feet above the water. He scanned the sea for submerged rocks, then jumped in an open space, plunging feet first into the waves.

The ocean crackled in his ears, its waters cooler than Meribah Corner's hot-spring-fed lake, but warmer than the Yâm Sea, making it a comfortable swim to the gate. From water level, its weathered slats seemed to stretch to the sky.

If guards were posted inside, they would see his silhouette as he climbed. Swimming beneath the gate was the best way to enter undetected. Carmack inhaled as much air as his lungs would hold, then dove. The gate stretched another three body-lengths below the surface. He kicked to its bottom edge, but when he tried swimming under it, a rush of water pushed him back from the gate. Though he kicked furiously, the current was too strong. He changed his angle and resurfaced near the cliff.

With one glance at the waves breaking below the high waterline, Carmack realized the tide was receding, worsening the current beneath the gate. Either he waited until the tide changed, or he would have to muscle his way through. Carmack took another series of breaths, then dove again, descending the boards like an upside-down ladder. He shifted his body into the current and pulled himself around to the opposite side of the gate. Straining against the pushing water, he climbed the boards upward out of the current, then kicked off the gate's slats toward the side of the cave.

The turquoise water was milky with silt, but Carmack spotted a thin dark line just ahead. He grabbed what turned out to be a rope, slimy with algae, and followed its diagonal path. Pilings rose like pillars around him. He surfaced in the shadowy waters by the rocky cave wall. Above his head, a dock blocked his view. As he turned to face the cave, his breath caught in his throat.

Hello, beautiful.

Not twenty feet away, the *Brierstar* sat high in the water. All four masts, five decks, and ten glorious sails of her. Like an eel under a coral head, the *Brierstar* faced the cave's opening, her stern and sides tied to the U-shaped dock. The ship's captors had pulled her in backward, presumably with the ropes mooring her to the pilings. It must have taken at least two dozen men, even with the help of an incoming tide. Carmack would have to reverse their work with far fewer hands, unless he and Dunn freed the crew first.

The ship's deep-brown hull glowed, surrounded by fire bowls perched on the dock's upper pilings. Not even in the sea cave could Carmack escape the stench of incense.

He slipped underwater and swam into the ship's shadow, then surfaced by the stern on the starboard side. At the dock's far end, near the ship's bow, a guard in a black uniform and green sash paced near a spool of rope tipped on its side. No, not a spool. A winch with a large crank running through the middle of it. The attached rope disappeared into the water where Carmack had first surfaced.

From somewhere on deck, a deep voice called out. "Stack those empty crates on the dock. And bring that last trunk!"

Carmack dove beneath the *Brierstar*, nearly colliding with a huge wooden roller running along a slanted rail. Not much farther, he came across another roller and rail. Together, the pieces created an underwater ramp. The ship rested on top, leaving a gap between it and the cave floor. Carmack swam through to the port side, over a geared shaft running parallel to the keel. He surfaced under the opposite dock near the gangway and spotted a large capstan in the middle of the rear platform. When turned, the capstan probably spun the geared shaft and rollers to launch boats from the cave.

Along with the two guards, two eunuchs stood on the U-shaped dock along the back of the cave, each guarding a huge winch with brake levers as tall as the men. The spooled ropes as thick as Carmack's forearm stretched from the winches and crossed three massive beams spanning the cave's ceiling. They wound through several pulleys before attaching to the top corners of the gate. Like a drawbridge, the largest Carmack had ever seen.

Suddenly, the monstrous contraption made sense. Cranking the rear winches would raise the wooden barrier, but to lower it, the brake levers would have to be disengaged first. Then turning the two forward winches would raise the stone counterweights along the side beams, forcing the gate to tip into the sea.

"I'll be glad to get out of this cave and see dawn again," one of the eunuchs said.

"Tomorrow can't come soon enough."

Tomorrow? Jaira must have discovered Leif was missing. Perhaps she was moving the ship because she suspected trouble.

Carmack swam deep, letting a gentler current carry him under the gate. As he bobbed to the surface outside the cave, he knew Tara was right. He couldn't do everything himself. It would take a crew to free the ship from the cave.

Thankfully, the *Brierstar* had one. Carmack just needed to find them and break whatever spell they were under.

CHAPTER TWENTY-ONE
TARA

TARA WASN'T SURE WHAT WAS WORSE, a screeching gowzal or a yappy dog named after one. As she tiptoed past Jaira's door, the little mutt started barking. Tara clutched her basket and ran around the nearest corner, hoping to reach Mandzee's chamber before Gowzal's racket woke Jaira. She intended to get Mandzee's permission to sketch in the queen's garden. Hardly her real objective, but an honest request to pillage the garden seemed unwise. There were limits to Hamartano hospitality, even Mandzee's.

Tara knocked quietly on the princess's door, and footsteps approached from within. She muttered a thankful prayer, but it died on her lips when the door cracked open.

Jaira glared through heavily painted eyelids. "Why are you pestering my sister?"

Tara cleared the tightness in her throat. "Good morning, Jaira. I don't mean to bother, but I have a small favor to ask Mandzee." Tara raised to her toes and peered over Jaira's head into the room at an empty bed.

"She is not available."

A mumbled shout came from inside the suite.

Jaira rolled her eyes. She stepped into the hallway, pushing Tara out of her way, and yanked the door shut behind her. "What do you want?"

"I wanted permission to sketch in the garden near the main staircase. I have been enchanted by its unique scent since I arrived and hoped to draw its flowers." The words rolled off her tongue just as she had practiced, and she grinned.

"I already told you. The queen's garden is not for guests."

Maybe Tara should have foregone permission and sought forgiveness as needed. Too late now. "But perhaps Mandzee—" More muffled noises from inside the suite penetrated the door. "Is she all right?"

"She is fighting with her stays. She'll manage." A yelp from within made Jaira shift. She grabbed Tara's arm and dragged her down the corridor. "On second thought, if you want to see the garden, now is a good time, while my sister is occupied."

Tara glanced back over her shoulder at the door to Mandzee's suite. She should have offered her assistance, but she couldn't risk frustrating Jaira when she was about to give Tara what she really wanted—access to the queen's garden.

At the top of the stairs, Jaira stopped. "We also need to discuss your brother, Leif."

Uh-oh. "What about him?"

"He's missing."

"Is that all?" Tara rolled her eyes. "Let me guess, he disappeared without warning. I had hoped he would have outgrown that habit by now. I can't tell you how many times he ran off as a boy, scaring my parents witless."

Jaira leaned closer, nearly pressing Tara against the wall. "Do you know where he might be?"

Tara's pulse spiked. She'd have to give the performance of her life to fool Jaira. They'd been friends for too long. "Off galivanting among Jaelport's taverns, I imagine." Tara huffed. "Not that I care.

Last night, he didn't even have the decency to offer condolences or an apology."

"For what?"

The words had slipped out—Tara shouldn't have said them publicly—but this was Jaira. "Neither of my brothers protested my father's arrangement with Lord Gershom. In fact, Leif did not even bother attending the wedding."

Jaira's brow furrowed. "Last night, you embraced him like you were happy to see him."

"Yes, well, isn't that what we ladies do when on display? My mother always says, 'Keep familial discord close to your bosom, for neither are to be exposed in public.'"

Jaira proceeded down the stairs. "On another topic, Captain Myck confided you practically threw yourself out of the boat to avoid him yesterday."

"That's a sorry version of events. I was overcome with seasickness."

Jaira paused on the next landing and faced Tara. "I should warn you, Myck won't tolerate being toyed with."

And Tara couldn't tolerate Myck. "If my brief illness somehow damaged the captain's opinion of me, then I can surmise his interest is merely one of idle infatuation."

Jaira shook her head, her mouth agape. "I can't tell if you're an incurable romantic, a complete imbecile, or both. Myck is not infatuated with you. He sees exactly what every other man sees—a beautiful, wealthy noblewoman who would make an advantageous wife. If your stray king stood in Myck's boots, he would see nothing more or less."

Tara's body went numb. What Jaira said was true. King Gidon had spent less time with her than Captain Myck, and his proposal had come after her marriage to Lord Gershom. That was how little he had known her. At the time, Tara had cried, wondering why, if Arman knew all things, He hadn't allowed Gidon to propose earlier, sparing Tara from Lord Gershom altogether? But after further reflection, Gidon's proposal had stung for another reason. He was practically a stranger. Despite his declaration, he could not have loved her, only the idea of her.

"For Zitheos' sake, don't stand there looking shocked about it," Jaira snapped. "Your marriage to Old Man Gershom should have cured your girlish fantasies. No man will ever see you as anything more than a trophy wife."

Tara bristled. No. That couldn't be true. "You're being cruel, Jaira. Not just to me, but to the opposite sex. Not all men are blinded by money and beauty."

"Really?" Jaira cocked her eyebrow. "Name one who isn't."

Carmack had confessed that her tenderhearted ways had won his heart, not her beauty. "Master Demry."

"Your mighty Shield? I forgot how droll you can be." Jaira staggered down the remaining steps and doubled over laughing until Tara stomped off the last step. "Oh dear, you weren't joking." Jaira patted Tara's cheek, her mocking pity ten times worse than her laughter. "Carmack Demry left you once. The only reason he's with you now is because it's his duty—one, I'm sure, your mother pays him handsomely to do."

The accusation lanced Tara's heart. Mother did pay Carmack's salary, and his job had brought Tara and him together, but her heart clung to his words.

You are everything to me.

Jaira was cruel to make her doubt him, if only for a moment. Why had Tara ever considered Jaira her friend? She needed to escape her, this gaudy palace, and smoky Jaelport forever.

"I know the way from here." Tara stepped past Jaira into the garden and followed Carmack's directions to the blooming shrubs. She sat on a bench underneath a nearby tree and began drawing one of its hand-sized red flowers.

Unfortunately, Jaira followed. Stones crunched under her shoes as she paced along the gravel path. "This humid air will make my hair frizz."

Good. The sooner Jaira got frustrated and left, the sooner Tara could collect the roots she needed. "You needn't stay."

"You can't be here alone."

If Jaira's patience wore thin, she might demand Tara leave the garden. Tara couldn't let it come to that. If Kressy returned from the docks empty-handed, the roots of those plants were their only hope of an antidote for Uncle Chantry and his men. "Perhaps you're right. Maybe I am holding on to unrealistic dreams. Do you think if I spoke with Myck, I could repair the damage I caused yesterday?"

Jaira wandered to a trellis and picked a white blossom. "Words are meaningless to men like Myck. You need to prove you're not toying with him."

"How?"

Jaira rolled her eyes. "Did marriage teach you nothing?"

Tara hadn't experienced normal marital relations, but she understood Jaira's meaning. "If Captain Myck expects that, I—"

"Spare me your virtuous outrage. Myck knows you're not a common harlot. A kiss would suffice."

Tara willed her face not to wrinkle with disgust. "Very well. I will kiss him."

Jaira's jaw slackened. "You will?"

"Yes." Tara straightened. "Unless I lose my courage before I next see him."

"Stay here." Jaira strode out of the garden.

Mercy. Was Jaira off to fetch Myck this very moment? Regardless, Tara planned to be long gone before he arrived. She immediately dropped to her knees in front of the purple-flowered bushes and scooped away the sandy soil with the spoon she had tucked in her basket. After a minute of digging, Tara hit one of the shallow roots, a piece as thick as her index finger. She pulled it, and a short chunk broke free, flinging dirt across the front of her dress. She grabbed a thicker piece, but the root was woody and would not break. Not even the spoon would chop through its tough skin.

This was taking too long.

Tara clawed at the soil, finally finding a cluster of four fingerlike roots. She snapped them free.

Crunch, crunch. Footsteps on the rocky path.

Had Jaira returned? Tara quickly threw the broken roots in her basket. She hid them under her drawing parchment, then pushed the sandy dirt back into the holes.

"Gardening, Lady Tara?" Myck's voice spread like oil in her ears. "I thought drawing was your preferred hobby."

How in creation had Jaira and her blasted eunuchs found the man so quickly? Tara stood, holding her basket behind her skirt. At least he was alone. "It is."

"Silly me, you must be searching for your lost earring."

Keeping her basket hidden with one hand, Tara touched her earlobes with the other. Both pearl drops were still in place, and they were the only pair she had on her when she had left Meribah Corner. "Why do you say that?"

Myck fixed his gaze on her hand.

Tara took in her nails packed with dirt. She swallowed and dropped her hand behind her back.

Myck's gaze returned to her face. "I ran into your maid on her way to the docks. She said you sent her to my boat to look for a missing earring."

Oh dear. That would have been a brilliant excuse had Tara agreed to it earlier. She forced a grin. "Ah, yes, that. I had quite forgotten about it."

"Really? I got the impression the pearl bauble was quite dear to you." He stepped closer. So close that he was able to tuck a loose clump of hair behind her ear. His fingers tapped her earring and his eyes glinted darkly. "Though I can't think why, when you are wearing another pair exactly like the one you supposedly lost."

Okay, maybe not so brilliant an excuse. Tara hadn't expected Myck to remember which earrings she'd worn during their outing. She kept her grin in place by clenching her teeth together. "I'm afraid you have caught me in an untruth, Captain."

"Explain quickly, Lady Tara." He took firm hold of her chin, the corner of his mouth jerking upward. "Few people dare lie to me. I have little patience for it."

Tara trembled as her mind tried to stitch together a plausible explanation. "You misunderstood. I lied to Kressy about the missing earring. She suffers with homesickness, and I craved solitude . . . a respite from her sniveling."

Myck brushed her cheek with his knuckles. "You sent your young maid to Jaelport's seedy docks on a fool's errand to buy yourself a bit of peace?"

"I did." *Arman, forgive me for lying about lying.* Layers of deceit and trickery, yet her cheeks weren't even burning. If Tara didn't get out of Jaelport soon, would she recognize the monster she was becoming?

"Bart's blood, aren't you full of surprises?" Myck snickered and reached around her waist. "What's in the basket?"

Tara gripped the handle tighter. "Only my drawing supplies."

His eyebrow arched. He yanked the basket, whipping Tara around full circle, but she held fast. He grabbed her drawing of the flower and held it in the sunlight. "Where's that portrait you were so busy with yesterday?" He started rifling through her parchments.

Impertinent cad. "Leave it be!" Tara jerked the basket back.

"Why?" Myck stepped closer, forcing Tara against a trellis. The sharp thorns of its climbing vine poked against her dress.

"Ow! Stop pushing me."

"What are you hiding?" he asked.

Her pulse sped. "Nothing." She tucked the basket farther behind her. She needed a better explanation. Quick.

"Hmm." His thumb wiped the sweat beading on her upper lip. "Then why are you trembling?"

"I left your portrait in my room."

"Jaira said you wanted to give me something. What could it be, if not your drawing?"

Oh, help. What plausible excuse could she offer? "She . . . Well, I thought I should make amends for yesterday."

Myck stared at her mouth, his nose nearly touching hers. Saints, Jaira must have told him to expect a kiss, but every fiber in Tara's body balked at the thought.

Myck's lips twitched, then suddenly his wet mouth covered hers. Tara stiffened and her stomach roiled. Gash, his breath stank. She lifted her free hand to Myck's chest, about to push him away, but Jaira's warning echoed fresh in her mind. *He will not tolerate being toyed with.* Tara couldn't run this time. They'd know she'd been lying and would want to know why.

Trapped by her own games, Tara closed her fist and channeled every ounce of revulsion into the soles of her feet, anchoring herself to keep from running. His lips pressed harder against hers, and tears pooled in her eyes. She'd be ruined. Her reputation couldn't survive this, not after she'd sailed alone with him. She couldn't think about that now. Lives were depending on her. But saints, how long would she have to endure this?

Perhaps, if she kissed him in return, both he and Jaira would be satisfied and leave her alone. Tara screwed her lips together and pushed against his, but instead of stopping, Myck buried his fingers in her hair and spread his slimy kisses down the side of her neck. Tara cringed, screaming inside.

Finally, Myck broke away and chuckled. "Jaira suggested you'd faint dead away if I acted the rogue, but you did exceedingly well for what I wager is your first tryst." He closed in on her again, his arm wrapped around her waist. "Not the smallest complaint from those ravaged lips." His finger traced her bottom lip. When Tara turned her cheek, Myck nuzzled her ear. "I think our princess has underestimated you."

Tara's pulse raced. He was toying with her. And she had allowed it.

She bolted past him, not caring what he might say or think, and heard him chuckling. Her feet couldn't carry her away fast enough. She wiped her mouth with her dirty hands. Better to taste dirt than that cad. Tara reached the main courtyard, dropped her basket next to the reflecting pool, and plunged her hands into the water. She scrubbed them clean and splashed her face and neck, rinsing off Myck's disgusting kisses and her tears.

What would she tell Carmack? Myck acted the brute, but she had practically dared Jaira to foist him upon her. Tara never should have said she'd kiss him, and she certainly shouldn't have stood there, too terrified to push him away. She sat by the pool's edge, her soul heavy as she watched the ripples she'd made fade and her reflection come into focus. She had believed that all the wrong things—her fears and lies—would keep her safe and bring success. Instead, they'd left her with shame, emptiness, regret. And farther from Arman than ever. Maybe it was time to start trusting Him and His ways again.

"M'lady!" Kressy rushed into the courtyard, stopping next to Tara. "What happened to your hair?"

"Nothing that some pins can't fix." Tara stood. Had Kressy found the mage at the docks? Tara glanced at the screened windows surrounding the courtyard. Anyone could be lurking behind them, listening. "I did not expect you back so soon."

"The dressmaker promised your new gown today, so I hurried. Shall we go now?"

Tara eyed Kressy, sure she had mentioned how much she

dreaded wearing the green mourning dress. Kressy must have had luck, something she couldn't discuss openly. "Absolutely."

Tara and Kressy left the central palace, then passed through the inner bailey's archway leading to the trades quarter, home to Tenma Palace's skilled laborers and their workshops. Garish rose stucco walls and russet roof tiles lined the cobbled street, creating an echo chamber for every pounding hammer, grinding saw, and chopping axe. Tara walked by weavers, carpenters, ropemakers, and chandlers. The blacksmith banged his mallet next to a rack of fearsome blades, sharp poles, and multipronged hooks, and the sharp clanking made her jump.

Kressy knocked on a weathered door and ushered Tara inside a cramped room. Bunches of drying flowers and greens dangled from the timber-beamed rafters. Slapdash shelves, brimming with dusty bottles and pottery jars, striped the walls. Between an interior doorway obscured by a beaded curtain and a small window, a woman with graying black hair stood at the sole table, grinding petals in a stone mortar. The pungent scent of fresh herbs and ground spices burned Tara's nose, reminding her of Isbelda's shop. Why had Jaira gone to the bazaar for her supplies when the palace had its own apothecary?

The woman lifted her darkly lined eyes, giving Tara a full view of the triangular symbol drawn on her forehead. It matched the ones Mandzee and Jaira painted on themselves the night of the banquet. Without a word, the mage disappeared behind the curtain of clacking wooden beads.

"She is not the mage I saw," Tara whispered.

"No, but her daughter is." Kressy jerked her chin. "Look."

A petite figure with long braids pushed through the curtain. Betzi. She wore a white sleeveless tunic, a dark blue skirt, and a fringed crimson sash tied around her waist. Kohl lines surrounded her brown eyes. Faded blue and yellow spots covered her arms, and a fresh bruise that no rouge could hide colored a swollen cheekbone.

Betzi's appearance *did* match the young woman Tara had seen onboard the *Ruby Tanniyn.* Her crimson sash resembled those worn by the members of Myck's crew and Carmack's attacker in Meneton. Like the scarf Betzi had covered with cheap earrings and waved in Tara's face.

Bitterness rose in Tara's throat. Betzi hadn't led Tara to an inn. She had led them straight into an ambush, one that ended with Tara on Myck's arm. Tara clutched Kressy's wrist. "We should go."

"But m'lady—"

"Now, Kressy." Tara turned for the door.

Like a cat trying to trap a mouse, Betzi slipped around the table and beat Tara to the exit. "I thought you trusted me."

Tara saw her clearly for the first time, not from a distance on a bobbing boat or through a fog of exhaustion. With her makeup, Betzi was not the stubborn child Tara remembered, but a young woman close to her own age. A skilled trickster using her girlish stature to reel in a gullible mark. "A mistake I won't make again." Tara reached around her and opened the door.

"Your plan will fail without my help."

Tara glared at Kressy. How much had she blathered to Betzi?

"You should listen to what she has to say, m'lady," Kressy said.

"Why should I believe anything you tell me?" Tara asked Betzi.

Betzi's dark eyes flashed. "Because Jaira Hamartano sold me to that fork-tongued monster, and I want revenge."

Betzi's mottled skin suddenly took on new meaning. Tara knew well the bitterness that came with losing one's freedom, but she did not for a moment believe her miserable marriage to Lord Gershom was in any way comparable to Betzi's torment, being owned by a blackguard like Captain Myck.

Arman, what should I do? A soft breeze cooled Tara's brow and tugged the door closed. "Very well. I will listen."

CHAPTER TWENTY-TWO
CARMACK

ONE LAST AFTERNOON IN THE CESSPIT of Jaelport. That night, Carmack and Tara would leave the city of mages—Arman willing, with the crew—or tomorrow, the *Brierstar* would sail on without them, stranding them there.

Carmack trudged uphill from Dunn and Leif's safe house in a back-alley livery stable to Tenma Palace's main gate, sweat sliding down his back and sticking his damp tunic to his body under the midday sun. Ahead of him, Dunn drove his rented mule, its cart, and cargo up to the gate. With the ship found and Dunn's promising lead on the crew's whereabouts, all they needed was to put the pieces together. Hopefully, Tara had scored more roots from Mandzee's garden.

Dunn brought his mule to a stop, climbed down off the cart, and extended his hand. "Ho there, Rok."

The guard shook it. "What's in the barrel, Dunn?"

No coincidence they were using names, a product of Dunn's campaign to win over the palace guards.

"Some refreshment for the fine men of Jabal Tower." Dunn went to the back of the cart, opened the barrel's spigot, and scooped a handful of ale into his mouth. "Ahh! Nothing like good brew on a hot day. Care to taste?"

"Commander Seetin would have my head, but save me some." The guard waved him through, then turned to Carmack and patted him down. The guard jerked his chin, allowing him to pass. Halfway across the crowded bailey, Carmack caught up with Dunn.

"Master Demry!" Kressy weaved through the people milling around. "Did you find it?" she asked in a low voice. When he nodded, she clasped her hands together. "Praise Arman! Lady Tara asked me to fetch you to the trades quarter. Master Dunn, you best come too."

Dunn glanced back at the barrel. "What do we do with the . . . er, ale?"

"What in the seas are you doing with that?" Kressy asked. When Dunn whispered in her ear, her eyes widened. "Well, you best bring it along then."

They followed Kressy through the trades quarter to a stone shed tucked behind two larger shops. She urged them to unload the barrel and move it inside. Carmack and Dunn lifted the barrel out of the cart and carried it into a storage room full of garden rakes, hoes, shovels, and scythes.

They set the barrel in front of Tara, who stood in the center, wringing her hands.

"The *Brierstar*?" she asked.

"She's there," Carmack said. Her bright smile quickened his pulse. "Did you get the roots?"

Tara's smile faded and her gaze flitted to the barrel. "I did."

He didn't like that look. "What happened?"

"Nothing of consequence." She pointed at the barrel. "What's that?"

Something had definitely happened. Changing the subject, like Lady Revada was known to do, would not work with Carmack.

"Then why are you hiding in this shed? If the head gardener finds you—"

"He already did." Tara tipped her head to the corner, where a slender man—presumably the gardener—lay sprawled out between burlap seed bags.

Dunn glanced sideways at Kressy. "Break another flowerpot?"

"Didn't have to. Betzi put him under until tomorrow, or so she says. Betzi?"

From behind a stack of bushel baskets, their young guide from Meneton emerged, wearing a fresh bruise on her cheek and a frock that aged her. Worse, her eyes were darkly lined with kohl, and on her forehead, a small black triangle had been drawn, its tip pointed down onto the peak of a larger one.

Carmack's stomach sank. A mage in their midst.

"I thought I caught a whiff of foul spice in the air," Dunn muttered.

Carmack moved Tara away from Betzi. "Why are you consorting with a mage?" Then the pieces clicked together. Meneton. Betzi. Myck. Tension formed a knot in his forehead, and he gripped fistfuls of his own hair. "You went to back to Myck's ship looking for antiserum, didn't you? After I specifically told you not to."

"I didn't. I sent Kressy, but that's not important. Jaira gave Betzi to Myck, part of some business arrangement between the two," Tara said, "so Betzi has a score to settle."

"She *gave* her . . ." Being a street urchin in Meneton was bad enough, but for Betzi to belong to that snake was more than Carmack could stomach. Yet how could anyone trust a mage, considering their penchant for double-crossing everyone, even each other?

Dunn pried open the barrel, and a gasp turned everyone's heads. Leif, drenched in ale, lifted his arms above the rim. "Help. My legs have gone numb."

"Leif!" Tara cried.

Carmack and Dunn pulled him out, along with three swords

and a small collection of knives, spoils of an arm-wrestling tournament Dunn had won against the guards.

"I can't believe you came for me, considering what a dolt I've been." Leif hugged Tara, lifting her off her feet. She squealed, and he put her down. "Sorry, I've gotten you all wet."

"Dolt is right." She brushed the brown ale stains on her light blue dress. "You missed my wedding."

"Believe it or not, that was the best gift I could give you. I was furious with Father for bartering you away to that daft old pervert. I didn't trust myself not to make a scene, but I should have written to tell you. I'm sorry."

"All is forgiven." Tara wiped her eyes with the back of her hand. "I am just happy you are yourself again . . . well, almost. You smell like a vat of brewer's yeast. And now I do too!"

Tara and Leif laughed, and Carmack's chest tightened. Would Roxburg greet him as warmly? In a matter of hours, Carmack would find out. He turned to Betzi. "If it's revenge you seek, why not just poison Myck? Isn't that what mages do?"

Betzi crossed her arms. "Not all mages are what you think, though I do dream of killing him. But if he falls ill or I disappear, his crew will tell Jaira, and she'll have my mother killed."

Tara wrapped an arm around Betzi's shoulders. "Betzi's mother is the palace apothecary and loyal to Princess Mandzee."

"She's preparing the antidote for the crew," Kressy said. "Have you found them, Master Dunn?"

"I scoured the gardens and checked every silo but two," Dunn said. "A pair of testy eunuchs wouldn't let me search the ones in the far southwest terrace, but I saw them lowering food and water into one of them."

"Eunuchs rarely leave the west wing and never go into the gardens unless escorting one of the royal family," Betzi said. "One of those silos is quite large and could easily house an entire crew."

"Aye, most of the silos were twenty to thirty feet deep," Dunn said. "We'll have to haul them out with the pulley systems they use, like drawing water from a well. Not all of them have ropes though."

"I noticed that from the tower, but it's not an issue," Carmack said. "I'll bring up the ropes from the cliff."

"Someone will have to go into the silo first to give the tea to the men," Betzi said. "They need two swallows each but won't be conscious enough to drink it by themselves."

"Tea?" Carmack asked. "Why not panzehir?"

"I sold the last of it yesterday," she said.

"Can't you make more?" Dunn asked.

"Panzehir is a royal serum. Only the Hamartanos know how."

Perhaps whatever Betzi had been selling at the docks wasn't panzehir. It could have been worthless snake oil for all Carmack knew, but that didn't seem likely. Not when the dose Myck had given him worked. "Then where did you get the stuff you sold?" he asked.

"Every time we left Jaelport, Myck would hand me a vial or two—I assume it was from Princess Jaira—and tell me to multiply it. I'd pour a few drops of actual panzehir into new vials, filling the difference with dyed water. Myck would keep half for himself and tell me to sell the rest. The vials fetched top price on the streets, because even a few drops of panzehir will work to break a spell, though its protective effects don't linger."

Leif slouched against the wall. "We're doomed."

Betzi crossed her arms. "But you don't need panzehir. From what Lady Tara told me, I suspect Princess Jaira gave your friends mad honey. To treat them with panzehir would be like using a catapult to knock down a gnat."

"What's mad honey?" Leif asked.

"It's made from despalea pollen," Betzi said. "It's commonly used by mages to subdue men. It's delicious but causes paralyzing intoxication, hallucination, and despair."

Carmack shivered at the way she rattled off the symptoms as if describing a common cold.

"Aye, that's the stuff," Leif said.

"The good news is Betzi's special tea will counteract the honey," Tara said, "and will be ready tonight."

"No good," Carmack said. "We need it at least two hours before slack tide."

Betzi's lined eyes formed slits. "It's not breakfast tea. The roots and petals have to be soaked at low heat. Too hot, and the temperature kills the healing properties. Remove it from the fire too soon, and you'll only give your friends a bad headache."

"That rules out freeing the crew first," Dunn said.

"Wouldn't it be better to wait until dark?" Tara asked.

"We need a receding tide to pull the ship from the cave. The next slack tide is an hour after sunset, and it's our only chance," Carmack said. "The men guarding the ship said it sails tomorrow."

"I overheard Myck telling Axe they'd be sailing in the morning," Betzi said, "but the *Ruby Tanniyn's* hull is empty. I figure he's planning to sail another ship."

Finally. Carmack and Betzi agreed on something, and the information she'd shared confirmed Carmack's hunches. Maybe he could trust a mage after all. "So, we have to steal the *Brierstar* first."

"Dear Arman, give this man wisdom and a plan," Dunn said.

"He already has," Carmack said. "Knowing there was a chance we'd have to go in without the crew, I've been thinking one over since I left the cave. Dunn, you and I will take the mule and cart out the garden gate. It's closer to the cliffs and will save us time. Leif, you'll hide in the back."

"I'm not going back in that barrel, Demry."

"No, that might pique the guards' interest. We need something they wouldn't be keen on investigating."

"A load of stable muck would do the trick," Dunn said.

Leif glowered at him. "Traitor."

"We enter the cave together." Carmack spotted a hand basket with Tara's drawing supplies atop an empty planter. He pointed and asked, "May I?" When she nodded, he took a piece of parchment and stick of charcoal and sketched the cave, the drawbridge-style gate, the ship's location, and the U-shaped dock. "We dive under the gate here." He drew a down arrow on the left side of the gate, then explained the current and the need to hold onto the slats to pull themselves into the cave.

"The ship is facing out to sea. Guards are posted near the counterweight winches. Here and here, next to the winch brake levers." He drew an *X* on each forward end of the dock and dots for the brakes. "Two eunuchs guard the back winches and the brakes." He drew an *E* in each back corner with circles as the winches and dots for the brakes. "Leif, you should head to the ladder nearest the gangway, amidships on the port side." He drew that too. "It'll be your job to get her ready to sail. Dunn, you will head to the starboard side and wait until I draw the eunuchs to the port side." He drew arrows from the *E*s to the back corner. "Be ready to release that rear brake and take out the forward guard."

"What about this other guard?" Leif pointed to the *X* on the port side. "Is he mine?"

"No, you just worry about getting onboard," Carmack said.

"I'm no scholar, but I count one versus three in your corner," Dunn said. "Someone's not sharing."

"The first one doesn't count," Carmack said. "I'll take him by surprise. As soon as the second eunuch comes after me, Dunn, you head to your brake lever and release it. Once the brakes are off, we run to the forward winches—"

"Yeah, yeah … I know how to lower a drawbridge. What next?"

"Cut the mooring lines and turn the capstan." Carmack drew a big *X* with a circle on it at the center of the rear dock. "It's connected to an underwater axle and rollers that should boost the ship out of the cave. Any questions?"

"Yeah, how do we get here?" Dunn pointed to the gate.

"We jump off the cliff and swim."

"No boat?" Dunn moaned. "Blast it, Demry, even when you plan, it sounds like you're wandering without a chart."

"I have to get back," Betzi said. "If I'm not on the ship before sunset, I'll catch another beating. One of you will need to collect the tea from my mother when it's ready." She slipped through the door.

"I'll fetch the tea," Kressy said. "You men need to free the ship."

"She's right," Tara said. "We all have to play our part. Kressy and I will get the tea to the crew."

"I don't want you in the gardens without me," Carmack said, especially when she hadn't told him what trouble she'd gotten into that morning.

"Might be a tad ambitious to liberate both crew and ship from two locations at the same time," Dunn said. "Even for you, Demry."

Carmack threw him a dirty look.

"And what shall I do while everyone else is doing their part and you do mine?" Tara asked.

"Do what you always do," Carmack said. "Go to dinner. Keep up appearances."

Tara's face slackened. "Because that's all I'm good for? To dress up, be polite, and simper for male company, no matter how vulgar they may be?"

Carmack would never suggest such a thing. "What gave you that idea?"

"You just did." Tara's voice turned brittle. "Along with everyone else I've ever known."

"Master Dunn, Master Livna, could you help me check on that mule?" Kressy opened the door and jerked her head toward the animal, still hitched to the cart.

Dunn lit up. "Oh, yeah. It's probably needing some, uh, something." He grabbed Leif's arm, hauled him outside after Kressy, and shut the door.

"Why are you so upset?" Carmack asked.

"Jaira said the most horrible things. That I had nothing to offer but wealth and beauty. She seemed irritated because Myck told her how I avoided him yesterday. So, I said I would kiss him to prove I wasn't toying with him." She paced. "I didn't mean it. I only said it so she would leave me alone."

The hair on Carmack's arms rose. "And?"

"Jaira fetched Myck to the garden, and"—Tara wrung her hands—"well . . . he kissed me."

Bitterness rose in his throat. How dare that slimy eel take advantage. Carmack flexed his hands, forming tight fists, and he reached for his sword among the pile of weapons. "So help me, I will run him through."

Tara's eyes widened. "You can't. It was my fault—"

"No, the man is a lecher." Carmack clenched his jaw. He had known better than to send her alone. He should have been there.

"He is, but we can't let him throw us off course. It was a kiss. That's all. I hated every second of it, but it's over. I'm fine." Tara rested her hand on his arm. "*Really.*"

Her light touch barely registered compared to the tightness around his heart. Carmack couldn't stomach the idea of Myck bruising her delicate lips with his. Nor could he bear knowing how easily things could have taken a darker turn. The rage kindled in his chest burned hotter. "I failed you."

"No, my dearest"—Tara lifted her hand and gently stroked his cheek—"I failed you. And it won't happen again." Her caress ignited a very different fire inside of him, one of powerful longing to hold her, protect her, and never let go. He cradled her face in his hand and brushed her velvety soft cheek with his thumb.

Outside, the mule brayed, and they both started.

With a bashful smile, Tara brushed at the wet smudges of ale

Leif had gotten on her dress. "What a mess I am. I best collect my new gown before dinner."

Carmack rubbed his face. "We have to come up with another plan. You can't go back to the palace without me."

"You will never know what I am capable of until you let me try," Tara said softly. "Please, Carmack, let me go. I want to show you I am not a helpless damsel. There's more to me."

His resolve unraveling, Carmack lifted her chin and, in a hoarse voice, said, "Lady Tara, you don't need to prove yourself to me. You're already more than I can handle."

Tara leaned against him, her sapphire eyes sparkling.

Carmack knew what she needed him to say. He might die of worry, but she needed to know he believed in her, that she was capable of facing any challenge, dangerous as it might be. He wiped away a tear, then let his fingers graze her jawline. "Go then, but cut dinner short. Be ready to meet Kressy as soon as she gets the tea, then both of you meet me at the silo. Once you find it, promise you'll wait for me."

She smiled. "Absolutely, but how will you get back into the palace?"

"Ideally, over the garden wall, but I'm short a grappling hook."

"The blacksmith had a rack of hooks at his shop," she said.

"Good to know. You're turning into quite the spy, Lady Tara."

Her smile faded, and she furrowed her brow. "What if you can't get back in time?"

Carmack wrapped his arms around her and rested his cheek against her silky hair. "I will always come back to you."

Poised on the cliffside, his toes suspended over the edge of a narrow shelf of rock, Carmack could hear his father scolding him like it was yesterday. *If your friends jumped off a cliff, would you jump*

too? Roxburg had smugly answered, "He'll be the first to jump." Roxburg had always been a know-it-all. Carmack would jump off a cliff to save someone he loved. Prayerfully, before the day ended, his brother would finally see that as a good thing.

Carmack jumped from the cliff and plunged into the water. He swam out of Leif and Dunn's way, surfacing in time to see Leif's splash.

Leif looked up at the cliff, then swam over to him. "What's Dunn doing? Saying his prayers?"

In the pastel light of dusk, Dunn looked like a giant *X* splayed against the rock. Seconds ticked past. He never had been an eager swimmer.

"Arman better be quick with an answer," Carmack said. The three of them had no hope of freeing the *Brierstar* without the pull of the tidal current, and because they had waited for sunset to lessen the chance of being seen, slack tide was quickly approaching.

Dunn crashed into the water with the subtlety of a breeching whale, then popped up, coughing and spluttering.

"If you can't manage to swim quieter than that, you should turn around now," Carmack said.

"I still think we could have done this part in a boat," Dunn muttered.

Carmack jerked his chin up at the shadow of Jabal Tower, black against the dusky sky. "And give all your new friends target practice? Stop second-guessing the plan, and remember to follow the side of the gate."

"I remember," Dunn said, "but I can't tread water all night."

"All right, let's go." Carmack cut through the water, Dunn and Leif swimming behind him. Once they reached the gate's edge, Carmack took a series of breaths to pack his lungs with air, then gave the signal. All three men dove in unison.

In the scant underwater light, Leif's blurry form descended the slats and disappeared under the gate first. Carmack stayed close to

Dunn. When they reached the bottom edge, Dunn bumped into him as the current pushed their bodies away from the gap. With a tight grip on one of the slats, Carmack reached out with his free hand, grabbed a fistful of tunic, and yanked his friend back to his side. Gurgling bubbles erupted between them. If Dunn didn't win his battle against the current quickly, he wouldn't make it to the dock without surfacing for air.

Carmack slipped past Dunn and pulled him under the gate. Once they were both through the gap, Carmack kicked against the gate and swam hard toward the dock, dragging Dunn along. The current eased, and a brownish glow from the fire bowls on the dock pilings lightened the silty water. Once Carmack reached the darker waters under the dock, he surfaced.

Dunn gasped, and Carmack clapped his hand over his friend's mouth.

Too late. The guard posted above them walked to the dock's edge. Carmack pushed Dunn back underwater, and they pressed their bodies against the side of the cave. A man's reflection rippled on the surface of the water for several seconds, then disappeared. Carmack allowed Dunn to surface but kept his hand over his mouth.

Hot breath blasted from Dunn's nostrils, and he tugged free. "I'll be quiet if you stop trying to drown me," he whispered.

Carmack swam with Dunn to the back of the cave where the dock abutted the limestone wall. Under the dock on the *Brierstar's* starboard side, Dunn waited by the rear winch and brake lever, while Carmack crossed to the counterparts on the port side. He spotted Leif treading water by the gangway amidships. Above Leif, a guard paced. Four foes total. Two guarding the front winches at the forward ends of the U-shaped dock, and two eunuchs near the rear winches, same as that morning.

Carmack swam deeper into the shadows until he was right beneath the eunuch standing portside on the dock's rear platform.

Peering up through the wooden slats, Carmack began to hum softly, needing the eunuch—and only the one eunuch—to meet him at the dock's edge.

"You say something?" the eunuch above him shouted.

"You've been down here too long." This from the one near Dunn. "You're hearing things."

Carmack hummed again. His target stepped forward.

That's it. Carmack freed the knife from his belt and kept humming, inching toward the dock's front edge. The sandals above followed. Carmack reached the ladder and crouched on a rung, ready to spring. When the eunuch leaned over the water, Carmack grabbed his skirt and yanked him off the dock, pulling him down and pushing him underwater. Bubbling sounds erupted as the eunuch twisted, pushed, and kicked for the surface. Carmack caught the man's belt and buried his knife in the eunuch's side. The man twitched and kicked, but quickly lost strength, making it easier for Carmack to haul him to the bottom. When no more bubbles left the eunuch's lungs, Carmack fastened the limp man's belt around a piling and surfaced in the dark shadows, facing the cave wall.

"Ivo?" A man standing above him hollered. "Ivo!"

Carmack gulped in a deep breath, then answered in a Jaelportian accent. "I'm here. I slipped." Not a great imitation, but with the water sloshing around him, it might be enough.

"Clumsy fool, get back to your post."

Carmack exhaled as footsteps overhead retreated to the far corner. One down. He tucked his knife in his belt, scaled the ladder, and ran to the brake lever. He tugged the brake, disengaging it, but the gate didn't so much as shudder.

"Intruder!" The forward guard shouted.

On the opposite side of the dock, Dunn emerged from the water, clambered up his ladder, and sprinted toward the brake lever. He threw his weight into it with a loud grunt.

The eunuch between them turned his head, clearly trying to decide who to attack.

Carmack's heart pounded in his ears as time seemed to slow. "Hurry!"

Dunn pushed and pulled at the lever, his face red with exertion, but it did not budge. The brake on Carmack's side had taken hardly any effort to move, but Dunn's was stuck fast.

"Stop them!" The eunuch hollered, turning toward Carmack.

Carmack unsheathed his sword and drew it to meet the guard sprinting toward him from the gangway. At the last second, Carmack dodged and pushed him aside. Instead of whirling around, the man threw himself against the brake, snapping it back into place.

"Got it!" Dunn shouted, but his success came too late.

The guard and eunuch turned toward Carmack, the latter chewing something. Whatever it was, Carmack preferred to suffer their raised swords and backed toward the gangway. Metal clashed across the cave.

The guard stepped closer, then shrieked and bent toward his foot. The bloody tip of a long sword poked through a gap in the planks, skewering the man's boot and anchoring him in place.

Well played, Leif.

Carmack lunged, jabbing his sword at the trailing eunuch, who scrambled backward. The guard pulled his foot off the blade and howled. He swung his sword in a wild arc. Carmack parried and forced its edge down into his cross guard. With his free hand, he shoved the wounded guard into the eunuch. Brownish spittle sprayed from the eunuch's mouth into the guard's face, and the guard slumped to the dock.

Maybe anabas wasn't all bad.

Carmack and the remaining eunuch circled the guard's fallen body, the tips of their blades only inches apart.

Dunn let out a guttural shout followed by a splash. With the

Brierstar blocking Carmack's line of sight, he couldn't see who had fallen off the other side of the dock. His stomach clenched. At best, Dunn swam like a rock. If he was injured, he would need help.

Time to end this. Carmack leaped over the fallen guard and delivered a series of cuts and jabs with his sword, each met by the eunuch's blade. Carmack worked him backward. A half cut enticed the eunuch's full parry, leaving his sword arm vulnerable. With a slight change in angle, Carmack's blade sliced the eunuch's exposed forearm. As the eunuch turned to shield his wound, Carmack freed his knife and buried it in the eunuch's side. His opponent crumpled in a heap.

"About time!" Dunn yelled, limping into view. "Killing one eunuch shouldn't take you that long."

At the sight of him, Carmack shuddered with relief. "What do you mean, 'one eunuch?' I took out two."

"The first one doesn't count. You caught him by surprise."

Carmack glanced down at a bloody gash in Dunn's pants. "You okay?"

"Caught a scratch. I'll live."

Leif climbed onto the dock and sheathed his sword. "Are we here to chitchat or sail?" He removed his sword belt and tossed it to Carmack. "Take this for Roxburg."

Right. Carmack strapped it on. Roxburg and the crew were up next, but first, he had to launch a tall ship with a crew of two. "Dunn, let's pull both levers at the same time."

"I have a better idea." Dunn jogged over to the winch and, with two thwacks, severed the rope that stretched to the ceiling. The frayed end flew upward, and the right corner of the gate jolted forward.

Carmack did the same. The top of the gate pitched forward, creaking and groaning. The cut ropes whipped across the ceiling and unwrapped from the pulleys as the massive wooden door splashed into the cove. Carmack and Dunn raced to the forward winches to secure the counterweights, while Leif sprinted across the gangway onto the ship. After securing the counterweights and cutting all the mooring lines tying the ship to the dock, the only thing left was to turn the capstan on the rear dock to spin the underwater rollers and launch the ship.

"Ready?" Carmack asked as he and Dunn stepped between the capstan's spokes.

Together, they heaved, muscles straining as they fought to set the cylinder in motion. Carmack pushed until every muscle in his body burned. The capstan didn't budge. A growl ripped through his throat.

Dunn stopped pushing. "Let go, Carmack. We can't do it on our own. It's not Arman's will."

Carmack fell to his knees. Why had Arman brought them this far only to have them fail? He couldn't accept it. *Arman, what more do You want from me? What else can I do?*

No answer. Just the sounds of water lapping under the dock.

"I give up," Carmack muttered. Dunn offered him a hand, and he stood, then slumped into the spoke behind him.

It slipped.

Dunn's eyes widened. "Should have guessed. Everything is backward in Jaelport."

Carmack turned, and Dunn followed suit. As both pushed the spokes the opposite direction, water churned under the ship. By the time Carmack and Dunn completed three rotations, the *Brierstar* was drifting straight for the opening.

Leif peered down from the railing of the stern deck. "Dunn, get up here. I can't sail this ship on my own!"

Dunn sprinted toward the gangway, hitching every other step and hissing in pain, but as the ship gained momentum, the gangway splashed into the water.

Carmack pointed at the small wakes in the water in front of

him, formed by the severed mooring lines still attached to the ship's stern and dragging behind it. "Catch a rope!"

Dunn swore and belly flopped into the water. He raised his fist, holding fast to a line, and hollered, "Meet you at the beach!"

Leif tossed a jack ladder over the quarterdeck railing, and Dunn grabbed on to the lowest rung. Leif waved back at Carmack. The *Brierstar* was underway. In moments, the ship would be visible to the entire Jaelportian guard. Meanwhile, Tara would be on her way to the southwest terrace. If Carmack didn't hurry, she would likely rush headlong into a silo of deluded sailors alone. He dove in and swam hard.

Time was slipping by too fast.

CHAPTER TWENTY-THREE
TARA

Faking a smile through a dinner of over-seasoned vegetables was much harder in the middle of a hostage rescue. Tara needed to finish her food and get down to the gardens. Kressy should have the tea ready by now. Slipping away would be easier if Tara and Myck were not Jaira's only guests seated at the low table in the Hamartanos' private dining room.

"You two are awfully quiet this evening." Jaira tapped her fingernails against her goblet while Gowzal licked her trencher. She glanced between Tara and Myck, who was sprawled out on three cushions next to Tara, chomping on a roasted onion, its vapors pricking her nose. "Is something amiss?"

Myck appeared subdued in all black, but he sneered at her, like he'd done after his disgusting kiss.

"Nothing at all," Tara said. "I was just wondering why Princess Mandzee has not joined us."

Jaira whipped her napkin over her plate, chasing away a fly. "My sister is resting." She tossed aside her napkin and slapped the tablecloth, crushing the insect with her hand. "Your guards have been suspiciously absent again. I wonder why you brought them when they are so rarely at your disposal."

Jaira's mood swings were fast becoming impossible to navigate. Tara needed to tread carefully. "I hardly need my guards to watch the three of us eat." Though her tight stomach suppressed any appetite, she took a bite of boiled squash. "I notice you have given Larkos a similar reprieve."

"You see, Your Highness?" Myck plunged his bread into the oil dish. "Lady Tara is not the timid damsel you imagine her to be."

"Where is Carmack?" Jaira asked. "Another headache?"

"No, he's on an errand," Tara said.

"Lady Tara desires more . . . what was the word you used earlier? Solitude?" Myck licked his oily fingers and squeezed Tara's knee.

She jerked it away, turning back to Jaira. "I sent my guards to find Leif." That much was true, a day earlier. "You seemed concerned about his disappearance this morning, and I thought Carmack, being well acquainted with Leif's antics, might track him down." Never mind that they were already together.

Jaira ran her finger around her goblet's rim. "Is your brother usually found sea bathing?"

"Not usually. Why?"

"Carmack was spotted swimming near the cliffs south of the palace."

Heat prickled Tara's neck, and she hoped the high lace collar of her new mourning dress hid any flush. "Swimming is Carmack's favorite pastime, not Leif's. He will not be denied the exercise when the opportunity presents itself, and these warm waters have been too tempting for him to ignore."

Jaira's eyes narrowed. "Is that so?"

What else could she say? Better not to say anything that would further pique Jaira's interest. Tara popped a potato in her mouth and chewed. A eunuch she didn't recognize entered the room. Gowzal barked and growled as he whispered in Jaira's ear. Her knuckles whitened around her goblet, and her gaze slid to Tara, who fought to coax the potato past the knot in her throat. It had to be news about the *Brierstar*. The eunuch offered his hand, and Jaira rose from her cushion. Myck sat up.

Keep up appearances. "Is something wrong?" Tara asked.

"Do not trouble yourself," Jaira replied. "I was reminded the evening has cooled, and the sky is exceptionally clear. Let us move outdoors to enjoy the views."

This was Tara's chance to make her escape. She covered a yawn. "As lovely as that sounds, I must retire."

"And miss this opportunity to end your day as it began?" Jaira tipped her head at Myck. Apparently, there were no secrets between the two. "You must come with us."

It felt as if the ground shifted under Tara's feet. Either she stood up to Jaira, or everything Tara had set into motion would fail. She pressed her heels into the floor tiles. "Forgive me, but no. I rose early this morning and am quite exhausted."

Jaira glared. "You dare say no to me?"

"You dare to order me about like your servant?" Tara glared back. "You may be my host, but you have no right to dictate my schedule." So much for keeping up appearances.

"You were right, Captain. Lady Tara is not the lady I remember." Jaira snapped her fingers at the eunuch. "Take Lady *Gershom* back to her chamber. See no one disturbs her for the rest of the night."

The eunuch bowed.

No, this wouldn't do. How would Tara sneak out to meet Kressy in the gardens with a eunuch posted at her door? "That's really not necessary."

"I insist." Jaira stomped out of the dining room, Gowzal on one arm and Myck on the other.

The eunuch gestured, and Tara left the dining room. A string of unladylike words flooded her thoughts as he followed her to her tiny chamber, then closed the door behind her, trapping her in darkness. When the lock clicked shut from the other side, Tara pulled on the door's lever. It would not give.

"You have no right to lock me in!"

No answer. No receding footsteps. She dropped to the floor and peered through the crack under the door at the eunuch's sandals. He was standing guard. She pounded on the door. "I need to use the privy."

Still, no answer.

Now what?

The floor creaked under her feet as she turned a circle and glanced up at the window. Lavender twilight seeped through its lattice several feet above her head. Even if she could reach it and break through its covering, there was no promise anything would stop her fall to the ground on the other side. Perhaps Kressy would come looking for her. Although feisty as she was, Tara's young maid was no match against a eunuch's sword.

That left the door to Jaira's room. Ordinarily, Tara wouldn't dream of trespassing in Jaira's private chambers. If caught, she would be thrown out of the palace, or worse, into the dungeons. It was a risk she would have to take. At least Jaira had taken her yappy dog with her.

Tara twisted the knob. It clicked. Aha, unlocked.

She cracked open the door and peered across the long room. At the far end, fringed drapes billowed in a soft breeze. An open window? Tara skittered across the room, through the curtains, and onto a small balcony. Even better.

The air from the west wing's private courtyard smelled heavily of cinnamon, and a carpet of petals formed a slippery cushion under her shoes. A thick canopy of leaves and blossoms kept her in its lacy blanket of shadows. Tara had not climbed a tree since her mother ended Tara's afternoon escapades with her brothers. Hopefully, her body remembered how.

She slung her legs over the railing and stepped onto the closest bough. It bent slightly under her weight, and she stretched for a higher branch to anchor her as she shuffled toward the tree's center. Once she reached the trunk, she climbed down until there were no more branches under her, then dropped to the ground.

When she hit, her teeth clacked together. She pitched forward and landed on her stomach in a patch of tall grass.

"Let us through!"

Tara froze.

Swords clashed. Men groaned. Then the patter of running boots filled the courtyard.

What in the depths was happening? Was the palace under attack? Tara gingerly divided the grasses in front of her and peeked at an officer of the palace guard.

"Post a man at each entrance," he said. "Bring every eunuch to the tower for questioning. Princess Jaira couldn't have gone far."

So the guards were searching for Jaira, not her. Little comfort that was. With guards swarming throughout the palace, Tara's task of slipping out of the west wing would be nearly impossible. If only she could bloodvoice with Aunt Nitsa. She would know what to do.

Then it struck Tara—she knew exactly what her aunt would do, and it would not include cowering in tall grass.

Tara stood and marched straight up to the nearest archway.

The guard there turned. "Excuse me, my lady, the palace is on lockdown. You must return to your guest chamber."

"I intend to as soon as I find my lady's maid." Tara kept walking, but when the guard quick stepped around her, she stopped and lifted her chin. "Young man, you are blocking my way."

"But—"

"Was that your captain I just spoke with in the royal family's private courtyard?" Tara asked, sounding more like her mother than ever before.

He glanced over his shoulder. "You spoke with Captain Rok?"

"Of course, I spoke with him." Her clipped words drove the man back a step. "Do you think he would let me stroll by without asking where I was going? Perhaps you would prefer to call him away from his search to explain that he gave me leave to fetch my maid? I'm sure he'll appreciate your tenacity for interrogating widows while leaving your assigned post unattended."

Twice, the flustered guard's gaze darted between her and his archway.

The third time, Tara huffed and marched past him. "I assure you I will be back before anyone misses me."

Tara continued, and the young guard did not follow. She reached the Fountain Court and headed for the opening to the gardens in its far corner. The guard posted there took a step forward, and she waved. "Pardon me. Captain Rok sent me to collect my maid. She has blonde hair and wears a pale gray dress. She went into the garden to collect herbs for tea. Perhaps you've seen her?"

"A blonde maid passed this way a half hour ago, madam."

"What a relief you've given me!" The guard blushed and stepped aside. Something in Tara's gut prompted her to ask another question burning in the back of her mind. "Do you know why the palace eunuchs are being sought for questioning?"

"Queen Torrezia has died, and Queen Mandzee cannot be found. Has your ladyship seen her?"

Mandzee was missing? "Not since this morning, though I only heard her from the hallway outside her chamber. Her voice was muffled, but Princess Jaira assured me she was getting dressed."

The guard's face turned stony. "Princess Jaira's eunuch is also unaccounted for."

Larkos. Jaira's lies about Mandzee were as bald-faced as her eunuch. No wonder the palace was in complete turmoil, but Tara could not help Mandzee. Not tonight. She had to focus on getting her uncle and his crew out of Jaelport before a war broke out between its princesses, their guards, and their eunuchs, including those Master Dunn had suspected were guarding the crew. Perhaps Tara could use the turmoil to her advantage.

"Hmm, I wonder if Larkos was one of the eunuchs I saw in the gardens earlier."

"In the gardens? Where?"

"The lowest southwest terrace, though I can't say it was him for sure. I'm afraid the eunuchs all look so similar from a distance."

Tara entered the garden, not waiting to see what the guard would do with the information. She found Kressy on her knees near the gate to the trades quarter. What in the world was she doing?

"Kressy!" Tara hissed. "I'm here."

"Praise Arman!" Kressy picked up a bronze teakettle by its bail handle and a black shaded lantern. "When you weren't here waiting, I dropped to my knees and haven't stopped praying for your safety since."

"Mother always said the faithful prayers of a righteous person avail much. Considering all that has happened in the last hour, I believe Arman has answered yours."

Kressy lifted the lantern, its metal shade closed to hide the candle burning inside. "I thought this might come in handy down in the silo."

"Clever girl." Tara took the lantern. "Come."

She and Kressy jogged downhill through the gardens and stopped at the line of cedars on the edge of the stone steppe bordering the southwest terrace. From her vantage point between a pair of columnar trees, Tara scanned the garden for Carmack. He should arrive any moment. She didn't see him, but she spotted two eunuchs standing between the holes that matched Master Dunn's description of the underground silos. Tara pointed. "The crew must be there."

"But what do we do about the eunuchs?" Kressy asked. "I can't toss this teakettle."

"Even if you could, we're short one kettle." Tara surveyed the garden behind her. "Let's wait and pray Arman hasn't tired of helping us."

Within seconds, several guards raced along the garden wall into the lowest terrace.

"Seize them," a guard shouted.

The eunuchs abandoned the silos and met the guards with swords raised. A skirmish broke out, blades clashing and men howling. When all fell quiet, the few prevailing guards dragged away the eunuchs in ropes and carried off their injured comrades.

The coast was clear. "You check the silo to the right," Tara whispered and sprinted to the left.

Kressy called out in a soft voice, "Not here."

Tara stepped carefully up a small incline that circled the other hole. She leaned in but could see nothing. She opened the lantern's shutter. The candlelight flickered. Below, pinpoints of light reflected in a host of unblinking eyes.

Tara shivered. Men. Dozens, dressed in sailors' garb, lying on the stone floor. They looked *dead*. But they couldn't be. Dead men didn't require armed guards. She checked her urge to scan the faces to find her uncle. Not yet. There wasn't time. Tara beckoned Kressy with her arm. "The tea."

Kressy handed her the kettle. "Remember, Betzi said the men will need two swallows each."

A firm hand clapped down on Tara's shoulder. She gasped and whirled around.

Carmack. Coils of rope with a grappling hook were draped over his broad shoulders. His black jerkin, pants, and two sword sheaths were dripping with sea water. "You were going to wait for me, remember?" He shrugged off the rope.

Tara's heart danced in her chest. Saints, he cut a strapping figure, and as always, he was there, exactly where and when she needed him. She beamed. "Right on time."

"How did you get rid of the eunuchs?" Carmack asked.

"The palace is in upheaval. Mandzee is missing, and the guards are rounding up the eunuchs."

"Not all of them. The ones in the cave were working together." He frowned. "I hope Mandzee is found safe. Of the Hamartanos, I like her best." Carmack reached for the teakettle.

Tara pulled it out of reach. "Let me."

"Absolutely not. Your brother wasn't the most cooperative when I forced the panzehir down his throat. What if the men turn on you?"

"And if they turn on you? Kressy and I could not lift you out as easily as you could me."

Carmack huffed. "Fine, but you'll be the first one I pull out."

"But—"

"Negotiation over." Carmack wound the rope with a large grappling hook through the pulley hanging from a timber frame above the silo's hole. "Grab the rope and step onto the hook."

Tara slipped her wrist through the teakettle's loop handle, gripped the rope, and placed her foot in the curve of the hook, her other hand outstretched. "Now, the lantern." Kressy passed Tara the lantern, and she adjusted her hold on the rope, hugging it tight to her body.

"You sure you can hold on like that?" Carmack asked.

Not really, but Tara broke out in goosebumps at the thought of descending into the black pit without a light. "The work will go faster if I can see what I am doing."

Carmack and Kressy lowered Tara into the hole. When her whole body was below ground, she opened the lantern shade. The silo was a large bubble carved out of the rough limestone, and men's bodies covered the concave floor below her. A weight settled into her stomach. So many mouths, so little time.

When the hook grazed the floor, she stepped off and released the rope. Next to her foot, a young cabin boy stared up at her unblinking. She kneeled, set down her lantern, and propped his listless head on her lap. Tara then poured tea into his mouth, stopping after his throat bobbed twice. She repeated the process with the next sailor, then worked her way to the sides of the silo, sending up silent prayers of gratitude when she found her uncle and Captain Demry, who looked a lot like his handsome brother but with a sprinkling of gray hair at his temples.

After the last man, Tara returned to the spot under the opening. "I've finished, but I don't think the tea is working."

Kressy's voice drifted down in a patter of echoes. "Betzi's mother said it might take a few minutes."

Carmack leaned over the silo. "Grab the rope. You can wait for the tea to take effect up here."

And if it didn't? Heaviness settled in Tara's chest. They would have to leave behind anyone who did not awaken. She wanted to tie the rope around them all and pull them to safety, but Jaira's minions would not give them all night to make the attempt. She closed her lantern. As she reached for the rope, something slammed into her back.

"Wicked mage, leave us alone!"

Chapter Twenty-Four
CARMACK

CARMACK NEVER SHOULD HAVE LOW-ered Tara into the silo. The tea had worked on someone—a cabin boy, by the sounds of it—but it revived him in a foul mood, just as Carmack had feared. He peered into the hole, unable to see anything without the lantern's glow. "Tara?"

Footsteps scuffled below.

"Ye—ow! Let go of me!" Tara said. "I am not a mage."

Carmack took a firm hold of the rope, ready to plunge into the silo, when a deep voice reverberated through the night air. "Easy, Peck. Are you all right, miss?"

Carmack froze, the hairs on his arms standing on end. Roxburg.

The scuffling stopped, and someone opened the lantern.

Tara raised the light. "Captain Demry, it is I, Lady Tara. I have come to rescue you."

"Lady Tara, it really is you!" Roxburg said.

Other voices chimed in, as one by one, the men awoke from their stupor.

"Cursed depths."

"Where am I?"

"Who stole my shoes?"

"Silence!" The silo quieted as a middle-aged man with grayish red hair and beard approached Tara. "Niece, how are you here?"

"Uncle Chantry, you and your crew are prisoners of Jaelport," Tara said. "They have intoxicated you with poisonous honey so you would not try to escape. Master Demry and I will pull you out, but we must hurry."

"Carmack?" Roxburg's voice cracked as their eyes met, and Roxburg shook his head. "It can't be." Like he didn't believe Carmack would come for him, but why should he? Carmack hadn't spoken to his brother in over a year.

The painful knot in Carmack's throat nearly choked him. "I'm here."

"Men, you heard the lady," Captain Chantry said. "Everyone up."

"Lady Tara first!" Carmack called.

She grabbed the rope and jiggled it. "Ready."

It took longer to go up than it did going down, but Carmack and Kressy finally pulled Tara out of the silo. Carmack lowered the rope, and Tara grabbed hold between Kressy and him.

"Captain Demry, you go next," Captain Chantry said below. "They'll need your help pulling the rest of us out."

Roxburg grabbed the rope, and Carmack hoisted up his brother, hand over hand, pulling the rope quicker despite the heavier load. Tara and Kressy did what they could to help, but Carmack did the brunt of the work, though his arm muscles burned with fatigue.

At last, his brother emerged. Roxburg's wide smile flashed in the moonlight, and he clasped Carmack's forearm with his familiar bone-crushing grip. "Mackie."

Carmack hadn't heard his pet name since he and Roxburg were boys. Blast, it was good to see him. Carmack smiled back. "Join us."

With enough hands to use the spare rope, they pulled out the remaining men two at a time. Carmack paused only twice to hug

Vexley Larr and Cerdic Ironblade, men he knew well from his days with the Fighting Fifteen.

Captain Chantry, the last to emerge, grasped Carmack's hand. "Master Demry, I am in your debt." He returned the lantern to Tara, who shaded the flame. "Now, where is my ship?"

"I'll lead you to her, sir, but first, Roxburg, take this." Carmack unstrapped the extra sword belt and handed it to his brother.

Roxburg donned the belt and Kressy grabbed the teakettle while others coiled the rope. Carmack led the group toward the garden gate. Inside the hollow box of stone, a lantern illuminated a narrow, keyhole-shaped gate—an oversized replica of other palace doors. This one, painted dark brown, resembled a slab of iron.

Carmack had found it on his first day in Tenma Palace when two men had stood guard. Now there were six. He motioned for his group to take a knee. "Roxburg, are you, Ironblade, and Larr fit to fight?"

"Fit enough to take on that lot. Besides, Arman is on our side, and we want to go home more than they wish to keep that gate closed."

"Captain Chantry," Carmack said, "we will do our best to distract the guards and reduce their number but have your crew ready to rush the gate. Tara, lead them to the beach past the royal cove."

"Please, take care," she said.

Captain Chantry's gaze darted between them. "Carmack is a Demry, better known for tackling danger head-on. Captain Demry, take a few of my men with you to help even the odds." Captain Chantry gestured at a group of six who joined Roxburg. "Lady Gershom, you best stay close to me."

Carmack flinched at Tara's title and married name. He'd forgotten to use both, and he'd also forgotten that the captain and his crew didn't know that Lord Gershom had died. Carmack cut an angle through the orchards to the gate's far side. He peeked through the branches covered in sweet-smelling blossoms. The three guards in front of the tower faced the orchard, and the three above faced outward.

Roxburg stepped next to him. "Simple mob and muster," he whispered.

"No stiffs," Carmack said. "If these men stand with Princess Mandzee, I don't want their blood on my hands."

Roxburg grunted. "That makes things more difficult."

And then some. So, why wasn't Roxburg taking charge and dictating his own plan, like usual? "Let's lure as many as we can away from the gate," Carmack said. "Maybe send a runner so they'll give chase. Trip them with the rope, grab their weapons, then charge the archers at the top of the gate."

Roxburg blew out his cheeks. "Okay, sounds good."

"That's it?" Carmack had expected Roxburg to list at least three reasons why his plan was rubbish. "No argument?"

"We've wasted enough of our lives arguing. If your plan doesn't work, we can always improvise."

A grin tugged at Carmack's mouth. The two of them, together again, doing what they did best.

Roxburg tapped Vexley Larr and Cerdic Ironblade, and they spread the rope across the petal-strewn path, ready to pull it taut. Carmack and the others hid among the fruit trees, and Roxburg whistled a merry tune. Two guards approached, their swords drawn. As Carmack stepped around the tree to get a better look, a twig snapped under his boot.

The guards stopped short of the orchard's edge.

"Who goes there?" one shouted.

When the other guard stepped forward, the first grabbed his gray sash, holding him back. He whistled shrilly and waved his arm. Three more silhouettes joined them.

Time to improvise. Carmack reverted to his training from his days in the Fighting Fifteen. He held up all five fingers on one hand. Roxburg stopped whistling and whispered to his closest man, who spread the word. They would be ready. Carmack waved his fist, and Roxburg's runner stepped onto the moonlit path between the tree rows.

"You there!" one guard shouted. "Stop!"

The runner sprinted away, and the guards gave chase. Larr and Ironblade pulled the rope off the ground, tripping the first three guards and sending them tumbling. Chantry's men leaped out from the trees. Fighting broke out. The two trailing guards stopped short of the trip line and pointed their weapons at the writhing heap. Roxburg sprang out from the trees and blocked one of their outstretched swords with his own. Carmack dashed behind and swung the pommel of his sword into the back of the other's head. When the guard stumbled forward, Larr pounced on top of him and stole his weapon.

Carmack turned just as the other guard's sword sliced toward his neck. He sprang out of the way, but a stinging cut bit through the collar of his jerkin, and he hissed. Too close. Way too close.

Roxburg lunged between them. Swords clashed again, but a woman's scream cut above the noise.

Carmack's heart jumped into his throat. He whipped his head in the direction it had come, back toward the gate. *Tara.*

"Go!" Roxburg shouted, but Carmack was already racing through the trees.

He emerged from the orchard, and the gate stood open. Captain Chantry's crew must have rushed the tower. Carmack caught a glimpse of blonde hair. The lone guard gripped Tara's arm, his sword keeping a handful of the crew at bay.

Tara stomped on the guard's foot and thrust her open palm into his nose. Good technique, but not enough power. The guard staggered but held fast to her wrist.

Carmack charged. His arms burned from the weight of his sword. He grunted as he lifted it, ready to run the guard through, but Kressy swung the teakettle, smacking the guard in the face. His jaw whipped sideways, and he collapsed.

Carmack skidded to a stop above the guard. "Well done, ladies."

The women exchanged shaky smiles. The guard at Carmack's feet writhed. Carmack gently pressed his sword tip to the guard's chest. "Stay."

Roxburg and his group arrived with five more stolen swords.

"What have you done with the guards?" Carmack asked.

"Gagged and tied them to the fruit trees," Roxburg said.

"Any rope left for one more?"

"Aye." Roxburg ordered three others to haul the last guard into the orchard.

The crew helped Captain Chantry to his feet, his forehead bloodied by a nasty gash, but true Livna stock, the captain steadied himself. Most of the tension in Carmack's shoulders melted away. Captain Chantry was alive. They all were, and their path to freedom awaited. "Hurry, everyone, through the gate."

"I must tend to my uncle first," Tara said. "Kressy, fetch the lantern. I dropped it near the wall, and we can use it to signal the boat."

Kressy untied her apron and handed it to Tara. "Take this," she said, then sprinted away.

Tara twisted the apron's skirt around its band, then tied it lengthwise around her uncle's head wound. Carmack ushered them and the rest of the crew through the gate. When everyone was through, Roxburg and Carmack wedged the doors closed with the crossbar to prevent anyone from tailing them to the beach.

Carmack stayed at the rear, watching the group's flank and listening as Tara led everyone past the royal beach. Frogs croaked in the surrounding trees, accompanied by the shrill-pitched buzzing and chirping of insects. Once everyone reached the next cove, they huddled into groups on its crescent of pale blue sand, thin like the moon above.

Carmack found Tara and Kressy with the lantern, its candle sputtering as the flame neared the wick's end. Tara's hair glistened, the tousled strands the only sign of her struggle. Her gaze was fixed upon Carmack's throat.

She reached toward him, and her fingers grazed his neck, lifting goosebumps with her soft touch. "You need a bandage too."

A powerful warmth spread through his chest. Saints above, Tara and moonlight were a heady mix. "Naught but a hangnail." He winked and she smiled. "Peck!" He waved over the cabin boy. "Take this lantern and stand at the water's edge to signal our boat. Master Dunn should not be far from shore."

The frogs fell silent, and Carmack glanced backward. The dark hillside blocked any view of Tenma Palace, but he spotted Roxburg not far away, an expectant look on his face.

"Go," Tara said. "Make peace with your brother."

His energy spent, Carmack struggled to think. What would he say after so long? Even if he found the perfect words, the most eloquent apology, would it be enough? This was as good a time as any. Like Roxburg had said, they'd wasted enough of their lives arguing. Carmack strode over to him. "I know we haven't spoken in a while, so I'm just going to come out and say this. I'm sorry I lost my temper. I hope you can forgive me for the awful things I said."

Roxburg gave him a bear hug. "I forgave you a long time ago, Brother. I knew you only said those things because you were hurting."

Carmack's chin quivered. "And can you ever forgive me for not saving Pa?"

"What . . ." Roxburg grasped his shoulders. "There is nothing to forgive."

"But it was my fault he drowned. You said—"

"What did I know? I was barely seventeen and grieving, both Pa and my carefree youth. I knew, with both our parents in Shamayim, you were my responsibility. Arman knows, I've failed you so many ways. Can you forgive me?"

"Yes." A tight knot formed in Carmack's throat. "Thank you, Brother, for all you've done for me. I know I haven't made it easy for you."

"True." Roxburg chuckled. "Why do you think I made Dunn train you?" He lifted his chin toward the sea. "Speaking of, that must be our ride."

The shadowy form of a longboat pulled over the breaking waves beyond the shallows. The crew rushed out to meet it, but Tara hung back with Carmack. "This is where those scratchy sailor's pants would come in handy." She fisted her skirt and lifted it out of the surf.

Though Carmack's arms still burned from hoisting the men out of the silo, he grabbed Tara's hand. "Wait. I'll carry you." He swept her up, and she wrapped her arm around his shoulder. He strode into the water, cradling her in his arms, suddenly amazed so much spirit and courage could be housed in such a dainty package. Everything in him longed to kiss her, and when their eyes met, he saw that same longing peering back at him.

"I'm relieved to be going home," she said, dashing his hopes. "But also reluctant. What will things be like when we return?"

"I'm sure your brother has sorted Meribah Corner since you left."

"I was not thinking of Meribah Corner. I was thinking of us."

Carmack's heart jumped so hard that Tara probably felt it through his tunic. *Us.* How had such a simple word become so hopelessly complicated? He reached the boat and lifted Tara inside, next to Kressy and Roxburg. Once she was settled, he climbed in and wedged himself between her and the hull. There wasn't an inch to spare in the overcrowded vessel.

As the crew grabbed the oars, Carmack turned to the man at the rudder. "Dun—Leif? Why aren't you with the ship?"

"Dunn's injured."

It wasn't like Dunn to surrender to an injury. "He said it was just a scratch."

Leif's gaze stayed on the horizon. "I'm the better sailor."

True. Dunn and the sea weren't the best combination, but Leif's curt tone didn't sit right with Carmack. As the splashing of the ocean pulsed in his ears, soreness seeped into his limbs and exhaustion into his bones. Even his tongue felt too heavy to form words. Leif likely felt the same.

Tara folded her hands, and Carmack gently squeezed them. If the moon were full, he could admire her sparkling eyes and flushed cheeks better, but the night dulled their color. Probably for the best, because when he glanced past her shoulder, he caught Roxburg watching them.

Carmack released Tara's hands. He'd heard Roxburg's speech before—how Carmack and Tara were dancing on a dangerous line. Roxburg knew about Carmack's vow, the one Carmack had considered a small price to pay to stay close to Tara. Now he felt the true cost. Tara was safe, Gershom was gone, and Carmack was *too* close to his heart's desire. Every fiber in his soul wanted to break his vow and claim her as his own. And though it seemed like she might want that too, he couldn't allow himself to dwell on impossibilities.

When the longboat pulled alongside the *Brierstar*, Leif said, "Captain, to save time, I suggest we board by ladder and tow the longboat until we clear Jaelportian waters."

"Agreed," Captain Chantry said. "All aboard. Prepare the ship's boat to tow."

Two crewmates secured the longboat to the ship. Leif clambered up the side ladder first. Chantry went next, followed by the others, until only Carmack and Tara remained. They peered upward at the darkened ship towering above them.

"We did it." Tara leaned against him, protecting his wet body from the night air. "We can go home."

Carmack cradled her face in his hands. "Tara, I . . ." Her strong, beautiful chin tilted upward, and with her jasmine scent filling his senses, his memory pieced together their first kiss. This time, his mind was clear. He ached to taste her lips again. Carmack pressed his forehead to hers. "This isn't proper. I'm your Shield."

Tara wrapped her arms around his waist, setting off alarms in his head. "You have always been more to me."

The words he'd always longed to hear ripped open his soul. All he ever wanted, and all he could not have. "I cannot return to Meribah Corner with you."

Her body stiffened. "Why not?"

"It would be impossible for both of us to stay apart."

"We won't have to forever, only until we find a way to dissolve your vow." Tara tucked her head under his chin and pressed her face to his chest. "Please, do not leave me again."

Carmack didn't want to ever leave her. That was the problem. Above them, an orange glow brightened the night. Someone must have lit the *Brierstar*'s lanterns. That seemed risky. Carmack expected to see some of the men staring down at them. Strange that no one was—not even Roxburg. "We'll talk more later. Hurry, before they wonder why we're taking so long."

Tara sighed and climbed up the boarding ladder.

Carmack waited until she was on deck, then stepped onto the ladder and let out the boat's tow line. He climbed up over the railing. "All on board."

The bleary-eyed crew was on their knees around the mainmast. A flickering fire bowl hung above them. He scanned the crew's faces, frozen and staring up at the stern deck. Stupefied. Had the tea worn off? By the capstan, Roxburg lay face down on the deck. Beyond him, Kressy lay on her side, a trickle of blood at her temple. Carmack started. What in the depths had happened? Where was Tara?

"Tara?" Carmack shouted.

"Stay where you are, or he'll run him through," Leif shouted from the stern deck where Larkos held the tip of his sword against Captain Chantry's belly.

How had Larkos gotten onboard? Carmack's gaze jumped around the ship. "Tara!"

"No need to shout," a man called from under the near ladder to the stern deck. "She's here." Myck emerged from the shadows, an ugly gleam in his eye. One hand covered Tara's mouth, and his other arm wound tightly around her ribcage. "Men, escort our guests below deck." His ugly first mate, Axe, was the first of Myck's crew to emerge from the main hatch.

Carmack's hand went to his sword.

Tara wrenched her face away from Myck. "Look out!" Her gaze darted above Carmack's head.

Above him, a lithe figure dangled from the ratlines like a spider on its web.

Jaira.

She blew a cloud of red powder from her mouth. The dust settled on his face, filling his nostrils, replacing the scents of brine and incense with that of burnt sugar. Not anabas. Not love dust. Some other concoction, but to what effect?

"Welcome aboard, Master Demry." Jaira cackled as she climbed higher into the ratlines.

Carmack was surrounded, lethally outnumbered, and about to be bewitched, like the others. Odd. He did not feel the powder's pull, but he was powerless to save Tara. He'd only die trying.

Like his friends, Carmack sank to his knees, surrendering to fight another day, and praying he'd get that chance.

CHAPTER TWENTY-FIVE
TARA

No!" Myck's hand muffled Tara's cry as Jaira's red dust settled on Carmack's face. He sagged to his knees. No! She bit Myck's fingers, and he jerked them away. "Carmack, get up!" she screamed.

But he didn't move. He didn't even glance her way.

Myck grabbed her again and hauled her across the deck. Tara swung her elbows, stomped on his feet, and pitched her head. Anything to break free and get to Carmack.

Myck chuckled and dragged her inside a small officer's cabin. "I do like this side of you," he said in her ear, then threw her to the floor.

Tara scrambled to her feet, but he quickly slipped out and locked her inside. With both fists, she pummeled the door. "Release me!"

All this was her fault. When Leif had helped Tara over the railing without a word, she should have known something was wrong, but by the time Tara realized he had been enchanted again, Myck had caught hold of her, his grimy hand over her mouth. If only she had fought back sooner—screamed, kicked—anything to give Carmack fair warning. Instead, she had just stood there, panicking.

Not anymore. She wailed and pounded until the door swung open.

Larkos shoved Kressy's limp body into Tara's arms. "Quiet! Or I'll feed your maid to the Eversea."

Tara crumpled under Kressy's weight. Tenacious Kressy had launched to Tara's defense, but Myck had struck her down and delivered another punch to keep her from getting up. She was still out cold. After several failed attempts to revive Kressy, Tara finally settled her maid in the bunk and lay next to her. Exhausted, she stared up at the small dark porthole and dissolved into tears.

CARMACK

Was Tara safe? Carmack had no way of knowing, chained with the others deep in the *Brierstar*'s belly. He was sure of one thing though—Jaira's magic had never taken effect. The others weren't as fortunate. In the pitch black surrounding him, men moaned and heaved. "Dunn? Roxburg?" Carmack asked. "You okay?"

"My head's pounding," Roxburg answered, "and my stomach feels inside out, but I'll live."

"Same." Dunn grunted. "Eben's breath, I can't say who I hate worse, mages or their eunuchs."

"What happened, Dunn?" Carmack asked. "How did they get on board?"

Leif answered. "Larkos was belowdecks. From the helm, I saw him knock out Dunn with his powder. Only muddled memories after that."

"I was the last one to board, and by then you were all out of your minds," Carmack said, then described the scene.

"So how is it you remember everything?" Roxburg asked.

Did he dare say it out loud? He whispered, "Lady Tara gave me a dose of an antiserum called panzehir the night before we freed you. I suspect it still lingers in my body."

"Strange," Leif said, "it didn't work that way for me."

"Your dose came from Myck. Betzi said she diluted his vials, remember?"

Heavy footsteps thudded above, and they all fell silent until the sound faded.

Roxburg whispered, "You were wise to play along. No antiserum will protect you from their swords."

"I just hope it lasts until landfall," Carmack muttered. Only the next blast of magic would tell.

TARA

Two days cooped up as a prisoner provided enough time to think, but Tara still had no answer for how to get out of this mess. She couldn't even get out of the miserable cabin that offered only a sea chest and narrow bunk to sit on, and not enough floor space to stretch out. Next to her, on the chest, sat Larkos's daily delivery of cider and crackers. Tara resumed concentrating on Aunt Nitsa, awaiting her voice inside her head. Several times, she'd fooled herself into believing she had heard it. Cruel, wishful thinking.

Outside the salt-encrusted porthole, thick clouds cloaked any hint of the *Brierstar*'s direction. The dreary light dimmed everything in the musty cabin, including the violet bruise surrounding Kressy's eye as she slept. Since Myck's blow, Kressy had roused several times during bouts of seasickness and complained of a headache, then dizziness. Tara worried Myck may have broken something inside the poor girl.

The ache in Tara's neck tightened, so she stood. As she stretched, Kressy squirmed in the bunk, her chapped lips pulling apart.

"Thirsty?" Tara asked.

Kressy nodded, but when Tara handed her the goblet of cider, she wrinkled her nose. "I'd rather sip sour goat's milk," she whispered.

"I don't blame you." The cider tasted bitter and a bit like rotten fruit, but Tara's thirst demanded a drink several times a day. "Unfortunately, I have nothing else to offer."

Kressy took one gulp and screwed up her face. "I swear, it's getting worse. Do you think it's poisoned?"

"I have suffered no ill effects, though it matters naught. We're still doomed."

"Don't give up, m'lady." Kressy winced and lay back down. "Someone has to keep fighting."

"I no longer know how," Tara muttered.

"That wicked mage could have left us in her dungeons to die. She wants something from you. When you find out what she wants, you'll know how to fight back."

Tara thought over Kressy's words until a key scraped in the lock. The door opened, and Larkos stepped inside, taking up what little space remained in the cabin. "Princess Jaira desires your company."

Tara glared into his kohl-lined eyes. "I do not desire hers."

"It was not a request." Larkos yanked Tara up by her arms, and she yelped.

Kressy sat up. "M'lady?"

"I'm fine, Kressy." The last thing Kressy needed was another blow to the head, and Larkos was sure to give her one if she got in his way. "Rest. I won't be long."

Larkos pushed Tara out the door and down the familiar passageway toward the great cabin. The sounds of laughter and clinking glasses grew louder with every step. He swung open the door to Uncle Chantry's spacious cabin, where the Livna family had often gathered during voyages around Er'Rets. The honey-colored paneling usually filled the cabin with golden light, but now the indigo curtains behind Chantry's desk blocked all but a sliver of daylight from the rear bay of windows. A smoky haze further dulled the halcyon glow of Tara's memories, and the acrid stench of Jaelportian incense made her nose water. Several empty wine bottles clinked together and skittered across the floor as the ship rolled over the waves.

Larkos pushed her to the mahogany dining table at the center of the room. Jaira sat at one end, a scroll and quill in hand, while Myck stood, reading over her shoulder. Jaira's gown sparkled with gold beading, its rich fabric matching Myck's coat. Both blood red. How fitting.

"Ah, Tara." Jaira bared her teeth. "We were just talking about you."

"Then I will leave you to your gossip." Tara spun on her heel, but Larkos stood with his arms crossed, a wall of bronzed muscle blocking her way.

"Did you hear that, Captain? The virtuous Lady Gershom is attempting to be catty."

"Charming." Myck collapsed in the chair to Jaira's right, grabbed an open bottle from the table, and put his booted feet in its place, one after the other. "Perhaps some of her uncle's excellent wine will set her more at ease." Myck lifted the bottle to his lips and gulped until it was dry. Wiping his chin with his sleeve, he dropped the empty bottle to the floor, where it joined the others. "Bart's blood, I'm afraid that was the last of it."

How had Tara ever attributed an ounce of grace to this uncouth wretch of a man?

Jaira motioned with her fingers. Larkos immediately pulled out the chair across from her and shoved it into the back of Tara's knees, forcing her to sit.

Of all the infernal, rude . . . "What do you want, Jaira?" Tara snapped.

"My, my, you are shrewish this morning." Jaira set down her quill, rose from her seat, and crossed to Uncle Chantry's desk.

She scattered his belongings, grabbed a large chart from beneath the pile, and carried it back to the table. "Can you guess where we are sailing?"

Taunting Tara with secrets had always been one of Jaira's favorite games. Did she honestly think Tara would play along anymore? When she didn't answer, Jaira flung the chart across the table, grabbed a knife, and buried its point in the heart of Er'Rets.

"Easy on the finishings, love," Myck said. "We don't want my new ship tattered on our first journey together."

"This ship belongs to my uncle, not you," Tara said.

"Quaint thought." Myck pulled a folded piece of parchment from his jacket and revealed Uncle Chantry's signature and seal. "But your uncle signed her over to me yesterday."

Lies. "Uncle Chantry would never surrender the *Brierstar*."

"Unless a certain beautiful princess suggested it." He and Jaira exchanged smirks. "Made quite the fool of himself, displaying his admiration for Princess Jaira."

"A small price to pay for violating Jaelport's imperial waters," Jaira said.

The thought of Jaira manipulating Uncle Chantry with her magic made Tara's stomach hurl. She returned her gaze to where the knife pierced Lake Arman. "We're sailing to Armonguard?" Home to King Gidon and Queen Averella. "That's the last place in Er'Rets you would be welcome."

"I intend to negotiate with the stray and his Council. Your uncle and his crew for an end to the blockade. Your so-called king has no right dictating Jaelport's affairs, and I mean to end his heavy-handed interference for good."

"You *mean* to steal your sister's crown, but it won't work. King Gidon will not hand over an entire city or abandon those he promised to liberate to spare one crew."

"I understand my opponent perfectly, which is why I so appreciate your support."

"You do not have it."

"Tsk, tsk . . . I thought we were friends. Your guards I suspected from the start, constantly skulking around my palace, but to the very end, I thought better of you . . . until you climbed out of that longboat and onto this ship. Clearly, you've been conspiring with them all along." Jaira stared Tara down. "Do you treat all your friends with such contempt?"

"Only those who capture, entrance, and imprison my family. I believe that evens the score."

"Hardly, but all will be reconciled once you convince the stray that my offer serves his best interests. By releasing Jaelport, he will avoid another costly war and liberate his wife's cousin, uncle, and the crew in one fell swoop. Well, all except Leif. He belongs to Zitheos."

Typical Jaira, always shifting the game pieces on the board. "Leif's pledge was not voluntary, as you well know."

"Nonetheless, a sacred rite cannot be undone by anyone other than Jaelport's queen."

"Then I will share my concerns with your sister."

Jaira slammed both hands on the table, and Tara jumped. "Mandzee will never be queen! Once I secure Jaelport's independence, my people will demand I take the throne."

Myck stood and approached Tara. He draped his arm across the back of her chair. "Allow me to share some advice. The only way to survive business with the Hamartanos is to side with the most ruthless one." Lowering his lips to her ear, he hissed, "Because unless you do exactly what Princess Jaira says, she will never gift your brother to us."

The hairs along Tara's neck lifted. What did he mean? Jaira was in the habit of receiving gifts, not giving them. "Gift? To *us*?"

"Leif's pardon will be your wedding gift." Jaira pushed a scroll of parchment across the table to Tara.

Tara reached for the scroll and unrolled it. She skimmed the first few lines of a marital contract, designating her as the bride. She released the scroll and clasped her hands together on her lap to keep from screaming. "You cannot bully me into marriage." Her gaze shifted to Myck. "I do not love you, nor will I. Ever."

"You're not my type either." Myck chuckled as he sauntered around to Jaira's chair. The oozing timbre of his voice made Tara's skin crawl. "Scoundrel that I am, the thought of marriage initially left me as frigid as your northern climate, but after seeing the untapped potential of Meribah Corner, I warmed to the idea." He and Jaira exchanged devious smiles.

Tara didn't believe him. Few people visited the remote corner of Er'Rets, and news of an ostentatious sea captain would have spread quickly among the locals. "When were you in Meribah Corner?"

"Around the time of your husband's death, on my way home from Ice Island."

Tara's stomach dropped. Her eyes fell on the document between them. Othvold Myvick. The name niggled at her, foreign with a touch of familiar. She *had* heard of him. He'd been the subject of Carmack's meeting in Meribah Corner the night Lord Gershom had died. "You're the fugitive slave trader."

"Yours truly." Captain Myck dipped his head in a mocking bow. "Princess Jaira was kind enough to help me out of those uncomfortable accommodations and give me a ride home, a favor I plan to pay forward once we are married."

Another dose of betrayal singed Tara's composure. What hadn't Jaira lied about? "You told me you were collecting your father's body."

"I was, but ship captains like Myck are scarce," Jaira said. "I needed someone skilled at transporting human cargo and running blockades. What a stroke of good fortune that my father should die the same week that I captured Tsaftown's flagship. His death provided the perfect excuse to visit Ice Island, though only Myck made the return trip. His charming company far surpassed that of Father's rotting bones."

"The pleasure was all mine." Myck caressed Jaira's shoulders, his eyes gleaming.

Saints, he was besotted with her. Why hadn't Tara noticed it before? And with a constant supply of Betzi's panzehir at his disposal, his infatuation was one of his own choosing.

Tara pushed the parchment back to Jaira. "I would prefer marrying the rotting skeleton."

Jaira rolled her eyes. "You did that when you married Gershom. Let's try something new, shall we?" She motioned across the room. "Larkos, bring him in."

Tara teetered on the edge of her seat as Larkos shoved Carmack into the cabin. His aloof expression never wavered, not even when Jaira approached him, dipping her fingers into a small purple pouch from her belt.

Tara sprang from her seat. "Leave him alone."

"I will consider it, once you cooperate." Jaira blew a puff of silvery powder into Carmack's face.

He rubbed his eyes. When they reopened, his lips lifted in an uneven grin.

"Anything you'd like to say?" Jaira asked him.

"I'll say whatever you wish."

If Carmack were himself, he would snap Jaira's arm in an instant. Instead, he stood captivated, allowing Jaira to whisper in his ear. The muscle in his cheek bunched like a fist, the same way it used to when Lord Gershom spat obscenities at him, but he dipped his head toward Jaira. Carmack lifted the mage's chin and kissed her squarely on the mouth.

The air rushed from Tara's lungs, pushed by an invisible dagger twisting in her heart. She'd seen the powder fly. She knew Carmack wasn't kissing Jaira willingly, but the sight twisted Tara's stomach. She turned away, unable to watch.

As strong as Carmack was, Jaira's magic was stronger. Aside from meeting Jaira's demands, Tara could not spare him. There had to be some other way. *When you find out what Jaira wants, you will know how to fight back.* Tara's gaze shifted to the contract on the table, and she picked it up, knowing what she had to do.

Arman, protect us.

CHAPTER TWENTY-SIX
CARMACK

THINK GINGERY SWEET BAKED GOODS. The familiar smell of love dust was far more appealing than the wine lacing Jaira's morning breath. It had taken everything in Carmack to act as bewitched as the rest of the crew, especially when he entered the cabin and saw Tara standing there, her face pale with shock. Jaira's blast of love powder gave him a warm, fuzzy feeling that made it easier to follow her disgusting order. Praise Arman, the panzehir still coursing through his blood quickly cleared his mind, but the clarity it brought was a two-edged sword. Every fiber in his body tensed, as if screaming he was kissing the wrong woman.

Carmack fought the urge to look at Tara, to reassure her in some way that this was only an act. He wanted to kiss *her*. He loved *her*. Instead of stroking her soft curls, his fingers were caught in Jaira's coarse braids, but if he drew back, the mage might get suspicious. The slightest glance in Tara's direction could give away their one advantage—the panzehir protecting him. A ripping sound coaxed his gaze to Tara's trembling hands as she flung pieces of parchment to the floor.

Jaira pushed away. The angry flush darkening her face made Carmack's cheek twitch.

"Stupid girl," Jaira spat, "Either you agree to my terms, or I will destroy everyone you tried to save."

"I don't believe you." Tara's icy tone would have made Lady Revada proud. "What other prize can you offer King Gidon for Jaelport?"

So, that was Jaira's scheme. A hostage swap for Jaelport. King Gidon was unlikely to cede control of the port city, especially considering his determination to end slavery throughout Er'Rets, but if Jaira were to negotiate a compromise, she might wrest the city's allegiance from her sister. How typically Hamartano.

"You underestimate me." Jaira snapped her fingers. "Larkos, take her outside."

No way could Carmack let Larkos manhandle Tara. He stepped between the two women, faced Jaira, and forced honeyed words from his tongue. "My beloved lady, please, allow me to remove this annoyance from your exquisite presence."

"Even better. Master Demry," she said, "you dispose of her."

Tara's eyes shimmered with tears as he took a firm hold of her elbow. He marched her quickly out of the room and past the other officers' cabins. If only he could get Tara out of earshot, he could reassure her, but Jaira, Myck, and Larkos were right on their heels.

On deck, the salty sea breeze snapped at Tsaftown's flag, which hung from the foremast. Despite the steady winds, a pall of smoke reeking of Jaelport clung to the deck.

Jaira marched past the mainmast. "You there!" she called out to a group of deckhands milling about. "Fetch the plank."

While the crew obeyed Jaira's bidding, Tara shook Carmack's arm. "Please, Carmack, don't listen to her. You are my Shield, not Jaira's, and I need your protection. She means to force me to marry Myck."

Before he could answer, Jaira spun around and snapped her fingers. "Master Demry, leave Lady Gershom and come here."

Carmack walked over to Jaira, Larkos, and Myck, fighting to keep his face flat. Their scheme had more teeth than he thought. Jaelport's independence made sense if Jaira believed herself a more capable queen than Mandzee, but why chain Tara to that sea rat? How would Jaira benefit from the arrangement? Whatever her reasons, the marriage would not happen, not while Carmack drew breath.

Jaira raised to her tiptoes and murmured in Carmack's ear. "Take Lady Tara onto the plank. Make her think you mean to push her off, but do not let her fall. Once she agrees to marry Myck, you may bring her back on deck."

Carmack bowed. "Of course, beautiful princess. I will not stop until you get what you deserve."

Jaira stepped back. Her eyebrows arched unevenly. "And what is that, exactly?"

Eben's breath. Carmack hadn't meant to say those words aloud, much less in that icy tone. If the ship were closer to land, he wouldn't explain. He'd toss Jaira to the fishes faster than she could bat those spiderlike eyelashes, then grab Tara and swim for shore.

Instead, Carmack forced himself to kiss Jaira's hand. "Whatever your heart desires."

Jaira cackled, her eyes flitting to the sailors sliding a plank through the rail. "Get on with it then."

Carmack returned to Tara. "Come with me."

She pulled away. "Please, don't do this."

When he grabbed her arm, her lacy sleeve slipped through his fingers. If he squeezed any harder, he might bruise her, so he swept her into his arms and carried her to the plank. Though Tara wriggled against him, Carmack cradled her tight until she panted with exhaustion. "You cannot fight this."

Tara stared up at him, her lips trembling. "You only think you love Jaira, but the Carmack Demry I love would not do this."

Love. She had said it so clearly his legs weakened. He stutter-stepped, fighting to keep his balance, waiting for the tightness in his chest to release his breath. Carmack softened his hold on Tara and forced himself forward, hoping Jaira hadn't noticed the effect Tara was having on him. "Trust me," he whispered as he lowered Tara onto the plank, which was not much wider than her shoes. Her sapphire eyes seemed to double in size as he stepped onto the plank with her and turned her to face the ocean. "Walk the plank," he said for Jaira's benefit.

Tara shuddered, then lifted her chin. She slid her feet along the plank, past the notch in the deck rail. She twisted around, her face white, and clutched his arms. In a hushed voice, she asked, "How can I trust you?"

Only one answer would convince her. The truth. Carmack looked deep into her eyes and lowered his voice. "Because I love you too."

Tara's lips parted. "You're not—"

"Bewitched? No." Carmack stayed close behind, steadying Tara's waist with every dip and rise of the ship. If the waves were stronger, staying balanced near the board's end would have proven difficult. As if accepting his unspoken challenge, the plank surged upward with a larger swell. Tara's knees buckled, and she screamed. Carmack lurched with her, and the ship dropped again. Pulled off-center by Tara's frantic movements, Carmack strained every muscle to check his balance and keep them both on the plank. Neither had the sea legs to survive this stunt much longer.

"That was a close call, Tara," Jaira shouted. "Have you come to your senses?"

Tara looked to Carmack.

"Call her bluff," he said, keeping his voice low.

She glanced warily back at their audience. "But they'll kill us."

"No, they won't. Jaira instructed me not to let you fall. She needs you to win over King Gidon. She's only using me to manipulate you."

"And the others?"

"She needs them alive, especially your brother and uncle as the queen's relatives. Without them, she'll have less to offer King Gidon." That made Carmack Jaira's most valuable pawn, the piece that could push Tara into position against her king. Carmack wouldn't allow it any more than he'd allow Myck and Tara to exchange wedding vows. "Promise me that no matter what, you will not marry Myck."

"I promise. I would rather die." Tara turned toward Jaira. "Do you hear me, Jaira? I would rather die than marry Myck."

Jaira screeched in frustration, unleashing a barrage of curses and slurs. "You will regret this, Tara. Get her back onboard."

"Told you," Carmack whispered in Tara's ear as he shuffled her back to the ship. As soon as Tara's feet touched the deck, Jaira grabbed her arm. "You selfish twit! Now your Shield will suffer because of your stubbornness."

Carmack stepped off the plank, and Jaira pulled something from the folds of her gown. A small jar. She opened it and flung a green jellylike substance at Carmack, spattering his face and arms. The stench of rotten eggs filled his nostrils, and his skin burned wherever the drops fell. Another potion. But how should he react? The tingling from Jaira's attack was already fading.

Jaira leered at him. "Why are there no blisters? What in the . . ." She scrambled up the ladder to the stern deck as if she'd seen a monster. "Seize him!"

Myck, his eyes bloodshot, wobbled closer, pulling a knife from his belt. "Bart's blood, I'm going to enjoy this."

Larkos followed, his sword drawn.

Carmack saw no way out of this other than to stay clear of the biting end of their blades long enough to think of something.

He sprang forward and blocked Myck's swinging arm, the impact sending shock waves into Carmack's shoulders. He pivoted and pinned Myck's forearm at his side. A sting lashed Carmack's back. He hissed and shoved Myck toward Larkos's bloodied sword tip. Larkos leaped out of the way as Myck took a sprawling dive onto the deck.

Warmth trickled down Carmack's back. He tapped the cut in his jerkin, and his fingers returned slick with blood. Only a flesh wound. He and Larkos circled each other.

"Leave Master Demry alone," Tara cried, then raced up the ladder to the higher deck. "Jaira, stop this. He's injured."

"Accept my terms, or Larkos will cut him to shreds," Jaira shouted from the front railing.

"I will plead your case before the king, but I cannot marry Myck."

"You'll do both, or Demry dies."

Carmack's heart sank. One shallow cut to his back, and already, Tara's resolve was cracking. He feared fate would play out this way. As Lady Tara's Shield, Carmack was her strength, but as her love, he was her weakness. At any moment, she might sacrifice herself to save him.

Unless he removed himself from Jaira's game.

Carmack leaped onto the plank. Larkos lunged after him, but Carmack skittered beyond his reach. When Larkos began pulling the plank back through the notch, Carmack timed his steps backward until his heels teetered over the end. He could go no farther. Trapped, with no moves left but one.

His eyes found Tara's. Those beautiful eyes, the same mesmerizing shade as the sea. *Arman, be her strength.* "Keep your promise."

Then, Carmack took one last step and fell into the deep.

CHAPTER TWENTY-SEVEN
TARA

N o!" Tara's scream ripped through her throat, and she flung herself against the *Brierstar*'s railing. *Arman, no.* Not Carmack. He wouldn't jump. He wouldn't tell her he loved her, then leave her alone.

Tara searched the ship's rippling wake. Where was he? Why could she not see him? He should have floated to the surface by now. Which bubbles in the waves were his? She must not be looking in the right place. She ran along the rail, her gaze skimming the water. Why was the ship still sailing on? Hadn't the crew seen?

"Man overboard!" Tara shouted and raced up to the stern deck, but no one moved. "Heave the anchor!" She spun around, shocked to see the men on the lower decks standing there, staring out to sea. Did they see him? She ran to the port rail and studied the ship's expanding wake.

Jaira walked up beside her. "I thought you said he was an avid swimmer." She scowled as though Tara had ruined one of her games.

Tara grabbed Jaira's arms and shook her. "Stop this madness! Carmack is drowning."

"That's your fault, not mine. Were it not for your selfishness, he'd still be in the cargo hold with the others."

Tara squeezed Jaira's arms harder. "I am begging you. Please—"

"Stop." Jaira jerked free. "You know I detest beggars. If Carmack is so important to you, agree to marry Myck, and we'll turn back."

"I . . . I . . ." Tara's memory flashed to her last glimpse of Carmack's mahogany eyes staring into her soul, pleading with her. *Keep your promise.* Tara shook her head. "I can't."

"Then you have chosen. You have until dawn to reconsider, or more of your loved ones will join your Shield at the bottom of the Eversea. Larkos!" Jaira flicked her hand.

Larkos climbed to the stern deck and escorted Tara to her cabin. Tara went willingly. What was left to fight for? The cabin door shut behind her with a loud clap.

A stabbing pain lanced her heart, and she dropped to her knees between the bunk and the sea chest. She clutched her sides, bracing against whatever was breaking inside her. *Why, Arman? Why bring us all this way together only to tear us apart again? You could have separated us a million ways. Why this?* Unable to hold her head up, she crumpled to the floor. The rough planks rubbed against her cheek as violent sobs rattled loose.

Kressy rose from the bunk and knelt next to Tara. A slice of warmth cut through the numbness as Kressy rubbed Tara's shoulder. "What have they done to you, m'lady?"

Tara could not answer. They had done nothing to her, but because she had so horribly underestimated Jaira, the man she loved was gone. Her chest burned and ribs ached, but how much more was Carmack suffering? His lungs filling with saltwater, gasping for a breath he'd never take. Her mind was trapped there, drowning with him, until her body wrung itself. Emptied of all energy, she could cry no more.

The ship's creaking brought her back to the cabin and to her maid, still sitting beside her. Tara lifted her head and sat up. "H-he's g-gone." The words scratched her raw throat. "Carmack is dead."

"I feared as much," Kressy said, sniffing. "Only a broken heart could make a woman cry so." She helped Tara off the floor. As they sat together on the side of the bunk, Kressy used her sleeve to wipe the tears from Tara's cheeks. "Poor man. Tormented by that cursed mage."

Oh, the cruel irony. "Jaira did not kill him, nor Myck or Larkos. They tried, but he jumped into the sea." The pain resurfaced, rippling through Tara, making her eyes well with fresh tears. "He must have known he couldn't win."

"Master Demry doesn't give up," Kressy said. "Did he give any clue to what he was thinking?"

"His last words were 'keep your promise.'"

"What promise?"

"I promised him that I wouldn't marry Myck."

"I see." Kressy's frown softened to almost a smile.

Tara went to the window and pressed her forehead to the cool glass. "I can't believe I thought we might have a future. I feel like he's abandoned me all over again."

"Don't be daft," Kressy muttered. "You've never been abandoned a day in your life."

Tara turned her head sharply. "Kressy!"

"Forgive me, m'lady." Kressy clutched her forehead with both hands. "With my head throbbing, I can't mince words. Master Demry danced you across many a hall in your youth. Nearly got discharged for them dances, had not his brother sent him with the Fighting Fifteen. And still he returned to be your Shield. He stood at your side while you married another. Remained faithful to you for over a year. Worked to keep you away from that old lunatic. If that isn't true love, I know not what is."

The words, put like that, felt like a locked trunk being opened for the first time. Why had Tara never thought of their story that way? Love had been beside her all along, but she hadn't recognized it. She'd tried to earn her family's love and that of society with obedience, compliance, service . . . perfection. But with Carmack, she had only ever been her imperfect self, and he loved her anyway.

"How many times did he risk his life just in the last month to keep you safe?" Kressy asked.

Shaking, Tara hung her head and whispered, "That's enough."

Whether Kressy didn't hear or was too agitated to listen, she continued, "Even in death, he's protecting you from that two-faced pirate. Abandoned? Psh. It's like saying Câan abandoned us when He sacrificed Himself to free us from death itself."

Everything clicked. Carmack gave his life to save her, to free her from Myck's trap. That's how much he loved her. As Câan had done—the same and yet even more.

Oh, Arman. Tara's knees weakened, and she sat on the sea chest. *Now I see.*

"M'lady!" Kressy clutched her arm. "Ugh, sorry. I shouldn't have scolded you, not when you're grieving. I wasn't thinking. Not sure I can with my brain sloshing around in my skull." She sniffed. "I ought to be sacked."

Tara rubbed her hand. "Calm yourself, Kressy. I won't sack you. You spoke from the heart, and you were right. I have been daft."

Kressy shook her head, wincing. "I had no right to say such things."

"But I am thankful you did." Tara nudged her friend. "Lie down. Your head needs to heal. And I need to pray."

Kressy gave her a quick hug, then returned to the bunk. Tara knelt, her hands folded on the trunk.

Arman, forgive me. I lost sight of You, too fixated on what I thought love should be, instead of who You are. I loved You with the same imperfect love others have shown me. Help me love as You do, as Carmack did, to sacrifice myself for others, not to win their love or approval, but because I have always had Yours. Help me trust Your plan without doubting Your goodness when things go differently than mine. Arman, I made a promise not to marry Myck. I want to keep that promise, but I don't see how I can and still love these captives as You have loved me. Câan, You have redeemed my life and forgiven my misdeeds. You freed me from a loveless marriage once. I believe You can do it again. Guide me, I pray.

Tara rose and went to the porthole. With her sleeve, she rubbed at the glass, cleaning away the salty film, while outside, a ray of sunshine pierced through the thick clouds.

CHAPTER TWENTY-EIGHT
CARMACK

PAPA. CARMACK WOULD SEE HIM AGAIN. The sea crackled in his ears, much softer than the brittle ice when it collapsed under his father's feet. *Papa, swim!* But this time, Carmack had splashed into the water. Saltwater stung across his back worse than the blade that had cut him. He exhaled slowly. Heaviness pressed in around him, pushing him farther into his watery grave.

It's no use, son.

Carmack's legs and arms twitched, wanting to swim, unwilling to accept the finality of what he'd done.

I can pull you out, Papa.

NO! Stay there. You're not strong enough.

Strength hadn't been enough.

Do you love me, Mackie?

I love you, Pa.

If you love me, promise me you won't come closer. Go. Get help. Pray. I love you, son.

Carmack had considered Tara's love her greatest weakness, until his heart remembered the power behind a promise bound by love.

Oh, Arman, help her keep her promise.

A spasm jerked his chest, his lungs burning for air.

Forgive me, Father. I failed. I couldn't save any of them—Pa, Roxburg, Tara. Only You can save us, so I surrender all to You in Câan's name.

Another spasm. This one from the outside. Something had knocked into him. Something big.

A rush of water rippled along his body, and Carmack opened his eyes. Nothing but inky blue water. Something clamped onto his foot, and his entire leg jerked upward. The rest of him was dragged behind, shooting through the water at tremendous speed. Was this what it felt like to pass through the Veil, from this world to the next?

Carmack left the sea. Weightless, he flew toward the sky, and warm air filled his lungs. He was still very much alive. Whatever had grabbed his foot suddenly released it. Carmack blinked the saltwater from his eyes, catching a glimpse of sky and three whip-like tails as he plummeted back into the water. He surfaced and panted, his breath the loudest sound as he treaded water in a rolling sea.

A *tanniyn!* A breaching sea serpent.

Carmack twisted in the water, searching the glossy surface for any change. When none came, he widened his gaze, seeking out the *Brierstar.* The ship seemed to shrink as the wind carried it over the waves, too far ahead to hear his cries. He'd be no more than a speck if anyone should look back.

An object nudged his back. Carmack turned and glimpsed a sleek, greenish-gray form studded with long spines glide past him.

Arman, why? Sinking into a peaceful slumber on the seabed was one thing. Being ripped apart by the jaws of a sea monster was another. The long, dark creature dipped underwater, then re-emerged, heading directly for Carmack, and there was absolutely nothing he could do to stop it.

Very well, Arman. If this is Your will, so be it.

A snakelike head with a fanged maw split the waters, but at the last second, it again brushed by Carmack.

Grab hold! a feminine voice shouted in his mind.

Carmack didn't have time to question it. He reached out and grabbed one of the spines on the tanniyn's neck, swung himself onto the creature, and used his legs to hold on. The tanniyn did not dive or writhe to shake him loose. Instead, it swam along the surface like an arrow through the waves. Carmack pushed his wet hair away from his eyes. Saved from drowning by an overgrown tadpole with too many teeth. Only Arman could orchestrate such a rescue.

Duchess of Carm.

"My lady," Carmack gasped, "it was you who spoke to me."

I am sorry I could not explain. I had to focus my energy on convincing the tanniyn not to taste you. He rather likes your smell.

Carmack shivered at the idea of those teeth in his flesh. "Much appreciated. Have you been watching this whole time?"

Unfortunately, no. The city of Jaelport is under an enchantment that keeps my magic out. Two days ago, the king received a report that the Brierstar *left Jaelport under Tsaftown's flag. We assumed your mission had been a success until I could not reach my niece. Nor could I find the* Brierstar *anywhere in the waters between Jaelport and Meribah Corner. This morning, another report reached us that a ship under Tsaftown's colors had been spotted near Er'Rets Point. I had been searching the seas from the Veil when I spotted the tanniyn. The creatures have been known to trail ships, so I followed it. Shortly thereafter, I spotted a ship clouded in a strange patch of fog. I suspected some enchantment was cloaking the* Brierstar, *much like the city of Jaelport. Those suspicions were confirmed when I saw you jump overboard.*

"You must think I am a coward for abandoning ship."

On the contrary, Master Demry. I beg you'll forgive me, but to make sense of your actions, I read your thoughts. You gave your life to ensure Tara lives free. That took immeasurable courage and self-lessness. Since she cannot, I thank you for your sacrifice.

Carmack swallowed. "It was the only thing left I could do."

I know. I see an alarming similarity between you and my niece, each carrying an enormous sense of responsibility for others. You both would do well to remember this world already has a Savior, and He alone sets the number of our days.

Yes, for too long Carmack had overestimated his ability to control fate. "Thick headed as I am, I think I know what you mean."

On the horizon ahead, the afternoon sun pierced through the clouds. The tanniyn was headed west. As the sea breeze dried Carmack's skin and hair, the shock of nearly drowning wore off. Had he done the right thing? Could he have done something—anything—else?

For apart from me, you can do nothing. Câan's words from the *Book of Arman* answered. Without Him, Carmack's efforts were futile. He could protect Tara in many ways, but Arman was his real strength. And hers.

Arman, forgive me for forgetting.

A dark line appeared on the horizon. Land—the duchy of Arman to be exact. The tanniyn didn't slow until ripples of beige sand appeared through the teal blue waters beneath it. Mere yards from shore, the tanniyn shimmied, as if to say the ride was over. Carmack slid down the monster's scales into the water and swam for shore. He looked back once, but the creature was gone. Just a little farther. He swam until his feet touched a sandy ocean floor. Then he stood, his legs weak, and trudged up out of the water. He collapsed on dry sand, his body shaking with exhaustion and hunger.

Rest here, Master Demry. The duchess's voice faded to a whisper. *Help is coming.*

⟵   ⟶

Carmack woke to a slow thumping sound. He lay on his stomach in the sand, and he lifted his head as two legs, wide like tree trunks and strapped in leather, approached him. Another thump brought with it a spray of sand. Carmack flinched, then as the feet stopped before him, he strained his neck to see the mountain of muscle that loomed over him. The huge man, draped in a Kingsguard cape, had a pair of thick black braids and a bushy beard that hid most of his face. While Carmack hadn't seen many giants in his life, there was no mistaking that this soldier was one.

"You must be Captain Demry's little brother," the giant said.

No one had called Carmack "little" since childhood, but the giant was a fair exception. "Yeah, that's me. I'm Carmack."

"Jax mi Katt, at your service. The Duchess of Carm sent me." Jax helped Carmack up. Even when Carmack stood, the giant's dark eyes were still several hands above his own. Jax opened the leather satchel hanging across his body, pulled out a bundle of waxy brown cloth tied with string, and handed it to Carmack. "Here. She mentioned you were hungry."

Carmack untied the bundle and inhaled the smell of fresh bread. He tore off a chunk and shoved it into his watering mouth, his stomach grumbling with impatient gratitude. "Did she also mention I need to catch a ship?"

"Aye, the *Brierstar*."

"It's bound for Armonguard. Jaira Hamartano plans on addressing the king and his Council."

Jax's eyebrows shot upward. "That's audacious, even for a Hamartano."

"Audacious only scratches at the surface. She plans to negotiate a hostage swap—Lady Tara and the *Brierstar*'s crew in exchange for Jaelport."

Jax grunted. "With these winds, they'll reach the Port of Arman tonight. My guess is they'll anchor there until morning, then hire horses to reach Armonguard before the Council adjourns. Have to be honest with you, I don't see how you can catch them. We're over twenty leagues from Armonguard."

Carmack couldn't cover that much ground in a day, not without a series of fresh horses. Maybe it was never Arman's plan for Carmack to go to Armonguard. Maybe he could stop Jaira before she got there. "What about the Port of Arman?"

"Eighteen leagues, maybe less by water, but there's no good road along the coast."

So much for that idea. "We'd need another tanniyn," Carmack muttered.

Jax cocked his head. "Another?"

Carmack motioned to the sea as he chewed. "The duchess used one to haul me ashore."

"Did she now?" Jax scratched his beard for a moment, then grinned and strode off toward the water.

"Where are you going?"

The giant held out his arms. "Ask and you shall receive. Let's just hope it didn't wander off."

Carmack scarfed down the rest of his bread, then joined Jax at the water's edge. The giant was kneeling on the hard sand, his eyes closed but fluttering. Carmack cleared his throat.

"Shh, I'm reporting our plan to the duchess."

"We have a plan?"

Jax opened his eyes. "Her grace sends her blessing." He rose to his feet. "And of course, we have a plan. It was your idea. He's coming."

"Who's coming?"

"There!" Jax pointed as a tanniyn breached the waves and splashed into the shallows. "Praise Arman! I may not be as gifted at bloodvoicing as Duchess Amal, but I do have a way with tanniyns."

Chapter Twenty-Nine

Tara

Another morning, another nightmare. That would be the pattern of Tara's life if she signed that marital contract. She sat up in the narrow bunk, her young maid still asleep beside her. This could be Kressy's last morning. If Tara did not sign, Jaira would have her innocent maid thrown into the sea. Tara remembered her promise to Carmack. His death left a hole in her heart, but better to break her promise than make that hole bigger.

The cabin door flew open. Tara startled. *No, not yet!* Tara still hadn't figured her next steps. Axe lunged in and dragged Kressy from the bunk. She shrieked as he muscled her into the corridor.

"Be gentle with her." Tara charged through the door after him. Larkos grabbed her by the arms. "Unhand me!"

Larkos pushed her down the corridor, out to the *Brierstar*'s main deck. The sails were folded and tied to the masts, affording a full view of the familiar pastel buildings lining the Port of Arman's shorefront.

Though the sun had yet to rise on the eastern horizon, the captives all stood at attention, the haze of incense smoke polluting the air around them. Leif, Uncle Chantry, and Master Dunn stood near the mainmast. A long chain shackled their ankles together. The cut on Uncle Chantry's forehead had scabbed over, and Master Dunn's pant leg was crusty with dried blood. Myck's crew formed a circle around them.

Axe tied Kressy's wrists and placed her next to Master Dunn, who whispered something that Tara could not hear as Larkos pushed her up the ladder to the stern deck.

At its front railing, Jaira held a scroll next to a table set with quill and ink, as if setting a stage for the audience of prisoners below. She even had the perfect costume—a dark green gown that made Tara hate her mourning dress even more. They would arrive at Armonguard matching in Jaelport's colors.

"Together again," Jaira said. "Do not keep us in suspense, Lady Tara. Have we gathered to congratulate your upcoming nuptials or for a mass burial at sea?"

Myck sauntered over, his boots thudding across the deck. He still wore black without a stitch of gold. A cunning choice for a fugitive seeking to blend in. "If it makes your decision easier, know that I don't want a traditional marriage. After our wedding night, I fully intend to move you to a small cottage, as far from Meribah Corner's keep as possible."

Tara bristled. How dare he think he could evict her from her own castle? She gave him a brittle smile. "A most generous gift to be spared from your presence."

Myck raised his hand as if to strike her. When she flinched, he laughed and lowered his arm. "Careful. Your temperamental brute is no longer here to protect you."

"Time is up!" Jaira slapped the table with a scroll of parchment. "We've drafted a new marital agreement, giving your groom full and immediate control of Meribah Corner. Will you sign or not?"

"No!" Leif lunged forward, tripping on his shackles.

"Don't sign, Lady Tara," Dunn said.

The circle of pirates, some with swords drawn, tightened around the captives. Tara held up her hand. "I have no choice."

Jaira grinned smugly. "I'm glad to see you've finally come to your senses."

Tara swallowed the bitterness rising in her throat, grabbed the quill, and dipped it in the inkpot on the table. She held the wet, black tip over the scroll and froze. Something inside whispered, *Too soon.*

"What's the matter?" Jaira snapped. "Sign it."

"Uncle Chantry," Tara said, "isn't there a law against contracts made under threat of violence?"

He lifted a quizzical brow. "You mean duress."

"That's the word." Tara raised her chin. "My aunt will undoubtedly ask if I signed this willingly." Tara tipped her head. "With her and the Council's bloodvoice mediators measuring the truth of my every word, a lie will fool no one."

"Who cares?" Jaira said. "You will have already signed away your property."

Myck shifted. "What Lady Tara is saying is that if she signs the contract now, the Council will not enforce it because it was executed under duress, which makes me wonder ... why warn us?" He loomed over Tara. "Why not simply sign now and challenge it later?"

Jaira stomped her foot. "What difference does it make when or where she signs?"

"Because when I sign, it must be my choice," Tara said. "The contract will not stand unless I enter it willingly, not because I am afraid of your childish temper tantrums or heartless games. And I am tired of lying. I will sign in Armonguard with your promise before the bloodvoice mediators that the captives will be released."

Tara laid down the quill. *That was for you, Carmack.*

Jaira's face reddened. "Launch the boat to shore! And get those prisoners belowdecks. If we're not back by sunset, kill them all."

Tara would do everything to make sure it didn't come to that. Arman willing, King Gidon would reach a compromise with Jaira to spare their lives.

While the crew readied the longboat, the first rays of sunshine splashed across sky and sea. Tara took a steadying breath. Her promise would stand for a few more hours. After that? Only Arman knew.

CHAPTER THIRTY
CARMACK

RMAN, KEEP TARA SAFE. HELP ME MAKE it on time, but if that's not Your will, then show me what is.

At dawn, Carmack caught his first glimpse of the Port of Arman, a small village of weathered huts overlooking a tranquil bay. The tanniyn had covered eighteen leagues in one night, and Carmack's aching back felt every one of them. The *Brierstar* was anchored offshore. Carmack glanced back at Jax and pointed. "There she is."

Sneaking up to her was going to be the hard part. A giant riding a sea monster was likely to draw plenty of attention. Maybe Carmack could use that to his advantage.

"Jax, can you guide the tanniyn to the *Brierstar*'s starboard side? Once we're close enough, I'll swim to the opposite side. I'll need you and the tanniyn to distract the crew long enough for me to crawl aboard and free Chantry and his men."

"And if we can't hold their attention?"

Improvising wouldn't be enough this time. Carmack had no hope of dispatching the enemies on his own, but he wasn't alone.

Arman was with him. "I have hope it won't be an issue, but can I count on your help onboard if needed?"

"Of course."

Carmack clapped the giant's broad shoulder. Once the tanniyn slowed, he slipped down the creature's side and caught hold of a shield-sized scale, only his head out of the water. Underneath him, the beast's long tentacles, covered with suckers, undulated through the water.

Shouts rang out from the *Brierstar*. They'd been spotted.

Carmack measured the remaining distance and the tanniyn's speed. At the right moment, he filled his lungs and slipped farther down the tanniyn's leg. He stuck his boot between two of the platter-sized suckers and held fast as he whipped through the water.

When the tentacle stretched out, Carmack let go and kicked away from the tanniyn, swimming underwater toward the *Brierstar*. With the last of his air, he surfaced where the longboat bobbed amidships on the port side, and climbed the boarding ladder. He peered down into the longboat. Blast it, the blades of the oars were already wet, so they must have taken passengers to shore earlier, likely Jaira and Tara. Carmack was too late to intercept them. He glanced at the port town, wanting to give chase, but somehow knowing he shouldn't. There must be a reason Arman did not give what Carmack had asked.

Stay the course. Trust Arman's timing. He scrambled up the ladder and peered through a scupper hole in the bulwark.

Across the main deck, Myck's crew stood with their backs to him, hollering and pointing out to sea. Jax's diversion was working.

Carmack slipped over the side and, within moments, reached the door to the officers' cabins. He ducked into the empty hallway. The surrounding cabin doors were all closed. Near the opposite end of the hallway, he spotted the ladder that would take him to the cargo hold-turned-dungeon. He rushed toward it.

Mere steps from the ladder, a door cracked open.

Carmack skidded to a stop and locked eyes with a young woman standing on the cabin's threshold, her hands behind her back. Betzi. The sleazy captain hadn't left Jaelport without his mage slave.

"You!" she exclaimed. "Your God really does bring people back from the dead."

"Shh!" Carmack pressed his finger to his lips.

"Bring him inside and close the door." This spoken from within by a woman with a thick Jaelportian accent.

Carmack clenched his jaw. "Who's with you?" He stepped past Betzi and peered into the small cabin. Across from the bunk, Princess Mandzee crouched next to a flat-lidded trunk, her wrists bound to it with iron cuffs and a chain.

The air left Carmack's lungs. His issues with Roxburg were nothing compared to the Hamartano sisters'. "Your Highness?"

"Get in here before you're discovered. Betzi, the jelly. Quickly," Mandzee said, holding out her wrists.

Betzi rushed to her with a small glass jar and paintbrush.

Carmack slipped inside the cabin and closed the door. "We heard you were missing."

"Larkos has had me trapped on this ship since before you and your friends liberated it," Mandzee said while Betzi brushed a glob of green jelly from the jar onto the chain link between the cuffs. The metal sizzled and bubbled under the jelly. "When my mother's health took a sharp decline, he and Jaira tied me up, threw some of my clothes into this trunk, then brought me onboard and chained me to it. When I get my hands on her . . ." Mandzee yanked her wrists apart, and the link broke. "Aha!" She took the brush and jar from Betzi and inserted a dollop of goo into the trunk's lock.

Outside, the shouting ceased, and Carmack's pulse quickened. "Your High—Majesty, we really need to go."

"Patience," Mandzee said, tipping her ear toward the sizzling metal. "What's inside is worth the wait." With one jerk, the padlock popped. She threw back the lid, dug around, and tugged open a compartment buried under her clothes. From it, she grabbed two wide green sashes covered with small pockets of different colors. She put on one and handed the other to Betzi. "I know your mother taught you the sash code well enough to best me at our last tournament."

Betzi nodded and tied the sash diagonally across her body.

From a golden pocket on her own sash, Mandzee pulled a tiny vial surrounded by the same silver filagree as the one Jaira first gave Tara. She handed it to Carmack. "This will protect you from accidental exposure."

"Ahh, panzehir." He was about to break the glass when Mandzee put her hand over it.

"How do you know of panzehir?"

"Jaira gave a vial like this to Tara, and Tara gave it to me in an hour of need."

"How long ago was this hour of need?"

"The night before we left Jaelport."

Mandzee's eyes narrowed. "And you did not succumb to Jaira's powder the following night or yesterday?"

"But that's impossible," Betzi said. "The only panzehir that lasts that long is—"

"Mine. That thieving minx!" Mandzee stamped her foot. "I knew she was stealing from me. This ends now." She tucked the panzehir back in its pocket. "You don't need this. Your last dose will last another three days. Which way to your friends?"

Carmack cracked the door. The corridor was still empty, so he led the mages down the ladder. Two decks below, the overpowering reek of urine and waste made Carmack's eyes water.

Betzi tugged his arm, then tapped her chest. The thought of her going down first didn't sit well, but if Myck had posted guards at the hatch, she could approach without alarming them. Carmack let her pass.

When Betzi descended, a man below said, "Hey, mage, what yah doin' down—"

Two heavy thumps followed.

"All clear," Betzi whispered.

Carmack and Mandzee clambered down the ladder, joining Betzi in a dry storage room. Barrels were stacked along the walls. As the ship rocked and groaned, a lantern swayed from the overhead beam, its dull rays lighting swaths of the wooden floor, a square hatch, and two fallen men. Betzi tugged a set of keys free from one of their belts and unlocked the hatch.

Carmack pulled it open. "Captain Chantry?"

"Who's asking?" This from the feisty cabin boy.

"It's Carmack!" Roxburg exclaimed. "They told us you jumped."

"Your brother's got more lives than a chatul cat," Dunn said.

Roxburg and Dunn, both alive and in their right minds, though Dunn sounded weak. Carmack released a breath he hadn't realized he'd been holding. "It's time we take back this ship for good. Can you climb up?"

"No," Roxburg said. "We're chained to the bulkheads."

"I have the keys." Betzi handed Carmack the lantern.

He climbed down first, and Betzi followed, the key ring jingling around her wrist.

One sailor growled, and several murmured.

Another shouted, "Mage!"

"Easy, men." Dunn sat propped up against the bulkhead, his complexion sallow, a sheen of sweat along his brow. "Betzi is on our side."

Betzi unlocked the men's shackles, silencing any further complaints.

Carmack crouched beside Dunn. "How's the leg?"

"A bit angry," he replied. "It'll do much better once I'm out of this grimy hold."

A knot formed between Carmack's eyebrows. What Dunn

considered a bit angry, most would call near gangrenous. He was clearly suffering, which would make it nearly impossible for him to walk, much less fight.

Captain Chantry, Roxburg, and Leif joined Carmack in a huddle beside Dunn. "Myck's men all carry blades. We'll be massacred if we storm them unarmed."

"Then we head to the armory first," Leif said.

Captain Chantry scratched his straggly beard. "We'll have to cross through the sailors' berth."

"Most of the crew in the berth are resting between shifts," Betzi said. "I can make sure they don't wake up."

"Ever?" Carmack asked.

"If you wish," Betzi said without blinking.

"Though these men sail with an enemy of the crown," Captain Chantry said, "the king might prefer we take prisoners for questioning. Can you put them to sleep for a few hours, instead?"

"Certainly." Betzi handed the keys to a sailor still bound in chains, then started up the ladder. "You men will be safer waiting here until I finish." Carmack followed her, and she scowled over her shoulder. "Stay with Queen Mandzee. You'll only be in my way, and your friend needs healing."

When Mandzee descended into the hold, Carmack said, "You should wait above. It's filthy down here."

"Betzi said Master Dunn is badly injured," she said. "Jaira may be the more powerful mage, but I surpass her in the healing arts. Please, allow me to help him."

Dunn wouldn't like it, but Carmack nodded.

Mandzee knelt next to Dunn, set down her lantern, and reached for his leg.

Dunn pushed her hands away. "Nope, no touching. I'm not that bad off."

"If you don't let me tend that festering wound, it could kill you." Mandzee's husky voice dropped. "Normally, that wouldn't bother me, but your friends and I require your help clearing this ship of pirates. Understood?"

She was right. They'd lost friends to shallower cuts than Dunn's. Carmack hovered over him. "Either cooperate with the lady, or I will make you cooperate."

Dunn glared. "And you call yourself a friend." Mandzee grabbed hold of Dunn's torn pants, and he hissed. "Easy."

She ripped the tear wider. "You whimper like a little girl."

He groaned. "I'm going to be sick."

"Don't you dare," Mandzee commanded. "The smell of this wound is bad enough. Here, swallow this." She handed him the panzehir from her sash, then dipped her fingers in several other pockets and sprinkled the contents over Dunn's wound.

"Carmack." Roxburg turned his attention back to the others. "Captain Chantry and I agree our best course of action is to split into two groups. He, Ironblade, and I will lead the larger group from the armory to the main deck using the forward ladder. You, Vex, and Dunn will wait with the second group by the main hatch. Once we draw the enemy to the bow, your group will attack them from behind."

"As good a plan as any," he said. "Let's go with it." While Roxburg and Chantry split the remaining men into the two groups, Carmack glanced over at Dunn and Mandzee. Dunn's scowl had left his face. Mandzee's powders were working their magic. The vial in his fingers was empty, so he must have taken the panzehir, just in time too.

Betzi reappeared at the top of the ladder. "It's safe to come up."

"So soon?" Dunn said.

"Never underestimate a mage," Mandzee said, helping him to his feet.

Carmack made his way from the cargo hold to the armory with the others and grabbed a sword and knife from the stash. Once everyone had weapons, he and his group returned to the main midship ladder and waited.

Arman, give us victory. And be with Tara . . .

Shouting erupted on deck, and steel blades clashed. When the thunder of running boots passed overhead, Carmack charged up the stairs, his group on his heels. Sword ready, he dashed toward the melee at the bow. Crimson flashed to his left, and he dodged the bloodied steel that whipped the air against his cheek. Carmack jabbed with his sword, just missing his attacker—a familiar bare-chested, pock-faced brute. Myck's first mate, Axe, spun around and did a double take. He countered, and Carmack deflected his powerful thrust.

Carmack's blade slid down Axe's until their swords' guards slammed together. Carmack threw his full weight against his opponent. Both men collided against the railing, their weapons still locked against each other. Sweat poured down Carmack's brow, burning his eyes. Axe bared his teeth, thick veins popping from his temples as his body dipped under Carmack's assault.

Carmack shoved Axe off-balance and kicked his legs out from beneath him. The brute's thick skull smacked against the ship, his eyes rolled back, and for a moment, his body slackened against the deck.

Carmack kicked aside Axe's weapon and poked the flesh above his heart with his sword. "Surrender."

Axe scowled and spit on Carmack's boot.

Carmack ground his teeth. Scum like Axe never respected mercy, only pain. He poked harder until blood seeped into the front of the man's tunic. "Or die."

Axe bellowed, "Stand down!"

Around them, the clashing ceased as, one by one, Myck's crew dropped their weapons. Carmack flicked his sword toward the mainmast. "Join your crew."

Axe got up and shuffled away. When Carmack turned to assess

their losses toward the bow, a deep voice shouted from above. "Look out!"

Carmack spun around. Axe had returned with another sword, thrusting it toward Carmack's chest. He lifted his sword to parry but knew he was too late.

Water poured down on his head as a fanged mouth snatched Axe off his feet. Carmack scrambled back. The tanniyn's neck rolled as it lifted its head high above the capstan. Axe screamed and stabbed the sea serpent, the blade skittering off a shell of hard scales. He dropped the weapon.

"Make way!" Jax slid down the creature's coiled neck and landed on deck. He looked up and waved at the serpent, who threw back its head, swallowed its catch, and retreated to its watery home.

Carmack trembled, awestruck by the creature and his creator. He had almost died. He lifted his arms in the air and shouted. "Arman is God, Arman is One, Arman is Three in One."

Several voices called out, repeating the prayer.

Roxburg yelled, "He delivered us in the name of Câan!" Capturing Carmack in a bear hug, Roxburg lifted him off his feet. "Well done, Brother." He set him back down and held him at arm's length, smiling. "If I'm this proud of what you've done, imagine what Arman must feel."

Carmack returned a bear hug of his own. "I've missed you."

All around them, the *Brierstar*'s crew cheered.

Roxburg patted Carmack's back. "Come on. Let's go get your lady."

Carmack cocked his head. "*My* lady?"

Roxburg only grinned. "Vex! Ironblade! Get this lot to the cargo hold," he said, then with the help of a few others, he escorted Myck's crew at sword point to their new lodgings.

Carmack's back stung. The cut from Myck must have reopened. He licked his dry lips and spotted Jax, Leif, and Captain Chantry gathered around a cask, drinking. When he joined them, Jax passed him a metal cup, and Carmack drank. On his third swallow, the sour bitterness choked him, and he coughed, clearing his throat of the worst brew he'd ever tasted. "Any word from the duchess?"

"No." The giant studied the cask suspiciously. "What is this foul drink?"

Mandzee walked over, opened the spigot, and dipped her fingers in the liquid. As she sniffed it, her nostrils flared. "This is not of Jaelport." She smelled again. "It's magen, a cider from Magos, mulled from fruits, herbs, and seeds."

"And âleh?" Jax asked. When Mandzee nodded, Jax tossed the cup aside.

"What's the matter?" Carmack asked.

"Âleh suppresses bloodvoicing magic," Jax said.

"When did you last speak with the Duchess of Carm? Does she know we've freed the crew?"

"I haven't spoken to her since yesterday. My mind's been tied up with the tanniyn all morning. I meant to send word but didn't think it would hurt to quench my thirst first."

That meant neither the duchess nor the king could communicate with them. The Council wouldn't know the *Brierstar*'s crew was safe. Carmack turned to Mandzee. "Your Highness, can we use your panzehir to counteract it?"

She shook her head. "Panzehir is an antiserum for harmful toxins. It has no effect against protective substances like âleh or runic incense."

"What's runic incense?" Dunn asked.

"A type of magic cast over Zitheon powders with the use of sacred symbols," Mandzee said. "Like these." She pointed to the lines Betzi had drawn on her forehead.

"Is that what's constantly burning in the smudge pots around Jaelport?" Carmack asked.

"Yes," Mandzee said. "It wards off unfriendly spirits."

Or, as the duchess had suspected, the mages used the incense to hide their activity from King Gidon. "And bloodvoicers." Carmack grabbed the nearest smoking lantern and tossed it overboard.

"Tossing lanterns won't help," Betzi said. "The incense lingers within the runes for hours after the smoke clears."

"Where are these runes? How do we destroy them?"

"We can't. The powders are nearly invisible, and Jaira likely painted them throughout the ship." Mandzee pursed her lips, as if she regretted sharing too much. "To try would waste time we don't have. She left with Lady Tara over an hour ago."

"Then we're too late," Jax said. "On horseback, it's but a two-hour ride between here and Armonguard."

"If I know my sister," Mandzee said, "Jaira would've hired a coach."

Hope eased the invisible weight Carmack carried on his shoulders. A coach would nearly double their time. "Seems an unlikely choice for someone in a hurry."

"Why would Jaira hurry?" Mandzee asked. "She thinks she has already won. Besides, it will be a cold day in the Temple of Barthos before my vain sister arrives in Armonguard sweaty and smelling like a horse."

"Then you still might catch them," Jax said. "There's a beacon tower between the sea and the eastern shore of Lake Arman. Tell the Kingsguards posted there that I sent you. They'll take you across the lake to the castle by boat. That'll be your best chance to catch up with Lady Tara and Princess Jaira."

"You're not coming?" Carmack asked.

"I'd only slow you down. You'll need to hire horses to reach the lake, and the livery isn't likely to have a festrier for me."

"Then might I ask your assistance, Sir Jax?" Captain Chantry asked. "I intend to stay with my ship and guard the prisoners, and we could use the extra help. I want no more surprises." Jax nodded, and Captain Chantry turned to his crew. "Man the longboat to shore, mates!"

Roxburg returned from the hold, and Carmack filled him in.

"I've been to that watchtower before," Roxburg said. "I'll go with you."

Carmack couldn't shake the feeling he was forgetting something, and then it hit him. "Betzi, where's Kressy?"

"I nearly forgot—she's still locked in the officer's cabin. She's been sleeping a lot since the captain struck her down."

"She should stay and rest." Princess Mandzee pulled a small lavender vial from her sash and passed it to Betzi. "Watch over her, Betzi. Give her a drop of this thrice daily to help the swelling, and do what you can for the others."

Betzi bowed her head. "Good health, Your Majesty."

Where did Mandzee think she was going? "Your Majesty, you should sta—"

"Master Demry, don't you dare suggest I stay behind while my sister incites a war." She glared up at Carmack.

How could he refuse after all Mandzee had done to help him? "Very well, after you." He escorted her to the ladder, and Dunn's uneven gait thumped behind them. As soon as Mandzee descended, Carmack slapped his shoulder. "Listen, I know you hate to miss a party, but Roxburg offered to go with me and Captain Chantry could use your help."

Dunn straightened his shoulders and crossed his arms. "After all this, there's no way your scrawny carcass is leaving me behind."

No time to pick a fight he wouldn't win. Carmack extended his hand. "Like old times?"

Dunn clasped it. "Aye, except it's morning."

"And we're stone-cold sober."

Carmack followed Dunn down the ladder, gazing at the brilliant blue skies. Almost as pretty as Tara's eyes.

Please Arman, help my lady keep her promise awhile longer.

CHAPTER THIRTY-ONE
TARA

UNLESS TARA CONVINCED KING GIDON to give into Jaira's ridiculous demands, a ship full of good people would die. Leif, Uncle Chantry, Kressy, Master Dunn, and Captain Demry—their faces flashed through her mind. Her bones ached from the jolting coach ride, her patience taxed by hours of awkward silence interrupted by Jaira's snippety comments and Myck's and Larkos's leering.

Outside the coach window, the whitestone towers of Castle Armonguard rose majestically beside Lake Arman. Breathtaking, and a vivid reminder she was subject to a powerful king. Far greater than Gidon was his God, whom Tara knew and loved, and who knew and loved her. Perhaps Aunt Nitsa was praying, because an unexplainable peace washed over her. Arman was with her.

Guards blocked the gatehouse entrance, forcing the driver to stop. A rotund Kingsguard, presumably the man in charge, approached the coach's window. "Announce yourselves."

When Jaira snapped her fingers at Tara, Tara's ears burned. "I am not your herald, Jaira."

"Bart's blood, enough quibbling," Myck muttered, then gestured to Tara. "Lady Tara Gershom of Meribah Corner, cousin of Queen Averella."

The guard nodded. "Lady Gershom, please identify your companions."

"Lady Jaira Hamartano," Tara said.

The guard's jaw slackened.

"And her Shield, Larkos, and Capt—"

"Me!" Myck interrupted. "Carmack Demry, Lady Gershom's Shield."

Tara's heart panged. How dare that coward hide behind Carmack's name?

"Beg your pardon, Lady Gershom," the guard said. "You and Master Demry are always welcome in Armonguard; however, your . . . er, friends from Jaelport, are not."

Tara took a deep breath. In Jaelport, she had emulated Aunt Nitsa's confident manner to slip out of Tenma Palace, but she couldn't muster up another performance like that. Tara had promised Arman and herself no more lies. How the truth would help her past the gate, she did not know. Tara opened the carriage door, biting back a groan as she shifted her sore body past Myck, so repulsed by his forked-tongue lies she nearly tripped climbing out.

She stood toe-to-toe with the guard on the wooden drawbridge of the castle. "These people are not my friends. Lady Jaira is the king's enemy and mine." When the guard reached for his sword, Tara lightly rested her hand on his. "Please, do not arrest us. If Lady Jaira does not address the Council and leave freely, she will have my brother, my uncle, my maid, and dozens of Tsaftown's sailors killed. A few days ago, my guards and I attempted to save them but failed." Tara couldn't save anyone, not even herself. Her voice caught and her vision blurred with hot tears. No more lies. *Arman, help me in my unbelief.* "So, I seek the king, and trust that, through him, Arman will accomplish what I cannot."

"I'm sorry, m'lady. All the more reason I cannot let them

through." The guard's gaze softened. "But Sir Gavin should hear of this. Wait in your carriage."

A small spark of hope kindled in Tara's chest as the guard entered the gatehouse, and she climbed back into the carriage. She had met Sir Gavin Lukos on several occasions, most recently in Meribah Corner when he and the then-prince were running from the imposter claiming to be Gidon Hadar. Tara had provided them food and shelter, and Sir Gavin had been most appreciative. Surely, he would remember her.

The guard returned alone. "Seems the Council was expecting you. I will escort you to the Veralla Room, but the eunuch must surrender his sword."

Jaira flicked her wrist, and Larkos handed over his weapon.

"What about him?" Tara pointed to Myck.

"Master Demry may keep his."

"But—"

"Now, m'lady"—Myck's fingers wrapped around her arm and squeezed—"we shouldn't keep Sir Gavin waiting." Once the guard was past earshot, Myck's harsh whisper grated in her ear. "Try something like that again, and you'll spend our honeymoon paying for it."

Mounted Kingsguards flanked their coach as it proceeded into the bailey, and four more surrounded Tara and the others when they alighted from it. The guards led them inside, up the grand staircase, and past several rooms to the Veralla Room's doors, where two additional Kingsguards stood post. Tara couldn't know exactly what would happen in that room, but their entrance was bound to create a scene. She glanced down at the sword hanging from Myck's belt. Violence seemed the only certainty, with a room full of innocent bystanders at risk.

Tara pulled Captain Myck aside, and Jaira followed. "You should wait here."

"Have you forgotten my warning already?" he asked.

"Do you honestly expect King Gidon to extend diplomatic courtesy to an armed fugitive who entered his household under false pretenses?" Tara asked. "Unlike the guards, King Gidon has met Carmack. At first glance, you will be found out, and getting caught in a lie is the worst way to begin a negotiation."

"She's right," Jaira said. "Wait here. Larkos will fetch you once the king agrees to our terms."

Myck's face twitched. The slug actually looked nervous.

Tara and Jaira stepped past him into the Veralla Room, a circular two-story hall with a high ceiling. The royal dais stood straight ahead, covered by a purple canopy embroidered with Armonguard's crest. Below it, King Gidon sat on his throne. The young man cleaned up extraordinarily well, dressed in a dark blue doublet, his hair and beard trimmed. Tara's cousin, Averella, was well deserving of such a fetching husband, but the young queen was not present. An armed Kingsguard in chainmail stood at each of the king's shoulders. Two curved tables flanked the dais and were filled with members of the Council of Six, each wearing black robes.

Aunt Nitsa occupied the chairwoman's seat immediately on the king's right. She wore a tall drum-shaped hat that signified her position. Next to her stood Lord Orson of Berland, who was reading aloud a report, something about increasing cultivation of farmland in the duchy of Therion. At the other table sat Lord Dromos of Xulon and Duke Pitney of Nesos.

Well-dressed spectators stood around the room and filled the second-floor balcony, transforming the Veralla Room into a circular theatre of sorts. These were likely noblemen and women and merchants who had business with the Council or were interested in court politics. Little did they know the drama Jaira had scripted for them.

Larkos remained by the door while Tara and Jaira wove their

way through the crowd. Tara thought through what she might say when given the floor.

Your Majesty, I ask you to . . . no, I seek to negotiate an end to the blockade of Jaelport to save my . . . the crew of the Brierstar. Maybe Tara should switch that around. She paused at the front and raised her hand, trying to catch her aunt's attention.

Jaira elbowed her ribs. "Get on with it."

"Don't push me, Jaira." It was hard enough mentally rehearsing the most audacious request ever to be presented to the King's Council without Jaira prodding her. "We are not in Jaelport any longer. If I decided to permanently flatten your nose, you could do nothing to stop me."

Jaira bared her teeth. "Break my nose and your brother's shall also be broken."

Tara didn't blink. "I think Leif would agree it would be worth it."

Jaira's head jerked back as if slapped. Tara stepped forward into the open space under the domed ceiling, and Jaira scurried alongside her.

When Aunt Nitsa spotted them, she paled. King Gidon noticed them too and smiled until his gaze drifted to Jaira. His expression hardened, and he flicked his fingers. One of the Kingsguards—Sir Gavin!—tapped his halberd on the floor, doors on either end of the council tables opened, and a dozen guards filed into the room, encircling Tara and Jaira. Every head swiveled toward them. In the balcony above, spectators leaned over the railing, their murmurs swelling.

Aunt Nitsa rapped her gavel once. "Quiet in the gallery." She whispered something to the king, then said, "Lord Orson, we shall briefly suspend your report. I believe Lady Gershom of Meribah Corner and Lady Jaira Hamartano of Jaelport bring unexpected new business." She fixed her gaze on Tara, her brow arched.

Why wasn't Aunt Nitsa bloodvoicing her? Days had passed

since Tara had left Jaelport, and her aunt hadn't reached out once. If she had, this entire ordeal wouldn't be unexpected at all.

Tara curtsied and took a steadying breath. "Your Majesty, Madam Chairwoman, and esteemed members of the Council, I have come to negotiate for the release of my uncle, Captain Chantry Livna, his crew that serves aboard the *Brierstar*, Captain Roxburg Demry, and two of his fighting men from Tsaftown in exchange for the end of the Jaelport blockade"—a collective gasp arose from the crowd—"and a declaration of the city's independence from the kingdom of Er'Rets."

"Treason!" a man shouted.

At least four different people yelled, "Traitors!"

"Order!" Aunt Nitsa hammered her gavel against its block several times. "Or I will clear the chamber!"

The uproar quieted to a rumble.

"The *Brierstar* disappeared weeks ago, Lady Gershom," Lord Orson said. "With respect, are you certain these men are still alive?"

"Yes." As long as Jaira got what she wanted and made it back to the ship. "I am willing to testify before the Council's bloodvoice mediators to prove it."

"Shall I call them in, Madam Chairwoman?" Duke Pitney asked.

Aunt Nitsa sank back in her chair and exchanged a look with the king. When he shook his head, she frowned. "I'm afraid the mediators would be of little help to us, Lord Orson. I have not been able to use my gift to communicate with my niece for the past several days. Even now, I cannot connect with her or anyone aboard the *Brierstar*."

"Can we thank your dark arts for this, Lady Jaira?" King Gidon asked.

"Why suspect me?" Jaira asked. "It's well-known that women

are not susceptible to Jaelportian arts. How could I have meddled with the Duchess of Carm?"

Yet she sneered like a contented cat. Tara knew that look. Jaira may not have used her magic directly, but she was undoubtedly responsible for whatever was preventing Aunt Nitsa from blood-voicing with Tara. Proud of it too.

Jaira took that moment to step forward. "It seems the gods have blessed us with a level negotiating table, one restoring freedom of thought to all parties."

A murmur rose up in the balcony. Suspicion toward blood-voicers was common among the people. Even Tara sometimes felt uneasy about her relatives' supernatural abilities. Thankfully, none that she knew had ever abused their power to invade people's privacy or control their minds. Even rumors of such abuses could easily turn people against the gifted, especially the king.

"How interesting you should speak of freedom, Lady Jaira," the king said, "while your family continues to deprive so many people of it."

"Our workers receive shelter, clothing, and food for their toil," Jaira said, "not to mention a sense of purpose, which is far more than most strays receive in the northern cities of Er'Rets."

King Gidon's eyes narrowed. "I'm sure your workers would tell a different story if they were allowed to speak freely. No human being should be treated like property."

"Tell that to Lady Gershom." Jaira gestured to the audience with open palms. "Or any of these noblemen's wives and daughters."

The stands erupted. This time some shouted, while others applauded.

What was Jaira doing? Trying to incite a rebellion? If she got herself arrested, Myck's thugs would kill Leif and the other captives. "Quiet," Tara snapped. "If you want to end the blockade, you're not helping."

The king leaned over and whispered something to Aunt Nitsa.

She straightened in her seat and rapped her gavel. "Lady Gershom, before we discuss your request, we would like to know, where is Master Carmack Demry? Sir Gavin informed us he arrived with you."

Could this be the moment she needed? A chance for truth to be revealed? If Tara tried to explain what had happened to Carmack, she would come undone, but she would happily expose Myck for the liar he was. "Master Demry is not here. The man I arrived with is Captain Othvold Myvick, also known as Captain Myck. I am here to seek his pardon."

"Why?" the king asked.

"Because I plan to marry him."

King Gidon leaned forward on his throne. "Lady Gershom, when we first met, I was struck by your kindness. You showed compassion to an enslaved stray and stood up to your peers who did not. Othvold Myvick is a ruthless slave trader. You cannot possibly love such a man."

His words reminded Tara of a conversation they'd had during his only visit to Meribah Corner. "You once said the same of my late husband, sir. Do you recall my reply?"

The king straightened, moving his hands to his knees. "I do. You said, 'This is not a world where one marries for love.'"

"And you told me it should be," Tara said.

The crowd broke into a ruckus behind Tara. Aunt Nitsa banged her gavel.

Tara spoke louder. "Love is the only reason I have agreed to remarry. This is not the kind of love that united you and my cousin in marriage, Your Highness, but a love that sacrifices willingly for others, like the love Câan showed us all."

The kind that had driven Carmack to jump.

"Whatever your choice today, some will be sacrificed in order to save others. Jaelport's slaves or Tsaftown's sailors. May Arman give you wisdom to choose, but my choice is clear. To free my brother Leif from the order of Zitheos, I will marry Othvold Myvick."

CHAPTER THIRTY-TWO
CARMACK

JAX'S SHORTCUT ACROSS THE PRISTINE waters of Lake Arman was not what Carmack expected. Scenic, quiet, and pure torture. At least a punishing ride on horseback would have taken Carmack's mind off his worries. Though the westward wind pushed their boat at a steady clip, nothing short of a gale's speed would be fast enough for him. He stood between Dunn and Roxburg at the bow, with Mandzee seated behind them. At the rear of the boat, two Kingsguards manned the rudder and sails.

"Relax, Demry," Dunn said. "We made good time. May have even beaten them."

Carmack stared ahead to Armonguard. The largest castle he'd ever seen, its white towers gleaming, covered much of the island it was built upon, making it look as though it was floating on the lake. Behind the castle, a sprawling city that dwarfed Jaelport stretched up the hillside. "I'll relax once we're there." And he knew Tara was safe.

"At least let the blood back into your fingers, or you won't be able to hold your sword," Roxburg said.

Carmack relaxed his fists, flexing away a cramp that had set in.

He jerked his chin at the swatch of green bandage peeking through the tear in Dunn's pants. "How's your scratch?"

Dunn glanced over his shoulder toward Princess Mandzee. "Amazing. Hardly feel a thing."

"You were a terrible patient."

Dunn shrugged. "Trusting women doesn't come easy, much less mages."

Behind him, Princess Mandzee huffed. "Neither does wasting magic on ungrateful men."

Carmack expected Dunn to fire back a witty retort, but instead, his friend sheepishly tucked his head. Princess Mandzee had left him tongue-tied. Carmack glanced between the two, uneasy that another sort of magic might be at play.

"Ready the ropes, men," Roxburg said. "We've arrived."

Carmack and Dunn followed orders until the longboat rested secure along the jetty abutting Armonguard's eastern bridge. Carmack climbed out of the boat, raced along the waterfront and up a ridiculously steep and narrow set of stairs curving along the sea wall. Dunn, Roxburg, and Mandzee weren't far behind. They all reached the main gate gasping for breath.

Having played a key role in the Battle of Armonguard, Roxburg was no stranger to the soldiers posted there. One guard rushed forward. "Captain, welcome back! We feared you were lost at sea."

"Far worse, I'm afraid," Roxburg said. "Has Lady Gershom arrived?"

"Only minutes ago, with a couple of Jaelportians and her Shield."

"Did he perchance resemble Sir Rigil Barak?" Carmack asked.

"Aye, that's him!" the guard said. "I thought he looked familiar."

"That is not Lady Tara's Shield or Sir Rigil," Carmack said. "He's Othvold Myvick, a fugitive slave trader."

The guard's eyes widened. "They're with the king and the Council in the Veralla Room."

"Come." Roxburg marched straight into the keep. Three guardsmen trailed their group through a series of corridors, up a grand staircase, and along another curved hallway.

Carmack turned a sharp corner and came face-to-face with Captain Myck. Myck did a double take, then sprinted down the corridor, past a set of burlwood doors and the two guards posted there.

No way would Carmack let that eel slip away. "Stop that man!" He drew his sword and barreled after Myck, who spun around, his own blade in his right hand. Carmack made a swinging cut, drawing Myck's parry. Carmack used his forward momentum to push Myck's blade upward, locking it against Carmack's guard, and pressed close to Myck's body.

Carmack dropped his sword behind his own back, butted his head into Myck's chest, and with both arms, grabbed the back of Myck's knees. He picked Myck off his feet and threw him backward. Landing on top, Carmack pinned Myck's throat under his forearm and bore down against his windpipe. The guards rushed over and knocked away his sword.

The captain's cheeks turned from red to purple. "Th . . . is . . . again." His eyes rolled back, and his body went limp. Only then did Carmack ease off, allowing the guards to tie Myck's wrists and haul him away.

Roxburg swung the doors open, and Princess Mandzee bolted past. Dunn hurried after her, shooting Carmack a dirty look.

"What?" Carmack asked, rushing back to them.

"You should have made him suffer," Dunn said.

"That's what Ice Island is for." Carmack followed him inside.

"He escaped Ice Island once. He deserves a prison without doors."

Carmack entered the back of a round, two-story chamber and came to a stop behind Princess Mandzee. A balcony encircled the upper half of the room, and rising before them, the crest of Armonguard hung on a large awning over the throne. Carmack spotted the top of the king's head, crowned with a thin band of gold.

He craned his neck. Tara and Jaira stood near the center of the room.

King Gidon's voice carried over the audience. "Lady Gershom, when we first met, I was struck by your kindness. You showed compassion to an enslaved stray and stood up to your—"

"Move out of my way." Mandzee's regal voice mixed with the din of the crowd, preventing Carmack from hearing the king's speech. "Let me through!"

Spectators turned and shushed her.

"Stop yer pushin' and wait yer turn," one man told her.

"Your Grace!" Roxburg shouted at a striking woman up front who wore an ugly hat. The Duchess of Carm. Carmack hadn't seen her in years, but she was easily recognizable from her petite frame, fine features, and shiny auburn hair. The duchess sat at a table beside the king and pounded her gavel.

The smell of musty spice rolled over them. Roxburg wobbled on his feet, bumping into Carmack, then slumped to the floor. The guard next to Roxburg did the same. Wet brown flakes covered their faces. Anabas.

A woman standing nearby scowled down at them. "Shameful drunks."

Carmack whipped around. A bald-headed man slipped into a dark alcove at the back of the room. He tapped Dunn's shoulder.

Dunn turned, his gaze darting to the men on the floor. "What happened?"

"Larkos," Carmack said. "See if Mandzee can help them. I'm going after him."

Carmack ran to the back of the room and ducked into the alcove. A twisting stairway led upstairs, and he climbed slowly. Sweat and spice tainted the air. Larkos had to be close. At least Mandzee's panzehir had protected Carmack and Dunn against the eunuch's powders. Carmack reached the top step and peered around the corner. He was standing in the only doorway leading onto the horseshoe-shaped balcony. People lined the railing, facing the banner above the dais, and Kingsguards stood at the far ends, closest to the king.

Tara's voice rose from the hall below. "To free my brother Leif from the order of Zitheos, I will marry Othvold Myvick."

Marry Myvick? No! She'd promised. Larkos could wait. Carmack had to stop Tara, but as he cleared the doorway onto the balcony, Larkos stepped into his path. A heavy fist clipped Carmack's jaw, and pinpoints of light exploded across his vision. Carmack staggered backward onto the stairway landing, raising his arms to block, but another blow struck the side of his face, spinning him around. Ringing in his ears eclipsed all other sound, and the metallic taste of blood filled his mouth. A kick to his back sent Carmack sprawling down the stairs. Larkos landed on him, pressing Carmack's chest into a step's sharp edge. Fingers gripped his hair and slammed his head on the step below. Carmack sagged against the floor, feeling consciousness slip away.

"Stop!" Mandzee's husky voice echoed through the haze.

Carmack felt a tug at his belt where his knife was sheathed.

"You're not the only one who can kill with a stolen blade," Larkos whispered in Carmack's ear and climbed off his back. Carmack inhaled. Moldy spice. More anabas.

The world slowly came back into focus.

"My sister Jaira does not speak for Jaelport," Mandzee said. "Our mother has died, and I am queen of Jaelport now."

Something was wrong. Carmack's aching bones screamed it. His mind cleared as he crawled back up the stairs. He stepped back onto the balcony behind a row of spectators.

"You fool!" Jaira said. "You have no idea what you're doing."

"Nor do you, sister. Neither the *Brierstar* nor its crew remain under your control. Captain Demry is here now, though your eunuch has poisoned him."

The room erupted into chaos.

Larkos! Where was he? He had Carmack's knife, but who did he intend to kill?

A series of loud raps carried over the din. "Clear the room!" the duchess ordered.

To Carmack's right, a bald man moved against the exiting crowd. A Kingsguard was clearing the balcony from the opposite end, but his eyes were not on Larkos, who was getting dangerously close to the awning above the royal dais.

The king.

Carmack's heart leaped to his throat, and he pushed through the spectators. He was two strides from Larkos when the eunuch lifted his arm, a flash of light glinting from the blade. "Knife!"

Screams erupted. The whites of Larkos's eyes doubled in size, and he took aim.

Carmack leaped. His outstretched arm knocked Larkos's hand as he hurled the weapon down. Carmack tackled Larkos, and when they hit the balcony floor, the eunuch's body went limp, as if his spirit had left him.

Across the hall, a woman shrieked. Through the balcony railing, Carmack saw Dunn covering Princess Mandzee on the floor. Behind them, a man slumped against a hysterical woman. The knife, clearly meant for Jaira's sister, was buried in the man's belly. Larkos's target had not been King Gidon after all.

"Someone help that man!" The command came from the king, who stood against the wall behind his throne, two guards standing in front of him. He nodded at Carmack and called, "Good thing you were here, Master Demry."

Carmack stood.

Across the room, Tara paled and stared at him, as though she didn't trust her eyes. "Carmack?" She started forward, but Jaira grabbed her arm and yanked her backward.

"Larkos?" Jaira screeched. When her eunuch failed to answer, Jaira glared at King Gidon. "Have you stormed him like my brother Marken?"

The king motioned to the closest guard. "Seize Lady Jaira and her eunuch at once."

Jaira pulled a knife from the folds of her skirt. Her arm snaked around Tara's shoulder, and she pressed the blade to Tara's throat. "Call them off, stray, or Lady Tara dies."

King Gidon raised his hand, stilling his guards. The room fell silent.

Carmack broke out in a cold sweat. One wrong move, and Jaira would slit Tara's throat. But what could he do? He was too far away to help. Tara lifted her chin, and a tingle ran up Carmack's spine. She didn't need his help.

Tara grabbed Jaira's arm, her knuckles tight around Jaira's sleeve. Tara bent her knees, her upper body twisting and tucking, and Jaira sailed over Tara's shoulder, landing on her back. A perfect throw.

Carmack's heart skipped. The knife still flashed in Jaira's hand. Would Tara forget?

Not this time. She pinned Jaira's arm with her knee, grabbed the mage's wrist, and wrested away the weapon. Tara held the knife, firm and steady, to Jaira's throat.

Jaira glared at her, gasping for breath. "You wouldn't dare."

"Like you said . . ." Tara leaned forward, and Jaira yelped. "I'm not the lady you remember."

That was his girl. Carmack pumped a clenched fist in the air.

"Well done, Lady Tara!" said the king. "Guards, assist her."

The guards rushed over and seized Jaira. Carmack bolted for the stairs, taking two at a time down to the lower level. Tara met him halfway across the room and launched herself into his arms. He caught her and, wrapping his arms around her, crushed her against him, sure she could feel his heart jumping against his ribs as if it hadn't fully beat before. Carmack tucked his chin against her shoulder and breathed in the smells of the ocean from her hair and dress. She was trembling, but so was he. Her choked sobs hit his chest with puffs of warm air, and her tears ran hot against his neck.

Carmack stilled. If he held Tara any tighter, she might break in his arms. He slowly set her on her feet, then stroked her hair, from her shoulders to her waist. *Thank you, Arman, for sparing her and for this moment.*

Tara looked up, her blue eyes glistening. "You're alive!"

Carmack didn't care that most of Armonguard, including the king and Tara's aunt, were watching. He slipped his fingers into her silky curls, grazing the soft nape of her neck. He kissed her cheek, then whispered in her ear. "I love you, Tara."

Tara tilted back her head, gazing up into his eyes. "I love you too." Her words stole his breath away. "Please, don't leave me again. I'll go wherever you go."

His throat ached, everything he wanted at his fingertips, because she was willing to sacrifice all she had. Carmack shook his head, and his voice turned hoarse. "You'd have to give up your family. Your estate."

"And you, your duty." A tear slipped down her cheek into the creases of a wistful smile. "Would you break your oath if I were only Tara and not the Lady of Meribah Corner?"

"I would." A pang of conscience stopped Carmack from promising more. To do so would presume their fate was his alone to control. "But there's something we both must do first."

"Anything," she said.

"Pray." And let Arman's will be done.

CHAPTER THIRTY-THREE
TARA

CARMACK WAS ALIVE, AND HE LOVED her. That made Tara's morning nearly perfect. Lake Arman's sparkling waters had never looked prettier under a bright blue sky. She sat with Averella and Aunt Nitsa on the castle's rooftop terrace, safe and refreshingly clean in a gorgeous pale-yellow gown. The sun warmed Tara's cheeks, and she breathed deeply, no more noxious Jaelportian incense choking her. With Jaira and her cohorts locked in the dungeons, Tara had only one problem left to solve—Carmack's oath.

"Would you like something to eat?" Averella slid the breakfast tray, overflowing with berries and pastries, across the table between them. She wore a becoming gown of royal blue with silver lace. Her dark brown hair had grown longer and was styled in delicate waves around her lovely face. "Or something else to drink?"

"The tea is fine," Tara answered.

Her cousin frowned. "But you haven't tasted it. It must be cold by now."

Tara swallowed a tepid sip from her full teacup. "It's fine."

"Leif and Chantry should arrive from the coast later today," her aunt said. "We'll all be glad to see them."

"Oh, and Kressy too," Averella said. "So you will have your own maid to ready you for dinner."

Ugh. Hours of tedious talking and eating too much. Then again, Carmack would be there. Maybe he would tell her what he had decided.

"Tara?" Averella tapped a spoon against her cup. "What is wrong? You have barely said a word other than 'fine' all morning."

"Dearest, your cousin has suffered a great ordeal. Allow her some time to recover." Aunt Nitsa patted Tara's hand. "Though, we are here to listen if anything in particular worries you."

Averella gave a wry smile. "But if you don't hurry up and confess what it is, I will read your mind and find out for myself."

"Averella, really!" Aunt Nitsa took a long sip of tea.

"I am only teasing." As Averella studied her mother's face, her eyes narrowed. "You have already read her thoughts, haven't you?"

Aunt Nitsa set her teacup into its saucer. "I most certainly have not." She smoothed her napkin across her lap. "I have no need to eavesdrop on Tara's thoughts, and neither do you." With her napkin flattened completely, Aunt Nitsa proceeded to pick at the tablecloth.

Tara's aunt rarely fidgeted, but Averella did, every time she and Tara got caught doing something naughty. Tara's eyes locked with her cousin's.

"Guilty," Tara and Averella said.

Averella snorted, and Tara giggled.

"You two are incorrigible." Aunt Nitsa's mouth twisted, and her lips clamped together, clearly fighting back a smile. "To be clear, I did not read Tara's mind." She paused. "I read Master Demry's."

"Mother!" Averella gaped.

Aunt Nitsa fanned her face. "He was drowning. I was short on time and needed information. Anyway, it doesn't matter. If Tara doesn't wish to discuss it, I will say no more."

Envy pinched Tara's heart. What she wouldn't give to read that man's mind and know for certain where she stood. "Actually, I am relieved, because I need your prayers. Carmack may not return to Meribah Corner with me unless we find some way to release him from his vow."

"What vow?" Averella asked. "Tara, please start from the beginning. Or better yet, give me permission to use my magic, so I can catch up faster."

Tara supposed that would be all right. Averella had known about her true feelings for Carmack since Tara had gushed about their first dance together. It would be easier to let her cousin see her memories than to have to confess everything aloud. "Very well."

Averella grabbed hold of Tara's hand and closed her eyes. "Simply remember all that you and Master Demry have gone through since this began. It goes rather quickly, I promise."

Tara shut her eyes too. The memories came easy. The sweet moments training on the *Zephyr* and the dance at Tenma Palace. The way he kissed her after smelling the love powder, and the confession of his lifelong vow of chastity. Her heart ached as she recalled their ride on the longboat to the *Brierstar* and his words before everything went so very wrong. *I cannot return to Meribah Corner with you.* Her thoughts jumped to his sober expression on the plank, when he told her he loved her, to the warmth of his embrace in the council room after she had thrown Jaira. Tara would make certain that embrace would not be their last, even if it meant giving up her family and her estate to stay with him. She would not lose Carmack again.

Averella released her hand, and Tara opened her eyes.

"You poor dear." A tear rolled down Averella's cheek, and she wiped it away. "Mother, we must do something."

"It is difficult to know what can be done without better understanding the problem," Aunt Nitsa said. "Beyond the obligation of chastity, has Master Demry shared any other details about his vow?"

"Only the consequences of breaking it. If he marries, both he and his wife would be banished from the northern lands and would forfeit any property. In my case, I would lose Meribah Corner and all connection to my family in Tsaftown."

Averella's face fell. "That's terribly cruel. What was Aunt Revada thinking?"

"Let's not judge your aunt too swiftly, dear," Aunt Nitsa said. "She would not threaten such severe, lifelong consequences without careful thought."

"I believe that too," Tara said, "but Carmack has no hope that the charter provides a way out."

"Charter?" Aunt Nitsa slid forward to the edge of her chair. "Do you mean the Northlander Charter?"

"He said it governs his oath."

"Hmm, I wonder . . ." Aunt Nitsa gazed up to the lacy clouds above them, then her eyes fluttered shut.

Tara leaned forward. "Aunt Nitsa, I—"

Averella nudged Tara's foot under the table and shook her finger. "Give her a moment," she whispered.

Bloodvoicing again. Arman's gift wasn't something Tara would ever feel accustomed to.

Aunt Nitsa nodded her head several times. When her eyes reopened, she rose from the table. "Tara, your mother bids you well, and you too, Averella."

"You spoke with my mother?" Tara asked.

"I did. I wanted to confirm my suspicions about Master Demry's vow. The Northlander Charter is a very old code—some of its provisions are nearly forgotten—but I remembered one clause that created a limitation on its power."

Could this be the loophole Tara hoped for? "What kind of limitation?" she asked breathlessly.

"It's known as the divine supremacy clause," Aunt Nitsa said. "When our forefathers in Tsaftown wrote that document, they fully acknowledged the supremacy of Arman over their lives, and that extended to the kings chosen by Arman to rule Er'Rets."

"I don't understand," Tara said. "How does that help Carmack?"

"It doesn't," Aunt Nitsa replied. "Not on its own."

Averella rolled her eyes. "Mother, you are being cryptic."

"And you, my dear, are being impertinent," Aunt Nitsa said. "What I am trying to explain is that the charter's powers are superseded by the crown's, so if royal law covers the same subject, the charter's provisions become null and void."

How in the depths could this obscure clause free Carmack from his deplorable oath?

Aunt Nitsa seemed to sense Tara's lack of understanding and went on. "The same is true of any oath taken under the charter, should the party make a higher oath. For example, one of fealty to his king."

Tara shook her head. "But Carmack hasn't sworn fealty to King Gidon."

A sly smile danced on Averella's lips. "Then perhaps he should."

Aunt Nitsa's face lit up with a matching smile, leaving no doubt that the two were cut of the same cloth. "Will you ask him, or shall I?"

"I will. Right away." Averella closed her eyes.

"I am still lost," Tara said. "Ask who what? Carmack?"

"Merciful heart, no." Averella was back already. She picked up the teapot and topped off their cups. "My husband."

Tara clenched her jaw. Why wouldn't these two simply speak plainly? "Are either of you going to tell me what is going on?"

"I know I'm being vague, but trust me." Averella grinned and plopped a sugar cube in her cup. "You'll find out soon enough."

King Gidon strode onto the terrace. "Pardon the interruption, ladies." Tara and Aunt Nitsa rose from their seats to curtsy, but he waved his hand. "Please, no need to fuss."

Averella beamed up at him. "How fortunate you were so close."

The king slid the one empty chair at their table closer to his wife and sat. In many ways, he was still the young man Tara remembered, though a new air of confidence enhanced his fine appearance considerably. "I was on my way to seek your assistance. I wish to host a celebration tomorrow."

Averella rested her hand on his arm. "First, we must discuss Master Demry."

"You're not going to let me share my plans, are you?"

"My dear husband, this is more important."

Gidon sighed, sat back, and crossed one ankle over his knee. "Out with it, then."

Averella rushed on. "Considering all Master Demry has done to free the *Brierstar*, rescue the captives, and apprehend Captain Myvick and Larkos, it seems obvious that knighthood would be an appropriate show of thanks."

Tara nearly choked on her tea. Knighthood? That was definitely a higher oath, but would the king entertain the notion in Carmack's case? Their only previous encounter at Meribah Corner had not ended amicably. She could not imagine that the king had forgotten being thrown across the room.

The king crossed his arms. "Obvious *and* appropriate?"

"Your Majesty has awarded knighthood in the past for comparable acts of valor," Aunt Nitsa said.

Gidon lowered his foot and leaned forward, resting his arms on the table. "I agree Master Demry deserves recognition, but the man once tossed me through an embroidery frame." He glanced at Tara, one eyebrow raised.

Her face flamed. No, he had not forgotten.

"Under the circumstances, asking him to swear fealty to me would be highly presumptuous. Wouldn't you agree, Lady Tara?"

She cleared her throat. "That day was a series of unfortunate misunderstandings for us all. And while I cannot speak for Master Demry, we both heard your call to worship Arman during the Battle of Armonguard and sang praises with you to his son, Câan." If only she had lived out more days with such faith. "Master Demry believes Arman chose you to be our king, so I do not believe he would consider such a request presumptuous."

"Hmm, a sound answer." Gidon pursed his lips for a moment before his countenance cleared. "Now, about tomorrow—"

"Achan!" Averella nudged his arm. "You will ask him, won't you?"

He shook his head. "There's no need."

Averella's face fell.

With her hopes dashed, Tara turned to prayer. *Very well, Arman. Even through my disappointment, I accept this is Your will and trust Your ways.*

"No pouting, my queen," Gidon said. "We have a feast to plan."

Averella tossed her napkin on her plate. "Excuse me, but I don't feel much like celebrating at the moment." She stood and started away from the table.

King Gidon snagged her wrist. "That's because you haven't given me the chance to tell you that the reason for tomorrow's celebration is a knighting ceremony."

Averella narrowed her eyes at her husband. "For whom?"

"Isn't it *obvious*?" King Gidon grinned, glancing from face to face, waiting for their reactions. "Carmack Demry, of course. He accepted my invitation to join the knighthood earlier this morning." He reached across the table, plucked a blueberry from the breakfast tray, and popped it into his mouth.

Averella punched his arm. "Insufferable tease! How could you torture us so? You gave me no clue of your intentions this morning."

"Because I genuinely believed Master Demry would decline the honor. You know how I acted the fool in Meribah Corner. I hope I have your forgiveness, Lady Tara." His scarred cheeks betrayed a faint blush, and when his eyes met Tara's, she knew he wasn't referring to his present jesting.

"All is forgiven," she said.

"Thank you." King Gidon hopped to his feet and gathered Averella in his arms. "And you, my beautiful queen, will you forgive my teasing? As I forgive you for presuming I'm too slow to reach a sensible conclusion without your prompting."

Averella's eyes widened, and she whacked his shoulder. "I said no such—"

His kiss ended the argument before it began. Aunt Nitsa shook her head, grinning into her teacup. Warmth filled Tara's heart to see her cousin—now a queen—so happy and beloved by her king.

Yet something else stirred inside Tara—a fervent, reborn anticipation that she, too, would soon enjoy such a kiss.

Pacing the length of the Temple of Arman took fifty steps more than in Meribah Corner's small chapel, but Tara still made six trips from one end to the other before the ceremony started. When the horns blasted their first notes, she slipped into an empty spot next to Kressy by the aisle. The priest led the procession, which started in the back of the room. King Gidon and Queen Averella, dressed in matching finery of blue and gold, followed the priest up the aisle. Behind them, Carmack looked devastatingly handsome in a simple white tunic and crisp black pants. His hair and beard had been neatly trimmed. He caught her staring and winked. Her heart fluttered wildly in her chest, and she smiled.

Once the king and queen sat on their thrones, the priest faced Carmack, directed the entire assembly to sit, and recited a prayer to Arman.

Tara silently lifted her own—one of praise, thanksgiving, and apologetically, a tinge of impatience, trusting Arman would understand. The priest then read from the *Book of Arman*, comparing the fruits of Arman's spirit to the virtues of chivalry. When prompted, Carmack vowed to uphold them.

"Have you bound your honor by debt or oath to another authority?" the priest asked.

At last. The part Tara had been waiting for.

"I am bound by an oath of service to Lady Revada Livna of Tsaftown," Carmack replied.

"Will Lady Revada or her representative now come forward?" the priest asked the assembly.

Uncle Chantry stepped into the aisle behind Carmack and bowed. "I, Captain Chantry Livna, speak on behalf of my late brother's wife."

"Does Lady Revada Livna acknowledge said prior oath?"

"She does," Chantry said.

"And does she hereby release Carmack Demry from its obligations in subservience to his knightly fealty to King Gidon Hadar?"

"Lady Revada has given a statement to the Duchess of Carm to read before the king and this assembly," Chantry said.

Tara sat breathless as her aunt unfolded a piece of paper and read, "Your Majesties, King Gidon and Queen Averella, I, Lady Revada Livna, wife of the late Lord Edik Livna of Tsaftown, was greatly moved by the news of Master Carmack Demry's elevation to the knighthood. Master Demry has faithfully served the Livna family and the people of Tsaftown for years, demonstrating great skill, strength, courage, and above all these, honor, even when it came at great personal cost to himself. I can think of no other man in Er'Rets more deserving of this recognition. With my greatest appreciation and wholehearted approval, I hereby release Master Carmack Demry of his prior oath."

Tears flooded Tara's eyes, and she nearly cheered aloud. Had Mother been there, Tara would have given her a breath-stealing hug. As it was, Tara could only squeeze her handkerchief and wipe the river of happy tears blurring her view of King Gidon rising from his throne. Her heart pounded in her ears for the rest of their exchange, and she couldn't hear a word. Finally, Carmack knelt before the king on a small silk pillow, and Sir Caleb, the royal chamberlain, handed the king his sword, Ôwr.

The king tapped the flat edge of Ôwr on each of Carmack's shoulders. "Rise, Sir Carmack. Go and serve your Lord and king."

As Carmack stood, cheers erupted from the congregation, mostly from the back where Roxburg, Leif, and others from Tsaftown had assembled. A trio of trumpeters played a jubilant march as the priest led everyone out of the temple. By the time Tara headed down the aisle, a mob of well-wishers had clogged the temple doorway. Presumably, somewhere in the middle, was Carmack.

"Saints, what a crush," Kressy muttered. "Tomorrow will come before our turn."

Tara fought back her impatience and smiled. She had too much to celebrate, to anticipate. "I am willing to wait." For her knight, she'd wait forever.

She glimpsed Carmack nodding, grinning, and using his strong handshake to move people out of his way. Within seconds, he broke free of the mob and jogged to Tara.

She curtsied. "Congratulations, Sir Carmack."

"Lady Tara." He bowed, an irresistible grin dancing across his lips. Tara's memories of those lips against hers warmed her cheeks. "Glad to see you up and about, Kressy."

"Couldn't be happier for you, Master—no, *Sir* Demry . . . eh, Sir Carmack . . . whatever your name is now. I'll leave you two to chat." Kressy bobbed a curtsy and walked away.

Carmack scratched his beard. "She wouldn't be so happy with me if she'd heard what I'm about to propose."

Tara's heart fluttered, and the blood drained from her face. Was he going to ask her to marry him in front of all these strangers? She braced herself for that very question.

"Would you mind if we cut our visit to Armonguard short?" he asked.

Her ears rang. "Why?"

"The *Brierstar* leaves tomorrow. Your uncle and his men are eager to sail home, and I'd like to go with them."

The ringing stopped. "To Tsaftown?"

"No, my sweet lady." A mischievous glint lit Carmack's mahogany eyes as he kissed her hand. "Home to Meribah Corner."

CHAPTER THIRTY-FOUR
TARA

THREE WEEKS LATER

HOME. FUNNY, MERIBAH CORNER HAD never felt like home to Tara until the carriage she shared with Carmack entered the inner bailey. She squeezed his hand as they passed through the gatehouse. Their long journey to the end of Er'Rets and back was finally over.

When they cleared the second portcullis, greetings of welcome rang out from every corner of the bailey. Standing at the keep's door, Tara's mother, Eric, his wife Viola, and their daughter Nevandra waved. Carmack pushed open the carriage door and helped her alight. Tara grabbed hold of her purple skirt and rushed up the steps, skipping every other one. She embraced each of her family, saving her mother for last.

"Oh, my dear daughter." Mother kissed Tara's cheek. "I ought to remind you how a lady climbs stairs, but I am too proud. How I wish your father was here! He knew this day would come. The day of your wedding, he said, 'Revada, our daughter has more strength in her tiny body than both my sons put together. By her goodness, her loving-kindness, I know Arman dwells inside her. He will not forsake her.'"

The last chain of resentment binding Tara's heart broke with fresh tears. *I forgive you, Father, as You, Father Arman, have forgiven me.*

"Now, now," Mother said. "There are two things this world has little patience for—occupied privies and . . . ?"

Tara giggled. "A woman's tears."

"Precisely." Mother turned Carmack's way next, dipping her head. "Congratulations, *Sir* Carmack."

Carmack bowed. "Might I have a word with you in private, my lady?"

Mother smiled at him and glanced that same smile Tara's way. "You certainly may."

CARMACK

Carmack would rather face off with ten eunuchs than one Lady Revada, but he needed an answer to the question that had been burning a hole in his gut for the past three weeks.

"This way." Lady Revada led him inside the solar off the great hall. The sofa and chairs had been moved. They now faced each other in front of the fireplace, making the familiar room feel new and different. Lady Revada closed the door behind them.

Carmack stood near the sofa, Tara's favorite spot to sit. "Would you prefer to sit, my lady?"

"No, thank you." Lady Revada remained close to the door, her chin lifted. "What is it you wish to say, sir?"

Make it quick. Carmack clasped his hands in front of him. "First, thank you for releasing me from my vow. It meant more than I can ever say."

Lady Revada raised an eyebrow, rattling Carmack's nerve. "A

mere technicality, if you must know. A dowager like me can hardly deny a king's request."

Carmack felt as though he were shrinking. So much for thinking she had warmed to him.

"However," she said, "had I the power to deny the king, I still would have released you from your vow out of my appreciation for all you've done for my entire family"—a slight grin curled her lips—"especially my daughter."

Fresh hope zinged through every nerve in Carmack's body. "It was my pleasure, my lady."

"I can never fully repay you for your esteemed service, though I do have one complaint. Your elevation to the knighthood leaves me in a most uncomfortable situation. Tara is still a young widow in need of protection. Might you recommend your replacement?"

This was it. Charge ahead, Demry. He stood tall and lifted his chin. "Perhaps you might leave her in my care, not as her Shield, but as her husband."

After a beat, Lady Revada's grin broke into a wide smile. "That is what I hoped you would ask." She clapped her hands. "I knew the two of you were meant for each other since your very first dance together."

"Forgive me, my lady, but if so, why did you make it impossible for us to be married?"

"Nothing is impossible for Arman." She squeezed his arms. "Now go. Make my daughter the happiest young woman in Er'Rets."

Carmack wanted a better answer but decided he'd rather live for the future than mourn the past. He bowed deeply. "Thank you, my lady," he said and rushed from the solar into the great hall.

Kressy found him. The young maid was looking healthier, now that her bruises were gone, and happy to be home. "Lady Tara wanted me to tell you she took a walk to stretch her legs after the journey."

"Alone?" His heart hammered. "Where did she go?"

"Down to the waterfall by the lake."

Without another word, Carmack bolted out of the keep. He pumped his legs, frustrated they would not carry him downhill faster. The woods blurred around him like a never-ending tunnel of green leaves, thicker than he'd ever seen. Light had restored the forest, so abundant with fresh growth that Carmack nearly missed the fork in the path.

He turned and raced on, dodging branches and sweeping leaves out of his face until he burst into the small clearing by the creek. Tara stood on the bridge, gazing up at the waterfall. Sunlight trickled through the mist rising around her, and Carmack stopped dead in his tracks, captivated by the woman he hoped to soon call his wife. Her white-blonde curls shimmered in the soft breeze, as her head tilted upward, her face glowing. A formidable lady, as wise and kind as she was strong.

When she turned and their eyes met, Carmack felt as though he were floating. Her heart was truly his, that he knew. But he doubted he would ever shake the feeling that this was all a beautiful dream.

Carmack ached to hold Tara, to touch her and know their shared reality. He closed the distance between them. "What are you doing here?"

Tara smiled bashfully. "I wanted to be alone . . ."

She might as well have dumped a bucket of water over his head. Maybe this wasn't the right time.

". . . with you."

Oh, this was definitely the right time. Carmack dropped to his knee. "My dearest Lady Tara, I won't waste another breath without asking, will you marry me?"

Her sapphire eyes sparkled. "Yes. Yes," she repeated. Her third 'yes' brought Carmack to his feet, the fourth delivered her into his arms, and the fifth was lost in a kiss far deeper and more passionate than either could have imagined, one that swept away the past and promised a happier future, fulfilling a hope Carmack had surrendered so long ago. Tara was his, and he was hers, bound by a love stronger than any magic.

As their lips parted, Carmack breathed deeply. "At last."

"Indeed." Tara sighed. "Coming from a man who is always there when I need him, that kiss is woefully late."

He chuckled. "My apologies, my lady. I will not keep you waiting again."

"No, Sir Carmack, you will not." Tara rose on to her tiptoes and pulled him into another kiss, every bit as sweet.

TARA

None of Mother's proverbs came close to describing how wonderful it was for Tara to sit next to her betrothed, surrounded by her family as she presided over her own great hall and a feast of roasted pheasant, venison, and early summer vegetables. Most of the families in Meribah Corner filled the tables set before her. Those closest to her included the new steward Eric had hired to replace Ulmer, his wife, and their two sons; and Constable Becker and his family. The two men seemed to be fast friends already.

During the last course, Constable Becker approached the head table.

Next to Tara, Carmack stiffened. The night had been going so smoothly, she'd nearly forgotten their unresolved business, namely, the charges against Carmack for Lord Gershom's death and his escape from Becker's holding cell.

"Forgive me for interrupting your dinner, my lady, but I'm afraid we have something rather unpleasant to discuss."

"Can't it wait until morning, Constable?" Tara asked.

Becker pursed his lips. "It could, but I thought you might like to know that I have closed the inquiry into Lord Gershom's death."

Beneath the table, Tara clutched Carmack's hand. "In that case, go on."

"His late lordship's healer paid a visit to Meribah Corner to conduct an autopsy shortly after Lord Livna arrived."

Gershom's healer was a crackpot of the worst kind.

"I didn't know the man was a coroner," Carmack said.

A waggish glint lit Becker's eye. "A point I also raised, but as he insisted, who am I to quibble with a trained professional?"

"What did his report say?" Tara asked.

"He concluded the condition of his lordship's heart was much worse than feared and that it was a miracle Lord Gershom lasted as long as he did. However, based on the evidence he collected, namely an unopened bottle of stomach tonic, he concluded Lord Gershom succumbed to indigestion."

"Indigestion?" Carmack and Tara exclaimed simultaneously.

"Aye, so with that exculpatory evidence, the steward, Lord Livna, and I unanimously concluded there was insufficient evidence to support charges of foul play. Your name, Sir Carmack, has been cleared."

"Thank you, Constable," Carmack said.

"You're most welcome." Becker bowed his head and returned to his table.

Laughter filled the great hall in Meribah Corner with an energy so different from the dullness Tara remembered before her journey south. She gazed at the hammer-beam ceiling. How, dear Arman, could this be the same place she had fled only two months ago?

"Something wrong, my love?" Carmack whispered.

Her heart warmed. *My love.* "Just the opposite. Everything is right." Tara smiled and lifted a mouth-watering bite of rhubarb crumble from her plate. The tart dessert had arrived moments earlier, but the servants were already scooping up abandoned trenchers, while others stripped the tablecloths and disassembled the trestle tables.

"What's this?" Tara asked. "Eric, why are they clearing the hall so soon?"

"How should I know? This is not my house." Eric winked at Carmack.

Viola leaned forward, her pretty face glowing. "What are you two up to?"

"I arranged for an old friend to visit us." Carmack waved to a threesome in the corner by the entrance.

The men stepped forward, each carrying a stringed instrument. The thinnest one fidgeted with his harp, his eyes darting around the room.

Where had Tara seen him before? "Saints above, is that the same harpist Lord Gershom chased up the mantle?"

"That's him."

"How ever did you persuade him to come back?"

"It wasn't easy." Carmack's tone turned wistful. "I'm not the smooth talker Dunn is."

"Are you disappointed that Master Dunn remained in Armonguard?"

"Nah, the change of scenery will be good for him, but I didn't hire a harpist so that we could chitchat about that crusty codger's latest attempt at retirement."

"Why *did* you hire a harpist?"

"To make up for lost time." Carmack took her hand and led her around the high table to the middle of the floor. The music started, and he bowed.

"My dearest Sir Carmack." Tara lowered herself into a curtsy. "You forgot to ask whether I wished to dance."

Carmack drew her close as they turned a tight circle around each other. "My apologies, soon-to-be Lady Demry. May I have this dance?"

"You may." She stepped in closer to him. "And every one that comes after it."

Ignoring the proper footwork, Carmack lifted Tara off her feet and twirled her as she laughed. He lowered her back to the floor, and his arms circled her waist. Then, with so many witnesses clapping and cheering, they kissed until the great hall itself seemed to spin around them.

Bonus Epilogue

Thank you for reading *Lady of Shadows*. We hope you loved the story. Find out what happens next with our Bonus Epilogue, a special gift, available only to our newsletter subscribers.

This Bonus Epilogue will not be released on any retailer platform, so scan our QR code to get your free gift. You acknowledge you are becoming a Sunrise Publishing, Kelly Fernlake, and Jill Williamson subscriber. Unsubscribe from any of the newsletters at any time.

THANK YOU

Thank you again for reading *Lady of Shadows*. We hope you enjoyed the story. If you did, would you be willing to do us a favor and leave a review? It doesn't have to be long—just a few words to help other readers know what they're getting. (But no spoilers! We don't want to wreck the fun!) Thank you again for reading!

We'd love to hear from you—not only about this story, but about any characters or stories you'd like to read in the future. Contact us at www.sunrisepublishing.com/contact.

Sir Rigil Barak came to Land's End expecting a routine mission: investigate some rumors, spy on some nobles, and above all, play the perfect knight. Instead, he is reunited with his less-than-shining past--the same past that has kept him on the road for years, fleeing his noble father's scorn and grieving the woman he thought dead. Until now.

Because in Land's End, he sees a face he never thought he'd see again . . . at least, not outside his dreams. And if she's alive, he'll do anything for a second chance to save her.

Years of captivity to a madman left Sethe with a face full of scars and one rule: never be trapped again. Except, to keep that rule, she'll have to ask for help from Rigil, the thief who broke her heart and abandoned her long ago. Now, years later, he shows up to rescue her from Land's End like a knight in shining armor? Who does he think he is?

And even if the boy from her past has become a real knight with real honor, can she fall for a man who lied to her?

Maybe that doesn't matter now, because Sethe's old captor is hot on her heels with a new invention that could turn her into something worse than a prisoner. He could turn her into a weapon.

Fortunately, Rigil and Sethe always did know how to pull off a heist--and if they can steal the enemy's deadly new weapon, they can save the kingdom. For Sethe, this means trusting Rigil without letting him anywhere near her heart. For Rigil, it means a second chance with the woman whose heart he once broke.

And this time, failure could cost them everything.

CHAPTER ONE

RIGIL

THERE WAS MORE TO SPY CRAFT THAN being impeccably dressed, or so Rigil had heard. Perhaps one day, he'd test that theory.

Today called for rich dyes and a good tailor.

The blue ensemble Rigil had chosen for this mission was sharp enough for a Kingsguard ambassador, yet flimsy enough that a week of travel in torrential rain had left its mark. As he stood at Lord Coble's library window, water dripping from both his hair and the sword at his waist and pooling under his boots, he squinted through the blurry glass at the ramshackle village of Land's End—a picture of desolation. Spindly trees, soupy rain, a few low buildings hunched together like old men, it was a land that still thought it was living in Darkness.

Perfect place to hide a plot against the king.

Rain pounded the glass as Coble's servant set out goblets on a table behind Rigil, humming something almost as irritating as that saltbeetle trying to bash through the window.

"Wine, Sir Rigil?"

Rigil turned to face the speaker. For a servant, the man was oddly dressed. With opulent robes, flawless pearl skin, and glossy white hair tied back with a ribbon, he would likely be considered handsome if not for those eyes. Grey as shards of foggy glass, they pierced Rigil through the dusty air as the man held the bottle over the cups.

Rigil nodded. "Thank you, Master . . .?"

"Nedir." Wine gushed into the goblets, dark scarlet. "Raith Nedir of Har Sha'ar." An Avenis pendant around Nedir's neck jingled as he corked the wine. A servant of the god of beauty, then. Strange for a man from Har Sha'ar. Even stranger for a place like this.

If Coble's library had ever been beautiful, years of dust and abandonment had eaten at its charm. On one end of the room, a low fire added the smell of char to the musk of rotting paper. The center table was blanketed in so many maps that it resembled a four-legged parchment creature. Ghosts of students seemed to hover about, their education cut short years ago when the Kingsguard school was overtaken by black knights, then shut down altogether. Nedir, maturely handsome as he was, had an ancient, dusty aura about him that brought the room's history into sharper relief. He could have sat among the cobwebs and warped books without seeming out of place here. A relic, like them.

But a useless relic. Isemios's wit, where was Coble? Rigil had *not* crossed Er'Rets listening to his squire's endless rambling to meet with some valet.

A sharp stab burst in Rigil's temples just before his squire spoke telepathically inside his head.

Mezaedo Chevyah.

Speak of a storm, and there it stirs. As usual, the squire didn't knock to announce himself so much as pound. Rigil lowered the shields around his mind, the mental equivalent of opening a set of drapes to let light in. He usually kept his mind guarded that way, a mental trick known as *blocking* or *shielding* among bloodvoicers, basic common sense among nongifted men like Rigil. Thankfully, bloodvoicing was rare enough that he didn't expect anyone but Mez to attack his mind here.

Sirrig, I'm in, Mez bloodvoiced. *You were right about the tunnel. Straight shot to the kitchens. You wouldn't* believe *what passes for soup down here.*

Rigil crossed the room to feign interest in *A History of Sakin Mageia.* Though he had no ability to bloodvoice himself, Mezaedo could hear his thoughts while the magical connection between their minds was open. *I see you took my lecture about staying focused to heart,* Rigil thought.

Sorry, Sirrig, Mezaedo shot back. *Can't talk while I'm chewing. Lightness' sake, you* tasted *Coble's soup?*

I think you're missing the important bit. The broth. Is chewy.

"Enjoying the library, Sir Rigil?" Nedir appeared at Rigil's elbow, goblet in hand, his robe draped like a mantle against the falling dust. "I thought you might appreciate Lord Coble's collection, being from Zerah Rock."

Aye, it was all very nostalgic, down to the judgmental stare of a thousand books screaming at Rigil to read more, learn faster, work harder, be better. *There are two kinds of men in this world, boy . . .*

Strange. All these years, and books still screamed in his father's voice.

"Very thoughtful, Master Nedir." Taking his cup, Rigil pushed *A History of Sakin Mageia* back into place. "Remind me again why Lord Coble cannot join us?"

"His lordship is attending to a personal matter."

More personal than an accusation of treason from the king? "Forgive me, but what does that make you? His steward?"

Nedir laughed, an unwrinkled sound to match his unwrinkled face. "I am not a servant. Lord Coble is interested in my research. Every scholar needs a sponsor."

A gust of wind slapped wet leaves against the window as Nedir gestured for Rigil to sit. When Rigil declined, Nedir took his own suggestion.

So. A scholar. What for?

Mezaedo, Rigil thought, uncertain if the squire could still hear him, *tell me you've found the box.*

Nedir set his wine on the sideboard to wipe his hands with a kerchief from his robe. No, not a kerchief. The whiteish parchment was a little damp and more than a little crinkled. As it would be, after weeks in Rigil's pocket.

Rigil blinked. "That letter was for his lordship."

"Yes, and how very well-crafted it was." With a manicured nail, Nedir chipped the last of King Gidon's seal away. "I would like to assure you, Sir Rigil, that King Gidon has no reason to fear. Lord Coble is too prudent to attempt reopening Mageia's school for black knights. They are illegal, after all. I fear the king sent you all this way for nothing."

Sirrig. Mezaedo's bloodvoice slashed through Nedir's false decorum like a scythe. *No sign of a mirror in Coble's rooms. Maybe Prince Oren was wrong?*

Rigil kept his expression as smooth as the wine on his tongue. Rich, a tad plummy. And was that currant? *Prince Oren's informant saw the box himself,* he thought. *It's hidden behind a silver-gilded mirror.*

No gilded mirrors here, Sirrig. Coble's got all the style of a blind cabbage.

Keep searching, Rigil thought, then held his glass to Nedir, resisting the urge to rest his wrist on the pommel of his sword in warning. "This research of yours. Anything that might interest the king?"

A smile as Nedir tipped the bottle over Rigil's goblet. "I study bloodvoicing, mostly. Origins, implications, the like. I was working on my research when you arrived."

Bloodvoicing research? Almost involuntarily, Rigil snapped the mental drapes shut around his thoughts again. Mezaedo wouldn't be able to hear him think if he was blocking, but if Rigil was dealing with a bloodvoicer here . . .

Needing space to think, Rigil meandered over to a larger table in the center of the room, where a half-finished game of citadel rested beside a stack of maps. Mezaedo hadn't knocked again. Blight it all, this was supposed to be simple. Interrogate Coble, filch the mysterious weapon Prince Oren's informant had warned them of, and be back in Armonguard before anyone was the wiser. Rigil had learned the castle layout by heart. Where would a garishly ornate mirror be if not in Coble's quarters? A servant wouldn't have something so—

Wood popped in the hearth. Slowly, so as not to spill his cup, Rigil turned to face his host. Nedir, who had a study in this manor. Nedir, who worshipped the god of beauty, judging by that *garishly ornate* pendant around his neck.

"So." Rigil leaned his fingertips on the table. "Why Avenis?"

Smiling, Nedir crossed his legs. "Beauty is the muse of all great minds, Sir Rigil, and Er'Rets is full of sights that far surpass what one might find in a mirror. In my case, there is something exquisite about an ocean view that stimulates my thoughts like nothing else."

Interesting. Hoping Mezaedo had left his connection to Rigil open, he lowered his shields long enough to call out in his thoughts, the best he could do without being able to reach out and knock on the boy's mind himself. *Mezaedo?*

Look, Sirrig, the boy answered, proof that he *was* listening, *there's no moldy mirror in this—*

You're in the wrong place. Rigil bent over the map, where someone had circled Tsaftown in bloodred ink. *Try the south wing, on an upper floor. Look for a study with an ocean view.*

South wing. Ocean view. Right. The boy withdrew.

Meanwhile, Nedir was swirling his glass. "It is a pity, Sir Rigil, that you came so far for mere rumors. Not that I fault the king

for being cautious, what with that horrid business in Tsaftown."
Finger to chin, Nedir held Rigil's gaze. "Such messy things, coups.
I commend Lord Livna and, of course, Lady Viola for removing
the threat so decisively."

As usual, Viola's name bit like a gnat. Rigil covered it with a hard
sip. Decisive, clever, ambitious, advantageously married—Rigil's
dear sister was all of those things, along with extremely adept at
holding a grudge. "I must say, Master Nedir, you are surprisingly
well-informed about affairs in Tsaftown."

Nedir shrugged. "There are no secrets on this side of Er'Rets."

Somewhere in the castle, a bell chimed. Noon. Time for the
guard change. Mezaedo needed to be back in the tunnel before he
was caught nosing through the upper rooms. *Mezaedo?*

Moldy onions, Sirrig, there's a whole room *for gowzals up here.*
Mezaedo.

Hang on. I've got a good feeling about this door.

This was Rigil's reward for taking a squire who could bloodvoice. Oh, for the simple days of Bran . . .

Nedir was watching him when Rigil turned back from the table.
"Forgive me, Sir Rigil, but as we have nothing more to discuss, I
must return to my work."

Rigil straightened. Return to work. Return to his study, where
Mezaedo was currently elbow deep in Nedir's belongings and
hopefully a very incriminating box.

Rigil's cup met the table with a curt clink. "I'd hate to waste
your time."

And now for the second part of spy craft. Improvisation.

He made to follow Nedir out of the room but stopped beside
the citadel board to lay a finger on a rogue piece. This set was solid
oak. Not like his father's, which had featured one army of solid
silver, the other of dull birch. Rigil had never been permitted to
use silver. That was for future lords who had proven their worth.

Shifting the piece ever so slightly to the left, Rigil chuckled enough to be heard over the rain. "Lord Coble is not much of a citadel player, I see."

Nedir paused beside the doorway, his smile pulling taut from cheek to cheek. "Actually, that game is mine. A sort of ongoing competition with myself."

Rigil gave a laugh. Airy, with a touch of condescension. "Well, I suppose even a scholar can fall for a three-tower gambit once in a while. I did myself, when I was learning."

He tapped the rogue piece with its ruby accents. Fitting for an Avenis worshipper.

Nedir cast a cool eye on the trap Rigil had invented. A moment passed. Two.

"Oh, how right you are, Sir Rigil." Crossing to the table, Nedir tapped the board. "I don't suppose you would be willing to educate me?"

Too easy. The table was cleared, chairs pulled out, goblets forgotten. Rigil took his time moving his villager, a decoy to distract Nedir from his rogue.

"The game of lords, they call this." Nedir moved his citadel. "How *is* Lord Barak, by the way? I've always thought he must have high hopes for you, to name a second-born son his heir."

For half a heartbeat, in the rattle of the rain, Rigil was facing Lord Barak himself across a citadel board in Zerah Rock, his father's frown scalding as he shifted his paladin. *Only a fool fails the same way twice, boy. There are two kinds of men in this world . . .*

"High hopes." Rigil moved his own paladin. "I imagine he did."

The game discouraged any more talk. Between turns, Rigil spoke to Mezaedo in his thoughts, hoping the squire was listening. *Mezaedo. Are you in the study yet?*

There was no answer for a long time. Not unusual with Mezaedo. He was a spotty bloodvoicer at the best of times, even carrying Rigil's sword to strengthen the magical connection between them. Personal possessions were known to do that for bloodvoicers, but weak as he was, Mezaedo needed more than a bit of Rigil's clothes or hair to help him connect to Rigil's mind. Of course, Rigil would have cut off a limb before letting a squire wield his old sword, Keseel, but ever since he'd lost that blade in Allowntown . . . well, that was that. Whether the blade he carried now was his own or Mezaedo's, neither would ever be Keseel. And both would cut flesh just fine.

Still. Something in Mezaedo's silence, the keen edge of it, drew sweat to Rigil's fingertips as Nedir slid his paladin forward. He still hadn't seen Rigil's decoy. *Mezaedo?* Rigil thought. *Mez?*

This time, Mezaedo's bloodvoice carried a note of fear. *He's in the study with me, Sirrig. Coble and a few others, but Coble's is the only voice I recognize. They haven't seen me yet. Moldy onions, don't check behind the curtains . . .*

Rigil stopped seeing the board. Maybe that was why he shifted his villager, exposing it as a decoy. The saltbeetle was throwing itself at the window now, a frantic blur of wings.

"What is this?" Nedir examined Rigil's villager, then the rogue that had slowly, quietly, been sneaking across the board behind it. "Ah. You nearly had me."

With a ring of silver on silver, Nedir toppled Rigil's rogue. The piece rolled across the board, gathering speed as it neared the edge.

Mezaedo? Are you there?

The rogue hit the floor. Bounced, rolled. Went still.

Raith Nedir stood. "And that is game. Thank you for indulging me, Sir Rigil. Peyton and Kali will show you out."

Two guards appeared at the door, clad in Coble's gold and black, and Rigil nearly grabbed Mezaedo's sword before checking himself. Blight it all. Prince Oren should have known about Nedir. He should have sent Rigil in with better information, with a fellow Mârad spy instead of a half-cooked Kingsguard squire, should have—

No. This was what the Mârad had trained him for, what had

set Rigil apart as more than a soldier in Prince Oren's mind. Improvisation. *Delicacy.*

Rigil rose, pushing his chair back until it bumped the fallen rogue on the carpet. "This is farewell, then, Master Nedir."

Nedir cracked a smile. "So it would seem." And on that strange note, he swept from the room, leaving a faint musty odor behind.

The two guards, both Barthian by their ashy skin, flanked Rigil out of the library and into the dark-paneled corridor, leading him toward the foyer and the manor entrance. Nedir must have gone the other way, or else dissolved into vapor. Only the faintest mildewy scent of him remained in the corridor, and it faded as the guards led Rigil to the left.

Rigil fought to keep his hands loose at his sides. Improvise, improvise.

At the entrance to the grand foyer, the first guard slipped ahead. Rigil chose that moment to whirl on the second, bringing his foot down hard on the side of the man's knee and drawing Mezaedo's sword at the same time.

Bone cracked. The guard fell, fumbling for his sword. But Rigil reached his first.

By the time the second guard lunged back into the corridor, Rigil's sword was careening toward him. Coble's man parried; Rigil's sword skidded down his blade and embedded itself in the doorframe. He tugged to no avail, then let go, leaving the sword protruding from the wood like a misfired arrow. The guard jabbed, and Rigil jerked to miss it, his heel catching on the first guard's body. He stumbled backward as steel spliced the air where his gut had been.

Arman help him. Ducking inside the guard's next wide swing, Rigil grabbed the man's arm and wrenched until something snapped. The man's sword struck the floor in Rigil's first stroke of luck. His second stroke of luck was the knife holstered in the guard's sleeve, right under Rigil's hands.

In a moment, it was over. A quick jab, a tangle of limbs, and then Rigil was hobbling out of the melee, trying not to think of the time he'd have getting bloodstains out of his best tunic.

But first, Mezaedo.

He didn't have long. The foyer was empty, but the sleek black staircase amplified his footfalls as Rigil took the curving stairs four to a stride and charged onto the third-floor landing. All black paneling and star-gilded ceilings, Land's End was a maze, the south wing no exception.

Rigil threw open the first door he saw.

The only light in the room came from dim green lanterns on dark-papered walls. Hundreds of gowzals, feathered and rat-faced, screamed in cages as Rigil flew by. A whole room for gowzals, indeed. One door in the far wall opened onto a closet, the other into a room hung with paintings of Sakin Mageia, the man who had commandeered this school for black knights instead of the Kingsguard it had been intended for.

Only one door remained. Rigil snapped the knob sideways and charged forward into . . .

A laboratory?

It was a modest room. Modest but full, every wall of shelves laden with books and potted plants. In the middle of the room, a large desk flexed under the weight of inkpots and old maps and, at the moment, one very calm Jaelportian squire.

Mezaedo Chevyah's dark curls were dusted with cobwebs from the tunnel beneath the keep, his feet dangling over the edge of the desk as he held an apple in one hand and a sheaf of Nedir's papers in the other. Still scrawny for seventeen, he wore tight-fitting trousers and an oversized canvas shirt, the sleeves shoved past his elbows to expose the tiny scars that flecked his arms and the tops of his hands. The scars were one of many mysteries that composed Mezaedo Chevyah. Another swung on a cord around his neck in the form of a blue velvet pouch, its contents staining his apple and the corners of his lips orange.

Aye, the sky could be falling, and Mezaedo would still stop to season his last meal with his secret Jaelportian spice.

"Sirrig?" Mezaedo hopped off the table and grabbed the sword as Rigil entered. "What's wrong?"

Rigil kicked the door shut. "Where's Coble?"

"*Lord* Coble?"

"This is no time for games, boy. You said he was in the room with you." Barely bridling a curse, Rigil raked hair from his brow, scanning the room for threats. He needed to get ahold of himself. Mez was alive. Rigil hadn't failed him.

"I don't understand." Red-faced as a dawn sun, Mezaedo looked for all the world like he'd just been accused of murder. And Prince Oren thought this boy had Mârad potential?

"Never mind." Rigil jerked a thumb at the door. "I'll give you an earful later, but Nedir is on his way."

He was ready to haul the boy out by his hair, and likely would have if his eyes hadn't fallen on a blue spot on the desk. The tiniest of glints, so small he should have missed it.

It was an earring of painted blue porcelain, a common bauble in coastal towns, pinned onto a map of Er'Rets over the island of Hamonah. Someone had scrawled an inscription: *Strong Sarikar bloodlines. Descendants of Hinckdan Faluk?*

The earring was in Rigil's hand, then his pocket, almost before the porcelain could cool his skin. Around him, the room grew suddenly more vivid, from the papers on the desk to the symbols sprayed across them. The runes looked ancient Tennish, but Viola would know for certain.

So. This was Nedir's research.

"I think it's botany." Mezaedo had the decency to sound abashed, pointing at a sickly potted root on the desk. The odd scars freckling his hand—which had a different explanation every time Rigil asked—seemed starker than usual in the room's rainy light. "My third master used the same elixirs to make things sprout. And look." Grabbing a bottle off the desk, Mezaedo popped the stopper and took a whiff. "Ink from the Shelosh Islands. Poison. Worth a moldy fortune in Jaelport. *Not* friendly with fire."

So many questions. Prince Oren would have given his left hand to see this room.

"By the way, Sirrig." Mezaedo cocked his head at the empty scabbard around Rigil's waist. "Where's my sword?"

In answer, Rigil held out his hand. Reluctantly, Mezaedo returned the sword Rigil had lent him. No Keseel, this blade, but the hilt was warm and sturdy in his hand, the pommel decorated with the looped insignia of Prince Oren.

Prince Oren. The mission. The box. Rigil stepped back, scanning the room again. Sure enough, a silver-gilded mirror hung on the far wall, next to a window overlooking a moody view of the sea below the castle. But before Rigil could think of checking behind the mirror, a new voice chimed in.

"Trespassing, Sir Rigil? And here I thought you were a man of honor."

Something heavy thumped to the floor. He spun in time to watch Mezaedo's half-eaten apple lollop across the rug to stop at Raith Nedir's feet.

Rigil dropped to his knee, sparing a glance for Nedir only *after* he found Mezaedo's chest still rising and falling. Instinctively, he checked the block around his mind and found it holding strong. The scholar had dropped Mezaedo without lifting a finger.

Which meant—wonderful—he *was* a bloodvoicer.

"Don't fuss, Sir Rigil." Nedir fluttered a hand. "He is only asleep."

"He wasn't lying, then." Rigil kept a hand on Mezaedo's chest. Still rising. Still alive. "Coble *was* in this room. Mezaedo saw him. Why blot his memory?"

"To see if I could." Smoothing his hair with the same fingers that had set a goblet in Rigil's hand moments ago, Nedir gazed pensively at the unconscious Mez. "Without training, strays rarely learn even the most basic principles of shielding. Even *your* mind is better defended, Sir Rigil. Tell me, did your Jaelportian mother teach you that shielding trick?"

A dozen of Rigil's half-made plans fell to tatters when a phalanx of guards filed into the room. No, not mere guards. That sleek obsidian armor, those helmets, the stink of illegal magic . . .

Black knights.

Rigil glared at Nedir. "I want to see Coble."

"Alas, Lord Coble leaves housekeeping to me."

On cue, the black knights stepped forward, faceless in inky helmets. Rigil's urge to pray was short-lived, like every plea for mercy at his father's citadel board. If this was a test, he could not fail it. And it was always a test.

Jerking his sword from his belt, Rigil lashed out against the first knight within reach until a blow to the back of his head liquefied his bones.

Rigil's knees hit the floor, the room spinning. He could not fail. Mezaedo. He couldn't . . .

"Don't feel badly, Sir Rigil." Nedir's voice was warped, retreating. "Even the best player falls for the three-tower gambit once in a while."

Acknowledgements

The journey to this debut book started over a decade ago, when I first admitted out loud that I was writing a novel. Since then, the Lord has provided a wonderful support network. Without each of these people, I could not have reached this milestone, so my heartfelt appreciation goes out to all of them.

To Alex, Sam, & Nora, for your love, all kinds of support, patience and never-ending encouragement.

To Mom, my extended family, and friends, who never stopped asking, "How's your book going?"

To Jill Williamson, for sharing her world and characters, and for choosing me to write Tara and Carmack's sequel story. You've given so much of your time and energy to give Andrew Swearingen, Niki Florica, and me this opportunity. I struggle to find words to express how grateful I am.

And, speaking of Andrew and Niki, you two have been a boon to my creative process. I'm gobsmacked by your imaginative gifts and look forward to reading your books for years to come.

To Susan May Warren and the entire Sunrise Media Group family, for your vision and dedication to helping new authors make their way in a challenging industry and for your unwavering enthusiasm for our stories.

To Emilie Haney of EAH Creative for an epic cover.

To my amazing editing team, Katie Donovan, Megan Gerig, and Kristyn Fortner, for the attentive care you gave to make this story sparkle.

To Carla Hoch for invaluable insight on how to teach a lady to fight.

To Deborah Clack for the many hours of free author-to-author laugh therapy.

To Jeremiah Friedli, Cate Touryan, & Paige Reed, my Bookends friends, who propped up this book and me with their faithful prayers, encouragement, and advice.

To my women's bible study and home group prayer warriors—this book is the tangible fruit of your prayers. (The intangible fruit is immeasurable.)

To the Blood of Kings: Legends Street Team for doing all the cool social media stuff that I struggle to do. You amaze me!

To my readers, I've been waiting so long for my work to find you. You are each an answer to prayer.

All glory to my eternal Lord and King Jesus Christ, my Savior and Shield, who establishes the works of my hands.

Kelly Fernlake is an award-winning author of sweet romantasy inspired by timeless truth. In addition to reading and writing, her favorite things include travelling to places with castles; classic old movies; comfy sweatshirts; dark chocolate; and hockey. A North Dakota native, Kelly now lives in Florida with her husband, two teenagers, and a furball pup.

Connect with Kelly at KellyFernlake.com, where you can sign up for her newsletter and receive her FREE novella *The Library Smuggler*; or find her on Instagram (@kellyfernlake).

Jill Williamson is a multi-passionate creative who loves the arts. She's written over two dozen books for readers of all ages and is best known for her Blood of Kings fantasy series, two of which won Christy Awards and made VOYA magazine's Best Science Fiction, Fantasy, and Horror list. She produces films with her husband and teaches about writing at conferences.

Visit her at www.jillwilliamson.com.

BLOOD OF KINGS: LEGENDS

Award-winning author
JILL WILLIAMSON

with Andrew Swearingen, Kelly Fernlake, & Niki Florica

Return to the world of Er'Rets in an epic fantasy series brimming with richly woven tales of loyalty, love, and sacrifice...

We solve the problem of what we read next.　　　　Available on Amazon

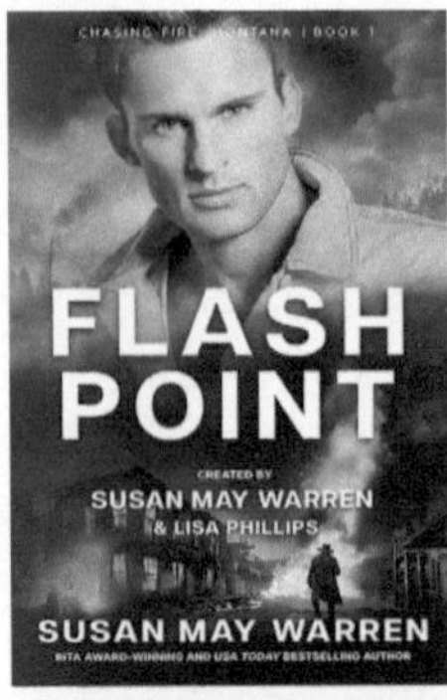

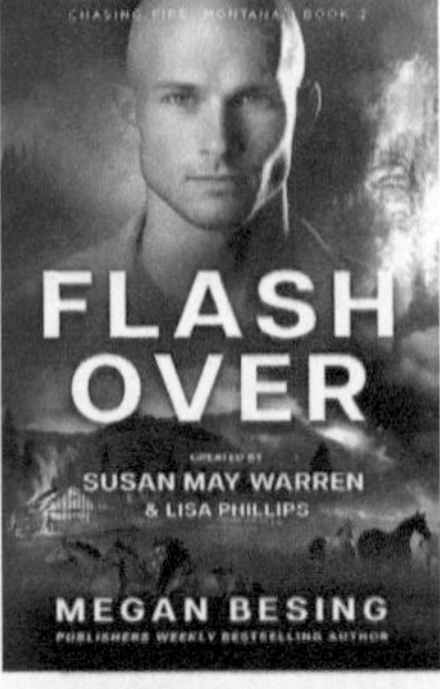

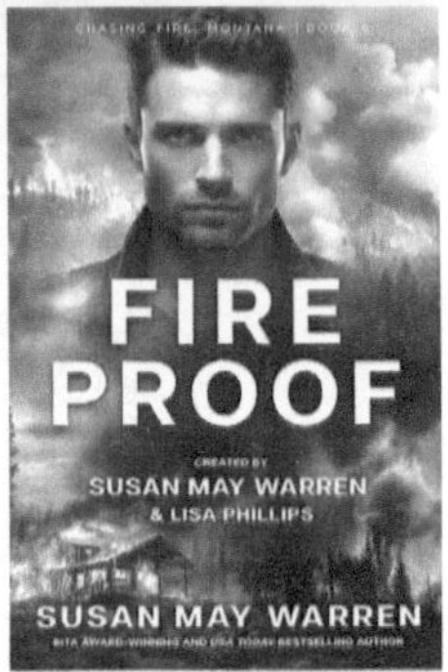

CHASING FIRE: MONTANA

Dive into an epic series created by

SUSAN MAY WARREN
and LISA PHILLIPS

We solve the problem of what we read next.

Available on Amazon

YOU MAY ALSO LIKE...

When a blizzard strikes Deep Haven and Megan is overrun with catastrophes, it takes a former Ranger to step in and help. But the more he comes to her rescue, the sooner she'll move out... Come home to Deep Haven in this magical tale about the one who got away... and came back.

***Still the One* by Susan May Warren and Rachel D. Russell**

Grace Howell leaves her life as a ballerina and returns to Heritage, Michigan, to heal. Teaching dance is just a temporary gig, until she finds herself unexpectedly charmed by small-town life and her growing attachment to Seth Warner, a man from her past with a troubled history of his own.

***You're the Reason* by Tari Faris**

Dani Sullivan is determined to revive Jonathon Island's fading charm and reunite her fractured family. Her plan? Reopen the Grand Sullivan Hotel. But without the funds to restore the hotel, Dani's forced to accept help from Liam Stone—a big-city hotel developer whose sleek, modern vision is everything she's trying to avoid.

***Meet Me at the Grand* by Lindsay Harrel**

We solve the problem of what we read next.   Available on Amazon

**WHERE EVERY STORY IS A FRIEND,
AND EVERY CHAPTER IS A NEW JOURNEY...**

Subscribe to our newsletter for a free book, the latest news, weekly giveaways, exclusive author interviews, and more!

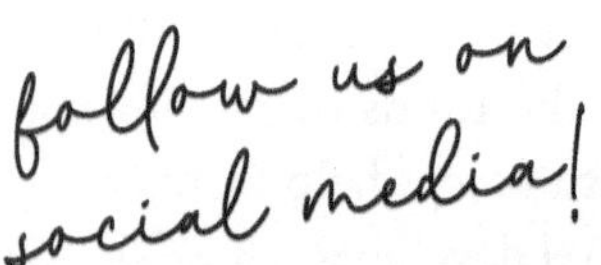

Shop paperbacks, ebooks, audiobooks, and more at
SUNRISEPUBLISHING.MYSHOPIFY.COM